THE UNBLINKING EYE

SCOTT LEIGH

Chiselbury

Published by Chiselbury Publishing, a division of Woodstock Leasor Limited, 14 Devonia Road, London N1 8JH

www.chiselbury.com

Cover design by Indra Murugiah

ISBN: 978-1-916556-86-7 (hardback)

ISBN: 978-1-916556-98-0 (paperback)

ISBN: 978-1-916556-99-7 (epub)

Again, for MAD, without whom none of this would be worthwhile

AUTHORS NOTE

The main characters in this book are fictitious and bear no resemblance to persons living or dead. The main protagonists from British and American Special Forces are fictional as are the various intelligence, communications, crypto and humint specialists. However, the historical narrative is as accurate as I can achieve and I have included, at the end of the book, a short chapter on what is verifiably true and what isn't. When fact is stranger than fiction, it is always worth including it in a novel.

As with 'Closer to Paradise' all real events depicted are from open sources available on the internet or in print. I have included no confidential or militarily sensitive information that is not in the public domain. The dialogue is, likewise, fictitious and is not intended to insult or impugn the reputation of any nation, army or indeed, religion. Banter and insults do not necessarily reflect my own views about people or events.

I have included some Arabic words which are in italics. There is a table of definitions in the back as an aide memoire but both spellings and meanings often vary.

There is also, apologies, a wealth of authentic military

jargon and some of these can also be found in a glossary at the back. For those to whom such words are totally alien, you might consider cutting out the glossary and using it as a bookmark.

I get a lot of help from friends and family, especially with read-throughs and editing, so, in no particular order, thank you to PEC, APMB, WAHC, JMW, GCM, JRCDN and, of course, my wife and daughters.

Of course, I need to thank Stuart Leasor and Chiselbury for publishing and you for reading.

Quae cum ita essent pleraque eorum quae sequuntur vera sunt – That said, most of what follows is true, as Cicero might have said.

YUGOSLAVIA 1991

The Bosnian War was a playground of the mind where the worst and most fantastic excesses of the human mind were acted out.

'My War Gone By, I Miss It So' by Anthony Lloyd, Old Etonian, Army Officer and Heroin Addict.

A decade after the death of the Communist dictator Josip Broz Tito, The Socialist Federal Republic of Yugoslavia began to break up into its old constituent parts. To the West, Croatia followed Slovenia's lead and declared itself independent. To the East, an irredentist Serbia, the largest of the Republics and whose people dominated the old Yugoslav army, began to carve out the new nation of Greater Serbia by invading Bosnia and parts of Croatia. Likewise, the new Croat government had designs on western Bosnia, where could be found ethnic Croat Christians. They supported them financially, militarily and politically, with the establishment of Croat Bosnian militias known collectively as the HVO. Caught in the middle were the Bosniaks, a South Slavic Sunni Muslim ethnic group predominantly from the central area of the former Republic of Bosnia.

They in turn, formed local self-defence militias loosely known as the ABiH.

Such was the complexity of the war, that in different regions and at different times, Bosniaks sided with Croats to fight Serbians, and Serbians sided with Croats to fight Bosniaks. Sometimes everybody fought everybody else. Stuck in the middle was a UN military presence whose duty was to deliver humanitarian aid. They were under strict instructions not to intervene in the war itself, except in self-defence. But the plight of the Bosniaks attracted the eye of the Islamic world, flush with victory against the Russians in Afghanistan and soon huge quantities of arms, money and men began to pour in.

All wars are bloody but civil-religious wars are especially vicious.

PROLOGUE 1

16 April 1993
Gornji Ahmići
Lašva Valley
Central Bosnia
0530 Local

The owls had been talkative that night. It had helped him stay awake after the ravages of his first ever hangover had wiped out the preceding day. He had only been in the local militia a fortnight, having turned seventeen a month ago. But now they were going to clear out the Turks, as they were wont to call Muslims, from the Canton. The word had spread rapidly amongst the non-Muslim population that the Turks were refusing to sign the Vance-Owen deal that gave Canton 10 back to the real people of Bosnia Croatia, the Christians. If he was honest, he didn't really understand the politics of it all. For the last year, he had been told the Serbs were the enemy, trying to force the Bosnian Croats into a Serbian Yugoslavia they now called Republika Srpska. Two nights ago, it had been explained to him again over numerous glasses of home-made slivovitz but he was not used to alcohol and the more it was explained the less he seemed to grasp it. After a couple of hours, the politicking had evolved into bawdy talk about girls, another subject he knew very little about. Finally, the drinking petered out in the early morning with singing around the dying embers of the campfire. What seemed an all-too-brief time later they were roused by an angry group of military police in black uniforms, kicking them awake and shouting they were going to cleanse the country of Muslims the next day, for the glory of Croatia.

And now, here he was, Luka Babić, aged seventeen, cradling an old Yugoslav AK47 with two spare magazines of bullets nestled in the webbing on his chest, waiting for something to happen. The cloudless sky to his left was beginning to bloom into purples and oranges and the birds were chattering away oblivious to everything that was about to happen. He looked to his front and could see the white houses of Gornji Ahmići in among the green fields. The mosque's minaret stood tall and bright and in the distance was a second minaret of the mosque at Ahmići itself. A small black and white cat was hunting around the piles of wood neatly stacked next to the houses. He was glad the headache of yesterday had receded and that he had not reported sick with a suspected malignant brain tumour that was disrupting his vision and had made him vomit twice after being kicked awake. He looked at the patch on his arm bearing the letters HVO - *Hrvatsko Vijece Odbrane-* the Croatian Defence Council, and felt a swelling of pride. He wished his grandfather were alive so that he could show him. Dida would also have been proud and would have once again told him of his fights against the Serb Chetniks in the last war. His grandfather had even kept his German coal scuttle helmet and the black uniform of the

Ustasha in the wardrobe but when he died, Luka's mother had thrown it all out. On his other arm, he wore an orange armband, which he was told was to help his fellow soldiers recognise him. The military police in black were wearing red and the regulars of the Vitěska brigade wore white. He was part of a group of five, led by a sergeant from the brigade and all he really knew about the coming action was that he was to stick close to his comrades and do everything asked of him by his sergeant.

There was stifled whispering and the order came down the line that they were moving forward in five minutes. Some of the regulars, with the longer rifles, now opened the bipods at the front and lay with the butts nestling into their cheeks, scanning the village. To the south, after the houses ended, there was a large expanse of meadow that went down to the main road to Vitez. He had seen no cars in the twelve or so hours he had been in the woods.

Along the line, the soldiers were getting up and walking down the hill towards the village, leaving behind the sharp-shooters. He followed suit, making sure he didn't lag behind or go too fast in front. He was expecting something to happen, rifles firing at them perhaps but the dawning day was still, save for the soft thud of numerous boots on the damp turf of the meadow. He looked for the cat but it had disappeared. He suddenly remembered with relief to click off the Kalashnikov's safety catch and kept an eye on his sergeant. All around him, men were moving towards the houses from three sides. There must have been dozens of them, all walking quickly down the hill. To his right, the flank had begun to jog down and the other two flanks began quickening the pace too. He was just approaching the nearest building, a white house with a red tile roof, when he heard his first shot. It was shockingly loud and the sound seemed to roll down the valley like thunder. He ducked down and then went onto one knee looking for the danger before the sergeant hissed at him to stand up and stop being a pussy.

There was shooting inside the village now and he saw that some of the fire was coming from houses' upper storey windows but it was not being directed towards the advancing troops.

'Calm down, everyone, they are ours,' the Sergeant shouted above the din of rifle fire.

The five-man team approached the house and he heard his named being shouted. 'Babić, get in there,' said the sergeant. The other teams were spreading out, each one taking a house. He tried the front door but it was locked and he looked at the sergeant for further guidance.

'For fuck's sake Babić. Stay here and don't let in anyone you don't recognise.' The sergeant kicked the door and on the third attempt the wood splintered and the door swung inwards. The sergeant went in followed by the three others in his team. He heard shouting and then a shot. Again, he involuntarily ducked his head and then peered into the building. A man, presumably the homeowner, had been shot and was lying in a corner gasping for breath. A second bullet hit him in the chest. He was in a dressing gown. Babić stared horrified. He looked away and kept his eyes looking down the valley. But he could not stop his ears from hearing. There were a woman's screams, again terminated by shots and then he heard something that would stay with him for the duration of his short life. Children's screams that were also cut short by shots. The four men came out, grim faced and marched to the next house.

Babić could now hear multiple shots throughout the village as the five-man teams were moving from house to house. There were screams and shouts mixed in with the noise of the gunfire. He hoped fervently that he would again be posted as guard on the door for the next one. It was not to be. The sergeant kicked the door and it swung open first time. He motioned with his rifle for Babic to go in. To his intense relief, there was nobody there.

'Clear upstairs'

He slowly climbed the wooden stairs, pausing briefly on the dog-leg landing, his rifle in his shoulder, scanning for movement on the floor above and desperately hoping there would be none. He crept up further but the wooden stairs creaked loudly so he decided to run up the stairs before the sound alerted anybody there. The landing was deserted and he tried a door. It was a child's bedroom but empty. The bed was unmade. He guessed from the Dinamo Zagreb poster that it was a boy's room. There was a smaller picture of Čelik FC, the local team from Zenica and a small trophy of a man kicking a ball. He tried the next room and it was equally clear that it belonged to two young girls but, again, no sign of the owners. Dreading the third and final door, he decided to open it and not go in. He waited a few seconds with his back to the wall before moving his head around the door frame and looking in. There was nobody there. He jumped as a burst of automatic fire from downstairs echoed through the house. He quickly glanced into the room to make sure it was empty and ran down the stairs. There were a further two shots coming from the basement and he descended the stairs into the cellar. He saw the family. One boy, probably twelve, two girls probably eight and six and the mother and father. All had been shot and were lying in a heap. From where they lay, it was evident that the father had tried to protect his family and the mother had died with her girls in her arms. One was clutching a well-worn teddy bear, its fur now seeped in blood. Tears welled up in his eyes and he turned away from the horror and vomited.

'Can't hold your drink, eh, Babić?'

He turned and ran up the stairs and out into the open before vomiting again. He reached for his water flask and took a swig, swirling and spitting out the water. All around him were the sounds of villagers being systematically killed. The four other soldiers came out and the sergeant, holding a leather wallet said 'Hey, Babić' and gave him a fifty deutschmark note before tossing the wallet aside. He took the note in his fist and crumpled it into his pocket. He sat on a woodpile and surveyed the carnage. Troops were now shooting the livestock, and sheep and horses lay dead in the meadows. He saw the little cat as someone fired at it but the bullet missed and the cat scampered off under a woodshed.

He looked at the meadow below the village and saw that the surviving villagers, mainly women and some children were running down the hill towards the main road. Shots rang out from the surrounding hills and he remembered the regular soldiers with the bipod guns and realised that they were shooting the fleeing inhabitants. Many lay still where they had fallen, some sat with their children weeping, either too terrified to move or already wounded. They, too, were picked off. Within a few minutes but what, to him, seemed both an eternity and immediately, there were thirty or more bodies in the field and shooting from the hills subsided.

Some cars came down the road and Babić looked to his sergeant.

'It's OK Babić, those are our boys.'

The leading car was an old Mercedes saloon which stopped near the Mosque. Four soldiers got out and the oldest looking one began issuing orders. Then a Gaz-66 jeep arrived and several jerry cans were off loaded. He was ordered to take a jerry can and go back to the houses he had helped clear.

'We are going to burn these Turk houses down. They are a stain on our great nation.'

The team entered the first house and sloshed petrol all over the ground floor and finished by tipping the last few litres onto the corpse of the man. The sergeant had a milk bottle half full of petrol and a rag in its neck, which he lit with a Zippo and tossed through the front door before they moved on to the second house. All over the village, houses were burning and a thick pall of black smoke hung over the valley. The houses that were spared, he was to learn later, belonged to the Catholic Croats who had helped organise the slaughter.

He heard an explosion followed by cheers and saw the minaret of the mosque teeter and fall. It crashed into the main building and the tower lay at an angle pointing an impotent finger accusingly to heaven. The soldiers were now milling around the main road, staying clear of the searing heat and choking smoke of the burning houses. The NCOs began to get a grip and marshal them into a column and they trudged down the road and out of the village. He saw that main town of Amići was also burning and that its mosque had also been destroyed. He could only see the uniformed men of the Croat Defence Council, the black uniforms of the military police already having disappeared. There were scattered bodies between the houses but he knew that many more bodies would be consumed by the burning buildings. His mind returned to the memory of the dead family and the screams of the children in the first house and he felt a profound loss of something he couldn't describe. Was it his innocence or was it his humanity? He felt there would be consequences for today and that they would follow him round for ever. The crime was too big to hide and he knew that the United Nations would be here soon with their white tanks and blue helmeted soldiers. He knew little of the British but he felt that this would be something they would find hard to forgive.

PROLOGUE 2

Almost exactly a hundred kilometres away to the south, on the very same day, a platoon of the Muslim Bosnian army, the ABiH, was observing a village. It was both typical and unremarkable for this part of the country. Stone built with tile roofs, perched on the slopes above Lake Jablanika, the simple dwellings housed families so far untouched by the war against the Serbs. The majority were Catholic but they had lived in amongst their Muslim neighbours peacefully enough for as long as anyone could remember. It was a rural community of farmers and herdsmen. A few days previously, the Bosnian Croat HVO had sent four soldiers to set up a roadblock and the villagers had been passing the time of day with them as they went about their business. Babushkas would bring tea and bread and other little treats to the extent that the soldiers were permanently stuffed and looked for excuses to avoid having to eat and drink more.

The observing platoon was from the Zulfikar 'Special Unit' of the ABiH – *Armija Bosnia i Hercegovina* – the armed forces of Bosnia Herzegovina. It contained at least twenty young men and several women. Other than their ABiH patches, they wore the uniform of the former Yugoslavian army and carried old Warsaw Pact weapons. They had been ordered to remove the Croat roadblock and take prisoner the Croat soldiers. Both sides were trying to dominate ground with roadblocks and, equally, both sides wanted to remove them and impose their own. Until now, there had been very few shots fired in these confrontations.

Ana Kovačević was playing with her puppy she had christened 'Sanel Zool'. He was a mischievous black sheep dog but she adored him. She knew that Sanel would eventually have to earn his living herding the sheep her father tended but for the moment he was too young to start the training and her parents had allowed her to adopt him as a temporary pet. He also adored Ana and followed her everywhere she went. He had already mastered sit but stay was still work in progress. He had learned, however, that the soldiers by the roadblock were a reliable source of titbits and treats and he would happily go with his mistress to visit them as she collected the milk for her mother each morning.

This particular morning, she was walking with Sanel towards the soldiers when she saw that, rather than lounging around by the makeshift barrier, they were crouching in the ditch or lying on the verge, their guns pointing down the road. Ana sensed all was not well and, scooping Sanel into her arms, ran back home. Once inside she called to her mother who was out at the back of the house feeding the half dozen or so chickens that they kept for eggs.

'Mama, there is something happening down where the soldiers are.'

'What sort of thing, dearest?' came the unconcerned reply.

'I don't know but they look as they are expecting some trouble.'

'This silly war' replied her mother 'It will be something they were told on their radios, I should think.'

Ana put Sanel down and went up to her bedroom from where she could see the soldiers. They were still lying in the ditch or on the verge behind the embankment. She heard a far-off bang and then the soldiers began to fire sporadically down the road. She watched through the window, on her knees so that just her eyes were above the sill. Two Croat soldiers got up and, still crouching ran back down the road towards the houses. They came to a halt and, kneeling, they fired whilst the other two also ran back. She could hear other shots being fired further away.

'Ana, get away from that window.' Her mother was in the room with Sanel at her feet. The puppy began to yap in excitement at the new game, running around the room in excited circles.

'They are shooting at something,' Ana explained, still transfixed with the unfolding drama outside. The soldiers were working their way back towards her house.

'Darling, come with me right this minute. This is not safe.' Her mother held out her hand and Ana picked up her wriggling puppy and, taking her mother's hand, reluctantly went down the two flights of stairs to the basement cellar where they kept the winter wood. Her mother closed the door but they could still hear the occasional shot.

'We will stay here until all this nonsense is sorted out' her mother explained.

'Do you think someone will kill the soldiers, Mama?'

'Hush darling. Of course not. They are just trying to scare them. This wretched war is getting too much,' she muttered.

The shooting had subsided and they both waited, listening. Ana sat on the floor and teased her dog, turning him over and rubbing his tummy. He then ran off and found a stick and brought it back, crouching down on his front legs with his tail in the air waving frantically.

'Darling, stop teasing the dog,' said her mother.

'But Mama, we are just playing.'

'Stop it at once, do you hear me.'

The mother's tone had changed and Ana let the dog have the stick. He began to chew it, holding one end between his little paws and splintering the wood into a messy pile.

There was a loud banging on the door above them. The mother put her finger to her lips and motioned to Ana to sit with her behind the door. There was more banging and then the sound of the door splintering and shouting above them. The two of them remained still and silent but Ana was more petrified than she had ever been in her life. She knew absolute silence was essential but it took every fibre of her being to stop herself crying. She gripped her Mama's hand so tightly her fingers were white. There were loud footsteps above them and doors slamming and she could hear but not discern talking. There was shouting down the stairs and they were saying if anybody is down there come out now. Her Mama motioned for her to keep still. And then Sanel yapped for attention. She grabbed the dog but this was just a new game and another few yaps broke the silence. Then in a horrifying sequence of events, there were boots on the stairs down to the basement and the door was flung open.

Two soldiers came in with rifles raised. One was a woman which gave a misplaced comfort to Ana.

'Out!' shouted the man, waving his rifle at them. They both

raised their hands and the mother began pleading, they were just two women, there were no soldiers, they were not part of the war, they knew nothing…

'Quiet. Out.'

The woman soldier grabbed Ana by the arm and pushed her up the stairs and straight to the front door. There were two more soldiers at the entrance, both kneeling with their rifles at the ready. One grabbed Ana's other arm and held her tight. She could see that they were also holding old Mrs. Horvat from next door. Two other soldiers appeared from the house opposite and they had Mr. Radić. One of the soldiers began shouting down the street for everybody to put down their guns. Ana assumed he was shouting at the Croatian soldiers who had been manning the roadblock for there were no other guns in the village. Ana felt herself being pushed into the middle of the road and her mother was now screaming, being held back by the woman soldier. They just stood there in road and Ana felt very alone, frightened and exposed. She could see no movement in front of her but could hear the Muslim soldiers moving behind her. She was crying now and she also wet herself but nobody seemed to notice or care. Absurdly, she wondered if any of the boys from her school were watching.

The soldiers were pushing the two grown-ups in front them, with Ana being marched behind, as they proceeded down the road. The shooting had stopped now and the village was quiet except for the sound of sobbing that seemed to come from all around. In front of her the four soldiers from the checkpoint stood up from their hiding places behind one of the houses. They had left their guns on the ground and had their arms in the air. The Muslim soldiers rushed forward to grab them and they were thrown onto the road. Several boots went flying in and each soldier was tied with his hands behind his back. A Muslim soldier tried to rip the army patches off one of the prisoner's arms but it was sown on too well. Instead, he cuffed the man on the back of the head, sending his helmet rattling down the road.

The prisoners of war and the hostages, for that is what they were now, were corralled into a tight group. As well as the four soldiers, there were about eighteen villagers, mainly women and old men but also some children. The woman let Ana go and she took the chance to run back to where her mother was tearfully calling out her name. She grabbed her mother's hand and hid behind her, glancing at what was happening. The Muslim soldiers split the group into smaller groups and the woman soldier and one of the other men led six of them away. Before long, this group was told to stop and were made to stand in a line looking out to the hills. Then the shooting started and all six fell. The Muslim soldiers continued firing into the prone bodies before one of the men went to check for signs of life. Satisfied that he had completed a job well done, he changed his magazine on his rifle and went to receive the praises of his comrades. There was further automatic fire in the village before the remaining villagers were told to return home.

The Muslim soldiers disappeared as quickly as they had come. The villagers, when they were sure they had gone, went out to find and identify the dead. There were twenty-two bodies, including the four soldiers and several children. The Croat Muslim civil war had now tipped past the point of no return.

PART I

Bosnia is under my skin. It's the place you cannot leave behind. I was obsessed by the nightmare of it all; there was this sense of guilt, and an anger that has become something much deeper over these last years.

Rt Hon Paddy Ashdown

At a certain moment, Yugoslavia stopped being rational, and then you end up going to war.

Emir Kusturica

1

Tuesday 6 July 1993
Maribor Airfield
Slovenia
260km South of Vienna
1900 Local

The drive south from Vienna had been simple enough. The evening traffic was light and the warm day had already begun to mellow by the time they pulled into the service station south of Graz for *Asr* prayers. They parked away from the main buildings with their garish advertisements and worked out the *Qibla* to face Mecca before unrolling their prayer mats. The Algerian had forbidden them from browsing the shopping mall and only the driver left the vehicle to fill with fuel before heading south towards the border with Slovenia. The Austrian customs officials had waved them through with barely a glance and they continued south to the airfield at Maribor.

As the minibus pulled up to the barrier the security guard

motioned to the driver to kill the engine. His ill-fitting corporate uniform, with its large Prevent Global plc logo, was in stark contrast to the smartness of the Austrian customs and border police they had encountered forty minutes previously at the border crossing at Spielfeld. He asked for the travel documents for all eight of the occupants which the Algerian in the passenger seat had already gathered. He took the passports and began flicking through them one by one. They were all brand-new Bosnian passports issued within the last few weeks by the embassy in Vienna. Folded into the passports were the letters of introduction written by TWRA, The Third World Relief Agency, a humanitarian organisation also domiciled in the Austrian capital.

'Abdel Kader Mokhtari?' he enquired vaguely.

The man in the passenger seat raised his hand. 'That's me' he said in German.

'Raus – out!' The Algerian opened the door and stepped out and stood in front of the guard, who looked at the passport and then at the face before him. He shut the passport and handed it back.

'Salim al Agayli?' For a second, Salim didn't recognise the nom de guerre, his *kunya*, he had chosen for his documents. It was also clear that all the passengers would have to get out of the minibus and they duly climbed out, stretching their stiff limbs, and stood around waiting to be called. The guard looked at each in turn, an officious performance more for the benefit of his own self esteem than any attempt at security. Once everybody had had their documents examined, his colleague sauntered out of the guard hut.

'These papers are not in order,' he announced, despite not having looked at any of them.

They had been told to expect this by Elfatih Hassanein, the Sudanese in charge of the TWRA in Vienna.

'What appears to be the problem?' said the Algerian.

'Airport is closed. No visitors.'

The Algerian dipped his hand into the side pocket of his cargo trousers and pulled out a wad of deutschmarks. He openly peeled four one-hundred mark notes and put them into his passport and handed it back to the second security man. The guard took them, removed the notes, stuffed them into his own pocket and handed back the passport. Saying nothing, he turned back to the barrier and lifted it.

They all got back in the minibus which then drove under the barrier and headed towards the runway. At the far end, parked on the apron outside an isolated hangar was an Iluyshin IL-76 transport plane. It had flown in from Khartoum that afternoon with a large quantity of humanitarian aid including uniforms, Kalashnikovs, RGP7s and several tons of ammunition. The minibus parked in the hangar and Salim got out with the rest of his fellow travellers.

Abdel Kader approached a man and handed him a docket. It was an irrevocable letter of credit made out by First Austrian Bank for three hundred thousand US dollars. The man took out a small Maglite torch and examined the letter. Satisfied it was genuine, he went into the small office at the back of the hangar and made a telephone call. A minute later he returned and gave the Algerian a quick emotionless handshake.

They stood around watching a forklift truck lift crates out of the aircraft. Someone offered Salim a cigarette, which he accepted gratefully and lit with the disposable lighter that he had bought from a kiosk in Vienna. He glanced at his watch and saw it would soon be time for sunset *Maghrib* prayers. He turned to a Saudi and enquired in Arabic if they should prepare for the prayers.

'Abdel Kader will tell us when it is time to pray. During Jihad, the strict observation of the Quran may be set aside for Sahwa.' *Sahwa*, they had been told in Vienna, is what they were in Yugoslavia for. The domination of the world by Islam. Their brothers were being attacked by the infidel Serbs and the cry for help had resonated all around the Muslim world. In their minibus alone, there were Mujahadeen from Algeria, Saudi, Yemen, Syria and Pakistan. Some were veterans of the war against the Soviets in Afghanistan, some, like Salim, young men not frightened of *Shaheed*, a martyr's death.

Salim sat on a crate of weapons and waited. At sunset, by which time the aircraft had been emptied, they did stop for *Maghrib*. As it grew dark, a chill descended and Salim wondered what the winter would be like in Bosnia. He came from an impoverished family living in the oasis of Bou Saada on the edge of the Sahara Desert. The youngest of seven, he had three older brothers. Actually, two now, as one had been killed in the last months of the war in Afghanistan. Another brother had survived to return home but had encouraged him to go to Yugoslavia with hair-raising tales of battles with the Russians and the shooting down of helicopters using missiles supplied by the Great Satan, America. His mother had tried in vain to talk him out of it but the Imam had requested volunteers, saying passage would be paid to the Jihad in far-off Europe. For the seventeen-year-old Salim, with a life of growing fruit and vegetables for the market stretching interminably in front of him, it was an easy decision.

It was getting chilly so he decided to put on his cheap black ski jacket he had bought in C&A with the weekly stipend they all received. He had never owned a warm coat before but enjoyed its weight on his shoulders.

Just before midnight, the group was stirred into life by the approaching headlights of a G-wagon with 'Eco-Trends' stencilled on the side. Two men got out and spoke in English to the forklift truck operators, which Salim neither understood nor realised was, in fact, spoken by an American. Shortly after, he heard the faint clatter of an engine and, for the first time in his life, saw a helicopter. It was displaying no lights and came in to land close to the hangar, blasting dust and litter into their faces.

The Algerian, Abdel Kader, told everyone that they were to wait for the cargo to be lifted onto the helicopter and then they would be transported to their destination sitting on the crates. The flight would be less than an hour. When Salim boarded, he made sure he was sitting near a window. He was nervous, having never flown before, but wanted to experience the exhilaration. The interior of the helicopter had red warning messages in Cyrillic Russian and he thought to himself of the irony that he was probably travelling in an aircraft that had been used to try to kill his brothers.

As the helicopter took off, he felt unbalanced and held tightly on to the crates. Transfixed by the flight and the smallness of the twinkling lights of the villages and towns far below, time passed quickly and he noticed that the helicopter was approaching another airport, this one altogether larger and busier and next to a black sea. They touched down with a bounce and Abdel ordered everyone to stay put. As Salim looked out of the window, he saw a fuel bowser approach and uniformed soldiers began uncoiling a pipeline. He reached idly into his pocket for his cigarettes only to be yelled at by Abdel. In a hail of curses, he was informed in no uncertain terms that smoking while a plane full of ammunition was being refuelled was the act of a madman and an idiot and did he want them all to die before they had even killed one infidel?

Embarrassed and chastened, he sat mute until the side door opened. Outside were two other uniformed soldiers with a forklift. One, with officer's rank on his shoulders, spoke briefly to Abdel. Then the forklift began off-loading crates until about half were neatly stacked on the runway. Abdel then reached for his small rucksack and took out a large clear plastic envelope with a thick wad of money in large denomination notes. Salim guessed they were US dollars. The transaction over, the side door slid shut and the Russian crewman indicated that they would soon be taking off once again.

Salim nudged his Saudi friend with a toe and gave him a quizzical look.

'It is the cost of waging war, my friend. We must pay the Croats in weapons and money for them to allow us to transport over their country. But do not worry, we have plenty of both for the fight against the enemy. And The Base will send plenty more of both should we need.

2

Wednesday 7 July 1993
Visoko Airfield
38 Kilometers South East of Zenica
Republic of Bosnia Herzegovina
0400 Local

They were called the 'Cricket Team' because they were required to be dressed all in white. Their official title was 'The European Community Monitoring Mission in the Former Yugoslavia' or ECMM for short, which had been set up at the start of hostilities in 1991. Their job was to report to the European Community what was happening in the rapidly breaking up former communist country, so that "Europe" could have a united response to what was fast becoming an escalating civil war. They were unarmed and forbidden from getting in the way of any of the factions, whatever it was that they might witness. And Eric Scott-Douglas, sitting in the driver's seat with a pair of binoculars pressed to his eyes, had already witnessed a lot of things he would rather not have seen. Next to him was Barbara Bishop. They had been working together in Bosnia for about two months but had met eighteen months previously in London.

'I can hear it but I can't see it, Babs.'

'Don't call me Babs,' said Barbara, also dressed in white, in the passenger's seat, also peering through binoculars.

'D'you remember Pans People? Top of the Pops?' he asked, not taking his eyes from the binos. 'There was one I especially liked, lovely Babs. Don't know her name.'

'Very funny,' said Barbara.

'Actually, that's stolen from Ronnie Barker in Porridge.'

'There it is. Hip. Coming over the high ground to the west.'

'Got it.' Eric tracked the helicopter, which was flying without lights, as it came into land on the grass strip. 'More weapons. How many have we had so far?'

'Must be eight, no, nine flights because we had two in on Thursday. What can they carry?' she asked.

'Um, I think for a Mil Mi-8 Hip it's about four thousand kilograms and twenty-four pax.'

'You are such a train spotter, Eric.'

'Bet you a pound to a pinch of pig shit that it's a mix of ammo and Muj.'

The hard topped Land Rover, also painted white, was parked on a bend in the mountain track high above the airfield. The area around them was forested but tree felling last year now afforded them a good view of the airfield and they had been up here for the last seven nights, logging the flights. The *Armija Bosnia i Hercegovina*, known as ABiH or just The Bosnian Army, was comprised mainly of Muslim Bosniaks. They had been recently formed to protect the local Muslim population from the depredations of the Serbian Army and, now, from the recently formed Serbian militias. As Yugoslavia broke up, the population of Bosnia Herzegovina, the most diverse of the Yugoslavian countries, had begun coalescing along ethnic lines. The Bosnian Serbs wanted to remain attached politically to Serbia, the Croats to Croatia, but the Muslims, always a minority, had no real homeland to speak of. Each group had suddenly discovered newfound fears and hatreds of the other two based entirely on religious grounds that were totally non-existent two years ago. But there was a new development that was beginning to concern those observing the conflict. The Bosniak Muslims were being supported by their brethren across the Middle East and Africa with both money for weapons and mercenaries. In the last few months, previously cordial if not friendly relations with the Croats had deteriorated to the point where the two former allies were shooting at each other in various parts of central Bosnia.

'Keep a note of what comes out will you, Barbara? I'm going for a slash and a fag.'

Eric laid the binoculars on the shelf above the instrument panel and opened the door, already putting a Marlboro Red into the corner of his mouth. He went behind the vehicle and relieved himself against a tree before returning to the Land Rover on Barbara's side. She slid open the window.

'Pass me the binos, would you?'

'Can you keep that foul smoke away from my window, please Eric. Asking nicely.'

Eric flicked the cigarette away and then thinking he didn't want to cause a forest fire, walked over and ground it into the dirt with his boot. They both scanned the helicopter and watched as the passengers disembarked.

'I can see ten,' said Barbara.

'Yup, agree with that. They look like foreign imports. They

are shifting out the weapons now. Nothing big by the looks of it.'

'AKs, RPGs and ammo?' asked Barbara.

'Yup.' He switched his view to the entrance to the airstrip. 'Here comes the transport. Zil 131, no, hold on it's a 157.'

'How can you tell?'

'Mudguards. 131 has angular front mudguards. The older 157 has a more sweeping design.'

'Really? Bloody hell,' said Barbara. Eric continued scanning the airfield but she saw a wry smile form and heard a muttered 'attention to detail.'

The new arrivals lifted the boxes into the back of the lorry which turned towards the road just at the helicopter's rotors began to turn.

'Do we know who is running the choppers?' asked Barbara.

'I'm hearing it's a newly formed PMC called "Eco-Trends". American-Russian joint venture believe it or not.'

'Sovs and Yanks working together in a new European war. Eric, the world has changed beyond recognition in the last three years.'

'Say that again. Gets worse, too. The Bosnians here are Sunni but they are being funded mainly by the Shi'ite Iranians. That wouldn't have happened five years ago either.'

'I'm hearing that there is money coming from Saudi as well,' said Barbara.

'Whole Muslim world is helping, from Algeria through to Pakistan by way of Turkey, Malaysia…'

'Even Brunei,' she finished for him.

'Yup, them too' agreed Eric 'but there's a shed load of cash coming from Sudan. There's some Saudi billionaire that has set up something called 'Al Qaeda' there and he's funding weapons. Was in Afghanistan in the eighties, apparently.'

'Do you think they are going up to the camp at Mehurici?'

she asked, still watching the departing truck through her binoculars.

'Probably,' replied Eric, 'or Polijanice maybe. Time to call it a night and return to the hotel.'

Eric started the Rover and put it into reverse and was just turning round to look behind when Barbara let out a little cough. He glanced at her and then continued the manoeuvre when she coughed again.

'You alright Babs?'

She was miming with her fingers, as if playing the piano. 'What?' he persisted.

'Notice anything?' she said.

'Um… your fingers appear to have contracted St Vitus's Dance?'

'No. Not that.' She wiggled the fingers on her left hand.

'Ah. Someone's given you a sparkler. And I'm guessing it's Captain Adam Lonsdale. Babs, I'm overwhelmed with joy and delight.'

'At least try and sound pleased' she said.

'No, genuinely,' Eric said with a laugh 'I'm really pleased for you. Come on, gimme a gander.'

She held out her finger and, as Eric craned forward for a closer look, she flipped him the bird.

'Oi!' he exclaimed and then, 'I hope it cost at least one month's pay.'

She laughed again, 'Come on, let's get back to the hotel and see if they have any fizz in the cellar.'

Babs sat back in her seat with a feeling of dreamy contentment. Though the ring was new, the secret she had shared with her soon-to-be husband was a month old. Only the parents knew. And now Eric. There would be a formal announcement soon, of course, but Adam had three months of his deployment with his infantry battalion in Bosnia still to run. After that, she would take some leave and they would spend a week in England with their families and friends. But first she was going to take some extra leave now and with her new husband-to-be, go somewhere nice. It was to be a surprise, paid for by the Lonsdales and chosen by Adam. He refused to let her know. 'You don't need any injections or any cold weather clothes,' was all he had said and she couldn't wait.

3

Wednesday 14 July 1993
Mehurici
Bilal Valley
Central Bosnia
1900 Local

Salim al Agayli had begun his training the very next day after morning prayers. They had all been issued with Yugoslav army fatigues and a webbing vest with pockets on the front in which they were to carry their magazines and ammunition. The first day had been loading and unloading drills and his fingers had become sore with the constant inserting, extracting and reinserting of bullets into the magazines and slapping the magazines into the housing on the rifles. The training staff, all ABiH regulars, had stressed that it should become second nature to them as, in the heat of battle, they could not afford to fumble. Getting shot fumbling with a magazine might be the Will of Allah but one could help oneself by not getting it wrong in the first place. To break up the lessons, they were made to run round a rudimentary assault course, leaping over barriers and crawling under barbed wire while the instructors fired into the air.

The next day they had sat in large circles with their AK47s in front of them and watched as the instructor took apart the weapon. They spent that day taking apart and assembling their weapons. He had learned the names of the various parts and how the two catches worked - the magazine release catch and the safety catch. The last hour of the day before prayers and the evening meal had been weapons cleaning and again their instructors had impressed upon them that a clean weapon was less likely to jam. At the final inspection the instructor took apart each weapon in turn. One of the new arrivals had misplaced his firing pin without which the gun would not work. The instructor screamed at him that not only might that result in him dying on the battlefield but also his friends dying with him. The miscreant, whom Salim recognised from the trip down from Austria as a Saudi called Nawaf, seemed unconcerned. Allah – *Subhanahu wa'ta'ala* - will provide he muttered, albeit not in earshot of the instructor.

In the evenings they lined up at the old Soviet field kitchens and received a generous bowlful of lamb or beef curried stew and some flat breads. Food was plentiful and the recruits never went hungry. Each day more new recruits would arrive, often three or four at a time, transported in via Austria, like he had been, or moved up through Italy and across to Split in Croatia. He never understood why the newly formed Croat state would allow that to happen. Most were ordered to pretend to be working for humanitarian agencies such as the "Advisory and Reformation Committee" set up recently in London and seemingly given the blessing of the British state. Others came in as journalists, also on spurious or forged documentation. Many had Bosnian passports newly issued by the embassy in Vienna.

After the evening meal and prayers, there were lectures from the mainly foreign fighters. Most had been in Afghanistan and originated from all over the Arab world. They were taught about 'Global *Ummah*' that all Muslims must come together for common jihad against the infidel and such an alliance would transcend race, nation or class. The main teaching was in the Salafi school of thought, a strict adherence to the ways of the 'Salafiyya' – the pious predecessors. Some of the Imams, mainly those from Saudi, were Wahabi, if possible, an even more puritanical form of adherence. Occasionally, they would encounter Shi'ites from Iran and certainly, some of the recruits were Hezbollah fighters from Lebanon. All teaching had the common theme of the mission to establish a devout Muslim country in central Europe. The more radical teachers were talking about global jihad and the setting up of a worldwide Caliphate. They were told about the local Muslims, who, because they were oppressed by the Christian majority, had strayed from the narrow path. However, in the new caliphate there must be allowances made until proper behaviour and customs could be retaught. They were advised to be tolerant of women showing their hair or wearing make-up, even drinking alcohol. Overzealous behaviour amongst the local population had led to some confrontations between Bosniaks and foreign in-comers. But, for the infidel, no such leeway would be allowed.

There were, amongst the new recruits, some veterans from the conflict in Afghanistan. They would listen to the stories of fighting the Soviets, of downing the feared helicopter gunships with American and British missiles and ambushing convoys of lorries and tanks from high in the mountains above the passes. Lurid tales of what they did to the captives, young Russian conscripts sent to fight as part of their National Service. The veterans would recount their stories with glee and pride; how they would cut a throat and pull the tongue through the slit, calling it the 'Afghan necktie'. The imams would nod sagely and approvingly, for the infidel was the enemy of God. His death was of no consequence. His killing a duty. There was *Dar al-Islam* or the *Dar al-Hab;* the House of Islam or the House of War. Nothing in between. The kuffir would be overcome, his men slaughtered and his women used as slaves and concubines. It was the Will of God. *In Sha Allah*.

Other recruits began to recount how they also were cutting throats here in Bosnia. One recounted how they had killed four Croat soldiers that April in a town called Miletići and another chorused with pride how they had dispatched eight wounded kuffir only a month ago in Maline. Salim listened to the teaching of the imams and learned from the actions of his fellow soldiers. Mercy was not to be given.

* * *

Salim was looking forward to firing the rifle he had been given and which he had taken apart and reassembled hundreds of times and cleaned and oiled until it gleamed. The day finally arrived and he lined up opposite the rough cardboard targets on the makeshift range. When it came to firing the first bullet, he forgot everything he had been taught. His heart was pounding and his breathing was rapid. He closed his eyes and snatched at the trigger. The other recruits, in a row either side of him, were firing away now but he decided he had to calm himself, remember what he had been taught and take his time. His next bullet was fired under much more control and he saw the splash as it impacted through the target. The kick of the rifle still took him somewhat by surprise and the deafening noise of gun was equally disconcerting. By the time he had fired five of his ten bullets, all the other recruits had finished. The instructor shouted for all who had finished to raise their hands and seeing Salim still pointing his rifle down the range, let him continue. Salim refused to be hurried and he squeezed off the next five in his own good time. When at last he raised his hand, they were instructed to remove magazines, lay down their rifles and walk to their targets. As he approached his, Salim looked nervously to see if he had hit it at all. But when just a couple of metres away, he saw the little rips in the cardboard. Most were grouped around the centre. He counted them. Then he counted then again. Nine. He had missed with one. The first one. That would not happen again. Walking back to the firing point, excited conversations ensued. Some of the recruits had failed entirely to hit the target with any of their ten bullets. He was top equal with nine and the instructor had praised him for the closeness of the hits. The instructor explained the tighter the group, the better the marksmanship. He felt a glowing pride and was desperate to give it another go.

That would not happen until the next day, when once again they lined up at the range. This time, he registered ten hits out of ten and then, in a second session another ten. At the midday meal, the instructor singled him out and told him he would be undergoing further training in a group of the best shots. There were six of them and the new instructor would be a Bosniak instructor from the former Yugoslav army. The instructor was from the 7th Muslim Brigade of the ABiH. He told them that the foreign volunteers would be formed into the El Mudzahid battalion and attached to the 7th. His job was to turn them into snipers. From now on, they were to hand in their AK47s and instead learn to use a Zastava M72 rifle. This was based on a Russian AKM Kalashnikov and was a precision weapon with a longer barrel and much higher accuracy. Furthermore, it had an integral bipod and could be fitted with a scope.

For the next week, most of his days were spent on a secondary range where the distances to the targets could be extended out to nearly a kilometre. Rather than joining the rest of the Mujahadeen mixing range work with patrolling skills and assault courses, the snipers had lectures on camouflage and concealment. He learned about how to construct fire positions, how the giveaways were movement, shine, shadows and noise. They learned how to read the contours on a map and to use them to their advantage, moving through dead ground so that they were not in view of the enemy. They were split into pairs and worked in turn as spotters and firers. Each evening, he took apart his rifle and cleaned it meticulously. He kept it with him and let nobody touch it. He was particularly careful when it had the telescopic sight fitted as he now knew that a slight knock could put the sight out as much as a metre over five hundred metres meaning that the shot would both be wasted and possibly fatal if it gave away a position.

This evening, they had been told that a VIP was visiting the camp. Nobody knew the identity of the person but there had been various visitors over the last week, most of them foreigners from the Middle East. However, this one seemed to have galvanised their officers and instructors and Salim felt that whoever it was might be different and more important.

The snipers had been informed that the next day they were to put on a sniping demonstration, shooting targets out to seven hundred metres. It filled him with trepidation but also excitement and a sense of achievement. He had been chosen, after just a few days, to be part of a display for an extremely important visitor.

When dawn broke, Salim was already up and had checked and rechecked his rifle. The final thing he had done yesterday was zero the sights, so he was confident he could hit his targets. Overnight, he had carefully lain his weapon on its side so that nothing could disturb the alignment. He kept telling himself that he had to remember both his training and not to inadvertently knock the sights. Now he was at one end of the range and he could see the lines of targets laid at varying distances from the firing point. His spotter, Khalid the Saudi, was at his side with a rare and prized pair of Spetznaz issued binoculars. Before too long a gaggle of men arrived at the firing point. In amongst them and obviously the focus of attention, judging by the fawning that was going on, was a very tall thin man, with an Afghan headdress and a sparse beard. His angular features and small dark eyes gave him an authority and charisma that immediately impressed Salim.

Their orders were to shoot each of the targets twice, starting with the closest at about a hundred metres and working progressively further down the range until putting two bullets through the final target at seven hundred metres. Salim looked through the sight, adjusted his scope for a hundred metres and saw that the cardboard target was absurdly big in his view. He calmed his breathing, reducing his heartbeat, steadied the rifle on its bipod, held his breath and gently squeezed the trigger.

'Right through the middle my friend' observed Khalid through the binoculars.

Salim could see the strike mark and, repeating the process, put another bullet right next to it.

'Similar my friend, but that was the easy one. We now go to the two hundreds but this is good shooting. God is with you this morning.'

The next two were also fine central shots but at four hundred metres, the target was beginning to look smaller and the shake of the adjustments made steadying the aim harder. He adjusted the sights for range and then squeezed off two more hits. But this time they were not so central and not so close together. But a hit was a hit. In battle, it would take a man down, removing him from the fight as well as striking fear in those that remained. At seven hundred metres, the central aiming point of the sights seemed to cover the whole target and his breathing seemed to move the centre mark wildly. He took more time, concentrated on calming himself before firing. The first bullet went short, kicking up a small dust cloud some five metres before the target.

'You are indeed lucky today, my friend' remarked Khalid.

Salim looked at the target through the scope and saw that a ricochet had taken the bullet through the target despite falling short. For his final shot, he adjusted upwards as best he could and fired.

'Again, God is smiling' said Khalid, putting down the binoculars and himself smiling at Salim. He handed over the binoculars and Salim saw that he had clipped the top of the target. Ten bullets, ten hits. He was hoping that the ricochet hadn't been noticed by the dignitaries who were now milling about talking with the tall man.

Salim stood at his firing point whilst Khalid collected the spent cartridges. The group wandered over and the tall man congratulated him on his shooting. He didn't mention a miss so Salim thought perhaps they had not seen it. The tall man then asked if he could shoot his AK down the range. Salim was taken aback that such an honoured guest should ask him and, of course, gestured to him to take a shot. The man squatted awkwardly at the firing point and Salim noted that he was left-handed. He had been carrying a standard, albeit new looking rifle and, with it in his left shoulder, fired an automatic burst at the nearest target until the magazine was empty. Bullets flew everywhere, some, but not most, hitting the target, the rest flying off down the range with the ricochets whining through the air. His left-handedness made firing the rifle difficult as the spent cases were ejected to the right-hand side, close to his face. The group behind him clapped and congratulated him. Salim looked on thinking that the man had just committed every basic mistake his instructors had just spent the last week drilling out of the recruits.

The tall man, having fired his gun, then addressed them all.

He spoke of the importance of their mission in Bosnia and emphasised the need for the establishment of a devout Muslim country in the heart of Europe where Islam could flourish and spread. He said their fight against the infidel was God's calling and, one day soon, the whole of Islam would be united into one great Caliphate. His mentioning of the 'Base' led Salim to assume he was the Saudi that had funded the Mujahadeen and their weapons. Some of the senior officers then announced that soon they would be ready to strike at the enemy and that plans were already advanced for an attack on the infidel Croats.

4

Friday 16 July 1993
Municipality of Bugojno
130km Northwest of Sarajevo
Central Bosnia

The foreign battalion, El Mudzahid as they now called themselves, was attached to the 7th Muslim Brigade and they were put on notice that they would soon be leaving the camp at Mehurici for the front. On the final day before moving out, they put on one last demonstration for their benefactors, including the tall man, that consisted mainly of choreographed assault course clambering and stylistic shooting. It appeared rather stupid to Salim, especially the simultaneous synchronised forward rolls. He was spared participating in this show and had been continuing to practise his marksmanship whilst the others had been learning their dance moves. As a finale, the El Mudzahid had formed into columns and had jogged past the dignitaries and senior officers. They had been issued green headbands which they all wore with pride and the El Mudzahid had been given their own black flag which was carried at the front of the column.

The next day, at dawn, they had formed up and climbed into the back of a fleet of assorted old trucks that would take them through the countryside to where the fighting was happening. Salim was full of nerves, telling himself that this was what he was here to do whilst still being unsure of what the future may bring.

The journey took about three hours, climbing up through the wooded hills of Bosnia passing villages and small towns on the way. He was relieved to see that the towns often had the minarets of mosques and he passed the time smoking and chatting with his fellow volunteers. He could see no signs of war and the inhabitants were going about their everyday chores without much of a care. At one point, after about an hour, he saw a white painted jeep with two occupants both also dressed in white and asked his companions who they were but nobody knew. They waved and the occupants waved cheerfully back.

When the trucks finally stopped in the square of a small town, they all got out and stretched their legs, many relieving themselves in corners of the buildings. Someone built a bonfire and soon there was water boiling for sweet mint tea. Their officers formed them up into two columns and they began to march out of the town and up into the hills. They walked through the fields but it was clear that many had gone before them because the grass was worn through to the mud and the pathway was littered with discarded food wrappers water bottles and other rubbish. After about two hours walking uphill, Salim heard distant gunshots. A murmur spread through the columns that this was the front line to where they were heading and indeed, after another hour or so, they stopped. There were numerous Bosnian troops all around them now and they were told wait in line for food at one of the old field kitchens where a cook was doling out two ladles each of goat curry. They sat around in the sun eating and then smoking. Most began to doze as the afternoon drifted slowly by. The shooting sounded closer now but was not intense, just the occasional shots or the rapid chatter of automatic weapons breaking into the summery afternoon.

In the early evening, they were again formed into columns but this time rather than just two abreast they were separated into smaller groups. Each group was given a guide and they set off in various directions up the hill. Salim, with his long rifle, trudged along at the back of his group, his legs becoming weary. Most of his fellow soldiers carried their AKs on their shoulders as they struggled up the hill through the woods. Some had the heavier belt fed machine guns and had opted to carry the belted ammunition crossed on their chests Rambo-style. Finally, they came to a stop and were told they were to be as quiet as possible and there was to be no smoking, lights or talking. As they approached the crest of the ridge, Salim saw the front line. A roughly dug trench in the soft earth on the ridge with the occasional structure made with felled trunks of the ubiquitous pines. There were soldiers with their rifles at the ready looking out into the gloom in front every five or so metres. When he got into the trench, the parapet only came to his chest so he bent down as he walked along to one of the bunkers cut into the side of the mountain.

The old hands were sitting around in the bunker chatting and smoking but none spoke Arabic so he found it difficult to gather what was going on. Eventually, one of the El Mudzahid NCOs told him that they were to hold this part of the line whilst some of the 7 Brigade units would be taken back to the rear. He was to set up his sniper's rifle and look for any opportunity targets to the front of the trench. He would be relieved by someone at some stage in the night. He was led out of the bunker and placed about two hundred metres away. He took off his backpack and set up his rifle. He ensured he had a bullet in the chamber but kept the safety catch on. By now it was dark and he could see a myriad of stars above him through the trees. To his front all he could see were the trees descending gently into the valley but the thick forest made it difficult to see very far ahead. He calculated that it was probably only fifty or so metres. Nevertheless, he settled down to scan the woods for what he thought was the inevitable attack by the Croats up the hill and on to their positions.

The soft drizzle on his face woke him. He had dozed off and now sat up with a start before realising his head would be in full view of the assaulting enemy. But the wood was quiet and as he looked to either side of him all he could see were the shapes of his fellow soldiers in the trench. The rain had soaked him and he now felt a chill in his bones. He shifted position to get some circulation back into his limbs and waited for the dawn.

The rain abated just before first light and with the dawning of the day came the first shots. Wherever the enemy were, he couldn't really tell. The shots sounded out in front but he could not see where they were landing. Certainly, nobody close to his position seemed to have been hit. Some of the soldiers either side of him began shooting back down the hill and again, he could see nobody in front of him. Using the scope of his rifle was not helpful either as all he saw were large trees in his field of view. Nevertheless, the noise of the exchange of fire excited him and he forgot the endless dull night and kept a vigilant look out to his front. Somebody close by opened up with a heavier machine gun and the sound cascaded down the mountain into the valley below.

Salim remembered that he was supposed to have been relieved in the night and wondered if they had found him asleep and just left him there. If that was the case, would there be consequences for being asleep at his post, he wondered.

After an hour or so, the sun came out and warmed his soaking uniform. As it grew hotter, he realised he was steaming. He ate one of the flat breads that he had kept from his last meal at the field kitchen, grateful he had had the foresight to keep some for later. He then decided he needed to go, so he moved down the trench to his neighbour, who was also a Mujahadeen and asked where he could use the toilet. He was told that they had been told to go behind, up in the woods. Salim felt very vulnerable as he dashed out and over the crest to find a quiet spot for this morning's ablutions. He then remembered, with some shame, that he had not yet done his *Fajr* prayers so he slipped back down to his position and, judging from the sun, orientated as best he could and said his prayers. There was still some shooting from his side but the more distant reports had subsided and now he could hear nothing of the enemy. He wondered if his own side were just shooting for the sake of it or because the noise gave them comfort. At what he judged to be midday, he again said his prayers but noticed that he had not seen any of the others doing likewise and wondered if they were using the excuse of jihad to absolve themselves of their duty. Finally, a working party came down the trench and he was told to go back to the bunker. He collected his kit and headed back down the trench where he was told to leave the front line back the way he had come the evening before. In the lee of the hill, he found that food had been brought up by another working party and he sat down with his comrades for lunch. The gossip over the meal was that the Croats had withdrawn from the hill and were moving down the valley to the town.

They did another night in the trenches before being ordered to go back down the mountain to the town from whence they had started. There they got back onto the trucks and set off again to who knew where.

5

Saturday 17 July 1993
Bugojno Town Centre
130km Northwest of Sarajevo
Central Bosnia
0915 Local

Eric drove his white Land Rover up to the HVO roadblock but was waved through by the guards without having to get out and show his papers. The soldiers by now were getting used to the white vehicles of both UNPROFOR, the United Nations Protection Force, and ECMM. He followed the main thoroughfare towards the town centre where he knew the HVO garrison commander had set up his headquarters in the Kalin hotel. There was a constant boom of gun fire from the hills that surrounded the town and it echoed throughout the valley. There were still civilians going about their daily business but Eric thought there were less than yesterday. He also noticed that there were more Croat troops in the town centre, many looking dirty, tired and dishevelled and he wondered if the HVO lines in the hills around the town would hold.

He parked his vehicle outside the hotel.

'Come on Barbara, another day another dollar.'

'If I must, Eric. It's meant to be the weekend.'

'Typical civvy,' and he harrumphed out a little raspberry of disdain.

'As you well know, I was a captain in the Women's Royal Army Corps.'

'Three years in the WRAC doesn't qualify you as a soldier.'

'It jolly well does and it was four.'

'Warm Round and Cuddly.'

'Cheeky.'

'Or, alternatively, Weekly Ration of Army Cu…'

'Thank you, Eric. I have heard them all before. Please not the slivovitz. You don't think they'll make us drink at this time of the morning?'

'They make you drink at any time of the day or night. Anyway, you need the practice. In a few months, you are going to be an army wife.'

Barbara let out a little groan as Eric skipped up the stone steps of the hotel giving a quick handshake to the guard on the door before reaching into his breast pocket and flicking a cigarette into his mouth. He strode into what used to be a main meeting room on the ground floor but had now been converted into an operations room for the local army commander. His cigarette remained unlit.

The commander was leaning over a large map on a table with two of his sub-unit officers. They stopped what they were discussing and looked up to see Eric's beaming smile and outstretched hand. The main Croat garrison was the Eugen Kvaternik Brigade and, until recently, they had remained friendly with the other occupiers of Bugojno, the 307th Mountain Brigade of the Bosnian Muslim army, the

ABiH. Even whilst the rest of Bosnia had divided up between Croats and Muslims, the two opposing units remained, if not friendly, at least cordial to each other. This was now rapidly changing as the ABiH began to have military successes in the hills.

'Good morning, gentlemen,' boomed Eric.

A pretty young translator echoed his greeting in Serbo-Croat.

'I am here to discuss whether you are considering evacuating the town of its civilian population. Especially the women, children and the old,' said Eric, who noticed the translator was talking even before he had finished.

The commander reached into his pocket and proffered a cigarette lighter. Eric accepted and then, as an afterthought, produced five packets of Marlboro cigarettes from his pocket and put them on the table. The commander took the offering and dished out cigarettes to everybody in the room, including the translator.

Barbara knew better than to comment as, it seemed to her, almost everybody over the age of ten smoked in Bosnia.

'We can provide an UNPROFOR escort from the British battalion at Gornji Vakuf if required,' she added.

'The British commander was here yesterday and I will tell you what I told him. We have no need to evacuate the town as there is not the remotest possibility that the Muslims will enter here. Our army is defeating them everywhere we encounter them.'

'Aren't they already here? And we are getting reports that your troops are falling back towards the town,' countered Barbara.

'I would respectfully suggest your information is incorrect,' said the commander.

At this point, the door to the meeting opened and a member of the hotel staff came in bearing a tray of shot glasses and a bottle without a label. He poured a measure in each glass and then offered them to the two Brits.

'Um… I'm driving so I'd better not…' stammered Eric.

'Come, my friends, we toast Her Majesty the Queen and President Tudjman of Croatia,' and with that he knocked the drink back in one.

Eric looked at Barbara and then they both drank as well.

The waiter filled the shot glasses immediately.

'Honestly,' said Eric, 'I really can't be drink driving in my Rover.'

'But we need to toast the British and Croatian armies,' countered the commander and knocked back a second shot. Eric and Barbara did likewise but this time they both held onto their glasses with their fingers over the top to prevent any refills, hoping the waiter would not insist.

'Where does your day take you next?' enquired the commander.

'We are going to see your Bosniak counterpart,' replied Eric.

'Send him my compliments. You may assure him that both his soldiers and his people are safe in Bugojno and that my troops will respect the "no hostilities" convention.'

'That's good to know, Commander,' said Barbara. 'We will be sure to pass on your kind words.'

As they were returning to the Land Rover, Eric asked 'What do you think?'

'I think he was bullshitting us and I think he's in denial. The ABiH won't observe any ceasefire and they will be in control of Bugojno by the end of the month.'

'Yup, I think you're right,' said Eric, climbing into the driver's seat and starting the engine. 'I reckon they outnumber them here three to one.'

'If they have a set to,' said Barbara, 'it's going to be messy'.

'Sure is' replied Eric. 'Let's go and talk to the Muslim commander, see what he's got to say.'

'What are you going to do once this is all over?' said Barbara, changing the subject.

'Me?'

'Who else do you think I'm talking to?'

'Oh, I dunno. I think I want to see if DIS would have me.'

'Defence Intelligence? That would mean sitting behind a desk in Whitehall.'

'I know,' agreed Eric, 'but, to be honest, I'm getting a bit old for all this driving around the areas. The pay's good but… you know… what about you?'

'Think I'm going to try for the Foreign Office,' replied Barbara.

'Foreign Office as in cocktail parties in Paris and schmoozing dictators and international criminals or Foreign Office as in MI6?'

'Like you, I rather want to stay in intelligence.'

'The name's Bond. Babs Bond. Shplendid Moneypenny.'

'Don't call me Babs…'

'Oh lovely Babs.'

'And please don't tell me that Ronnie Barker thing again or I might actually scream.'

'Do you know what, Babs, I mean Barbara, I think the SIS would be lucky to get you.'

'Thank you, Eric. That, I think, is the nicest thing you've said to me for a while. Maybe ever.'

'I see that Adam has had the good sense to chuck you.'

'What?'

'You're not wearing your ring. You back on the market again, Babs, or just looking for a bit of commitment-free fun while you can?'

'Fuck off, Eric. My engagement ring is safely in the hotel strong room with my passport. And, for your information, I'm hoping to meet up with Adam in a few days. If you play your cards right and aren't a total dickwad, I may even introduce you to him.'

'Well, that would be nice. And now, with the Muslims, don't forget to stand behind me and agree with everything I say.'

'Fuck off, Eric.'

'Actually, I've got an idea.' Barbara recognised the glint in his eye and knew, somewhere, that a penny had dropped.

* * *

The white Land Rover retraced its journey out of Bugojno passing through various roadblocks and identity checks back to where they had seen the halted column of Muslim transport.

'You going to tell me what this is all about?'

'It's a hunch. Something I learned at BRIXMIS and which you would do well to observe.'

'So, suddenly, you are now Yoda, are you?' said Barbara.

'Who's Yoda?' asked Eric.

'Never mind.'

Eric pulled into the town square and parked the vehicle. 'In the glove box are some blue vinyl medical gloves. Get me a pair too, and a placcy bag.'

'That's why it's called a glove box, I suppose,' replied Barbara, opening the compartment. 'These look faintly kinky, Eric.'

They both got out of the Land Rover and Barbara followed Eric over to where they had seen the soldiers cooking. With his hand he tested the heat coming from the pile but the overnight drizzle had extinguished everything. He then began digging through the ashes. He picked out some half-burnt papers and put them into his plastic bag. Some had been printed material and some were handwritten, mainly in Serbo-

Croat. He and Barbara searched around all the fire pits picking up any remnants of paper that had been used to start and sustain the fires.

'Eric, check this out,' shouted Barbara from beside one of the piles. She held up a half-burnt school exercise book. Some of its pages had been torn out, presumably to start the fire, but the rest had failed to burn. It had several pages of handwritten Arabic script.

'Bingo, Barbara. I told you you would make a good spy. Now for the part that you will like less.'

'What's that?'

'We are going to find where they had their craps and look through what they used for bog paper. High chance that they used official material to wipe their arses.'

'You're not serious?' There was a look of horror and disgust on her face.

'Deadly serious, Ms Bishop, soon to be Mrs. Lonsdale. Ever been stopped at customs?' said Eric, snapping on the blue gloves. 'Seriously, actually we could find all sorts of things. Radio frequencies, ORBATS, letters from home. Prime source material. Follow me.' He sped off to the nearest field and into the wood line. There, indeed, were the remnants of an ablution area. Treading carefully, they looked on the pine needle strewn ground. Many of the little deposits were without any evidence of paper.

'The Islamic ritual for this sort of thing is different to the Western,' observed Eric. 'They tend to use a left hand followed by hand washing. Which means a lack of intelligence for us.'

'Eeewugh.' Barbara had found evidence of make-do toilet paper.

'Well, pick it up then, woman.'

'You pick it up. You're the man.'

'Might I remind you that sort of sexist talk is no longer tolerated in Her Majesty's Forces.' Eric bent down and picked up the smeared paper. 'Serbo-Croat. Looks like a radio log.' He placed the paper in a plastic bag and made sure the Ziploc seal was fully closed.

'There's a bit over there Barbara…'

'It's your turn.'

'I picked up the last one.'

Barbara bent down and, between forefinger and thumb, gently picked up the offending scrap. Wrinkling her nose, she peered at it.

'Arabic in biro. Possibly from that exercise book we found at the fire. Oh my God, I've actually got shit on my fingers.'

'Lucky you are wearing gloves then. Barbara, don't be stupid…stay away from me, two can play at that game.'

Barbara resisted the urge to attack Eric with the soiled paper and placed it into her bag. 'There's some more over there for you, Eric.'

'I hope SIS will appreciate the lengths you are prepared to go to ingratiate yourself to them,' said Eric.

6

Saturday 17 – Friday 23 July 1993
Vicinity of Bugojno
130km Northwest of Sarajevo
Central Bosnia

The lorries carrying the El Mudzahid fighters drove for several hours before stopping in a village square. To Salim, the villages all looked much the same. White houses with red roofs, churches if they were Catholic, or mosques if they were Muslim and sometimes both. Central Bosnia was essentially rural and agrarian in nature and the pace of life was slow. He had spent the previous night camped in the school of such a place before again getting on the transport this morning.

They were ordered off the vehicles and stood in groups talking and smoking before an officer of the 7th Muslim Brigade asked for the sniper teams to separate themselves from the rest of the troops. There were half a dozen teams of two, each equipped with their telescopic-sighted rifles and powerful binoculars. They were told they were joining a new unit and that they would be going to support an assault on a Croatian held town about an hour away. The assault would start at first light tomorrow.

They climbed aboard a new vehicle and set off once again. Salim spent the journey looking out of the back. He still had not got bored of the greenery of the landscape nor the vast expanses of wooded hills, which were so different to his homeland. Here it could be both rainy and sunny in the same day and repeat the same sequence for a week. The rivers were many and full, the grass was lush and green and the fields dotted with fat and happy cows. He had even seen his first ever rainbow. He liked the prevalence of dogs much less as he had been brought up to consider them dirty. They should be confined to guard duty on the end of a chain, not permitted to wander where they liked. He assumed that once the caliphate had been established, such infidel habits would be quickly prohibited.

The lorry came to a stop. Salim stood in the back and, holding on to the roof stanchions for support, looked around the canvas to the front. They had stopped at a roadblock but the guards appeared relaxed and were talking to the driver. After a minute or so, they started again and as they passed the guards, they waved at him. Salim waved back. They were on the outskirts of a town and the road was crowded with the townsfolk making their way out on foot or on horse drawn carts. The numbers impeded the convoy's progress and they were constantly stopping and starting. Eventually, they pulled into a square and were ordered off. They were formed up and marched in file to a deserted factory where they were told they would spend the night.

In the factory were perhaps two hundred Bosniak soldiers, standing around or sitting in groups, talking and smoking. At midday, some said their prayers but others didn't seem to care.

Shortly after, food was brought in by working parties. It was the same food as they had had every day since leaving the training camp. Lamb curry and flatbreads.

Shortly after lunch, the snipers were once again gathered and briefed on the next day's events. They were told they were in the town of Bugojno, which was jointly held by both the Muslims and the Croat forces. Tomorrow, they would attack the Croats and seize the whole town. The local commander told them he expected the takeover to be quick and simple. The Croats were undermanned, he explained, as they had sent half their troops to reinforce the units fighting in the hills around the town. He expected most of the Croats would lay down their weapons but there may be pockets of more determined resistance. The sniper teams would be deployed to support the infantry as they advanced into the Croat held areas. Any Croat soldier, from tomorrow, was to be shot and the sniper teams would be expected to engage any target that became visible. They were told that shooting the infidels at longer range would keep the defenders' heads down whilst the infantry closed in. They would leave the factory at last light and take up positions, as directed by their commanders, in upstairs windows overlooking the planned axis of advance. Each team was issued extra ammunition in magazines as well as loose bullets in cardboard boxes of twenty.

Salim raised his hand and asked if they would be able to zero their sights as he had been taught in the training camp. He was told that surprise was the priority and so any zeroing had to be done during the battle.

That evening, Salim and Khalid were led through the back streets of Bugojno. There were very few people to be seen. They arrived at the rear of a large block of flats and were ushered in by the Muslim guards on the door. They were led up several flights of stairs and then into a flat on the top floor. Opposite the front door was a window looking out over a large main street. The window was open but the curtains were drawn. A gentle summer's breeze wafted through the flat. The commander explained that this was to be the axis of advance and that at the end of the road was a school that was being used to house a Croat company of soldiers.

Salim took the binoculars and gently parted the curtains so he could scan the road up to the school. It was an impressive structure, built of contrasting pink and white stone with a crenelated roof and large windows that owed at least some of their heritage to the Ottomans. The road was mostly deserted but for a few people, mainly elderly, going about their usual business. He looked at the school and could see sand-bagged guard posts manned by several soldiers. They were standing around unaware they were being observed and that tomorrow they would be attacked. He used the stadiometric graticule on his sights to estimate the range to be three hundred metres.

Once it was dark, Salim organised his firing point. In another room he found a table that he and Khalid moved into position so that he could rest the rifle's bipod away from the windowsill. They found two kitchen chairs and, finally, Salim got a few books to raise the rifle to the correct height. He looked through the sight, wondering how badly it may have been knocked out of true. Only tomorrow would tell. He focussed in on the guard post and even in the dark, could set his aiming point on the chest of one of the guards. His earlier estimation had been three hundred metres and so he set his sights accordingly.

Sniping was an art form that was best done slowly. Most military training is about the speed of engagement but snipers were trained to wait. Rushing the process led to missing the target and possibly exposing the position. He inserted his magazine into the rifle and laid a second one on the table. The rest he put on the floor behind his chair. Khalid could fetch more ammunition if required and would load empty magazines with the bullets from the cardboard boxes. After several days of constant training, three hundred metres was a distance at which he seldom missed. Even so, the slightest tremors made the target dance around in the sights.

He left the rifle on the table and he and Khalid went into a next-door room to search for somewhere to sleep. There was a sitting room with a sofa and some armchairs and Salim let Khalid have the sofa and he arranged the cushions from the chairs on the floor. They sat talking and eating flatbread which they both now held back from meals in case of times like this when they knew not when food would be next available. Water came from the tap and they could use the toilet. He could hear muffled comings and goings in the rest of the block and presumed that there were other soldiers waiting for the assault to begin the next morning.

* * *

Salim was dozing in that strange land between sleep and awake when the opening of the door brought him back to full consciousness. Whispered orders were given by the visitor that they were to take their positions and so they went next door and took the opportunity to say their *Fajr* prayers. It was earlier than orthodox but they both knew that God would overlook strict adherence in times of Jihad.

At just before first light, they both heard the first rifle shots break out somewhere in the town. It sounded as if it was possibly behind them but it was close. Salim looked through his scope at the Croats in the school. The sentries behind their sandbags cautiously looked out and he put the central aiming point on the head of one. The target kept moving, in and out of sight, bobbing around so that he couldn't acquire his central aiming point before it was gone. He put down the rifle to take a moment to relax and then pulled the cocking lever to slot a round into the chamber. He flicked the safety down and off and then looked to reacquire a target. The man at the other end had taken up a fire position with just the top of his head showing. He had on an old Yugoslav helmet and was pointing his rifle down the street looking for any signs of imminent danger.

Salim centred his aiming point onto the helmet, slowed his breathing, then, as he had been taught, stopped breathing and squeezed the trigger. The report of the rifle was deafening and the kick made him briefly lose sight of the target. He turned to Khalid who was still looking through the binoculars.

'Difficult to say, my friend. I think the shot was high and to the right.'

'Pass me the binoculars,' ordered Salim, irritated and disappointed. He began scanning the target area. The sentries had ducked out of sight but he couldn't see where the impact was. He needed the splash mark to adjust his sights.

In his intense concentration, he had shut out all ambient distractions but he was now aware that the whole town sounded as if it were engaged in a gun fight. The rapid staccato of automatic weapons could be heard everywhere. He could also hear the louder reports of larger calibre weapons and remembered that some of the lorries he had seen were towing double barrelled anti-aircraft guns. As the air threat was considered non-existent, these had been converted into ground use weapons that could rake rapid fire onto buildings at considerable range.

Salim once again put the rifle into his shoulder but this time he traversed his aim away from the sentry post at the entrance to the building and onto an expanse of brick wall.

'Khalid, look to the wall on the left. I am going to shoot the second window from the right.'

He settled his aim on the centre of the window and squeezed. Again, the kick made him lose the target in the sights but he saw the puff of red brick dust. It was half a metre or so to the right and low. He adjusted the sights, stopping to think which way he should turn the dial. He set his horizontal hash-marks onto the impact mark in the brick and then used the adjustment screw to put the centre chevron back onto the window. He settled for a second shot, squeezed the trigger and was pleased to see the glass shatter. He couldn't tell the exact point of impact, so he decided to use the original splash mark in the brick as a secondary aiming point. His fourth shot hit within a few centimetres of the impact point. He decided this was good enough and again settled the stock into his shoulder to wait for an opportunity target.

Throughout the day, the two of them waited. The Croats had disappeared and neither of them had seen movement at the front of the building. He wondered if perhaps they had evacuated from the rear. All around them they could hear activity in their own building and after several hours, Salim decided to see what was happening.

Outside the flat he could hear animated talking from down-stairs and through the windows looking out to the rear of the building, he saw that there was grey smoke hanging over the whole town. He went down the stairs and found a group of Bosniak troops in the lobby part of the block. They were talking and shouting but his command of Serbo-Croat was not good enough to grasp what was happening. A commander with a radio was shouting into his microphone and Salim's general impression was one of chaos. He decided to go back up to his firing point and wait until either he saw a target or was told to move.

At about midday he was beginning to think about going to try to find something to eat when Khalid hissed at him that he had seen something. He put the rifle into his shoulder and scanned the building.

'There. There. A man. Shoot him.' Khalid urged.

'Where? You need to give me better directions than that, my friend.' Then he saw the movement on the roof of the building. The Croats were setting up a machine gun on the roof to fire down the street. Three soldiers were lifting a gun and fitting it onto a tripod, using the low parapet wall as cover. He had an unhindered view and selected a target. Once again, the movement of the men made selection difficult but he decided to wait until they had set up the weapon. The firer was sitting behind the gun and his number two was crouched at his side loading the belted ammunition. He put his chevron onto the chest of his target, squeezed and fired. The man dropped from sight and his number two also ducked down below the parapet. Salim kept looking and heard Khalid say that he had hit his target. He felt emotionless at his first proper kill.

Three hundred metres away, the Croats were swarming around the casualty, dragging him away from the gun and presumably down into the building. They kept low and out of sight and the only brief glimpses he had were of bobbing heads as they tried to manoeuvre the gunner back into the building.

'Salim,' said Khalid 'look to the left side of the building.'

He adjusted the gun and the bipod fell off the books. Cursing under his breath, he rearranged the books under the legs and looked again. He saw a team of three or four soldiers looking around the side of the building. They fired down the street and then, one by one, soldiers began crossing the road and entering the building opposite. He selected his aim in the middle part of the road and waited.

'Now,' said Khalid when a soldier made a dash. As the man crossed through his telescopic sights, he pulled the trigger. The man kept going.

'Close my friend. Just a bit behind.'

He lined up again and waited. Another soldier ran across and he fired again. Once more the man got across unharmed but Salim saw the strike a hundred metres or so behind. He fired a third time but also missed. He had not trained on moving targets and at this range it was difficult to gauge the lead. He had no real feel for where his bullets were landing. He adjusted his grip and waited for the next soldier to cross. This time he would concentrate on the door into which they were going and fire as they arrived.

7

Thursday 22 to Friday 23 July 1993
Gimnazija Bugojno
Bugojno Town Centre
Central Bosnia
0915 Local

After the slaughter at Amići, Luka Babić had been assigned to
the 3rd Battalion of the Eugen Kvaternic brigade and had travelled by lorry through Travnik to the town of Bugojno some
fifty kilometres to the west. He was told by his superiors that
the fighting in the surrounding hills against the Muslims,
although going well, would need reinforcements. His unit was
on standby to go. In the meantime, they were to remain in
barracks. Over the weeks, soldiers were loaded on to the transport and driven away towards the ominous sound of gun and
artillery fire which was constantly rumbling in the background.

The troops were on frosty, but not violent, terms with the
Muslim soldiers in the town. There was often a patrol of

NATO armoured vehicles operated by the British who were there to discourage any open warfare. He occasionally saw white vehicles he was told were driven by European observers, often parked outside the headquarters building in a hotel. There were also some foreign television crews including a reporter, also dressed in a white suit, who could be found speaking to camera. He wondered why all foreigners dressed in white in Bosnia.

The platoon sergeant, a red-faced alcoholic with a reputation for violence named Ivica Nakić, had ordered them to collect together all their equipment and be ready to redeploy. They were not going to the mountains but to the local school. It was a short walk from the barracks but they should expect to be there for some time and that coming back to collect anything left behind would not be possible. Luka did not have anything with him other than his issued kit which he stowed in his backpack.

The Gimnazija Bugojno was an impressive building of pink candy-striped stone and a castellated roof. It had large arched windows and an Arab style patterned fresco of *girih* tiles running along the soffit. Outside, at the rear of the building, was a full-sized football pitch. The two hundred or so soldiers had the place to themselves and Luka bunked up with the rest of his platoon in one of the upstairs classrooms. Aside from guard duties at the two entrances, where a sandbagged position had been placed, the days were not filled by much. They had played football, conducted some radio and weapons training on the football pitches and eaten their meals, cooked in the school kitchen, in the refectory. With permission from their commanders, soldiers were allowed out locally to the shops but had to go in groups of more than two. There was a strict curfew.

All that changed in the early morning of the 18th. Luka had been asleep when the first shots shattered the early morning peace. Everybody was instantly awake and there was a scramble for boots and equipment. Soldiers looked out of the windows until Sgt Nakić yelled at them all to stay away and not present targets to any snipers. The sentries behind their sandbag walls at the entrances peered out cautiously into the breaking dawn. Babić was ordered by the sergeant to go down and join them and to act as a link with the interior of the building. The rest of the platoon were to help with hauling a Zastava M84 machine gun and heavy tripod up onto the roof.

Word came through on the radio that the perfidious Muslims had launched an attack on all Croat HVO forces in the town. The barracks, where they had been until recently stationed was being mortared and shot at with an anti-aircraft gun. There was also heavy fighting at the Kalin hotel where the HVO military police had their headquarters. As of yet, nothing had happened at the Gimnazija but they could hear the shooting and crump of mortars all around them.

Luka crouched in the doorway, unable to see anything except the sandbags in front of him. The sentries had small gaps through which they could keep watch but the road in front was clear and the surrounding buildings were quiet.

'We are fucked if they bring a tank down the road,' he whispered.

'We are fucked anyway. We have only our rifles here and the Zastava,' replied the sentry.

'Can you see any movement?' asked Luka, glad to be breaking the silence, albeit in a whisper.

'Nothing. Want to take a look?'

'Sure.'

Luka stood up and started to peer over the sandbags.

'Keep your head down, mate,' warned the sentry as a zip and a crack sounded.

'What was that?' Luka was now crouched down, almost on his belly. He had an urge to go back into the safety of the building behind him but knew he couldn't without encountering Sgt Nakić. On balance, he preferred to take his chances here.

There was another zip and crack as a second bullet went into the wall somewhere above them. A third blew out a window on the first storey to the left and half a pane of glass smashed on the pavement below.

One of the officers appeared in the hallway behind them and ordered them back into the building.

'You are no use out there. Go upstairs and look for snipers. Don't get close to the windows. Stay back in the rooms.'

Luka and the sentry did as commanded and they went up the broad stairs to join the rest of the platoon. They found them in a room overlooking the front but everybody made sure they kept down below the level of the windows. They had rigged up a periscope and were surveying the buildings around them.

Towards midday, there was another shot but this time it was followed by panicked shouting from above. The machine gunner on the roof had been hit in the head. Luka went out onto the stairs and watched as four soldiers carried the body of the stricken gunner down the stairs to the medic. The casualty's head lolled and bounced with the steps and a steady stream of blood flowed out from under his helmet and onto the stone, leaving a crimson trail.

'Got him,' shouted the soldier watching through the periscope. 'He's in the top floor of the block of flats in front of us.'

'The one directly in front of us? The big building with the red roof just to the right?'

'Exactly sergeant. He's in the…third window from the left.'

Sgt Nakić rushed off to inform his platoon commander and together they reappeared a few minutes later.

'Let me look,' he said, crawling to the window and taking the periscope. 'Which window? Ah yes.'

He gave the situation some thought and then said 'We will draw his fire. Sgt Nakić, I need you and four volunteers. Leave the building by the side entrance and cross the road into the building opposite. We have a section in there. Don't dawdle on the road and cross at irregular intervals.'

'Right, Babić, you little cunt, you can be one. Which other of you wankers has pissed me off?' Soon the five of them were at the side entrance where there was also a sandbag sentry point. They looked around the sandbags down the street. All was quiet. Sgt Nakić would go first, because the first was less likely to get shot. From then on, the danger would become progressively greater as the snipers picked up on the movement. Luka was to be last. He watched as the sergeant leapt out of the shelter of the sandbags and jogged across the street and into the door opposite. The second man then sprinted across and a shot rang out. He made it to the other side and through the door. The three remaining soldiers now knew the sniper had spotted them. The next to go was trembling, ashen faced trying to pick the right time when he could summon enough courage. He was mumbling a Hail Mary over and over and then, without warning he was off. Again, a shot rang out and again it missed. There were just two of them and Luka knew that the sniper would be learning from each miss. He had a desperate urge to take a piss but knew he just had to get across the road.

As the penultimate soldier was about to dash out, there was the deafening retort of a rocket propelled grenade. Almost instantly, it detonated just below the window line of the block of flats and a wild cheer emanated from above them. This was quickly drowned by rapid rifle fire from a dozen or so Kalashnikovs which were spraying the outside of the building. Then a second rocket hit and a ball of flame and smoke ballooned out of the brick wall. Luka decided it would be an opportune time for him to follow quickly on behind the next volunteer, thinking that if the man in front was shot at, it would be too difficult to pick him up in the sights, for a second shot.

He dashed across and leapt through the door and into the hall of a house. The other five, including Nakić, were there looking back across the road to the school. The chaos of rifle and machine gun fire was intensifying. Further away, there were booming detonations.

'That will have sorted those Turkish cunt snipers,' Nakic said with a grin. 'Gone to their ugly-as-fuck virgins in the sky.'

It wasn't clear who was winning the battle to take Bugojno. From their position, they could see the outside of the school take hit after hit on the pink stone walls. To Luka, it didn't seem like they could hold out for very long. Once the Muslims had worked their way around to the rear of the building, it would be a matter of time. He wondered where the rest of the Croat army was.

8

Salim lined up the sights on the opening through which the Croats were entering the building. Through the sights he put the graticule on what he estimated to be chest height.

'Khalid, I need you to tell me when the next one runs across.'

'If there is a next one, my friend.'

There was a flash and all he saw was the window in front of him shattering and spraying shards of glass into the room. A searing hot blast knocked him off his seat and momentarily stunned him. Bullets began peppering the inside of the room as both he and Khalid lay on the floor. The Croats had identified their position and were now pouring fire into the room. On his hands and knees amid the splintering of wood and through a haze of plaster dust, Salim grabbed the rifle and his spare magazines and began to crawl towards the door. Khalid was also shuffling out muttering 'Allahu Akbar' constantly to himself. As Salim reached the door, there was a second ear-splitting detonation and the room filled with acrid smoke. Both men lay prone on the floor with their hands over their heads before rolling through the open door.

Once in the corridor, they ran crouching down the stairs to the floor below and flopped into a rear facing room. The flat was empty and they sat on the floor, catching their breath. Outside, all hell seemed to have broken loose and they could hear the impact of bullets hitting the building and the walls of the front facing rooms. Salim looked at Khalid and started laughing. His friend's face was covered in white dust giving him the appearance of a clown. Just his dark eyes and his mouth, the red of the lips accentuated by the white dusty matted beard, stood out.

'Your face, my friend, is indeed a sight.' His voice reverberated in his head and he realised he had a ringing in his ears.

'Eh?' said Khalid also finding it hard to hear. 'If I look anything like you, then I see why you might be laughing,' Khalid also began to laugh and they sat there looking at each other whilst the battle raged on.

'We had overlooked that the infidel also fights back. But for the grace of God, we might have been killed,' said Khalid.

'Indeed, my friend. God is with us. I think that may have been a rocket grenade they fired at us.'

They both got up and made their way downstairs, mindful that the building was the only thing between them and the enemy. On the ground floor, they encountered more soldiers from the brigade. The talk was of numerous dead on both sides and Salim described how they had hit a machine gunner on the roof of the school. Nobody appeared particularly interested and so he and Khalid decided to find a new firing position upstairs.

When they reached the top floor, they got down on their bellies and crawled to the half open door. Salim looked into the room and saw that the table was on its side, blown over by the explosion. There was a large hole next to the window through which the street could be seen. The floor was covered in shattered glass, pages from his books and the curtain had been blown to who knew where. The gaping hole made him feel very exposed and Salim quickly shuffled back out into the corridor.

'We need a new firing point,' he murmured to Khalid and they wriggled to the next-door room. They found it in an almost identical state. The windows were shot out and the back wall was riddled with holes. The Croats had poured fire into all the windows facing down the street and, by now, almost certainly had them under observation for any signs of movement. The curtains here had been burned by the tracer rounds. Neither of them wanted to be on the receiving end of another RPG, so they withdrew again to the corridor.

They sat with their back to the rear wall as they assumed the Bosniaks held the area behind the building. The sound of battle continued outside but it was impossible to know from where the gunfire was coming or, indeed, from whom.

Finally, they went down the stairs again. There were fewer soldiers and they found a group of Mujahadeen that they recognised from the training camp. They were told that the Croats were outnumbered and withdrawing. Many had already been killed and that the force had now been split into three, each fiercely defending an enclave. The Muslim commander, Tahir Granić, was trying to move his troops up to encircle the Eugen Kvaternic barracks. They were waiting for a guide to come and take them to the front-line positions to help with the attack.

Salim and Khalid decided that they would go with them as they felt more comfortable among Arabic speakers. They could offer their services as sniper support providing there was a suitable firing point they could occupy. That night, as the shooting died down, they were led out of the block of flats. Salim recognised the school and was nervous as he walked down the road towards it in the dark. Underfoot was broken glass so that it was impossible to walk quietly. He was at the back of a single file of soldiers, with Khalid in front of him and they kept close into the side of the buildings. Salim had decided, should they be fired upon, he would dart into the nearest doorway and seek cover. They went past the school where the sandbagged guard post had been and there was a corpse lying on his back. Someone had put a carpet over his body but his legs and arms were still exposed. He saw the HVO insignia on the sleeve. They walked round the building to where the Croats had been running across the road and he had so unsuccessfully shot at them. He paused and looked back to where he had been sitting but in the dark it was impossible to identify the exact window. They continued on in the dark until, finally, they arrived at a park. There was a large number of soldiers, possible eighty or even a hundred, sprawled in small groups on the grass.

He and Khalid sat next to a mortar team that had two mortar tubes with them. They communicated through sign language and the mortar team were excitedly demonstrating how they had blown up scores of Croats. They offered them both some clear alcoholic drink, which, of course, the two Arabs refused. At around midnight, the food arrived in the back of a lorry and an orderly queue formed. Bottles of water were handed out and Salim realised how thirsty he was. Having eaten and drunk and with a couple of flatbreads each tucked away for later, he settled down to sleep.

* * *

The Bosnian Croat forces had been forced to withdraw into three fortified enclaves in Bugojno. One, an elementary school, was now the scene of fierce fighting. The Muslims had surrounded the area and were subjecting the defenders to constant fire. Salim had been tasked to take opportunity shots at the Croats and had spent the early part of the day finding firing points. The two lessons he learned from the previous day was that firing points only had a limited life span and shooting a constantly moving man was infinitely more difficult than hitting a static target on a range. Two or three shots and then it was time to move. Equally, it was important that the escape was kept clear. With so much concentration going into acquiring target in front of the point, it was easy to forget that the enemy could come in from the rear.

He was now lying on the floor in the upper storey of a house. He had knocked out a small hole about twenty centimetres up from the floor with a hammer he had found earlier that day and now had a good view into the school grounds. Most of the fighting men were holed up in the main building and he watched as the face was peppered by gun fire. Small spouts of brick dust erupted from the wall and the was a pall of smoke coming from one of the windows. Khalid was keeping his binoculars trained on the open area. He was lying to the left of Salim, so as not to be hit by the ejecting cases. He nudged his friend, who moved the rifle sight. The Croats were setting up a first aid post and he saw a stretcher team bring out a man and lie him on the ground.

'What are you waiting for, Salim?'

'If I shoot him now, they will bring no others. If I wait, I will be able to shoot many more,' replied Salim.

They watched as a second casualty was brought out on a stretcher and laid next to the first. Four more were then brought out in turn. A medic appeared with a red cross armband. He knelt by the stretchers, administering to the wounded. Salim watched him through the scope as he rigged up a saline drip. Salim put the centre point on his head and began to slow his breathing. Khalid had begun his ritual of *Takbeers*. The medic was still whilst trying to find a vein and Salim held his breath and squeezed the trigger. The medic fell on to his front. Salim changed his point of aim and quickly put a bullet into first one and then the other wounded man. Without waiting to see the result, he was folding the bipod and collecting his magazines before Khalid had time to congratulate him. Three shots, three kills, all in less than a minute.

Downstairs, Khalid congratulated Salim on the hits but asked why he hadn't waited until the wounded area was full.

'I wanted to kill the doctor. A dead doctor will mean more of their wounded will die,' he replied without emotion.

* * *

Salim and Khalid watched as the Croat defenders of the elementary school, outgunned, exhausted and suffering numerous casualties, surrendered on the Friday. White flags were raised and the firing stopped. A soldier appeared at the door waving a sheet and behind him trooped out 73 soldiers, some of them wounded. They had left their weapons behind. Voices shouted, unseen, from the surrounding buildings. They were ordered to sit on the road outside the school with their hands on their heads. ABiH soldiers emerged from the doorways of the surrounding houses, rifles pointing. There was a lot of shouting and the Bosniak soldiers came to separate them into more manageable groups. Some began hitting and kicking the prisoners, who, defeated, offered no resistance for fear of escalating the violence. Rifle butts crashed into backs and heads, often knocking over the victims who would scramble to their feet and shuffle along behind the man in front.

The long shambling column of prisoners were marched

out to the football stadium of FC Iskra. Along the way, they were told to stop and an officer of the Bosnian 7th Muslim Brigade began selecting some of the prisoners. He tried to identify the officers or members of the military police. About twenty were separated and told to wait whilst the rest of the prisoners carried on their trudge to the stadium.

Salim and Khalid recognised some of their fellow Mujahadeen from their training and approached them. There was a lot of gabbling of war stories, shaking of hands and even some firing of Kalashnikovs in the air, much to the immediate alarm of both the prisoners, who thought they were being murdered and the regular Bosniak troops, who thought the battle may not yet be over.

'How many infidels did you send to hell with your sniper's rifle, Salim al Agayli?'

'At least a dozen, my friend. God guided the bullets. I was but a servant to his will.'

'We found a group of six hiding in a house and Omar cut their throats in the traditions of our forefathers.'

Omar stood beaming, holding a large kitchen knife in his hand. His sleeve was brown with the blood of his victims.

The selected prisoners were escorted to a nearby bank. Inside, it was the temporary headquarters of the AbiH military police. The Mujahadeen accompanied them, giving them kicks or smashing rifle butts into their backs. Some of the civilian population had come out of hiding now and were jeering the prisoners or throwing stones. One had a tyreless car wheel which he tried to smash into the faces of the prisoners as they passed. The escorts looked on, neither preventing the beatings nor helping the prisoners other than to encourage them to get back to their feet with further kicks and threats. Inside the bank, the twenty were pushed downstairs in to the large underground vault.

They were sorted into rough groups of five and made to sit

with their hands on their heads. The Mujahedeen guards began beating some with pick helves, police truncheons and shovels. The victims tried to protect themselves with their arms around their heads, curling into balls on the ground, but the blows kept coming. At last, it stopped but not before several of the prisoners had succumbed to unconsciousness or death. They were kept in the vault without food, water or medical aid. There were no toilets and, before long, the atmosphere was rank with the odour of urine and faeces and the floor was awash.

It was, in fact, two days later that a detachment of the Muslim brigade was ordered to take eight prisoners back to the barracks at Mehurići. Salim and Khalid were detailed to ride in a jeep, escorting the old soviet minibus with the hostages.

'Omar tells me,' Khalid said, 'that he executed twenty infidel prisoners at Bikoći in May who were being taken back to our base.'

'Do you think this fate awaits them today?' asked Salim.

'Only time will tell whether God requires it.'

The little convoy set out from Bugojno through the shattered streets of the suburbs. As they drove out, Salim noticed painted graffiti on walls *"Pazi Snajper"*. He asked the driver what the words meant and was told "Watch out for Snipers". It occurred to him, then and there, that people were terrified of the death he could bring. As the jeep left the suburbs and wound up the twisting roads into the wooded hills, he realised that the sniper could be an important part of subjugating the infidel and bring the Caliphate in Europe to reality.

* * *

Luka Babić and Sgt Nakić had surrendered with the other seventy odd defenders of the school. They were lined up against a wall and a grinning oaf with a kitchen knife insisted that he would cut their arms off. He picked on the youngest of them, a mere boy of sixteen who was terrified into tearful pleading before being let go. Since then, they had been badly beaten and thrown into the vaults of a bank. There they had been savagely beaten again, this time by foreign mercenaries. They had been warned about the Islamic Jihadists, who had a reputation for violence and cruelty. In the vault, Luka's face had received a kick that had broken his nose and several teeth. One eye was closed and his left wrist was probably broken too. Sgt Nakić had also been subjected to a ferocious assault and had been lying unconscious for half an hour before coming to. He sat slumped against a wall with his eyes closed. Nobody dared speak.

When the door opened again, Luka was desperately hoping for water and dreading further beatings. He wasn't sure if he would survive the next one. It was the Muslims with the green headbands and they selected eight of them including him and Sgt Nakić. They were led upstairs and out of the bank into the hot sunny day, the light causing them all to screw up their eyes. They were pushed on to a minibus with an AHiB driver and then with a jeep in front and one behind, they set off out of the town into the hills.

After half an hour, the little convoy entered a small village. The sign said Ravni-Rostov. They pulled up outside a motel. Sgt Nakić decided to chance that the driver was friendlier than the other Muslims.

'Why are we stopping here?'

'I don't know,' said the driver 'probably a food and toilet stop.'

'That would be most gratefully received. We have had no food or water for several days.'

'Well then you must ask your God to allow you to eat and drink but it is probably for the Mujahadeen to say their prayers.'

They were taken into the motel, which was deserted and then out the back into a yard overlooking the hills.

The Mujahadeen arranged the prisoners into a line with Luka and Nakić on the far end. They were forced to kneel. Nakić whispered to his side 'Babić, you were always an annoying little cunt, but you would have made a good soldier eventually. I think this is the end for us.'

'What do you mean, the end?' There was now panic in Luka's voice.

'The Turks kill their prisoners usually.'

As they knelt in the sun, looking out over the wooded hills of Bosnia, the first rifle shots rang out. The Mujahadeen were shooting the prisoners one by one in the back of the head with a Kalashnikov. Each body tumbled forward. Before they got to Luka, Sgt Nakić held out his hand and grasped Luka's. Luka looked at the old man. He had tears streaming down his bruised and bloody face.

* * *

The Mujahadeen arrived later that evening in Mehurići to find there had been an intake of new recruits from around the Muslim world. Salim was told that he would be taking the best of the shots and turning them into snipers. His fellow jihadists had named him 'the Sniper of Bugojno' a moniker of which he was immensely proud. In Bugojno, he had bought an expensive ink pen and a hundred white cards and had sat down to write in beautiful script "The Sniper of Bugojno" in Serbo-Croat, which he had been taught to do by a local soldier. He would leave the cards at his firing points with the empty shell case so that everybody knew. He was also proud that he had caught the attention of the patron of Al Qaeda. During their talks at the camp, they had discussed all aspects of the new Caliphate in Europe, including the coming together of all

Muslims. They both agreed that it would be perpetual Jihad against the infidels until Islam had triumphed. Salim had argued that the role of the sniper was integral to the struggle. He had argued that the snipers in Bosnia should be used as a weapon of terror as well as a tactical resource. He learned that the Serbians were shooting civilians in Sarajevo for that very reason and morale in the city was suffering as a result.

That evening, after prayers and the evening meal, Salim was informed the tall benefactor wished to see him. He remembered him from a few weeks back, recalling how he was rumoured to finance much of their weaponry and uniforms.

He entered the tent and the tall man was sitting cross-legged on a carpet. He did not stand but rather gestured to Salim to join him on the floor.

'*As-salamu alaikum*' – 'peace be upon you,' he said in greeting.

'*masaa al-khayr*' replied Salim.

'I am told that you are a most devout Muslim and follow the word of God. You never miss your prayers and you never miss your target,' he said.

'You are most kind. I try to follow the true path of God and to protect my fellow Muslims as you yourself have taught me, Master.'

Salim and the Benefactor spoke long into the night. The tall man treated him with gentle courtesy and was politely curious about his opinions. He found out that they both shared the same vision of the two main factions of Islam coming together. The Shi'a and the Sunni, uniting against the Infidel. The tall man explained that here in Bosnia, the Shi'a and the Sunni fought side by side but, all over the Muslim world, the biggest killers of Muslims were other Muslims. Salim had not given it much thought and had never met a Shi'a Muslim until he had joined the 7th Muslim Brigade. He agreed that they were brothers united in their faith in God and should never be enemies in the face of the Infidel. It was only by uniting that they would form the Caliphate and spread the Word of God throughout the Christian World. And with the Word of God would come Sharia Law, the Law of God. Sharia was the only valid law and those that dissented would be seen as heretical. The Quran was clear what was to be their fate.

As the night began to lighten into dawn, the tall man stood to go to his sleeping quarters. Beside where he had been sitting, there was a pile of Qurans and as Salim stood up, the man picked one up and gave it to him.

'I wish to give you a Quran to remember me by. It is from a town in my new home, for I have been forced to live in Sudan. It was printed by a factory I have recently purchased in Juba. Keep it with you and let it guide you to a life of righteousness.'

Salim had barely known where Sudan was and had never heard of the town of Juba.

'You will be a famous warrior, like your famous ancestors, and when you are old and living in the Caliphate, you will tell your grandchildren about this Quran and how it was given to you by Osama bin Laden when you were fighting for him and 'The Base' against the infidels. He was speaking in Arabic so he called 'The Base' "Al Qaeda".

9

Friday 30 July 1993
HQ BritBat Forces UNPROFOR
Gornji Vakuf
Lašva Valley
Central Bosnia

Eric and Barbara had decided they had some vital intelligence to share with the British Infantry Battalion stationed at Gornji Vakuf. Or, at least, Barbara had persuaded Eric that they should pay the infantry battalion a visit so he could meet Adam. As they drove through the picturesque countryside, it was easy to imagine that the war was a million miles away. But in the town itself, nestled among bucolic pastured hills and woodland, tensions were high. Both the Croat and the Muslim armies had numerous soldiers stationed in and around the town and, after the fall of Bugojno, Vitez was considered by both sides as a vital strategic node and Gornji Vakuf lay in the way. The British Battalion kept an uneasy peace between the two warring factions.

'So, Babs, he's the one, is he?'

'Yes, Eric, he definitely is.'

'You were his battalion's assistant adjutant were you not?'

'Yes, my last six months in the army were with them in Northern Ireland.'

'Sleeping with the staff. Contrary to military standing orders.'

'Two consenting adults of similar rank, Eric. All above board.'

'And when's the big day going to be?'

'We were thinking of Christmas, maybe in London. I don't want anything too big and swanky but Adam has a trillion friends and family plus the whole of the officers' mess has to be asked, so it's going to be quite a do.'

'Can't wait,' said Eric.

'And what makes you think you'll make the cut?'

'You can't not invite me, I'm just about your only friend.'

Barbara bashed Eric on the side of the arm in frustration. 'Fuck off and if you want to come you can stop calling me Babs.'

'Easy, Tiger, we don't want to go into a ditch.'

As they arrived at the guard post to enter the camp, an armed sentry stopped them.

'Eric Scott-Douglas and Barbara Bishop here to see Captain Lonsdale.'

'Check in at the Guard Room, if you would, Sir.'

The guard checked their IDs and then raised the barrier. They drove up to an agricultural building where the duty officer came out to greet them.

'Ah Barbara, you've come to see Ken?' he said in broad Northern Irish accent.

'Um, no, here to meet Captain Lonsdale.'

'Yeah, sure. I'm Paddy, I'm attached with a platoon of Irish Rangers. I'll take you up to the officers' mess. It's not much to look at but they are expecting you. I think Ken's been buying up all the mess champagne.'

The Irishman sat in the back of the Rover and directed them up to a big army tent outside of which was a couple of trestle tables with white tablecloths. Atop the tables were two dozen glasses and several bottles stuck in a bucket of ice.

'Corporal Luscombe, can you fetch Mr Lonsdale and let him know his guests have arrived.'

'Paddy, I've got to ask. Why do you call him Ken?'

'Well, you are Barbie, so he's now Ken.'

Barbara inwardly groaned as Eric hissed 'Yeeessss. Brilliant.'

They were each handed a glass and Adam appeared from behind the tent. He bounded up and gave Barbara a big bear hug, his face a picture of pure happiness.

'Oh my god, Barbara, you look ravishing, Darling. Love the white trousers.'

Barbara blushed but looked suddenly radiant. The surrounding officers all made either vomiting noises or jeered, which then turned into cheers and clapping. Adam was immediately fined a bottle for 'public displays of affection.'

She wished they could just be alone together but knew it was impossible. His fellow officers, or at least those not out on patrol, were here to meet her and drink Adam's champagne. Operations continued twenty-four hours a day, seven days a week but Friday afternoon was still Friday afternoon and they were going to make the most of the excuse. Battalion Headquarters at Vitez had been informed and the Commanding Officer had given the impromptu party his blessing, albeit with dire warnings about 'not getting out of hand' and 'we are in a war zone.'

The subalterns and captains made short work of the two bottles and another two were brought out with Corporal Luscombe discreetly informing the Company Commander that they were down to the last six bottles.

'It's not every day that the 2ic gets engaged, so crack on, Corporal Luscombe. Once the fizz is expended, we will swap to white wine.'

After a short while, once everybody had admired the engagement ring and asked questions about the wedding, the mysterious honeymoon and did Barbara have a load of cute friends, three tracked armoured reconnaissance vehicles appeared at the gate and, passing under the barrier, parked up next to the line of Warrior armoured fighting vehicles.

'Ah, that will be our resident cavalry officer,' said Adam. 'Hey, Tom, over here.'

A tall young man eased himself out of the turret, unclipped his radio harness and took off his helmet and jumped to the ground. He sauntered over to the mess tent, his face caked in dust save for where his goggles had been. The piercing blue eyes seemed to convey a sense of humour and an insouciant attitude to life.

'Tom, meet the future ex-Mrs Lonsdale' said Adam and received a similar bash on the arm as Eric had previously.

'I won't kiss you, or indeed shake you by the hand, as I am covered in shit,' said Tom. 'But it's lovely to meet you. Ken's told us all about you. How's the ECMM?'

'Oh, it's fine Tom. This is Eric Scott-Douglas, he also ex-cavalry.'

Eric extended a hand which Tom shook, clearly less concerned about dirtying the hand of other males.

'Tom's with the Light Baboons.'

'I'm not actually a Light Dragoon, just attached from KRH.'

'He wants to join the SAS. He's easily the warriest officer here.'

'When are you thinking of doing Selection?' asked Eric.

'Dunno, I am going to complete this tour and then see what's next. Maybe start work-up training next summer.'

'Summer selection or winter?'

'Summer. I know it's more competitive but I don't fancy tabbing the hills up to my goolies in snow.'

'Best of luck Tom. Many come, few are chosen.'

'Yeah, I know. I'm not really expecting to pass. Just doing it for a laugh.'

'Not sure there are many laughs to be had on selection.'

'How was your patrol, Tom?' asked Adam.

'Routine. Escorting a food convoy up route Diamond.'

'Any sign of the Fish Heads?'

'Who the fuck are the Fish Heads?' asked Eric.

Tom gave a grin 'They are a gang of local pointy heads that rob the cars and lorries on Tunnel Road, a few miles away from here.'

'They take the aid meant for civpop and then sell it on the black market. An Associated Press journalist called them the Fish Heads because he was stopped near the trout farm up there and they demanded money with menaces.'

'They killed three Italians up there a while back. They mean business and now that law and order has gone to rat shit, they operate with impunity.'

'There's a book open for the first officer to encounter them,' said Adam.

'They'll get a burst of seven-six-two if it's me. Robbing and killing aid workers trying to feed their people,' said Tom.

'They say western civilisation is only five days' worth of meals away from Armageddon.'

'Sounds as if they are north of here, so hopefully your

blushing bride and I can wend our way home without meeting them. We should get going before dark.' Said Eric.

'Should be ok in a UN Rover,' said Adam, 'but make sure you look after her.'

'If we do get stopped, I'm trading Barbie for a free passage. Just saying.'

Which resulted in another bash on the arm and demands made on the busy Corporal Luscombe to open more wine.

10

Saturday 25 September 1993
Colombe D'Or Hotel
Saint Paul de Vence
West of Nice
South of France

The day after the impromptu engagement drinks, the Bosnian Muslims attacked and occupied most of Gornji Vakuf and all leave had been cancelled or postponed, including Adam's. But the battle had not lasted long and the Croat irregulars of the HVA had deserted the main part of the town and fallen back to a small defendable suburb to the southwest, that they renamed Uskoplje. The Croats were still entrenched on the Podovi Ridge to the southwest of the town and from there their artillery had shelled the town centre for a while. Once the Croat counterattack had petered out, the fighting ground into a stalemate, with the two opposing lines digging in whilst the strategic point of focus moved further north to Vitez.

But for Barbara and Adam, that was all far away. Adam had insisted he was a war hero as a mortar round had landed close to his vehicle and spattered the armoured hull and turret with white hot shrapnel. Fortunately, both Adam and his operator beside him in the turret were unhurt. The only casualty was Adam's cup of tea, which he dropped into the turret traverse at his feet.

'Worth at least a Mention in Despatches,' he said.

'Darling, I'm sure they're discussing your MC as we speak,' laughed Barbara, keen not to talk about the war or be reminded that each day was held hostage by Lady Luck.

'And Tom found a sniper's firing point. The bastard was probably shooting at the civvies trying to get away from the bombardment. Anyway, we despatched Corporal Yardley with a section to clear it, but they'd buggered off before we could get them.'

'Let's not talk about Yugoslavia, darling…'

'OK. But the strange thing was he found this sort of calling card. On the card, written in black ink in Serbo-Croat was "The Sniper of Bugojno".

But they had had five blissful days in the Colombe D'Or hotel nestled in the hills of Provence. The September weather was soft and sultry and they had eaten out on the terrace or driven their little Fiat hire car down to the coast and wandered around Cagnes-sur-Mer with its dominating hexagonal keep and winding Provençal streets. They had found little deserted coves and skinny-dipped in the Mediterranean before finding a small bistro in the back streets for dinner. They went shopping in the little stores that proliferated the old town. Barbara was already beginning to nest build and was buying local hand-crafted ceramics such as salad bowls.

'Why don't you try this on?' Adam was holding a turquoise blue sun dress. 'You would look fabulous in this. You would look fabulous in anything, really.'

The lady showed her into a small changing room and Barbara put on the dress.

'Ta Da…' she said, doing a twirl.

'Looks great,' said Adam 'other than your big mummy-bra.'

Barbara turned her back on Adam and using a complex set of manoeuvres, removed the underwear without removing the dress.

'This better?' she asked, with a bashful smile.

'Just jump up and down for me.'

She looked round to see whether anybody was watching and then did a few jiggles.

'Perfect, I'll take it,' said Adam.

'Would Madame like to keep it on?' asked the store owner appearing from nowhere.

Barbara blushed and giggled and Adam said she would. The price was eye-watering for a simple piece of cloth but there was no price to be put on style. Or so he told himself as he handed over his credit card. A small gold crucifix on a chain caught his eye at the counter and he asked for that to be added to the dress.

'Plastic Santa can take the strain for now. Luckily, Her Majesty sees it fit to pay us good Local Overseas Allowance and there's not much to buy in Gornji Vakuf other than booze in the mess.' He turned her round and clipped the gold chain at the back of her neck.

'Oh Adam, I love it,' said Barbara 'even if the whole world gets to see my bosoms every now and again. I can perhaps get it tailored in UK when I get back.'

'You'll do no such thing,' said Adam. 'It'll be for our warm weather excursions after the big day.'

'I'm certainly not wearing this for my going away. It'll be December in Blighty and I don't want the whole regiment gawping at my tits.'

'Darling, I didn't mean as a going away outfit but rather first day of the honeymoon outfit. You know, when we are on our own.'

She slipped her arm through his and drew him tight. He gave her a hug and she felt more happiness than she thought it possible to feel. Even when his arm snaked through hers and bounced her braless breast, she didn't mind. She just gave him a big kiss, giggled and squeezed his bum. This was their last night in France and she wanted to make memories to tide her through the ten cold weeks in Bosnia until the wedding.

11

Monday 15th November 1993
Gornji Vakuf
Lašva Valley
Central Bosnia

Since her return from the pre-moon in France, Barbara, often with Eric, had watched the former Yugoslavia descend into a bloodlust madness, as the ethnic cleansing in the Lašva Valley gained momentum. But all anyone could do was watch. Even Adam, with the BritBat battalion in Gornji Vakuf, complained of not being allowed to help prevent the now frequent massacres that were taking place all through Bosnia. The Muslims, especially the foreign fighters of the 7th Mujahadeen Brigade, were continuously cited as having killed and raped Croatian civilians, including children, often in the most barbaric way. The ECMM headquarters, at the Hotel I in Zagreb, would send its Mission Officers to report and acquire evidence. But they were strictly prohibited from intervening.

The Croats, for their part, would massacre civilians less often. But when they did, they did it on a greater scale.

Eric had visited the aftermath of a Muslim slaughter of civilians at Uzdol where thirty-four Croat civilians, including women and children, had been butchered. Some had their throats cut in what was becoming a trademark for the foreign Islamist mercenaries. Some of the women were raped.

A month later, they were told to visit the town of Stupni Do to investigate crimes committed by Bosnian Croat troops. The Apostoli and Maturice units had entered the village and systematically set about destroying it. First, they raped the women and then killed everyone they could find; the bedridden, the children, the elderly, everyone. Then the houses were looted for anything of value before the bodies were carried inside and the buildings set on fire.

By the time Eric and Barbara got there, in the last week of October, there was little remaining other than burned houses and charred bodies. In the days before, other ECMM personnel had visited the village, high in the hills above the strategic Croat enclave at Vares and reported back about the charred bodies in the burned-out houses.

'This is going to be grim,' observed Eric as the white Land Rover wound its way up the narrow road and through a tunnel in the mountains. 'Listen, Babs, when we get there, you stay in the Rover. I can gather the info for the report. No need for both of us to…'

'No Eric. These crimes need witnesses and the more witnesses the better. When this nightmare is over, there will be court cases, like Nuremberg for our times. Crimes against humanity.'

'Suit yourself, but these things stay with you. I'm still getting nightmares from the Gulf War.'

They parked the vehicle in the village centre. As they got out, the smell hit them. A thick odour of burnt wood mixed with the deathly aroma of a charnel house. There was an armoured vehicle from the Nordic battalion and Eric asked a Swedish Lieutenant for a quick summary. He told them in faultless English there were charred corpses in numerous houses, some burned beyond recognition. The Swede was ashen faced and Eric wondered if he would be able to control his emotions as he described what had been found.

'There are reports of an outhouse with some bodies in it. Do you know where that is?'

The Swedish officer said 'When we came here, we found upwards of thirty civilians killed. But also some survivors who told us what they witnessed. Come with me.'

He led them through the town to a burned-out house. 'Here we found two women and three children, all murdered. We believe this was the house where they lived. Inside, was the half-burned body of a man, probably a husband and father to the three children.' He looked blankly at the ground and then wiped the corner of his eye with the sleeve of his combat jacket. He paused and then walked on. Eric and Barbara followed in silence.

'Seven members of the same family, including three women and two children were murdered inside their shelter. Our medics estimated that both the children were between two and four years old.'

After a few minutes, he stopped and said 'There was an ECMM monitor here recently. A German air force Colonel. I think he took pictures but I wasn't here at the time.'

'Thank you,' said Eric 'we can find out who that was from our local Headquarters at Zenica.'

'He tried to get into the village but the HVO didn't let him. He said they blocked the road. By the tunnel. They were dug in and had mined the approach. They were drunk and yelling. Saying they had been forced to do it.'

'Do it?' asked Eric.

'I think kill the villagers. They were saying they don't like their commanders but were forced to obey orders.'

'"I was just following orders" is no defence for this,' said Barbara. 'That was established at Nuremberg nearly fifty years ago.'

'Exactly right, Barbara,' said Eric.

'My men are bagging the bodies for removal and identification,' said the Swedish officer. 'You know, we watched as they loaded the looted gear on to lorries in the middle of the night. They were also beating people up and raping women up the road at Vares.'

'I heard that,' said Eric. 'We've been asked to visit two schools used as "detention centres" but they are not allowing us access. They claim they are doing their own internal investigation. You tell them, that according to the Brioni Agreement, that their government signed, we have complete freedom of movement and they laugh and tell you it is too dangerous and they cannot allow it. Nothing you can do.'

'Some British UKLOs were up here as well, helping us with the bodies.'

'UKLO?' asked Barbara.

'United Kingdom Liaison Officers,' said the Swede. 'But we all know them to be Special Forces, your SAS. They are famous, no?'

'They carry a certain notoriety before them,' said Eric.

'Three men in a car. They helped us with the bodies. Some of the victims had been burned with their animals, as we found sheep in amongst the human bodies. They were children.' Once more the soldier paused, staring at the ground. He sniffed and wiped his eye again with his sleeve. 'The smell, it stays with you, you know.'

'Have you seen any signs of combat?' asked Eric, to change the subject.

'No. Nothing. You can see there is no shell damage, no

shrapnel damage on the walls, nothing. All we found were the empty bullet casings where we found the bodies. Five of them where we found the five burned bodies in the cellar. That's all.'

'They are trying to tell us that these were all victims of Bosnian shelling and heavy fighting,' said Eric 'but I can't see any evidence of that. Clear to me they were murdered.'

'Bloody obvious,' said Barbara.

12

Wednesday 3rd November 1993
Gornji Vakuf
Lašva Valley
Central Bosnia

The El Mudzahid battalion of the 7th Muslim Brigade once again found itself loaded into lorries and driving through the wooded hills of central Bosnia. Salim had taken his favourite seat at the back so that he could look out at the rolling country-side, now covered by snow. It was dark, wet and cold and the rear wheels of the lorry kicked up a fine mist of mud that covered the front of the vehicle behind. His breath condensed in the air.

This evening, they were heading towards the town of Vares, twenty kilometres to the southeast to take the fight to the infidels. They were supporting the 317th Gornji Vakuf Moun-tain Brigade who had redeployed their forces from the north-west, north and east of the town. Their orders where to retake any ground lost after a counterattack by the Croatian militia who were attempting to retake the town they lost in the summer. As evening fell, the Croat assault intensified.

Salim and Khalid were part of a sniping team that were to pick off Croat militia as the main Bosnian forces advanced through the streets to the town centre. Salim now knew to select vantage points that commanded good views of the enemy, preferably higher and with easy escape routes. They chose the attic of a three-storey house that had a sweeping command of the axis of advance. He had kept the hammer that he had found in Bugojno and with it he now made a small loophole in the brickwork of the outside wall. The assault started with the mortars being fired from the hills behind the town and the two men watched as the projectiles whistled over-head and landed with a puff of black smoke, followed by the crump of the explosion. The infantry below them were working their way along the street, using the doorways for cover whilst Salim, with his telescopic sights and Khalid with his binoculars looked for movement or light in the gloom. Within ten minutes, it was clear that they would have to move to keep up with the advance and so the two men picked up their equipment and moved downstairs onto the street.

'We must be careful not to be victims of the infidel snipers ourselves, Khalid. We move one at a time. I will watch as you go to the doorway there, in front.'

Khalid darted forward, the broken glass underfoot crunch-ing. When he was in the doorway, Salim ran to catch him up. They jockeyed down the street for a few hundred metres before finding the first of the advancing Bosnian troops.

Their lack of Serbo-Croat meant that communication had to be in a primitive sign language but they were eventually directed to an Arab speaker who told them that fifty metres ahead there was a defensive position that was stubbornly holding out. The man described the building and Salim decided to go into the house to find a firing point. He made his way up the stairs with Khalid following. It was a residential building of six flats over three floors. Reaching the top floor, Salim tried the door but found it locked. He pounded demanding entry, knowing that his Arabic would be incomprehensible and terrifying to any occupants hiding within. No answer came so he kicked the door several times and then remembered the hammer in his knapsack. He made short work of the wooden door frame and they entered the flat. It had been abandoned, presumably within the last day or so as everything was neat and looters had yet to ransack it. Salim cautiously approached the window overlooking the road below. He peered through the glass by crouching below and to one side, mindful that in poor visibility, movement was most likely to give their position away. He identified the house which held the enemy and then retreated to the back of the room. He pushed aside furniture and found a table and a chair and set up his firing point. They were too close to make a loophole or even risk knocking out the windowpane. He would shoot through the glass.

With his sniper's rifle on its bipod, he and Khalid observed the building and soon saw flickers of movement on the first floor. Before long, there was a muzzle flash from the back of the room and Salim set his sight. He waited for the second flash and then pulled his trigger. It was impossible to know if his shot had found his target but they were not going to wait anyway. As soon as the shot rang out, Salim picked up his weapon and moved back out into the corridor and then onto the stairs.

Down on the street level, he found more Bosnian infantry and he followed them as they moved from doorway to doorway. The advance had now passed the house but Salim indicated to Khalid that he wanted to check out his shot. On the first floor, they found an open door and, cautiously, Khalid

looked into the flat, his AK47 at the ready. They moved
through the door, checking each of the rooms for signs of life.
In the room overlooking the street there was a body, lying still
on the floor in a pool of blood. Ignoring the casualty, they
ensured that the rest of the flat was empty before they
returned.

The Croat was in uniform but had no weapon. He had
probably been abandoned by his comrades and left for dead
but his eyes were open and he watched as the two Arabs
entered the room. He tried to speak but was unable to. His
breaths were coming in short rasping pants. Khalid was
nervously watching the man down the barrel of his rifle. Salim
looked the infidel in the eye, raised his rifle and shot him in the
chest. The body jerked with the impact. He fired a second
bullet, also in the chest and the body was still, the eyes still
open. From the side pocket of his combat trousers he pulled a
card and placed it carefully on the corpse before picking up the
ejected empty case and putting it next to it. The case rolled off,
so he took the card and placed it on the floor beside the dead
man's head with the cartridge standing up on top of it.

'What does the writing say?' enquired Khalid.

'The Sniper of Bugojno.'

'The Sniper of Bugojno, my friend?'

'Sniping is a strategy of war and will be used as a weapon
of terror in the coming fight to establish the Caliphate in
Europe. Everyone will learn to fear the Sniper of Bugojno.'

'The Croats will punish you severely if they capture you
with those messages in your pocket, Salim.'

'If it is the will of God, so be it.'

The two men left the room just as the Croat artillery in the
high ground surrounding the town began again to shell the
Muslim occupied half. The blasts of the high explosives shook
the buildings and panes of glass fell and shattered on the street.
The explosions were followed a few seconds later by the soft

boom coming from the hills. The Croats did not have enough artillery to fire more than three or four shells a minute but the barrage kept going for most of the morning and Salim and Khalid sheltered in the basement of an abandoned flat with a platoon of Bosnian Muslim soldiers.

At midday the shelling ceased and the silence enveloped the town. Word came in that the British had organised a cease-fire so that wounded civilians could be evacuated. Salim decided to go to an upper story room to see what he could see. Khalid followed, grumbling about leaving the safety of the basement.

Salim picked a vantage point overlooking the town centre and set up a firing point, more out of habit than anything else. His view took in the town centre and a concrete bridge over the River Vrbas. He could hear the movement of tracked vehicles, the powerful diesel engines whining in the still of the ceasefire. A white tank moved into view on the bridge and he could see, through the scope, the two blue helmets of the British soldiers in the turret. Their bodies were halfway out and one of them was directing people on the ground who he couldn't see from his position. As the vehicle moved forward, a plume of diesel exhaust erupted skywards and the tracks squealed as the heavy vehicle turned. Behind it was a Yugoslav ambulance with its lights flashing. He zeroed in on the soldier in the turret, calmed his breathing and squeezed the trigger.

The report took Khalid by surprise and he gave a start. Salim kept his scope on the turret and watched as the soldier slumped forward, his head bouncing off the armour as he slid down into the open hatch. The second soldier also ducked inside and the turret swivelled towards them. Salim picked up the expended case and stood it upright on top of another card announcing the presence of the 'Sniper of Bugojno' and indicated to Khalid that it was time to leave.

13

Thursday 4th November 1993
Regional Headquarters of the ECMM
Busovaca
Lašva Valley
Central Bosnia

Barbara entered the headquarters building with a sense of trepidation. She had not been summoned there urgently before and she could not supress the feeling of foreboding. She wondered if it was anything she had done wrong. She was shown into a meeting room where Eric was sitting. He stood up immediately, a look of blank pain on his face. He said nothing and she knew at once that something was terribly wrong. He walked towards her and gave her a big hug, something he had never done before in the two years they had been working together.

Seconds later, the door opened again and the Regional Head of Mission entered with a British army major. Barbara looked at the two of them and felt an overwhelming sense of dread. She didn't want to hear what was coming next. She knew now.

'Barbara, this is Major Stevens. He is regimental second-in-command at Gornji Vakuf. I'm afraid we have no good way of telling you this. Peter, please…'

'Yesterday afternoon, at about thirteen hundred hours local time, Captain Adam Lonsdale was hit by a sniper in the town of Vares. He was killed instantly, Barbara.'

She said nothing. She felt nothing other than a weight on her whole being. Tears began rolling down her cheeks and she blinked them away and wiped her eyes on her sleeve. Eric handed her a box of tissues and she grabbed a handful.

Major Stevens continued, 'Adam was at the time organising the evacuation of some seriously wounded civilians from the fighting. He had put himself in the middle of the danger zone and, with his customary bravery, was leading his men from the front without thought for his personal safety.'

'But why…why would they shoot at UNPROFOR?' she stammered.

'We think the attack on Vares was in retaliation for the massacre at Stupni Do. Or, at least, the ABiH justified it to themselves like that. There had been numerous complaints that Nordbat soldiers had done nothing to prevent the slaughter there.'

'But I was there,' she protested 'they kept everyone out by mining and guarding the tunnel entrance. Nobody could get in.'

'I know Barbara.'

'They tried. They fucking well tried…'

'Adam's body has been evacuated to Split where an RAF Hercules will take him back to Lyneham. Adam's next of kin, that is to say, his mother and father have been informed. I'm afraid we couldn't tell you until we had told them. I'm sure you understand. For your information we found a card at the firing point. It said, "Sniper of Bugojno."'

'We were getting married next month…' Barbara now broke down in a fit of racking sobs. She bent over double in her chair, hugging herself and rocking too and frow. Eric awkwardly came over and place his hand on her back. He too wiped his eyes on his sleeve and, taking a tissue, blew his nose in a great elephantine trumpeting sound. Barbara looked up and laughed before her face crumpled into tears once more.

The Head of Mission coughed and announced 'We have organised a flight back to London. We will get you on a chopper to Zagreb and then a civilian flight to Heathrow. Major Scott-Douglas has asked if he can stay with you until you board the flight. I would like you to know that you have our deepest condolences and sincerest sympathy.'

'I am sorry, Barbara. Adam was a close friend of mine and highly regarded by all ranks within the regiment. He will be sorely missed by everyone. I am hoping to come back for the funeral with some of the officers. We will also be dedicating our Remembrance Day service to him on Sunday week as will the regimental rear party back in Colchester. We have extended an invitation to the Lonsdales to attend that service as a guest of the regiment. I am also personally recommending him for a Military Cross.'

Barbara nodded mutely, the ball of tissues held to her nose. The two men turned and left. Eric sat down and said gently 'Let's get a cup of tea shall we and then I'll drive you back to get your kit.'

'Eric?'

'Yes Babs?'

'I think I may be pregnant.'

14

Tarnak Farm Compound
Karez-i-Zarq
30 Km Southwest of Kandaha
Afghanistan July 1998

Salim had not seen his patron and benefactor Osama for three and a half years and was very much looking forward to meeting again as he had much to discuss. It was a requirement of the Dayton Accords that had brought the civil war in Bosnia to something of a conclusion, that all foreign fighters leave Bosnia and so he had left Europe to return to Algeria. But he could no more be a fruit seller in the family business than an astronaut. He felt his whole being was now dedicated to God and the earthly struggle of *Ummah* and *Sahwa*. To his mind, despite the Muslim Bosniaks gaining political control over half the territory of Bosnia, the struggle, the *jihad*, had not succeeded. They had given in to democracy and secular law and the European Caliphate was just a distant memory. But worse for him was that the coming together of Muslims of all persuasions was, if anything, further away than ever.

The past three years in Algeria had reinforced that sense of failure. His homeland was going through what later would become known as the 'Decennie Noire' – the Black Decade. The country had descended into a vicious civil war, with Muslim killing Muslim. On his return, he had been quick to join the 'GIA' – the Armed Islamic Group, which was dedicated to the overthrow of the incumbent military-backed government that had seized power in a coup, following the first ever successful political victory by an Islamist party, the FIS – the Islamic Salvation Front.

But, to his dismay, the GIA began making the same horrific decisions that he now recognised as a pattern. It launched an increasingly violent campaign against all Algerians that it considered were not supporters, including ordinary people trying to go about their business and avoid being killed. Perhaps they were not true adherents to the strict teachings of Salafism, but that true purity cannot be forced upon whole populations. He had seen that in Bosnia, where the Muslims were happy to allow make up and dancing, even alcohol and fornication. The sins of the West, so addictive to mankind, could not be eradicated by decree. So it was with predictable déjà vu, he once again witnessed Muslims slaughtering their brothers. It was the cycle of *takfiri*, where one Muslim group's interpretation differed from another's and so both denounced the other as *Kuffirs* worthy only of slaughter. Caught in the middle were the ordinary people. Groups of GIA had begun systematically murdering schoolteachers for incorrect religious teaching – what they called 'taming the youth' and over two hundred had now been killed. All foreigners were told to leave the country and those that didn't or were too slow were also killed. Non-Muslims were considered targets as well and those that hadn't already left were also being murdered.

Salim had preached that the true enemy was the infidel West, led by the Great Satan, America and his allies in Europe. In Algeria, the militants were less interested in hitting the Americans than the French. For historical and colonial reasons, they launched their attacks in mainland France. Salim had helped plan these, including a bold attempt to hijack a jet liner and crash it into the Eiffel Tower. The plan had initially gone well and the four martyrs, who had called themselves 'the Signatories with Blood' group, had succeeded in boarding an Air France plane in Boumedienne International Airport in Algiers. However, they deviated from the agreed plan and landed at Marseilles to take on more fuel, the bigger to make the explosion when it was crashed. A stand off ended with French Special Forces storming the plane, killing the martyrs and freeing the infidel passengers. But it had got him thinking, and it was something he was keen to discuss with Osama.

The reaction within the GIA was to run an internal investigation whilst preaching to the West about the success of the mission, with the GIA leader, Damel Zitouni saying,

"The escape of the plane and its passengers was not because of the bravery of these special forces, but because of the Will of Allah, the four kilograms of explosives onboard did not detonate. Oh Martyred convoys, Oh Deathmakers, know well that you have made for the khilafah a new height with your blood, and a towering structure from your body parts. In conclusion... this operation is the start of a new phase which is the Martyrdom phase in which the enemy will be completely overwhelmed by the attacks. This is a result of an organized Mujahideen army which now includes a huge number of Muslim youths... Mujahideen have the resources, the personnel, the ability and the power to do that. The operation will be imprinted forever in our Islamic history."

As recriminations increased and attitudes hardened, an internal civil war had started within the GIA. The Algerian military government had also begun to arm the villagers and the flow of young willing recruits began to dwindle. For Salim, it was too much and he decided, once again, to leave his country of birth and follow in the footsteps of his benefactor and mentor. As he left, the GIA broke into factions and the Salafist Group calling itself the Group for Preaching and Combat was born.

In its Al-Qitaal newsletter, the GIA elite defended their unyielding policies in the face of *"the cowardice of the sick-hearted people who have broken away from the straight path."* The group further ordered its fighters to resist any call for peace or reconciliation with the Algerian government:

"Mujahideen never felt a day of truce with those apostates who sold out their religion and waged war on Islam with everything at their hands... It is a cry repeated today by every Mujahid youth of GIA, he repeats it with courage and steadfastness and do not fear anyone of the apostates... it is the cry of No Truce, No Reconciliation and No Dialogue... Repeat it, my brother, while you are in your trench awaiting the soldiers of the apostates despite their hate. Repeat it while on your way in a raid over the Mubtadi'a despite the hate of the hypocrites and rumour spreaders. Repeat it while you are beheading France."

✳ ✳ ✳

Osama himself had returned to Sudan but he was also destined for disappointment. He helped fund the purist spiritual leader of the country, Hassan al-Turabi, but once again, the hardline stance that Turabi demanded had both alienated the ordinary Sudanese as well as come to the attention of the Saudis and their friend, the Great Satan. Osama's Islamic Army Shura had once more pleaded for the unification of all Muslims to fight the West but, once again, they found more urgent and local enemies amongst their own brethren.

By this time, Osama had been stripped of his allowance of seven million dollars a year by his family and with the Government under increasing international pressure and then sanctions, his businesses began to fail in Sudan and his presence was becoming embarrassing to the government. They expelled him in 1996 and he returned to the place where he had found the greatest success, Afghanistan.

Nursing a strong grievance against the United States in particular but against the West and their allies in general, he began to form the philosophy that would stay with him for the rest of his life. He based it around the presence of infidels in Muslim lands, especially the American Air Force presence in Saudi to enforce the Iraq no-fly zone and the existence of Israel in the occupied lands of Palestine. In Afghanistan, he had found a sympathetic benefactor in the Taliban and he was soon recruiting again around the Muslim world. He announced a declaration of Jihad against America in 1996. This was followed by a series of further announcements that outlined his burgeoning philosophy of the 'Clash of Civilizations' – Islam against the West.

Osama framed his new war against the infidel as a response to *"new crusade led by America against the Islamic nations,"* And he urged the whole Islamic world to unite as one homogenous people, or *umma.* He urged all Muslims to choose their own leaders of a *"pious caliphate"* governed by under *Sharia* and to emulate the regime imposed by the Taliban in Afghanistan as an example of the model Islamic state.

In 1998, he issued a *fatwa* against the United States, arguing that the Muslim world must fight a defensive Jihad as the Americans had *"declared war against God, his Messenger and all Muslims".* He also announced *"The World Islamic Front for Jihad against the Jews and Crusaders,"* and began his now infamous campaign of bombing American targets, starting with the US Embassy in Tanzania.

To Salim, this was all a crystallisation of the philosophical topics they had begun discussing in Bosnia seven years previously. Furthermore, in the Taliban, Osama had at last found a country that, even if they didn't share his views exactly, were willing to let him have the freedom to develop them without hindrance. Very soon, he was setting up militant training camps and welcoming the numerous young Muslims that had responded to his clarion call. Moreover, the Taliban had allowed him to take over, in all but name, the Afghan national airline and it was on an Ariana Airlines jet that Salim travelled, via the UAE, to Kabul. He was then driven to the Tarnak Farms complex outside Kandahar, where Osama had set up his own base. The military vehicle in which he travelled had Taliban military number plates but was driven by an Al-Qaeda soldier. The plates meant that they were waved through the numerous Taliban checkpoints with the minimum of fuss.

He arrived at the compound as the sun was setting after a cloudless spring day. Exhausted from his travels, he nevertheless felt the exhilaration of being at the heart of Al-Qaeda. His first action was to prepare for evening prayers and then, once he had given his praises to God, he met with Osama. He'd forgotten how tall he was. His beard was greyer and he was somewhat stooped but the sparkle in his eyes was still there. They discussed how the great clash of civilisations would finally unite the Muslims and defeat the Crusaders and the Jews. Afghanistan, under the Taliban, was the perfect launch pad for Global Jihad.

A spread of goat stew and flatbreads had been prepared and the two old friends reminisced about Bosnia, joking that all they ever seemed to eat was goat stew. Salim noticed that the Mujahadeen sitting with them looked so young. Osama himself was forty-one years old and Salim was approaching twenty-six but they were surrounded by beardless youths who gazed upon their benefactor with adoration. There was much talk about striking at the 'Far-Off' enemy, the United States in retaliation for the sin of placing crusaders in the holy lands of the Saudi peninsula. Salim remembered his first day in Bosnia had started with a ride on an American sponsored helicopter ferrying weapons that the Americans had helped pay for.

Osama believed the coming war against the infidel would take place in the Middle East over the decaying carcass of the atheist nation of Iraq. The Muslims would unite, the Shia in the south and the Sunni in the north and destroy the crusader armies in a crucible of fire. The Holy Lands of Palestine would be purged of the Jews and Jerusalem, the third city of Islam, would be rightfully taken back. Once the Caliphate had been established, the apostate states of Syria and Egypt would soon fall to the word of God and Muslims of all denominations, through the Levant and the Maghreb, down through Africa and up into the former Soviet Union and Turkey would turn to face the Christians in Europe. What had once been the indomitable Empire of the Ottomans, stretching from northern Spain across to Vienna, would be restored according to the teachings of Mohammed, Praise be Upon Him.

Salim recounted the plan he had helped devise to fly a plane into France and crash it in Paris, full of fuel. They had chosen the high-profile target of the Eiffel Tower. But the plan had failed for the simple reason that it had landed in Marseilles. What if, instead of hijacking a plane in Algeria, they assembled a Mujahadeen force to hijack a plane just after it had taken off in America? What if the force had the capability to fly the plane and choose the target without having to coerce the pilots? What if they hijacked a number of planes at the same time, from different airports and crashed them all, simultaneously, into chosen targets? The White House, the Pentagon, New York, Los Angeles? They spoke long into the night and Salim knew that Osama was intrigued by the concept of taking the fight to the heart of the enemy. He shared with Salim the advanced plans to attack the Americans in Africa, hitting their embassies in Kenya and Tanzania but he clearly liked the idea of a spectacular attack on mainland

America. Bombs were being prepared and would be exploded within the next two or three weeks.

The following day, Osama showed Salim around the Tarnak compound and invited him to shoot on the range. Osama himself, left-handed as he was, was not a good marksman but Salim felt comfortable with the AK47 he was handed. He drilled two rounds into a target at a hundred metres and then two more at two hundred and then a final two at four hundred.

'You have lost none of your skills, Salim al Agayli.'

'I had plenty of practice slaying infidels in Bosnia,' he replied, 'and some more defending the faithful in Algeria. But my true skill is teaching the art of sniping.'

'I have another request, should you be pleased to hear it,' said Osama.

'Say it, and I shall grant it.'

'I have need of ears and eyes. Not those of a warrior, although undoubtedly you are the bravest of the Mujahadeen. No, the ears and eyes of a brother.'

'You wish me to be a spy?' asked Salim.

'No, my brother. Not a spy. I myself will find it harder to travel to the places where Jihad will occur. I cannot lead men in battle and must rely on others for that honour. But I need to know what is occurring. Only the pure truth as witnessed by God. For that I need the trust of a brother.'

Salim knew that Osama's whole family, not only his brothers, had already forsaken him. He also knew, from bitter experience in Algeria, that factions erupted out of nowhere and that Muslims could start fighting Muslims at the slightest provocation.

Osama wanted Salim to be his scout when the great battle against America began.

15

Mazar-i-Sharif
Balkh Province
Northern Afghanistan
August 1998

The new rulers of Afghanistan, the Taliban, were crushing all resistance until only a few enclaves were holding out by the summer of 1998. The main military opposition, the Northern Alliance, consisted mainly of Uzbeks and Hazaras and had retaken the provincial capital, Mazar-i-Sharif, the year before but were now under siege once again. The Hazaras, said to be descended from the Mongol armies of Genghis Khan, had been persecuted for centuries. They were Shia and therefore the sworn enemy of the Sunni Taliban. Furthermore, they had readily identifiable central Asian ethnic features that made them instantly recognisable to the Pashtun Afghans. A hundred years previously, it was estimated that sixty percent of all

Hazaras, some one hundred and thirty-two thousand families, had been systematically slaughtered in an ethnic and religious genocide. Those that did survive had been stripped of their possessions and sold into slavery. Throughout the twentieth century, the Hazaras that remained scratched out a meagre existence in the infertile, rocky hills of northern Afghanistan.

Such enmities live long in the minds of the Afghan and the Hazara militants, the Hezbi-Wahdat, had executed Taliban prisoners in 1997 when they retook the town. Since then a fatwa had been declared.

"Shias are infidels. There is no doubt in their infidelity… We demand that the Shia shall be declared a non-Muslim minority on the basis of their non-Muslim beliefs."

Salim had left the Al Qaeda compound the day before yesterday and was now sitting in the front of a jeep travelling from Kabul the nine or ten hours north in a convoy of Taliban vehicles. For nearly all Afghans, the journey would have been impossible but their progress was unimpeded by the numerous roadblocks that prevented all but the shortest journeys. The Taliban were getting a reputation for extreme and unprovoked violence and nobody who was not a member would stand in their way. The local warlords, all themselves allied to the new regime let them through the numerous checkpoints as soon as they saw the Taliban military number plates and the numerous black turbaned warriors travelling in the backs of the lorries.

For Salim, it was a new country and a new experience. On the roads, even in Kabul itself, there was an almost complete absence of women and children. What women there were, were covered from head to foot in the traditional Burqa and accompanied by a male family member. To do otherwise would be to invite a random whipping at best and the very real possibility of arrest and death by stoning or beheading. Salim thought back to Bosnia and the Muslim women with their hair on view and their faces and nails painted. He wondered if the Islamic world could ever be united.

The road out of Kabul had few cars and trucks. It was lined with single storey concrete shops where locals tried to earn their living selling food and goods or mending cars and bicycles. But there was a noticeable lack of a joy for life. As they passed, everyone would look down, fearful of catching the eye of the soldiers in the back of the vehicles. Every few kilometres the vehicles would slow down for a speed bump that had to be negotiated at walking pace for fear of bursting the already worn-out tyres.

The driver was playing takbeers on a cassette player, all other forms of music having been banned, as Salim looked upon snow-capped mountains for the first time. He had encountered snow and steep wooded hills in Bosnia but nothing compared to the sight of the Hindu Kush through the dusty and cracked windscreen. In the towns through which they passed there would be gangs of men standing around waiting for casual work, hoping to make enough that day to feed their families tomorrow.

'What do they grow in the fields here?' Salim asked the driver.

'This area is famous for grapes, cucumbers, pomegranates and opium,' he replied. 'Opium is taxed by the Taliban and much money is raised but there is a problem. Too many farmers are now growing and there is not enough food for the people.'

'Is not opium *haram*?'

The driver didn't answer. Salim kept his thoughts to himself about the double standards he was encountering everywhere in the country. For the Muslims to be united in *Ummah*, then such hypocrisy must be eliminated. He had witnessed the depravities of some of the Mujahadeen in Bosnia who would routinely round upon civilians for some mild misdemeanour in the street but themselves would partake of alcohol and other sinful behaviour when it suited them.

They followed the main Kabul to Kunduz highway, beside the shallow Kunduz River. Kunduz itself had been taken from the Northern Alliance the previous year before the Taliban turned their attention on to Mazar-i-Sharif. As the road climbed towards the Kaoshan Pass, the land became arid and sparsely populated. Even in the height of summer, the temperature began to drop and the vehicles struggled with the lack of oxygen. They stopped for *Dhuhr* prayers after which they ate some chicken skewers and cold sabzi, a local Afghan spinach dish, before driving towards the pass. At the summit they paused for people to stretch their legs, relieve themselves and take in the stunning panorama of the snowcapped mountains. It was nearing last light as they left the road to Kunduz and headed west towards Mazar-i-Sharif. There was now a considerable military presence on the road, with some broken down former Russian tanks beside the road, their crews crouched cooking over small fires. It was dark by the time they passed through the canyon at Saighanchi, the enormous cliffs on either side of the road blocking out all the stars, and headed for the palace at Kholm for the night.

The next morning, the convoy headed into Mazar-i-Sharif, flying the white flags of the Talib. The Taliban had already begun their assault and were now driving through the narrow streets killing everything that moved. The city, which had been briefly held by the Taliban the previous year, was being held responsible for the massacre of Taliban prisoners and the retribution being meted out was unrelenting and uncompromising. Salim saw numerous women and children dead in the gutters and on the pavements. Black puddles of congealing blood were alive with feasting flies. Smoke was rising from every district and the familiar sound of automatic fire echoed through the surrounding hills. All Hazaras were hunted down and killed mercilessly, whatever their age or sex. Uzbeks and Tajiks fared little better although Salim saw prisoners being herded onto trucks to be taken to the local prisons, where they would also be slain.

The convoy halted in a marketplace and the soldiers descended. Their commanders barked orders that they were to patrol the street looking for Hazaras. Salim went with a group of five as they kicked in doors and then dragged out anybody that had the features of an ethnic Mongol. He witnessed throats being cut and the quivering bodies being let drop in the street, the life blood gushing from their severed neck. Others preferred to shoot the prisoners with their Kalashnikovs, having tied their hands with their own turbans. Some chose to beat them to death with iron bars.

The witnessing of the atrocities did not perturb Salim for he was sure that it was God's will. But he did question, internally, why Muslim was once again killing Muslim. He understood the concepts of revenge on the Hazaras for their crimes against the Pashtun Taliban but he suspected, with a heavy heart, that it was also for the crime of being Shia and that made him sad.

Towards last light, the group knocked on the door of a handsome house that must have belonged to a rich merchant. There was no answer, so one of the young soldiers shot through the lock and pushed his way in. The house was deserted and they decided that it would do for the night. More young Taliban arrived and began to go from room to room ransacking the former occupants' possessions. Televisions and radios were thrown from the upstairs windows. Pictures and photographs were taken from walls and sideboards and smashed under foot. Someone demanded that no more glass be broken on the floors for it was to be their living quarters from now on. Instead, glass objects were hurled from the windows or taken outside into the yard and smashed with rifle butts.

The next day, the newly installed governor, Mulla Manon Niazi, began giving speeches at the Mosques and on the radio calling for Hazaras to be handed in by the inhabitants. Those found harbouring them would be severely punished. *"Hazaras are not Muslim, they are Shi'a. They are kuffir. The Hazaras killed our force here, and now we have to kill Hazaras. Wherever you go we will catch you. If you go up, we will pull you down by your feet; if you hide below, we will pull you up by your hair. If anyone is hiding Hazaras in his house he too will be taken away. What Hizb-i-Wahdat and the Hazaras did to the Talibs, we will do worse...as many as they killed, we kill more."*

Salim also heard that morning, the Taliban had entered the Iranian consulate and killed eight diplomats. Those that were being rounded up and not summarily executed were herded into metal containers. Upwards of a hundred and fifty were crammed into each container and driven out of the city to other Taliban-held towns. In the stifling heat, survival was all but impossible and he heard later that, on arrival, all inside were dead. More trucks arrived with containers and soon an orderly system developed for prisoners to wait in line until they were crammed in and driven off.

The bloodlust of the occupiers continued for almost a week. As Salim walked the narrow streets with his Al Qaeda soldiers, he witnessed many deaths of the Hazara men. Perhaps worse was the fate of the Hazara womenfolk, who would be raped, often multiple times by the young Taliban soldiers before also being despatched. Salim witnessed the aftermath of such a rape as four men dragged a young girl, no more than fifteen he estimated, out onto the street. Her clothes were dishevelled and she was screaming pitifully. She was forced to her knees as one of the men tied her hand behind her back with her own niqab before raising her head and plunging a dagger into her windpipe. Salim looked away as the body was left to bleed out its last few seconds of life.

He returned south the next day and learned of the news that the US Embassies in Tanzania and Kenya had been destroyed by Al Qaeda truck bombs. More than two hundred had been killed and four thousand wounded, the news services were reporting. The war to establish the Caliphate, put on hold since Bosnia, had restarted in earnest.

PART II

Those Brits are a strange old race. They show affection by abusing each other, will think nothing of stopping casually in a firefight for their 'brew' and eat food that I wouldn't give to a dying dog. But fuck me. I would rather have one British squaddie on side than an entire battalion of Spetznaz. Why? Because the British are the only people in the world who, when the chips are down and there seems like no hope left, instead of getting sentimental or hysterical, will strap on their pack, charge their rifle, light up a smoke and calmly and wryly grin:
"Well, are we going then, you wanker?"

Anonymous American Infantryman Iraq 2005

"People sleep peaceably in their beds at night because rough men stand ready to do violence on their behalf."

Attributed to George Orwell

"There are some among us who live in rooms of experience we can never enter"

John Steinbeck

Joint Special Operations Command Designations

Delta Force US Task Force Green
   Seal Team 6 (DevGru) US Task Force Blue
   Special Air Service (22 SAS) UK Task Force Black/Knight
   Parachute Battalion UK Task Force Maroon
   75th Ranger Regiment US Task Force Red
   UK and US Intelligence Groupings Task Force Orange
   160th Special Operations Aviation Regiment Task Force Brown
   Aka 'The Night Stalkers'

16

Wednesday 6 July 2005
Chelsea
London SW3
2015 Local

'If you ask me, I thought they were a bit standoffish.'

'Look, you wanted me to take you to my local, I said I didn't really have a local but I would take you to a good London pub that I sometimes go to and here we are. We had a pint, Ginge had a whisky and now we are going home.'

'But Boss, you said it would be rammed with posh totty. The only posh totty was talking to you,' said Ginge.

'I didn't say anything of the sort, Ginge. I merely intimated that sometimes the females in there can be better looking than average,' said the Boss.

'Definitely disappointing,' said Barnes.

'Might I remind you that you are happily married, about to

return to the loving bosom of your family before deploying back out to Iraq tomorrow evening?'

'There's nothing in the marriage contract that says you can't window shop,' muttered Barnes.

The three of them were walking back to where they had parked the Range Rover. After a long day briefing the Metropolitan Police about the Hereford response to a future terrorist incident, the Boss was looking forward to getting back home and prepping his kit for the deployment.

The Boss stopped walking and turned to his two companions. 'Right. OK. I'm going to give this to you straight because I think you need to hear it. Look at yourselves.'

Ginge and Barnes stopped and looked at him. 'What?' said Ginge.

'You are both dressed in desert boots, tight jeans, and t-shirts.'

'So?' said Barnes.

'And you both have short hair, sun tans and drooping Zapata moustaches. You are obviously trim and fit. Do you know what that says?' continued the Boss.

'What?' asked Barnes.

'Ninjas?' asked Ginge.

'It says gay,' said the Boss.

'Youse calling me a nosher, Boss? Because…'

'No Ginge, I'm not. Not that there would be anything wrong with it if you were. But look, you have a Dundee Utd tattoo on one big freckly bicep and on the other you have a heart with "The first woman I ever loved was another man's wife. My Mam" written in italics. I mean, what the fuck?'

Ginge looked at his arms. 'Got that in basic training when I were a bairn, Boss. Mistakes were made.'

'And nobody south of Edinburgh can understand a word you say. And you, John, you mumble so much nobody can actually hear what you're saying. It's not a total surprise you weren't an instant hit with the ladies.'

The Boss continued walking. Taking out the key fob to the car, Barnes pinged the remote locking and the hazard lights flashed twice.

'I love the way it does that,' he smiled.

At that moment, from the garden square along which they had been walking, two shadowy figures languidly vaulted the black railings and landed in front of them. Both were holding large knives.

'Gimme the keys to the motor, faggot,' said one, waving the knife in front of them.

The three stopped. 'See? I think that proves my point,' said the Boss.

Barnes stepped forward, his arms open 'There's no need for this. Leave us be and you can be on your way.'

'Keys, muthafucker. Less you wanna get shivved, bro.'

'OK, relax mate, here you are'. Barnes reached into his pocket and the Boss heard a high-pitched whine. 'Hold on a mo…' With the speed of a striking cobra, Barnes' left hand clamped onto the wrist of the knife hand, and using forward momentum, lifted it into the air and rammed his other fist into the man's armpit. There was a loud crack and a blue-white flash and the man went limp, still being held aloft by Barnes's grip on his wrist. The knife clattered onto the pavement.

The other assailant was looking down the barrel of a Browning pistol held six inches from his nose. 'Dids ye call me a faggot?' asked Ginge softly. The man dropped his knife and slowly backed away as Barnes released his grip and his mate slumped to the ground.

'You can fuck off now,' said Barnes. 'And don't forget to take your friend with you. He'll be a bit sore for a while.'

The three of them got into the Range Rover, having disposed of the two knives down a drain. 'What the fuck John?'

'It's a handheld taser I got in Dubai on the last decompression. Neat, isn't it. I've been dying to try it out. Trouble is, it takes a few seconds to warm up.'

'Fucking spare me. It's an illegal offensive weapon. And Ginge, what the actual fuck are you doing with the nine millie? It's meant to stay locked in the armoured compartment not taken into a pub and waved around in people's faces.'

'Well Boss, if the vehicle gets nicked, and I think we all agree it nearly was, then we don't have the hassle of reporting a stolen weapon.'

'It stays in the compartment. SOPs Ginge. Nobody gets busted for sticking to SOPs.'

'Dinna worry, Boss, it didna have a magazine.'

'What? That's even worse,' said the Boss, incredulously. 'You are waving an unloaded army pistol in the face of a man armed with a knife.'

'Did you see those knives?' said Barnes. 'More like Ninja Turtle swords. Young people these days.'

'Right,' announced the Boss 'nothing more shall be spoken about this episode. Drive to Hereford, do not go over seventy, don't get pulled over by the cops and let's put this behind us.'

'OK Boss, keep your hair on. Why don't you get your head down and we will wake you when we get there.'

Twenty minutes later, Barnes looked over his shoulder to see the Boss lying across the back seats asleep. 'Out like a light. He's never been known to get past the raised section of the M4 before nodding off. He'll wake up before Ross-on-Wye and demand we stop so he can have a piss. Right Ginge, get this vehicle back home. I don't want to see that needle drop below a hundred and ten and put on the blues.' Ginge flipped a switch and the blue police lights hidden in the front grill and the back light clusters started flickering as it accelerated past the other cars dutifully making way.

'Wilco, John. And I think some bangin' tunes to help us on the way.'

'Oh God, please not Wet Wet Wet'

'It's that or Bryan Adams.'

'Boss might be on to something.'

17

Thursday 7 July 2005
Defence Intelligence Staff
Old War Office Building
London SW1
0715 Local

'Got something for you here from Babs, Eric.'

'What sort of something? You know she really doesn't like being called that?' asked Eric, wondering why his mouse didn't work. He started to fiddle with the back. 'Fucking hell, why does this fucking crap never work? David, can I borrow you for a mo? Got a technical issue with my rodent.'

'Another picnic. Have you tried changing the batteries?' enquired David, not getting up to help.

'What do you mean, picnic? How do I change the batteries?'

'Oh dear God - Problem In Chair Not In Computer. The

safety of this great kingdom rests in his hands.' David found two batteries in his drawer, walked over to his supervisor and quickly changed the batteries, making sure it was all working.

'That's a brew you owe me, Eric.'

'Two hopes. Bob Hope and fuck all hope and…'

'Bob's playing golf?' finished David. 'Your favourite game, Eric.'

'Goff?' demanded Eric, 'Sergeants' Mess game. Don't let me catch any of you with goff bats.'

Eric had opened the jiffy bag and extracted a DVD.

'Hopefully a dirty home-made vid…' said David, who was loitering behind Eric waiting for the video to start.

Eric stopped and looked over his shoulder. 'Do you mind?'

'Nope, carry on,' said David, not moving. He was joined by most of the rest of the office in a little semicircle around his workstation.

The film was of an American GI standing by his Humvee, the camera-work shaky and unfocussed. There was spoken Arabic.

'Have we got a transcript of what he's saying?' asked David.

'Yup, Barbara's put one in here,' said Eric, pausing the video. 'It says *"Let's go in the name of Allah."* And then *"I just want him to stay still. Let him become still, let him become still, then I fire"*. He pressed play again and there was the sound of a gunshot and the soldier fell.

'Fuck me,' said David. 'Wait, he's up again.'

Eric clicked pause and read out, 'they say *"Fast. It's coming behind us, it's coming behind us."'* The video restarted and the film showed several Humvees pulling across a central reservation, their top gunners pointing straight at the camera before the screen went blank.

'Let's see what Barbara says,' said Eric, reading the typed

note in the case. 'This is a medic from the 256th Infantry Brigade, called Stephen Tschiderer. Shot in the chest by Ali Sayid Abbas on Saturday. Bullet failed to penetrate his body armour.'

'Explains why he bounced up so fast, then,' said David.

'Apparently,' continued Eric reading the note and talking to himself 'Dum de dum, er, yup, they gave chase, caught the two snipers. Amazing. The medic that was shot at the beginning even treated the sniper that shot him for gunshot wounds and… er, dum, dum de dum, ha, the sniper was shot in the arse. He was shooting out of a white van sound proofed with "diapers", whatever they are.'

'Nappies, Eric.'

'Actually, I know that. Interesting, says here the weapon was a Dragunov Soviet sniper rifle. Also had grenades and a pistol. Shot was taken at an estimated seventy-five metre range. Fuck me sideways, that body armour kept out the round at almost point-blank range.'

'There was a sniper in the States that shot people out of a car, wasn't there? Couple of years ago now,' said David. 'Google, "sniper in automobile trunk"'.

'It says here "Beltway Sniper, October 2002. DC and Montgomery County, Maryland. A hole was cut at the rear of the blue 1990 Chevrolet Caprice driven by Muhammad and Malvo, as a firing port to be used during their attacks. This allowed them to remain hidden and escape the scene following their attacks," read out Eric. 'Not much new under the sun. In fact, I think the Provisional IRA did it even before them in the mid 90s.'

'Remember that, actually. Was in Bessbrook Mill at the time,' said David, 'Mazda 626. Modified with armour and a loophole cut in the boot. Where is Barbara at the moment?'

'That's classified, but since we are all friends here, she's operating out of the Camp Slayer facility in Baghdad Airport. She hops between there and the US int facility at JSOC at Balad. Officially, we are not talking to the Shermans because of the special renditions malarky. But I think she's got a contact at Balad that gives her the occasional titbit.'

'I bet he does,' said David.

Eric ignored him and continued 'Barbara thinks this is a foreign trained Al Qaeda sniper and represents a change.'

'What sort of change?' asked David.

'Well, for a start, we are fucking around trying to run 'Former Regime Elements', the FREs, to ground. They aren't the problem.'

'No?' said David 'We are tasked with dismantling the former Ba'athist party infrastructure. They are the bad guys and them's the orders.'

'Well sort of. But we are wasting our time. At least Barbara thinks so. When she was last over here, she told me the Yanks were far more worried about Al Qaeda in Iraq. They are recruiting heavily and they are getting volunteers from all over the Arab world. And some of these are hardened veterans of Afghanistan, Yugoslavia, Lebanon and Algeria. The old regime is a busted flush and rounding up old men associated with Saddie the Baddie is not going to stop the attacks. We should be looking at the Sunnis.'

'Not many Sunnis in the Multi-National Force South East area though, Eric. Our problems are Iran and Shi'ites in the Mahdi and Badr groups.'

'Granted, Dave, absolutely, but the Regiment are operating out of 'The Station' or MSS Fernandez to you civvy fucknuts and they are taking down FREs around Baghdad. Not many of them are down south. They should be hitting Al Qaeda in Iraq, the AQI network. And another thing, this filming of sniper and bomb attacks, that is very Al Qaeda.'

'They do operate in the south,' countered David, 'remember G Squadron taking Mashadani after the telephone tip off? OK, he was only a second-tier hanger-on but the tip off system we are using is working well.'

'Barbara told me about him. She interrogated him at Balad. Said he was surprised they were arresting him when the whole of Iraq was being invaded by ultra-violent Salafi jihadists looking to set up the Caliphate. She was really pissed off that a textbook successful operation was dissed by the very person it had taken down. Humiliated, even. The problem is, we are pursuing the wrong hare.'

'Well,' said David 'AQI is being run by Abu-Musab al Zarqawi. The terrorist formerly known as Prince.' Nobody so much as smiled. 'Ok, formerly known as Ahmad Fadil al-Khalayilah. Designated an HVT by the Yanks.'

'We should be helping them find these High Value Targets, not rounding up some smelly old MPs hoping to have a quiet life now they've no longer got their beak in the trough.'

'Trouble is, Eric, it's not up to us.'

'We should escalate this up the chain of command. I'm hearing through the grapevine that Hereford are very pissed off at not being able to join in with Delta and the Seals. They live next door to each other at the Station, for fuck's sake.'

David considered this statement. Defence Intelligence also knew that there was friction between the American ground forces and their own Special Forces. The death toll amongst American troops was rising monthly and they felt that scarce intelligence gathering assets, such as drones, phone hacking equipment, sophisticated remote surveillance and all the other paraphernalia of intelligence work was being hogged by the SF community to hunt down their own priority list. At the same time, British special operations were answering to Joint Operational Command based at Northwood, outside London and the Chief of Joint Operations took his orders from the Prime

Minister. The penny had begun to drop with the PM. This was a very unpopular war based on what was fast turning out to be a tissue of lies about weapons of mass destruction and playing second fiddle to the Americans in the 'GeeWot' – The Global War on Terror. The post invasion plan, such as it was, was unravelling fast.

18

Monday 25 July 2005
Somewhere North of Habbaniyah
Ramadi-Fallujah Corridor
Anbar Province
0830 Local

Salim al Agayli had been up before the sun to escape the heat. His students, all six of them, had been on the makeshift range they had built in the desert north of the lake. It was his third intake of pupils and he had had them only for a month but already they were showing promise. All were foreign to Iraq, mostly from Afghanistan or Pakistan but also some, like him, from North Africa. They had come in through the so-called rat runs, either over the Syrian border to the west or over the Iranian border to the east. Of the twelve previous pupils, four were now dead and five in prison, captured by the Iraqi or American security forces. His star pupil, however, was Celebi

Othman, an Iraqi national. Of them all, he had understood the training and the message. Hitting the target was not enough. That just made you a sharpshooter. To be a sniper, one had to hit first time and then disappear. The Americans could cordon off a whole block in a matter of minutes and most of his former pupils had been caught by not moving away fast enough, or not planning the escape route thoroughly. If they couldn't catch you, they would bomb you. They didn't care about who was under the bombs and they killed many innocent women and children.

Celebi was different. He had lain in wait for three days in a top floor room in Ramadi, watching as the Americans patrolled below him. He knew they would have snipers overlooking their ground troops and he wanted to hit a sniper team. That he shot both the firer and the observer was testament to his ability and speed. He had disappeared before anybody realised both infidels were dead. But not before a fellow mujahadeen had stolen the weapons. Back at the farm, he had been given the American's M40 sniper rifle. But he declined. He was happy with his Tabuk rifle because he had grown up with it. He had to leave his Zastava rifle behind in Bosnia but his Iraqi-made Tabuk rifle was an exact copy. God had chosen his weapon of retribution and he was happy with the choice.

But this morning Salim had another thing on his mind. One of his pupils had filmed himself shooting an American. He had not learned the lesson Salim had spent so long teaching him and he was too greedy for glory and approval. For though he had hit the American he had not killed him and they had captured him running from his van. Foolish and vain, the infidels had shown the captured video to the world and had made a hero of the donkey that had been shot. The clip had been seen thousands of times all over the globe and it had sparked an idea. This morning, he had spent an hour firing his Tabuk with a camera taped to the side. It had not unbalanced his aim and the film was good enough to upload.

He would equip his latest pupils with Sony handicam video recorders and he would watch their shooting. He would keep the best videos and they would release their own. These would not contain Americans surviving. But first, he would give a message to the infidels. He walked to one of the cars parked at the front of the farmhouse and opened the door. Sitting in the front, wearing his black jacket and red and white kufiyah, he filmed his opening segment. Looking directly at the camera as it recorded, he said,

'I have nine bullets in this gun, and I have a present for George Bush. I am going to kill nine soldiers. I am doing this for the viewers to watch. *Allahu Akbar Allahu Akbar*. God willing, I will give America's dog Bush a simple present. I swear to God, I swear to God, I swear to God, I shot twelve bullets on an American camp. Only three bullets missed, with each of the other nine I killed a donkey. God is the greatest. In front of your eyes, this is a gift for Bush, America's dog.'

* * *

Salim had chosen an abandoned block in central Ramadi and had moved in after dark on a moonless night. Unarmed helpers had walked the route before him to check that there was no obvious surveillance and to ensure the roof was still vacant. It overlooked one of the main thoroughfare's junctions, where coalition mounted patrols would be held up by traffic gridlock. Ideally, he would target the top gunners in the Humvees but would take any opportunity target that presented itself. It was a difficult shot for many reasons. Top gunners were protected with armoured glass and the shield on their guns. The also wore body armour and ballistic helmets.

The ideal shot would be through the gaps in the armour or straight into the helmet. Helmet shots were more difficult because the ballistic nature of armour meant that bullets could hit the target but be deflected off without killing the wearer.

In his hide he had with him a new mobile phone and his Walkman and headphones. He had also brought some food and water. He had bandaged his elbows and knees with padding, anticipating the long uncomfortable vigil to get a shot. He would wait until his phone was texted by the lookouts, listening to verses of the Quran to while away the time. His own Quran, given to him by Osama, was safely in his breast pocket. He also had, of course, his prayer mat. To keep the sun from his head he wore his customary kufiyah. Also at his side were two grenades and a pistol in case he had to fight his way out. Finally, he had written in his beautiful cursive Arabic script a note on a white card.

"What has been taken by blood, cannot be regained except by blood. Baghdad Sniper." He would leave this behind with the single expended cartridge case as his calling card, like he had done in Bosnia.

His phone buzzed towards eleven o'clock. The heat of the summer was unforgiving but he knew that God made it so to punish the invaders and he felt blessed by the rays of the sun. He moved his rifle nearer to the loophole made in the wall of the parapet where the Americans often stopped. He switched off his Walkman and began his ritual of *takbeers* to bring him calm. "*Allahu Akbar Allahu Akbar*" "God is Great."

Below him, he could hear the convoy. The whine of the big diesel engines of two Bradleys and the clatter of the metal tracks on the tarmac of the road. As he had been told, they stopped at the junction, their evil main guns pointing towards the on-coming traffic. He watched as the American rose from the hatch and stood on the back decks. He unclipped his radio harness and then walked to the back. He was speaking to a soldier on the road below him.

Salim had the chevron of his sights on the man's neck. He calmed his breathing, stopped his *takbeers*, finally held his breath and squeezed. He collected all his equipment and, before leaving, he placed a beautifully scripted card under the spent bullet case.

19

Sunday 25 September 2005
Mission Support Site Fernandez
Baghdad Green Zone
1530 Local

'Right lads, gather round. Wolfie, where's Ron?' Staff Sergeant Barnes looked around at the circle of faces, mentally ticking off each of his troop.

'Dunno, John. Haven't a scoobie. Probably still stuffing his face with brekkie,' replied Harry Wolfson.

Breakfast was normally taken in the early afternoon because the relentless programme of night operations meant that the morning was for sleeping. Teams would deploy out after last light and depending on the mission, hit the target, always known as the 'alpha', at two in the morning. They would have limited time on target before the exfiltration back to The Station at around five. Any prisoners would be handed over to the first-line interrogators, known by all as 'the gators' and other intelligence such as documents, mobiles, laptops, passports and the like would go to the first line int team at JSOC, the Joint Special Operations Command at Balad, which everyone called Jaysoc. Then everybody just wanted to go to sleep, the come down from high adrenaline having a soporific effect that was almost irresistible. But for the Boss, there was the post raid report to write first. Barely had heads hit the pillow than SSgt Barnes would be coming around and shaking them awake again. Then it was rinse and repeat, day in day out, sometimes seven days a week.

'And where's the Boss? Anybody seen the Boss?'

'Probably still in his scratcher, John.' Stan was the medic and recently the Boss had been confiding in him the problems he was having with sleep, despite the exhausting pace of night operations. The first deployment had seen the Troop down south operating out of Basra but this time they were at Fernandez, in Baghdad. The mission had begun to change. Whereas previously they were hunting the fabled Weapons of Mass Destruction and tasked with taking down the Former Regime Elements of the Ba'athists, eighteen months on, the focus had changed and with it the tempo. No more lying around in OPs getting a tan.

'Fucks sake,' mumbled Barnes. 'Stan, go get him out of his pit. Everyone else take ten and we will reconvene here for the O group.'

At that moment, the Boss appeared with Ron. Both were fully rigged for the night's operation, wearing, like all the others, a mix of American and British special forces uniform, over which they had chest webbing with spare magazines and a Sig Sauer pistol.

'Nice of you to turn up, Boss.'

'I've been having a talk with a humint operator from Box

on the phone,' explained the Boss. 'She thinks tonight's target might have connections with a sniper team she's tracking based somewhere over towards Ramadi.'

'And?'

'And actually, she was the handler of the hostage release asset which was used to track those Americans we freed down south. She knows what she's doing.'

'Is she a looker, Boss?'

'Dunno. Not met her. Don't even know what she's called.'

'So, what are we looking for tonight?' asked Barnes.

'OK, everybody, listen in. Op BOSSINGTON 2. We are hitting the house of a mid-ranking Sunni who has connections to the AQI operating near Yusufiyah. We think he employs a driver and we think the driver also drives for an Imam. And Box think the Imam can lead us to the sniper cell. We get inside the house, do the sensitive site exploitation, bag anything we can find, cuff the MAMs and out. Back for tea and medals. Ops Officer will give us the full briefing at 1800.'

Barnes then took over for the administrative briefing.

'Right, listen in. Boss has given the outline, further details to be confirmed at 1800. What I do know is that we are using two choppers, the Puma and a Little Bird. Ron and Wolfie in the Little Bird for top cover sniping. Tonight, we are deploying with a team from Delta, who are taking down the next house, left of our objective. Was chatting to them and there is a big risk that this geezer will have armed response in the house. The Yanks have encountered bodyguards in suicide vests, so if you see someone sprinting out towards you, be aware he might be rigged to go boom. Ron and Wolfie, I want you to be especially vigilant. There will be a couple of guys from INIS coming for the ride plus Ibrahim as the interpreter.'

Ibrahim was an Iraqi who had moved to London in the early eighties with his parents. He had an engineering degree from Imperial College but had volunteered to help in the country of his birth. The Boss always tried to pick him as interpreter.

'If he does go boom,' added Stan, 'make sure you look upwards because when the suicide belt blows, the bloke's swede goes about two hundred foot in the air and it comes down with quite a thump. You don't want to be under that.'

'Oh, and another thing,' said the Boss, 'make sure you have fresh batteries in the new night vis goggles. They eat through power much quicker than the old sets, so fresh batteries for tonight and every night. Any questions, points or observations? No? Good. Go and see Banjo for the batteries and anything else. Ginge, make sure you have enough twelve bore shells for the shotgun.'

'Twelve bore, Boss?'

'Yes. Cartridges, Ginge.'

'You mean what everyone except Cav Ruperts call twelve gauge?'

* * *

It was approaching last light as the Boss and Barnes wandered up to the helicopter landing site. There would be two Black Hawks for the Delta team and the Puma and the Little Bird for the Troop. The Americans would also have a topflight of at least one Little Bird and some close air support from a couple of F16 fighter ground attack jets who would be stacked above the target in a holding pattern. The rest of the troop had already arrived and were chatting in a group.

'D'you know what?' asked the Boss.

'What?'

'It's a bit weird that we now think a night op like this is routine. Before Afghanistan, this would be headline grabbing but now it's just, well, run of the mill. Not sure anybody knows or cares in the UK.'

'Well, they don't know much about what we do. In fact, I'm not sure Brigade in Basra know much about what we do. They are down in the sleepy shires worrying about their own little corner. We are really part of the American effort up here.'

'Suppose you're right,' conceded the Boss. 'Still, each night op takes its toll out of the Boys. Certainly does with me.'

'Just got to take it one day at a time, Boss,' said Barnes. 'Looks like the Yanks are bringing dogs on this one.'

They watched as a Humvee unloaded two large dogs with their handlers.

'Afternoon,' said the Boss.

'Hi,' said a handler, shortening the lease to keep his dog close to his side.

'You coming on the op tonight?'

'Sure are buddy. Been told there might be explosives on the alpha.'

'Those Alsatians sniffer dogs, then?'

'Them's not Alsatians, son, they're Belgian Malinois. Can sniff out an IED and rip your arm off at the elbow, all in one big, fun, furry package.'

'What are they called?' enquired Barnes.

'This one is Baskie and that over there is Samson.'

'Baskie as in Hound of the Baskervilles?' asked Barnes.

'Yeah. PFC Baskie Hound and PFC Samson Dog.'

'Been to a pub called the Baskerville,' added the Boss. 'Just outside Henley-on-Thames. Quite nice, actually.'

'Any posh totty, Boss?' asked Ginge.

'Mainly yummy mummies with kids, Ginge. A lot of Range Rovers, so you would fit right in. Good food though.'

'Waddya you guys talkin' about?' asked the perplexed dog handler.

'Oh sorry,' said the Boss 'We are just discussing a bar in the UK called the Baskerville.'

'They named a bar after a dog? That's like super weird. Fuckin Limeys, no offence,' he observed.

'None taken. Yes, pub names can be like that.' Said the Boss, not wanting to get into explaining the dog was named after a family.

The loadmaster of the Puma called the troop over and they walked towards the aircraft, well used to the embarking drills, each member knowing where they were to sit. The engines began to whine and the rotors to turn as the Boss clipped into his harness. The use of harnesses had been much discussed. On a night infiltration, there was a risk that the helicopters might crash or be shot down. Some of the men preferred the freedom to get out of the plane as fast as possible, others preferred not risking being thrown out on impact. It was a personal choice and, like many procedures in the Regiment, personal choice was usually respected. However, much had been learned from the Americans who prepared for crash landings by always wearing helmets, eye protection goggles, fire-retardant gloves and ear defenders and many of the troop followed their lead.

As the rotors picked up speed, the airframe shook. Everyone went into their own personal routine, silhouetted by the dim red glow of the internal lights. People either checked and rechecked their equipment, or remained quiet, immersed in their own thoughts and possibly prayers. Before long, the helicopter lifted and the Boss looked out of the open door over the Green Zone. The lights of Baghdad appeared below as they gained height and he saw the two Black Hawks and the Little Birds also begin to lift off. He could see the barrels of Ron and Wolfie's rifles as they sat with their feet dangling onto the skids. Flight time to target, the 'alpha', would be no more than ten minutes. He went through the operation in his head.

They would land close to the target, a big villa in a once wealthy suburb. They would go straight through the front gate and in through the front door. Ginge and his shotgun would be first, making sure that any locked doors had their hinges blown out. If recent ops were anything to go by, they usually found a sleeping house roused into terrified panic. Speed, aggression and surprise would hopefully be enough to suppress any notions of resistance. The Boss knew that such an invasion of personal space was especially provocative to Iraqis. Women would be without head coverings, children would be screaming and the whole domain would be wrested quickly from the protection of the head of the household, who, amidst the screaming and wailing would be cuffed and led outside. They would then look for any evidence that the Int Section could use and leave before any serious local resistance could be mustered.

Before he knew it, the loadmaster was indicating that they were coming in. The Boss put his hand onto the harness quick release, did a mental check of his equipment and looked straight ahead at the door. Like the rest of the troop, he had a round in the chamber of his M4 and the safety applied.

The Puma bounced down onto sand, the rotors swirling up a storm, as Ginge jumped out. The Boss was fourth out and jumped down into the dust. They were fifty-odd metres from the villa, its big green iron doors closed. As he ran, he was aware that off to his left, the Black Hawks were also touching down, further adding to the maelstrom of grit and dust. Lost in the sound and fury of the four helicopters, he ran at a crouch towards the gates. Ginge had already checked and found the big iron doors were secured by a padlock. He quickly put a solid shot, made of a mixture of wax and lead dust, into the lock, blowing it apart. The doors were hauled open and the troop poured in, left and right. Ginge was running towards the front and quickly blew the hinges out of the wooden door which he kicked in. The interior of the house was dark. Operating in pairs, half the troop cleared the ground floor whilst the other half moved up the central staircase. Then the first shouting and screaming began. He could hear Cookie and Stan shouting to take command of the situation upstairs. Over the din of the assault, the Boss heard small arms fire coming from outside the house and assumed that Delta had hit armed opposition in their target. He shouted to Barnes to bag what he could find on the ground floor and leapt up the stairs two at a time.

Cookie and Stan had the family lying face down on the floor. There were two military aged males, one older man, presumably the head of the household, three women and three children. Stan was cuffing the MAMs and the older man. The three women were ululating, a series of high-pitched screams issuing from their mouths like a demonic chorus. The children were crying and clutching on to their mothers and aunts.

'Ibrahim,' shouted the Boss over the din, 'ask them where the electronics are.'

Ibrahim interpreted and then shouted that they denied having any computers or mobiles.

'Can you please ask them to shut the fuck up?' shouted Cookie.

The Boss ran down the stairs, jumping them three at a time, into the main living space. The lads were ransacking it to unearth anything of interest. They found an old AK in a cupboard and then Ginge found two mobile phones and a Japanese walkie talkie. That was the first major indicator that this was not an innocent household. It made the Boss feel better about the chaos they had unleashed on a sleeping family. Soon a Compaq laptop was also found under a pile of laundry.

<*Zero two zero what's happening outside*> The Boss pushed his headphone closer to his ear to block out the cacophony around him.

<*Two zero alpha, accompanying callsign in contact. Wait out*> The

gunfire he had heard while running to the house was indeed armed resistance and the Americans would be applying themselves to winning the firefight and suppressing any enemy fire. Wolfie and Ron would also be providing sniper cover.

<Two zero alpha, accompanying callsigns are on the alpha. Objective taken. Out> Wolfie, observing from several hundred feet above the houses, would be looking out for anybody leaving either of the premises, as possible suicide bombers.

The Boss decided to go out into the courtyard and then through the open iron gate to check that all was ok on the LZ. The Puma and the two Black Hawks were still grounded, their rotors turning, billowing dust. Through the green of his night vision, the tips of the rotors occasionally glowed white with little sparks of heat as they cut through the gritty dust. The loadmasters were beside the open side doors waiting for their respective troops to come out. Up above he saw the smaller choppers circling. They were in a holding pattern and were at their most vulnerable to ground fire at this point.

Then there was a flash and a blast. It was perhaps several hundred metres away and hadn't hit the choppers. 'Suicide bomber' thought the Boss and remembered to look up but he couldn't see any severed heads.

The three hooded males were being bundled out of the building, hands cuffed in front of them, by the Iraqis. They were pushed towards the helicopters and then made to kneel in the swirling dust, heads bowed. The American dog handlers came out of the neighbouring building, the dogs smartly at heel, unperturbed by the noise and chaos.

The Boss returned to the house. 'John,' he shouted, 'let's fuck off now.'

'Roger that, Boss.' Barnes shouted up to stairs as the Boss went outside to count his men out. Nobody had yet been left behind after an op like this but the Boss was paranoid that it could easily happen. He counted them all out, including the attached Iraqis and then jogged over to the helicopters. The prisoners had already been loaded and the troop swiftly embarked into the fuselage, taking their accustomed places. The Loadmaster was last in and gave a thumbs up to the pilots and the airframe shuddered as the pitch of the rotors changed and lifted the plane up into the night sky.

20

Saturday 1 October 2005
Camp Slayer
Baghdad International Airport
1830 Local

Barbara occasionally liked to have some of the early evening just to herself. The fierce heat was waning and she often went for a walk down by the lake. Although the time difference didn't correspond, she thought of bath time with her two young girls and the bedtime rituals of stories read and lights out. She was missing them growing up and, at times like this, she even missed her ex. He was a successful accountant; kind, clever and perhaps a little bit dull. But the constant travelling, long periods of separation and the clandestine nature of her work didn't give the marriage a chance. He had found someone else.

But, deep down, she knew the real reason. Barbara was damaged goods, never having really got over the death of her fiancé, Adam. And her eldest daughter had his eyes and she both loved and hated being reminded of that brief white hot period of happiness that had been taken from her by a Muslim sniper in Vares.

The better part of her nature was grateful that both the children were growing up in a safe environment like all children should, but, at times like this, she felt a resentment that someone else was being their mother. She dreaded the day that they called the other woman 'mummy'. But she was happy that Millie had a dad, even it wasn't her real dad and that Daisy, little Daisy-Doodah, had a settled ordinary life. Millie would be twelve soon and entering a new phase of her life and Barbara knew she should be there for her but couldn't. She buried the guilt in her work but it was always present, lurking in her subconscious and it was times like these that really hurt.

Many of her male colleagues, those that were married, were also failing in their relationships and toxic semi-serious semi-joking banter about ex-wives and girlfriends was commonplace. The singles did not even bother to have girls back home, opportunistically propositioning the numerous pretty girls that hung around the garrison towns when they returned on leave, or just buying some solace and release from the numerous professional girls that stalked the decompression resorts like Dubai and Cyprus. This seemed particularly true of the Task Force Black 'blades', as they liked to call themselves, from the Special Air Service Regiment based in Hereford. She'd talked to one on the phone and wondered what he was like.

She looked out at the domed roof of the Perfume Palace, where she worked. Built by Saddam as a pleasure dome for his family and guests, she had heard that it served as a sort of brothel where his sons Uday and Qusay would rape and murder young girls before having their bodies dumped in the slums of Abu Ghraib nearby. Staff were ordered to go to prominent Iraqi families and demand that a young daughter was sent to a party, inevitably to be raped. Often preferring them to be between twelve and fourteen years old, they would be assaulted and then paid off like prostitutes. Any father complaining would be eliminated. During the "parties" all guests would be forced to down large quantities of cocktails. Those that couldn't or didn't were brought by the bodyguards and flogged on the soles of their feet in front of everyone *'pour encourager les autres'* as Voltaire might say. As soon as the drinking had taken its effect, out would come the guns. Gold plated Kalashnikovs and Glocks would be fired randomly and indiscriminately by the brothers. In the morning, the dead and dying would be swept up with the rest of the party's detritus.

After the invasion, the hunt for the family members had begun. Ironically, Uday was the Ace of Hearts in the infamous deck of cards. Qusay, always in his brother's shadow, was the Ace of Clubs. In the end, the two brothers had been betrayed by the owner of the villa in which they had sought refuge. Swayed by the absurd thirty-five million dollar reward, he had snuck off to the local US 101st Airborne troops up the road and dobbed them in. There was an intense gun battle with the American forces, backed up by Delta and some airborne gunships, killing the brothers eventually with a TOW missile. In the aftermath, the Sensitive Site Exploitation Team had found, amongst other weird things, in excess of a hundred million US dollars in cash. Which her ex-husband would think of as a gross profit of 65% on the reward.

Also, across the lake was the 'Flintstones' house, nicknamed by the American GIs because of its peculiar architecture which they thought resembled Fred Flintsone's cartoon home. It was here, apparently, that the most vicious of the sexual deprivations took place. It resembled a children's play area. Barbara shuddered at the thought. It had been hit hard in the initial assault by the Americans and was now covered in graffiti, weeds growing up through the paving. Newcomers to Slayer, on the official tour of the camp, would be taken there to gawp and listen to the lurid stories.

She looked back at the dome of the Perfume Palace. It had escaped destruction during the 'shock-n-awe' initial air assault because the planners didn't want to risk it being a mosque. It was now the US centre of operations where the daily battle update briefs were held. The Americans had built a scaffolding mortar protection roof above the dome to prevent a lucky shot killing a large number of high-ranking officers. At this moment, both the British and American governments could do without having to explain that to an increasingly sceptical populace.

A large but distant explosion brought her back to reality. Central Baghdad was only seven or eight kilometres away and in the still of the evening, the sound of the insurgency carried over the flat ground to remind everybody in the camp that there was a war on. She presumed it was a car bomb which was fast becoming the terror weapon of choice for the Sunni insurgents. Some poor sap would be persuaded by the thought of seventy-two virgins and eternal paradise if he volunteered to kill himself and dozens of innocent bystanders in a car packed with ammonium nitrate with an RDX or Semtex accelerant. It was happening on a daily basis and there was little anybody could do about it, but it was all she and her colleagues could think about here in what the troops the other side of the wire called 'The Pussy Zone'.

As the sky darkened, Barbara watched the bats gorge on the early evening insects. Tomorrow she would hitch a lift from the Liberty Helipad over to Joint Special Operations Command at Balad airbase and meet with the American and British special forces command. JSOC was run by General McChrystal, the famously ascetic warrior monk and his British counterpart, General Lamb. The latter, universally known as

Lambo, was famous for his intolerance of fools and a prodigious use of profanity. JSOC was where all intelligence was accumulated and shared. For her, as a humint specialist, it was where she could add little bits of colour to the reams of signal, internet, phone, interrogation and other intercepts that even she didn't know about. What she did know was General McChrystal was a man in a hurry and he drove the ever-enlarging JSOC operation mercilessly.

At the sharp end of this operation were the special forces soldiers. Tier One included the Special Air Service, - Task Force Black; Delta Force – Task Force Green; The Seals – Task Force Blue; and then there were the Tier Twos, including her unit bundled together as Task Force Orange; Task Force Red – 75th Ranger Regiment and Task Force Maroon, a British Parachute Battalion used by TF Black as heavy-hitting back up. Of course, the military being the military, these names were only sometimes used. The famous Seal Team Six, TF Blue, was often formally referred to as DevGru which she had only recently found out stood for Naval Special Warfare Development Group. The whole shebang was called Task Force 145. That was, of course, until they changed it. Which they would, to Task Force 714. How could anybody not living and breathing this daily possibly hope to keep up? Not that she could talk to anybody about it back home except to the analysts at Vauxhall Cross and Defence Intelligence at the Old War Office Building in Whitehall. She'd served with the notoriously contumacious Eric Scott-Douglas in Bosnia nearly a decade ago but she kept him on what they called these days 'speed dial'. He would effortlessly follow these numerical mutations even whilst being unable to operate the photocopier or the microwave in the office, barking swear-word ridden commands at his colleagues about coffee and standards. Eric understood and appreciated the structure of Sunni society in Iraq and it was always to him that she turned if something she picked up didn't make sense. He could normally tell her why she was seeing it wrong.

* * *

Barbara looked out of the porthole of the Puma helicopter as it came in fast over Balad. Below her was an American base the size of a large town. Twenty-five square miles housing over thirty-five thousand military and civilian personnel of all nationalities. The whole complex was run by KBR, Kellog Brown Root, the large services company that just happened to be owned by Dick Cheney, the current Vice President. But they ran it well and there was nothing the serving personnel could wish for, from Olympic sized swimming pools, through to every fast-food franchise you could think of as well as two large PXs and even a full tier-one trauma hospital.

The chopper veered suddenly and she felt the red webbing straps of her seat belt tighten as the airframe dropped. Unofficially, the base was sometimes called 'Mortaritville' on account of the daily attacks that occurred and the chopper pilots always liked to come in hot. She made a mental note to stop calling them choppers as she got some enquiring looks from her American counterparts to whom a chopper was something completely different. They liked to call them 'helos' or 'birds'. But to the British, of course, birds were girls. Maybe the birds and the choppers should get together.

'Ma'am?'

She came out of her reverie and saw that she was next to get out and a small queue of standing people were waiting for her to unharness and move along to the exit.

Outside, she was taken to the JSOC compound, known universally as the Death Star. She was here for the Battlefield Update Assessment, the BooHa, which took place daily. It was when all the prime intelligence from the raids the night before would be shared for analysis, the multitude of coalition bases all dialling in on the intranet. It was also the time when she could share what the Brits were thinking back at Slayer. It was all fed into a complex human computer comprising many hundreds of analysts. The machine never slept and Barbara had a little titbit she wanted to feed into its ravenous maw.

The drive over to the Death Star was short. Officially called the Joint Operations Centre, it was a large hangar filled with all the technology, communications and analysts that were needed to process huge amounts of data. From there, the next night's special ops would be tasked. Along one wall were three large plasma screens that relayed live information, sometimes from bodycams worn during operations or from Predator drones filming high in the sky, the all-seeing 'unblinking eye'. The wall of screens was known to everyone as 'Kill TV'.

The BUA was introduced by General McChrystal. As was his wont, he delivered facts over slides in a machine gun rattle, using a green laser to highlight points he wanted to get across. Other commanders also gave their own regional assessments as did the intelligence and surveillance units. All were fixated on two points. The first was who was co-ordinating the huge rise in attacks on both coalition forces and the general public, although these were often targeted at the Shia community. The second, how to stop them. It was generally accepted that the predominant force behind the attacks was orchestrated by Osama bin Laden's deputy in Iraq, the Jordanian Abu-Musab Zarqawi. He was running a group calling itself Ansar al-Islam or Al Qaeda in Iraq. This group of mainly foreign fighters had flocked to Iraq via the rat runs through Syria and Iran and were predominantly Salafist in nature. That is to say, this was a religious not a nationalist war. Their aim was to establish a caliphate in Iraq based on a puritanical interpretation of the Quran. Of course, any foreigner was a legitimate target but they held equal contempt for any secular Muslim government.

Zarqawi refused to let his followers compromise on his demand for visible viciousness. He was banking on driving out the foreigners by inflicting such huge casualties on the coalition troops that any democratic government would be compelled by its own electorates to withdraw their soldiers. He was also determined to foster a uniquely brutal civil war between the Sunni minority in the north of the country against the Shia majority in the south. And, to achieve this aim, he began using the technology that the Americans had so generously provided following their invasion — mobile phones and the internet. This was the chink in the armour that the coalition in general and Barbara, in her own particular small corner of the intelligence map, had picked up on.

After the BUA came the 'Huddle'. This was where a select few of the most senior commanders discussed the update and the actions it would engender. General McChrystal had said that Al Qaeda in Iraq was a network and that he needed to build his own network to take it down and that is exactly what he was doing. He dictated the general strategy but wanted sub-unit commanders to think and act on their own piece of the jigsaw without having constantly to centralise permissions. And the strategy was to eviscerate the middle management of the Sunni insurgency. To gut the beast.

In the gloom of the Death Star operations room, Barbara sought out her contact. Mendoza was foremost a cryptologist who existed at the far end of the spectrum. He wasn't the best communicator or the most sociable of humans but he was the best electronic communications expert she had met in the last ten years and she had spent considerable time at GCHQ. She had learned that he was instrumental in piecing together the electronic chatter that had confirmed the human source she used to run, codename Clocktower. The Delta team had requested he be taken out of FOB Echo and sent up to Balad. She spied him standing alone clicking on a mobile phone.

'Morning Brian.'

'Oh, er, yes er, good morning, Ms Bishop,' he stammered, blinking behind his round pebble glasses.

'Please, Barbara.'

'Er, of course. Yes Ma'am.'

'No. Not Ma'am or Ms Bishop, Brian. Just Barbara. I've got something I want to share with you.'

'G..g..good. Er what?'

Barbara wondered if the blinking was brought on by shyness or excitement. Mischievously, she thought she would test it out.

'One of our raids picked up a laptop and a telephone. We've managed to hack the password on the laptop but can't get into the really juicy parts of the hard drive and we can't get into the phone. The good news is we think we know who owned both.'

'Why don't you ask him for the passwords then?' replied the mathematically logical Brian.

'Because he's denying it's his phone and laptop.'

'Who is he?'

'We think he's a mid-ranking AQI commander recruiting foreign Mujahadeen into Ramadi.'

'Excuse me Ms Bishop…'

'Barbara, please' she corrected.

'Excuse me Ms Barbara…' Barbara let it go. They would be here all day otherwise. 'Ramadi is not in the British tactical area of operations.'

'Brian, I know that.' Clearly the Americans were still a bit sensitive about having their eyes wiped by the Clocktower operation. 'But we are all one team here now and British SF are working with Delta trying to take down the Al-Ansar rat runs. I think this phone might lead us to a significant foreign High Value Target.'

'Who is the HVT?' asked Brian. Barbara knew from experience that she needed to nurse him along and not rush him. Every fibre of her being was wanting to shout 'just fucking hack the fucking phone for me, would you Brian?'

'We don't know his name. But we think he goes under the moniker "Juba".'

'The Baghdad Sniper?' asked Brian.

'Yes. How did you know about…'

'He's becoming a pain in the ass, excuse my language Ma'am. Although, if you forgive me, we think Juba is a 'they' not a 'he.' Juba the man doesn't exist, even though, soon, every American GI will want to get the credit for killing him. But it's a wild goose chase. He's a chimera.'

'What makes you say that?' asked Barbara, impressed by the use of the Greek word.

'Because we've picked up video on some of the wiki sites that shows sniping films of coalition troops, mainly American, being shot. We don't think it's the same shooter. Juba is every insurgent sniper and he's none of them.'

'Interesting. But what if Juba is actually the link that organises the recruitment, training and deployment of the snipers. They may be working for him and acting on his orders.'

'We've thought of that as well. We don't think that's the case. It's propaganda.'

'Well, the phone and the laptop might well lead us to an answer, Brian.'

'Let me take a look. See what I can find out. But, Ms Barbara Ma'am? Next time, think about not taking the phone.'

'What do you mean, Brian?'

'We're now working with sim cloners. If your operators find a phone, pop the sim, put it in the reader and we can both alter the sim and clone the phone. In about twenty seconds. Then put it back and pretend you never found the handset.'

'What does that enable?'

'Well, that means we can do all sorts of things without the owner knowing.'

'Such as?' He had Barbara's interest now.

'Such as turn on the microphone clandestinely and listen to what's being said. Sneaky uh?' Brian grinned and blinked rapidly. 'We can send texts from another phone that looks like the phone we've cloned. And receive texts sent to the original phone. All without anybody knowing.'

'Are JOC publicising this to all departments?'

'Yes, Ma'am. General McChrystal and General Flynn want everybody bought into the same task. No more Chinese walls, guarding secrets, not sharing info. None of that parochial empire-building shit, 'scuse my language, Ms.'

'That's ok, I use worse sometimes, Brian.'

'You don't look as if a cuss word has ever escaped your pretty mouth, Ma'am.'

'No? Ask my ex. So, we should return phones to where we found them without the owner knowing having swopped out the sim?'

'Yup. But not necessarily laptops. We can do a certain amount here but the real expertise is at NMEC in Fairfax, Virginia.'

'NMEC?'

'National Media Exploitation Centre. They can hack a hard drive that's been shattered by a hammer. They then feed back to the collated data onto the intranet. Everybody can then access it here at the Death Star.'

'Good man, Brian. I owe you. Anyway, they're here in my bag.' She made a mental note that the stammering was improved by the idea of cracking codes. Which might indicate that it was aggravated by her initial presence. Which, in turn, meant he might find her attractive. '"Pretty little mouth". Still got it,' she thought to herself, 'even if it is only Brian Mendoza.'

21

Wednesday 19 October 2005
Somewhere North of Habbaniyah
Ramadi-Fallujah Corridor
Anbar Province

The old Toyota truck reached the farmhouse at last light. It had already successfully negotiated two Sunni insurgent checkpoints. The driver was used to such interruptions and knew how to deal with the nervous young gunmen. Out in the countryside, there was little chance of encountering an American or Iraqi Police patrol but, nevertheless, the journey had been both dangerous and high risk owing to the value of his freight. But once he was through the reinforced steel doors of the outer compound, he could relax.

The Mujahadeen at the farmhouse began unloading the truck of its cargo of fruit and vegetables, stacking each crate neatly. Once unloaded, they were left with three flat wooden boxes which they carefully unscrewed to reveal a dozen

Dragunov sniper rifles, still in their original boxing. With them were two thousand rounds of 7.62 ammunition.

There was a commotion at the gate, which then opened to admit a white Mitsubishi saloon with tinted windows in the back. It pulled up behind the truck and the driver smartly got out and opened the rear passenger door. Out stepped the supreme leader of Al Qaeda in Iraq, Abu-Musab Al Zarqawi. He had an M4 Colt carbine with him, which Salim knew had once belonged to a British unit ambushed in 2003. It was his pride and joy and he was never seen without it. Out of the other side appeared an Imam.

Al Zarqawi, a self-styled cleric in his mind, was a portly, smallish man in his late thirties, dressed in the flowing robes of a preacher. Yet he held all those gathered in the courtyard spellbound. Every one of them would gladly die for him as many before them had already done.

Inside the house, he greeted Salim al Agayli with a hug. *Subhanahue wa'ta'ala* – 'Glory to him the exalted.' Salim had prepared prayer mats and together, before anything else, they said their *Maghrib* prayers with the Imam. They started in the *qiyam* position, inciting God to ward off Satan and then went through the three obligatory *rakats* and then the two optional *sunnah rakats*.

Salim had the house staff prepare a welcoming feast of *masgouf* made with local carp, followed by goat meat *quzi* and rice. Sweet mint tea was served throughout and Salim noted that the Jihadist had a good appetite.

Yet Salim was wary of his guest. Although he was the chosen representative of Osama, he knew that the relationship between the two warriors was uneasy. Abu-Musab was notorious for his quick temper, ruthless intolerance and vicious, uncompromising violence. Despite this, Osama had helped him set up a camp for jihad in Herat, Afghanistan. It recruited mainly Jordanian Salafists and operated independently, moving men and weapons over the border from Iran. He had also read the letter Abu-Musab had distributed to the Sunni fighters and was uneasy about its content. When fighting in Bosnia, to establish the European Caliphate, Osama had emphasised 'ummah' or togetherness. Muslims should wage Jihad against the Infidel, not against each other. He had seen then, ten years ago now, how Mujahadeen could put aside religious differences to fight the common enemies, Israel, America and their allies. He had also witnessed in Afghanistan how Muslims seem to reserve their most bitter hatred for fellow Muslims.

Yet, the letter demanded that the war first be fought amongst themselves. His hatred of his fellow Muslims was most apparent.

They, the Shi'a, are the insurmountable obstacle, the lurking snake, the crafty and malicious scorpion, the spying enemy, and the penetrating venom. We here are entering a battle on two levels. One, evident and open, is with an attacking enemy and patent infidelity. Another is a difficult, fierce battle with a crafty enemy who wears the garb of a friend, manifests agreement, and calls for comradeship, but harbours ill will and twists up peaks and crests.

Salim watched as his guest ate heartily, knowing that he had already killed hundreds, if not thousands of Iraqis. He knew that this war against the Americans would be won using nationalism yet here was the leader of the resistance, second only to Osama, fomenting sectarian civil war amongst Muslims. This was not a strategy he could support but Salim knew better than to share his concerns with anybody but himself. He was, after all, an Agayl, the warriors of the Hashemite kingdom and the most revered fighters in the Arabic cause. Yet here was a Jordanian prison thug telling him that his men should kill fellow Muslims. He already knew that the Sunni sheiks of Northern Iraq would not tolerate either his violence or his wanton habit of *'takfir'* the denouncing of fellow Muslims as apostates in order to justify their killing. In short, Abu-Musab al-Zarqawi was a murderous psychopath whose presence in Iraq would be detrimental to the greater cause.

After the evening meal, the two men retired to discuss the war. It was clear that Abu-Musab had convinced himself and those around him that the only way to rid the country of Americans and prevent the establishment of what he called Greater Israel in the Land of the Two Rivers, was to awaken the Sunni sheiks from their slumber. And that would require a civil war with the Shi'a in Baghdad. In the midst of a civil war, the death and destruction of Multi-National Force soldiers would be too much to bear for their weak and feeble democracies and they would have no choice but to withdraw at the behest of their voters. Yet Salim felt the local people would not support such a plan.

They spoke long into the night, Salim keeping his guard up. He explained about the sniper school and how it was the most feared tactic after the roadside bomb. How using the internet and the mobile phone network, though the invention of Satan and used by the Crusaders, was a powerful weapon for them too. He described his war in Bosnia, knowing that Abu-Musab had missed the war in Afghanistan and then had spent the nineties in a Jordanian prison for a botched terrorist attack. They talked about Khalid al Mihdar, his spotter in the Bosnian war who had then gone on to fly an aeroplane into the World Trade Centre and bring Jihad to the Far Enemy itself and glorious martyrdom to himself. He showed him some of the videos he and his pupils had taken of the shooting of foreign infidels, acutely aware that there were no Shia targets. He explained how the infidels were already running scared of Juba the Baghdad Sniper. His guest nodded approvingly, seem-

ingly greedy for each new clip of death. He appeared unconcerned about the impact on morale such clips would have,
merely fascinated by the images of death itself.

In the morning, he summoned his most trusted driver using
his new mobile phone. Although he had many followers, his
guest would only allow this one driver to take him as he was
also, as on this occasion, the driver to the Sunni Imam to
whom he was closest. The roll out of mobile networks
throughout Iraq had enabled the Mujahadeen to dispense with
their Japanese walkie-talkies to which, they knew, the Americans listened. The new phones had a whole country range and
could transmit in coded words.

Just before getting into the car, Abu-Musab summoned him
over to offer the gift of a book. It was wrapped in a red and
white kufiyah.

'This is for you, my brother,' Abu-Musab said. 'It will
inform you how the infidels train their own snipers so that you
can learn and improve. I trust God will look benignly on your
jihad.'

With that, he got into the car. Salim unwrapped the cloth
and saw that the book was in English. He looked around and
called out to a man he knew spoke and read the language.

'What is this?' he asked.

The man took the book and said, 'It is called "*The Ultimate
Sniper: An Advanced Training Manual for Military and Police Snipers*"
by Major John Plaster USAR.'

22

Friday 21 October 2005
Defence Intelligence Staff
Old War Office Building
London SW1
0715 Local

'Right, everybody,' barked Eric, 'gather round. We've been sent something fresh in from the Defence HumInt Unit at the Joint Interrogation and Debriefing Centre at Slayer.'

'Another love letter from Barbie, Eric?'

'Never. Ever. Fucking. Call. Her. Barbie, David. Got that? Never. And that goes for all you other cunts in this room.'

The was a pregnant silence.

'Ok. Sorry Eric.'

'It was a nickname she was called when she was engaged.'

'Right. Yeah. Sorry again. Anyway, video must be important then. I'll put the kettle on.'

'Task Force Black brought in a hand-held wireless tele-phone a few weeks ago.'

David rolled his eyes and muttered, 'commonly called a mobile.'

'Yes,' continued Eric. 'Quite right, a mobile hand-held wireless telephone handset. The Yanks have hacked it and there's a list of numbers and names that Vauxhall want us to put through the database to see if we can ping any info we might have on them. First thing I want is a division into native Iraqi and foreign. JSOC is droning on about "reconcilables" and "irreconcilables" and we need to know the flavour of who is on that phone's memory. Just to be clear, it's not really possible, categorically, to know the difference but for us, a reconcil-able is someone who is fighting against the coalition for nationalist reasons rather than religious ideology.'

'The point being,' added David, 'that as we hand over power to the Iraqis and gradually draw down, the anti-coali-tion insurgency will diminish. "Irreconcilables" are those elements within the insurgency that are hoping to replace the State of Iraq with a hard-line Islamic Caliphate. Once we've gone, they will attack the government. Most, but not all, are foreign imports.'

'Correct, David, thank you. *Al Tawhid Wa Al Jihad*.'

'Eh?'

'"There is only one God and Holy War." Start with name analysis and see if you can identify known Iraqi-born insur-gency middle managers or Mujahadeen imports. I want to know if they are AQI, Ansar al Islam or the Mujahadeen Shura Council. We know that they are clustered to the north and west of Baghdad in what the Americans are calling the Triangle of Death.'

David went to the large map of Iraq on the wall.

'The triangle is made up of Doura, Arab Jabour and Salman Pak, here. Here is Ramadi and Fallujah is here.'

'I want to know if any of those numbers or names can be placed within or near that triangle.' Added Eric. 'I want to know tribal affiliations, family networks, business connections, foreign travel, names of mistresses, illegitimate children, drinking, gambling and drug habits and when they last took a dump. Most importantly, I want to know if those names appear anywhere else on sigint or any other fucking type of int. Get to work.'

The analysts dispersed to their desks to start on the task.

'David?' said Eric.

'Yup.'

'There's a word here that is really bugging me. "Agayli". Mean anything to you?'

'Nope. Can't say it does.'

'The Agayl are an Arab tribe that used to protect the caravans crossing the Arabian sand sea. They were famous for their navigation and fighting skills. They were predominantly from what is now Jordan but used to be the Hashemite Kingdom. The Hashemites protected Mecca from about the tenth century and were the rulers in many parts of the Ottoman Empire, from Syria and Palestine to Jordan and Iraq.'

'So, do you think this might be a link to al Zarqawi? Being Jordanian,' asked David.

'Maybe,' said Eric, 'But I can't quite put my finger on it. I've come across the Agayl somewhere before. They were much praised by Lawrence of Arabia in his Book "Seven Pillars of Wisdom", where he considered them the best fighters in the Arab Army but I'm thinking something closer to home. It'll come to me eventually. Let's start off by checking the Afghan references, see if we can pinpoint him there. Start with the Zarqawi camp at Herat.'

'I'm on it like a car bonnet,' David replied.

23

Saturday 19 November 2005
Mission Support Site Fernandez
Baghdad Green Zone
1530 Local

The Boss felt for his combat knife but he couldn't move his hand. It was in his webbing belt but he couldn't draw it from the scabbard. He didn't know where his rifle was. The shadowy figures of the insurgents were getting closer and he could hear them talking. His hiding place was small and cramped and he felt his pulse thumping in his temple. He struggled to control his breathing. They were very close now, torches flashing. When one was almost within touching distance, he leapt out and plunged the knife, which was now in his hand, into the man's neck. He felt the hot carotid blood seep between his fingers. He stabbed again and then again. The figure turned to him, grinning a toothless grin, his eyes unseeing sockets.

He awoke with a start, the sun streaming through the thin

curtains of his room. He sat up, getting his bearings. Already the dream was receding but he knew it would be back. He became aware of the mortar alarms and an urgent voice booming out over the tannoys ordering all personnel to go to the shelters. It was almost a daily occurrence but it still annoyed him that today it was so early. The nightmare would have woken him anyway, although he never knew if the alarms started the dreams or saved him from them. He got up and wandered over to the ablution block for a shower and then headed off to find something to eat. An army fights on its stomach, the saying goes, and the Americans in the Green Zone certainly lacked for nothing foodwise.

The relentless nature of the fight against the insurgency meant that all Allied bases in Iraq operated twenty-four hours a day and sleep was taken whenever possible. For Task Force Black and the other Tier One Special Forces at MSS Fernandez, this usually meant from early morning until early afternoon, as they were predatory, nocturnal creatures.

"Good morning everyone, you are listening to one-oh-seven point seven Freedom Radio. Here in Baghdad it's currently ninety seven degrees and sunny. Coming up next we have a special request for Weezer and 'Beverly Hills.'"

He spotted SSgt Barnes sitting alone at a table nursing a cup of coffee and so plonked his tray down opposite.

'Morning John.'

'Morning Boss. Unlike you to be up so early. What happened? Did you piss the bed?'

'Charming. Once the alarms wake me, that's it. Might as well get up.'

'What's on for tonight?'

'Dunno. I'll go and see Ops after my brew. No doubt they'll have a house raid or two lined up.' The Boss looked at his number two and saw that there was something on his mind.

'You look a bit liverish, John. All ok?'

Barnes looked around to check for people listening and then leaned in to murmur,

'Anything new from Mauritius?' Having delivered the question, he leaned back and faked a yawn and a stretch, with his arms going behind his head. He was referring to a large amount of money they had both liberated from an ambushed convoy in the previous tour and which was now sitting in a bank account in the Indian Ocean tax haven.

'When you finish with Her Majesty's Forces, there's definitely going to be a second career in acting.'

'Boss, I am deeply fucking uncomfortable about it all now.'

'It was your idea in the first place…'

'Our idea. It was our idea.'

'Whatever, it is what it is. Look, the account has been anonymised.'

'Can your banker mate guarantee that it's amonynous, er, anonymous?' asked Barnes.

'There are no guarantees but, apparently, according to him, if nothing happens, no transactions or stuff, then nobody is going to pick up on it. He's set up what he calls a complex filter system where the account is owned by another entity in the Cayman Islands. He tells me the amount is too small to alert the global money laundering authorities and, whilst it is what he calls 'dormant', it's safe.'

'What happens if we get slotted?'

'Then it stays in an account for ever.'

'Is there, you know, a thing whereby the missus can get money should I peg it?'

'Don't think so John.'

'Here comes Brent. We'll pick this up later.'

An officer from Task Force Green, Delta Force, approached carrying a tray.

'Mind if I join you, Gentlemen?'

'Be our guest, Brent.'

The American, Captain Brent Schapner, deposited his tray and sat down next to the Boss. They had first met on a hostage release raid a year and a half ago. That was before the senior commanders of both the UK and US Special Forces had knocked political heads together and formed a united response to the insurgency. Prior to that, there had been unhealthy rivalry and a dysfunctional reluctance to share information. This had led to an uncomfortable encounter with an American hostage release team, led by Brent, arriving after the Troop had already rescued two captured American soldiers. It had been awkward at the time but had helped push a new era of co-operation. The Americans had agreed to be more sensitive to 'human rights' and 'prisoner welfare' and promised to stop special renditions to 'black sites' for 'unconventional intelligence gathering methods' which may have included water boarding. Now they were neighbours at MSS Fernandez.

'Like the new arm patch?' Brent turned his shoulder to reveal a Stars and Stripes with 'Fuck Al Qaeda' embroidered above.

'Where did you get that, then?' enquired the Boss.

'The little tailor's shop next to the PX. Most of the guys are wearing them now.'

'Boss, you're not thinking…' started Barnes.

'We could get some Union Jack ones made,' said the Boss.

'No Boss, we couldn't.'

'Why not?'

'Because we just couldn't. Not right. Not in my troop.'

'I hear we are going out again together. Tonight.' interjected Brent, to break the awkward tension. 'House raids a go-go.'

'What have you heard?'

'Just more of the same. Seems one of the detainees at the Temporary Screening Facility is getting close to spilling the beans. You've got a smart lady running a humint team that's now moved him to Joint Interrogation Centre at Balad and is teasing stuff out of him bit by bit. He's given an address but I'm not cleared to know who we are after. Other than it's a driver, I'm told.'

'Driver for whom?' Asked the Boss.

'That I don't know,' replied the American.

'Can't wait.'

24

Monday 21 November 2005
Camp Slayer
Baghdad International Airport
1830 Local

Barbara had decided that she was going to transfer the prisoner to Balad. Currently, he was languishing in the Secure Confinement Facility at Camp Cropper, a temporary holding area for those brought in by the nightly house raids. Cropper was within the perimeter of Baghdad International Airport which also included Slayer, so there was no need for a heavily armed escort. They were not supposed to be held for more than seventy-two hours before either being released or formally processed. For the Taxi Driver, taken by the SAS two nights previously, life was about to change for the worse, because nobody had any intention of releasing him.

She arrived at the compound, run by the US Airforce, and signed in with the Interrogation Control Element sergeant.

Camp Cropper was next to Camp Nama. Most US camps were named after fallen American servicemen but Nama was just 'Nasty-Ass Military Area' and Nama already had a reputation for 'Enhanced Interrogation Techniques' with which Barbara wanted zero association. She'd recently had a tip off from Eric back in London that there was a gulf opening between what was acceptable to the US and what was to the UK. In her mind there was an existential dilemma with which she did not feel equipped personally to deal and about which she had received no guidance from above. In her room, she had a laminated definition of 'torture' sent by Eric in a secure email. He had warned her that the quest for high grade intelligence as fast as possible would be no defence against later accusations of prisoner mistreatment or abuse, even if it saved military lives.

Any act by which severe pain or suffering, whether physical or mental, is intentionally inflicted on a person for such purposes as obtaining from him or a third person information or a confession, punishing him for an act he or a third person has committed or is suspected of having committed, or intimidating or coercing him or a third person, or for any reason based on discrimination of any kind, when such pain or suffering is inflicted by or at the instigation of or with the consent or acquiescence of a public official or other person acting in an official capacity. It does not include pain or suffering arising only from, inherent in or incidental to lawful sanctions.

But it was not as simple as that. Things out here never were. There was also the question of 'complicity'. She should, she knew, report any concerns about prisoner abuse, regardless of whether she had actually witnessed any, which, incidentally, she hadn't. However, it was becoming apparent, most prisoners held in the detention facility were not being held to the standards which the British Government, safe back in London, would accept. Her own view was that beating up prisoners was exactly the wrong way to go about getting good grade intelligence. Eric had told her that the Argentine prisoners taken in the Falklands, on being given shelter and warm sugary tea, had divulged huge amounts of information about troop deployments within hours of being captured, just grateful that they hadn't been butchered and eaten by the Gurkhas. The shock and anxiety of capture was enough for most to spill the beans. Regardless, some of the hardcore prisoners had mentally prepared for resistance and the Coalition Forces could use any number of 'Enhanced Interrogation Techniques' and still would get nothing useful.

At Camp Nama she had witnessed some disturbing sights. The facility consisted of several interrogation rooms quaintly named 'Black', 'Blue', 'Red' and 'Soft'. She had been shown inside 'Black' which, indeed, was an empty windowless room painted black. It had hooks hanging from the ceiling and speakers in the corners and she was informed that it had been used by Saddam's secret police. In the rare occasions that she'd been asked to interrogate at Nama, she had always opted for the 'Soft' room which, in contrast, had comfy furnishings, leather chairs and nice prayer mats on the walls. There, she could offer detainees tea or soda and conduct a simple question and answer session. She made a point of never filling out the US interrogation printed-menu where you could order, in advance, such items as strobing lights, loud rock music, cold water soaking, stress positions and all the rest of the tricks of her trade.

But there was another problem. The Coalition was just that and the UK was a junior partner and she was working within the remit of the US run bases at Slayer and Balad. Although Joint Special Operations Command had worked hard to accommodate UK concerns, she knew that the Americans regarded prisoners in a different way. She had been told on numerous occasions by them that detainees were not Prisoners of War but rather Detained Unlawful Combatants. As such, the Geneva Convention didn't apply to them. Donald Rumsfeld himself, she had been assured, had said as much. But Barbara hadn't seen anything on official orders or written in Standard Operating Procedures. So, as far as she was concerned, any detainee was covered by the Convention.

Absurdly, the Americans, at the Temporary Screening Facility at Balad had erected a "UK Compliant" holding cell adjacent to their own holding pens. This was bigger and could be examined by third parties such as the Red Cross but frankly, it didn't really help her as the Red Cross were not allowed on that part of the base. Whichever way you looked at it, these were black sites and there was a very good argument that they were illegal. And Barbara knew she was not a match for some snake-tongued human rights barrister in a wig hat asking her why she was a war criminal in an Old Bailey courtroom five years from now.

What she would rely on, she had decided, was not to get involved in anything she couldn't happily describe to her granny. Granny Bishop was a formidable old bird who had looked after Barbara numerous times when she was a girl and to whom Barbara always turned in times of trouble. To Barbara, she was the font of all wisdom who brooked no nonsense. She had a robust Edwardian sense of fair play and knew with a certainty, derived from age, right from wrong.

To try to protect themselves, the UK members of JSOC had worked out a 'cheat'. The British house raids were very often accompanied by American operators, usually from Delta and all prisoners lifted in these raids were deemed 'American'. This relieved the responsibility, the theory went. If the Americans were the handlers, then the British could wash their hands of the interrogation. British prisoners could be sent down to

Basra, where things were done differently and she was familiar with the routine of flying down and conducting questioning or source handling.

But Abdullah the Taxi, currently languishing at Cropper and about to be moved by Barbara to the Temporary Screening Facility at Logistics Support Area Anaconda, at Balad Airbase, was different. She had asked the SAS to lift him because he was linked to a phone recovered from another raid. And, it would seem, he was potentially also on a computer captured during the same raid. Cellular terrorism networks are often described as onions. You have to peel slowly and carefully through the outer layers to get to the core. But a driver, if she could turn him, would negate all that. He might lead them straight to the centre of the onion without having to peel the layers of skin and avoid all that crying that went with it.

At the Facility, she signed the necessary documentation and picked her usual interpreter, with whom she worked well. The chopper, she must stop calling them choppers, would be taking off from the Liberty Command Helipad for the short hop up to Balad. She had a GMC Suburban and a driver and the four of them drove the ten minutes to the waiting Puma.

Once at Balad, she was escorted, with her prisoner, to the Temporary Screening Facility. She went past the sign that proclaimed, "No blood/No foul, The High Five Paintball Club". It referred to the common assumption that if you didn't draw blood, then you hadn't mistreated the prisoner. She had heard that some prisoners had actually been stripped of their clothes, sprayed with freezing water and then had paintballs fired at them. It was a puzzle to her what might motivate interrogators to act like that. Besides the humiliation, discomfort and fear it induced in prisoners, it was, to her mind, the least effective way to get good quality intelligence quickly.

She entered the low building, signed in and was shown to where they had an interview room waiting. She dismissed the

assigned armed Military Policeman and asked for the plas-
ticuffs that bound Abdullah's hands behind his back to be
removed. She then booked him into the medical facility,
mindful that she wanted a medical assessment done before she
started to question him. That way, all existing evidence of
maltreatment could not be laid at her feet. Twenty minutes
later, other than some bruising around the wrists from his
restraints and some further bruising on his legs, probably from
being bundled unceremoniously into the helicopter, he was
pronounced fit.

The interview room had a table and four chairs. She indicated a chair and Abdullah sat down. He kept his eyes down,
avoiding any contact, which, to Barbara, indicated he was
fearful of a beating that he had convinced himself would now
commence.

Barbara sat opposite him and removed the small backpack
she was wearing. She rummaged around and produced a
packet of Marlboro cigarettes, making her think of Eric and
the days back in Bosnia. Next out were two bottles of water
and a banana. She opened the cigarette pack and offered one
to her guest. It took a little cough to get him to look up from
his feet. For the first time, they had eye contact and that was
perhaps the moment when she knew she had got him. He took
a cigarette and she flourished a zippo that she had in her cargo
trousers' pocket. He bent forward, closer to the flame. Then
she unscrewed the top off a bottle of water and passed it to
him before opening her own. She took out her notepad, a biro
and a Dictaphone, which she turned on to record and sat back,
staring at the captive, a slight smile on her face. Then, as if the
thought had only just occurred to her, she offered a third bottle
and a cigarette to her interpreter, sitting beside her, who she
knew didn't smoke.

'Do you know why you are here?' She asked, the interpreter immediately translating.

'No, I do not,' replied Abdullah in English. 'I am taxi driver. Not terrorist.'

'Oh, we know exactly who you are Abdullah. We know where you live, where your mosque is, who your friends are. We know everything. But the question was, "do you know why you are here"'.

'The answer is still no.'

'We think you can help us. And by "we" I mean the British.' Abdullah just stared at her. She took a sip of her water to increase the pressure of the silence but he still said nothing. The interpreter butted in, in Arabic, to which he responded also in Arabic.

'He says he knows nothing. If he pretends to know something he will be killed.' There was another exchange of rapid Arabic.

'He says he can't help you and would like to go now.'

'The trouble is, Abdullah, I can't just let you go. Oh no. You see, all I can do is give you back to the Americans.' She waited, thinking back to her laminated brief on torture *"intimidating or coercing"*. Legally, she was already on thin ice. *'Play ball with me and all will be fine. Act the goat and you go back to Camp Nama and the Black Room, with the dogs, the hoses, the strobes, the sleep deprivation and the random beatings. Pick one'*.

'What happened to the last prisoner we gave back to the Americans?' she asked the interpreter. It was a loaded and rehearsed question.

'He was renditioned to Morocco. Then Guantanamo Bay. I think he is still there.'

Barbara looked into the eyes of Abdullah who refused to blink.

'Better than the black site at Bagram in Afghanistan, I suppose. What would happen to your son, Abdullah, if you were sent to Morocco? Or Lithuania? It's very cold in Lithuania. Food's not good at all and they don't care for

Muslims. Who would earn money to pay for food, and, you know, your family's other needs?' She knew now she was definitely on the wrong side of what was legally and, probably, ethically appropriate.

'Or you could co-operate with us. We Brits don't have special sites where prisoners are waterboarded. Do you know what waterboarding is, Abdullah?' He stared sullenly but she knew he was calculating the risks. 'Abu Ghraib was very mild,' she added, referring to the scandal of the year before about pictures of detainee abuse in the prison which were published throughout the world. 'Black sites like Bagram, well, there's no knowing what goes on inside them. But I can promise you this, it's not nice.'

'What do want from me?' *Bingo* it was now a negotiation.

'We want to know, every time you drive your taxi, where you are going and who you are taking. Very simple.'

'Why do that when you can just follow me?' Had a point, of sorts. What he didn't appreciate is that a constant overwatch on just a single vehicle requires a twenty-four-seven Predator drone presence and a team of at least four. Predators were a very scarce resource and they were hogged by JSOC, mainly for the American special forces. Even the SAS of Task Force Black complained they could never get hold of them even for short operations.

She ignored the question.

'Have you got a phone?' He continued to stare at her so she went on, 'I mean they are absolute game changers. Couldn't live without mine. Tell you what, we will give you a phone, not too snazzy, don't want people asking awkward questions.'

'What is snazzy?' He asked. The interpreter spoke in Arabic and for the first time there was a hint of a smile.

'Let's have a quick look.' She rummaged in the pack and pulled out and placed a phone on the table while looking at the prisoner. There was a tiny reaction in his eyes that told her it was his phone that had been brought in on the same raid that had taken him.

'This your phone, Abdullah?'

'I think you know it is,' he said.

'You're right. I do. As I said, I know everything about you. You keep using this phone. Don't change the sim or throw it away, because we will know and the deal is off. And, knowing the Americans, they might let it slip that you have been helping us.'

He looked at her with resignation and hatred in his eyes.

'And we will give you money.' It was the killer point to get him back on side willingly. Nothing worked better than money in this country.

'How much?' Now they were arguing over price and she knew she had him. Even if he wasn't who she thought he was, for a small stipend, he could be kept on the books. Once you accepted the money, you were owned. There was no going back.

'A hundred dollars a month.' It was a sizeable amount for a taxi driver in post invasion Iraq. The silence was broken by the loud, vicious barking of dogs. There was an indistinct American voice shouting and then the wailing of another man clearly in distress. She looked at Abdullah, her face expressionless save for a small arching of her eyebrows. He shifted uncomfortably in his chair, listening yet not wanting to hear.

She played her trump card, the deal sealer.

'And we will look after your medical needs. For you and your family.' Barbara knew from the post operation report that epilepsy drugs had been found in Abdullah's house. Mainly knock-off clone drugs produced in India and probably shipped up from Kuwait. These were not cheap for a taxi driver. She could give him a year's supply of, say, Oxcarbazepine. That wasn't just expensive in this country, it was unobtainable. She was taking a calculated risk that someone close to him, possibly his wife or one of his children, required seizure drugs.

'If I help you, you give me the money and the medicines?'

'It's that easy, Abdullah.'

'And I want asylum. I go and live in England? Me and my family.'

'Let's not get ahead of ourselves now. Let's get you cleaned up and we will take you back to Baghdad with your phone.

He continued to stare at her.

'When you get an order to pick someone up, call us and let us know who it is and where you are going. Couldn't be easier. Just don't get caught.' She smiled.

'Sometimes they don't tell me who and only where when he is in car.'

'Don't you worry about any of that. We will probably know you have been tasked for a job. But the more you tell us, the more you get paid. So try to find out who is telling you to pick up a passenger.'

Abdullah let out a heavy defeated sigh. Barbara pushed the banana towards him.

'Here, have a banana.'

25

Tuesday 22 November 2005
Defence Intelligence Staff
Old War Office Building
London SW1
0730 Local

'Morning Earthlings.' Eric had a jaunt in his step. 'Have I got something for you civvy filth today.'

'Eric, you are a civvy too, now,' said David.

'Have you got my coffee yet? You don't have permission to speak until then.'

'Literally fuck off. What have you got?'

'I have got a new film. Came in last night. Was given to some Aussie at the Sydney Morning Herald. Paul McGeough, currently stationed in Baghdad. Apparently, it's been on sale in the bazaars for a while but someone made sure it got wider publicity by handing it to a westerner.'

'Well, put it on then, man,' said David.

Eric made little coughing and gasping noises.

'Fuck's sake, Emma, get Eric a brew. Nato standard, no sugar.'

Eric sat at his desk and opened a drawer to extract a DVD. The office got up and gathered round his monitor. It started with the customary *nasheeds* as the video rolled and then a man in a black jacket and a red kufiyah addressed the camera from the back of a car.

"I have nine bullets in this gun and a present for George Bush."

Eric paused the video. The circle of on-lookers behind him waited but he stayed silent.

'It's a Tabuk,' he said, mainly to himself. Everyone knew to remain quiet as the cogs whirred in his head. 'It's a fucking Tabuk.'

'Er, Eric? What's a Tabuk?' enquired David.

'The rifle, it's a Tabuk. It's a Zastava. Of course. An M70 with a PSO-1.' He mused to himself.

David looked at the others in the circle and made a 'don't ask me' facial gesture.

'Emma darling? Once we've finished watching this vid, will you dig out the Bosnia archive? I want stuff on the ABiH 307th Brigade in Bugojno. Anything we've got on the 7th Muslim Brigade attached, especially foreign fighters.'

David said 'Do you mind, Eric, explaining what is happening in your head? Has insanity finally come calling to take you off in its clutches to the asylum?'

'Metagnomy, dear boy,' said Eric.

'Right, stop this now. Can you kindly speak in English rather than gibberish. Nobody in this room, me included, has any idea what you are talking about.'

'The rifle he's using in the video. It's a Tabuk. And a Tabuk is an Iraqi version of another rifle, the Yugoslavian Zastava M70. Now most snipers we've come across would use a Soviet

Dragunov rifle, wouldn't they? An SVD or something. The same as in the first video Barbara sent.'

'If you say so, Eric.'

'I do, so why is this man using a Zastava? It's because he's been brought up using one and that links him to Yugoslavia, specifically Bosnia.'

'Er…ok…' said David 'what about the "Metathingybollocks" you mentioned?'

'Metagnomy? That is the paranormal acquisition of information. Cryptesthia, if you like.'

'You're telling me that a poltergeist is telling you this stuff?'

'No, I'm telling you that the penny has dropped and I think we can find out who this sniper is. He calls himself Juba, which is his *"kunya"*.'

'His what? I think I'm getting a headache. How do you know he's called Juba?'

'It's on the video, Einstein. His nom de guerre. He's calling himself *"Juba Qannas Baghdad"*- Juba, Baghdad Sniper. Why Juba? David, can we assemble everything we've got on Juba? I think it's a town in Sudan. Maybe he's a Muj from Juba. So, we need to trawl anything we have on Sudanese Mujahadeen, including Bosnia, Afghanistan, the Maghreb and the Levant, especially Syria, Lebanon and Palestine.'

'OBL,' David used the acronym for Osama bin Laden 'was living in Sudan during the nineties.'

'It's hardly likely to be Osama. He's hiding in the Waziristan Badlands on the Durand Line between Pakistan and Afghanistan.'

'Really?' said David. 'Have you told the Americans this?'

'No, they told me. What else is on this vid?' Eric watched as a series of grainy sequences showed American and Iraqi soldiers being shot by snipers.

'That is grim viewing,' said David.

'It's meant to be. Straight out of the Al Qaeda playbook.

They are terrorists, after all and they want to show the world how they are taking on the Great Satan. David, the Yanks will have this. Can you find out if they have identified the locations and timings of each clip?'

'Best person for that is Barbara in Baghdad. She'll have discussed this with them already.'

'Yup, you're right. I'll drop her a line, see what's she knows. Juba seems to be an important asset for AQI. I can promise you this; Babs does not fucking like snipers.'

26

Monday 12 December 2005
Mission Support Site Fernandez
Baghdad Green Zone
1130 Local

Delta Force, known as Task Force Green, and the Special Air Service, now known as Task Force Knight, occupied adjoining houses in MSS Fernandez. There were seven two-storey trophy villas in a row on an elbow of the Tigris in the heavily protected Green Zone of Baghdad. Prior to the invasion and occupation, they had been the Baghdad residences of a well-connected elite but were now occupied by the men and paraphernalia of two combat squadrons. The Americans liked to call themselves 'operators' and the British 'blades.'

In the American villa, the operators had occupied the top floor as their living quarters, whilst downstairs, in what they called the basement, there was a holding cell and an interrogation room. Detainees were often taken to MSS Fernandez and held for twenty-four to thirty-six hours prior to being handed over to the interrogators at Balad. That period of time was usually extremely productive in terms of gathering intelligence. There were rumours, strenuously denied, that some of the interrogation techniques in these hours may not have strictly complied with the latest standing orders on detainee holding procedures. All US Special Forces operators had undergone SERE training – Survival, Evasion, Resistance, Escape which was taught at the John F. Kennedy Special Warfare Center and School, known as Swiks at Fort Liberty, North Carolina. The resistance part of this training had subjected those wishing to enter the hallowed inner sanctum of US Special Forces to such methods as sleep deprivation, time disorientation, white noise and stress positions. Recruits were also waterboarded, an ancient yet extraordinarily effective method of torture, first developed by the Spanish Inquisition. It was used by the Americans in Vietnam and was also now being used in their 'black sites' in Afghanistan and Iraq.

To members of Delta, who had all themselves experienced these methods in training, it was considered legitimate. And, strictly, they were right, as the 2002 Bybee Memo from the Office of Legal Counsel at the White House concluded that the technique did not amount to torture and that it could be used in the interrogation of enemy combatants. But ethical and moral considerations were another matter. However hard someone thought they were, it was unlikely to take more than thirty seconds to break their will. Normally, physical recovery was good but the mental trauma could and did stay with victims for a very long time. The beauty, if you could call it that, is that it left no physical marks on the victim and the results were near instantaneous.

In the Global War on Terror, quick information was good information and detainees that could provide the targeting for the next raid were encouraged to do so in the basement of MSS Fernandez. Last night's detainee was no exception.

Brent Schapke had not been present when it was revealed that there was a Baghdad internet café which was being used as a conduit for insurgent communications. This snippet had already gone into the machine of Task Force Orange. And now they had a rare opportunity to slot another jigsaw piece in the gradually expanding picture of the Sunni Insurgency.

* * *

The Boss was making the brews. This was good and bad news. Good in the fact that it was really his turn and he was confident he knew how to make a cup of tea. Bad in that it invariably led to discussions about the cavalry and Ruperts – the name generally used for commissioned officers from other regiments.

'So, Boss, did your batman teach you how to make the brews or was it nanny?' Wayne Bruce, since passing selection, had been called, obviously, Man Bat or simply Bat. He was white Zimbabwean by birth but had come to the UK to join the Parachute Regiment and from there it was a well-trodden path to the Regiment.

It was important, if you wanted to survive the banter wars, to nip back early.

'Well, Battyboy, old chap, it's a simple process that we exported to the colonies along with cricket and queuing.'

'Not really answering the question, Boss,' observed Wolfie, not looking up from a six-month-old copy of *Top Gear* magazine.

'Let's be clear,' said the Boss, pouring the water into six identical white china mugs, 'It certainly wasn't our Batman.'

'He's not worked out how to boil a kettle.' Cookie, usually the radio operator, was assiduously cleaning his Sig Sauer pistol that most of the Troop kept tucked into the front of their body armour in case of emergencies.

'Yeah, but Boss,' persisted Man Bat, 'You told us in the tanks your radio operator made all the brews. So, really, Cookie, you should be doing it. You are a cook, after all.' Man Bat was pleased with this observation and fruitlessly beamed a smile around the group.

'True, in the turret, it is usually the loader/operator that makes the brews. But that is a matter of ergonomics. He's the one that stands next to the BV.'

'The what?'

'Boiling vessel. All British tanks have a kettle. Every other army thinks it's British eccentricity until they see the practicalities. It was almost taken out at the design phase of the Challenger 2 new tank project but the civvies at Vickers were told in no uncertain terms it was a sine qua non.'

'Fuck's sake Boss, speak English.'

'Here's some English for you. Come and get your tea whilst it's hot. Help yourselves to milk and sugar, I can't be arsed to remember what you all prefer.'

At that moment, Staff Sergeant Barnes came in.

'You making a brew Boss? What did your batman die of? Wonders never cease. Yes please. NATO standard.'

'Fuck's sake, John,' muttered the Boss, refilling the kettle and getting out another mug and teabag.

'Must be a change for you, Boss, not having the loader make it.'

'John, we've already been through this conversation just before you arrived.'

'Well, in that case, we've been given a task. Boss, we need to go to the briefing, so forget my tea and drink up.'

'What's the task, John?' asked Cookie.

'Daylight trip into Baghdad. Going with Delta and some Mohawks.'

"Mohawks" were the Iraqi volunteers that worked with the coalition, especially Delta, on close-target reconnaissance, where it was too risky to use a westerner. A so called 'low-vis' operation.

'Come on Boss, get it down you. Can't sit around all day drinking tea. You're not in the cavalry now.'

The Boss abandoned his tea and accompanied Barnes to the briefing room. They learned that Delta had identified the exact computer in a downtown internet café that was being used to pass information. It was a modernised version of an old technique called the 'dead letter drop.' The insurgents would use password protected generic email servers to write emails and then save them to the 'drafts' file. That way, unless you had access to the log in and the password, it was virtually out of reach for the Int teams of Task Force Orange as the email was never sent.

The plan was simple. A three-car convoy, chosen from Delta's fleet of inconspicuous beaten-up local vehicles, would drop off a Mohawk short of the target. The Iraqi would walk to the café, identify the exact computer and, if it were free, download a trojan horse software virus. If the computer was occupied, he would occupy another berth and text the team when it became free. A second Mohawk would then be dropped off to occupy the now vacant seat. The virus, developed by a secretive organisation called the Computer Networks Operations Squadron in Arlington, Virginia, would then record and transmit keystroke combinations back to the Int guys. Data would also go straight back to Arlington, where it would be analysed and parsed and then fed back to JSOC at Balad, all in a matter of hours. If the computer had a built-in webcam, that would also be surreptitiously activated to get an image of the user.

Simple, but dangerous. Mohawks had been compromised, kidnapped and murdered on similar missions, their tortured bodies turning up floating face down in the Tigris or dumped in a rubbish pit in the suburbs. Delta operators would track the car with their own car and a van. Inside the back of the van, would be six of the SAS troop. The back window was covered in a translucent foil that gave the appearance from the outside that it was full of carpets but could still be used to view out from the inside. Back in the Green Zone, the Parachute Regiment quick reaction force would be mounted up, engines on and ready to deploy in case a hot extraction was needed. In the air would be a Predator drone, part of General McChrystal's 'unblinking eye.' A second turboprop would also be airborne to eavesdrop on any mobile phone traffic and could track any handset, even those turned off providing they had a battery and a sim card.

Low-vis operations always made the Boss nervous, despite the intricate preparations and the exhaustive "actions-on" contingency planning. If the op was compromised, they may have to fight their way out of a rapidly escalating, violent confrontation.

'Stan, you'll be driving as per normal. We'll be using the blue Nissan Vanette.'

'Great name for a van. Full marks to the Nissan marketing department for coming up with that one,' remarked Stan. The Skunkwerks team up at Logistics Support Site Anaconda had modified the back of the van to include seating and that was where the other five members would be. Cookie would be relaying any information from an encrypted two-way radio, especially possible threats identified by the aerial surveillance and the mobile intercepts.

The troops loaded up and then followed the two Delta Force cars out of the heavily fortified west gate. Baghdad Airport and Camp Victory was approximately five miles away and, in between, was Sunni territory. It was some of the most dangerous real estate in the world at the time, with the road connecting the Green Zone and the Airport the most heavily bombed carriageway in existence.

Outside the relative calm and safety of the Zone lay the chaotic mayhem of Baghdad. Nose-to-tail traffic moved agonisingly slowly, with a mix of trucks, cars, bicycles and donkey carts all vying for space. Beside the road were trestle tables, shaded from the searing heat of the sun by beach umbrellas, selling food and hardware items. Streams of stagnant water mixed with pools of sewage which did not seem to bother the seething throng of people. For the most part, they were all dressed modestly, since seemingly innocuous items such as blue jeans or patterned shirts could get you summarily executed by the Sunni insurgent enforcers that unofficially policed these ghettos. The few women were dressed in full face coverings, bobbing black shapes in among the men. There was no female hair or make up to be seen.

'Fuck me,' said Stan from the front of the van, 'No wonder they've got a shitty-on with us. This is considerably worse than even a few months ago. I can smell the stink of shite even with the windows up and the air con on.'

'Update from zero,' interrupted Cookie, 'No discernible uptick in mobile traffic and the eye in the sky tracking us is not picking up any hostiles.'

'Roger that,' confirmed the Boss. These expeditions always made him jumpy and a bit tetchy. It was not just that the existential threat was always present when outside the Green Zone. There was also an added layer of responsibility should things start to deteriorate. His primary mission, he had told himself, was to get his troop back home unscathed but equally, he had to execute the actual mission given to him.

They drove down an avenue that had blue Samsung flags hanging from the buildings on both sides and a herd of goats eating from a pile of garbage. Along an iron railing fence were hung black hand-painted flags commemorating the dead from previous roadside bombs.

The Delta car in front swerved around a blackened blast hole in the tarmac.

'That'll be where they died,' observed Stan, also avoiding the hole.

'Two minutes to drop off,' announced Cookie.

'Just hang back a tad, Stan,' said the Boss, his already heightened senses now threatening to overload his brain. The Delta car slowed and the Boss noticed one brake light was not working, almost certainly a deliberate part of the camouflage. The passenger door opened and a young Iraqi got out and was quickly engulfed by the crowd. The Delta car started moving again and they saw the internet café slip by before they turned right at the junction.

'Right, we are going to do a series of figure eights whilst the Mohawk does his stuff in the café,' said the Boss. 'Stick behind the Delta car, we don't want anybody getting in between us at this stage.'

'Mohawk is on the objective. Time to completion four minutes.'

'OK, Stan, keep up the chuff of the Delta guys, we will only be doing one circuit.'

Outside the vehicle, the world carried on with nobody seeming to give them a second glance. The number of people milling around was a comfort as were the hordes of children running errands or passing the time idly in the street. Whilst there was always the random chance of a suicide bomber detonating as part of the relentless tit for tat strikes that the Sunni and Shi'a fighters inflicted on each other, the real threat was that somebody in the crowd somehow noticing that the Americans were in the vehicles. If that happened, a large and angry crowd would swamp the little convoy and it would be a matter of shooting one's way out of the problem with massive civilian casualties. It would be difficult to explain why lethal force was required to extract his team, as in the cold harsh daylight of an enquiry a few years hence, nobody would remember the images of blackened bodies of contractors caught by the mob hanging from motorway flyovers.

'Mission accomplished, as George Bush might say,' announced Cookie.

The Delta car circled round again and paused just beyond the entrance to the internet café, the Mohawk knowing he had to turn right out of the door. The Boss spotted him as he emerged, walking nonchalantly along looking at a cheap mobile phone in his hand. As the Delta car pulled up behind him, the door opened and, without looking around, he got in.

'Right,' said the Boss. 'Let's get the fuck out of here.' That was when the bomb exploded in a side street in front of them. The pressure hit before the noise as the detonation blasted everything and everyone down the ally and into the main street.

The small convoy of Delta vehicles and the van were shielded from the main blast which had targeted an ice cream shop with a car packed with explosives.

'Fuck me,' said the Boss.

'What do we do, Boss?' asked Stan.

'Keep following Delta.'

As they drove past the side street, the Boss saw the carnage. The immediate aftermath of a car bomb has its own peculiar nidorous atmosphere. The smell of the explosive, probably a mixture of RDX and ammonium nitrate, was a sort of almondy flavour. It hung in the air amidst the billowing dust and smoke. There was a pitiful array of bodies, most blackened or covered in cement powder from the pulverised concrete walls. Some of the many wounded were either sitting or lying where they had been caught by the flying debris. Others, less badly hurt, were wandering around in a state of dazed confusion, the intense concussion having obliterated their ability for rational thought.

Quickly crowds gathered and soon the road was swarming with Iraqis, some trying to get to the scene, others trying to get away. The cars slowed to a walking pace, with the crowds surging around them. The Boss felt very conspicuous and the team had already made sure their weapons were out of sight. The Delta car in front was held up by the sheer mass of people and Stan waited patiently behind it, the front bumper of the van almost touching its rear bumper. He kept his eyes ahead, not wanting to catch the eye of the crowd. In the distance the sirens of the Iraqi emergency services could be heard wailing as they struggled to get to the casualties.

Inside the van, the Boss heard a few fists banging on the side, the angry crowd wanting instant revenge on anyone or anything that could be held responsible. In front, the first Delta car was now surrounded and a mass of young men began to rock it from side to side.

'Cookie, let zero know we have a situation.'

'Roger, Boss.'

The wail of sirens intensified as the Iraqi emergency services began arriving on the scene.

'Boss, there's a Humvee approaching. Looks American,' said Stan.

'Cookie, let them know we are in the vicinity.'

'Roger Boss.'

The little convoy slowly made its way through the throng, finally getting onto a wider street with flowing traffic and headed back to the Green Zone.

'Thank fuck for that,' said Stan 'thought we were going to have to shoot our way out.'

That day, more than one hundred and thirty civilians were killed in multiple car bombings in Iraq.

27

Tuesday 3 January 2006
Somewhere North of Habbaniyah
Ramadi-Fallujah Corridor
Anbar Province

There was no shortage of foreign volunteers for the Jihad in Iraq, with the fighters from the Maghreb usually coming in through the porous borders by vehicle. Some came from Europe through the equally porous border with Turkey but mainly they slipped into Syria having landed in Lebanon, making their way across country to the Iraqi border and into Anbar Province. The trafficking network couldn't work without the co-operation of the local tribal elders and sheiks, for despite the vast and open desert being able to conceal almost anything in its sandy wastes, it was impossible to exist without the help of the local population.

The first destination of this stream of bodies was usually the urban areas around Ramadi and Fallujah, where the insur-

gency kept the Americans penned into their Forward Operating Bases. Although interceptions did occur, many more
succeeded getting through than were caught.

Once they were accommodated in either the slums of the
towns or the dispersed farmhouses of the productive farmland
of the Euphrates, they were quickly assessed. To a western
observer, the unlucky ones, perhaps illiterate and stupid, definitely poor and destitute, were earmarked as suicide bombers.
They would be rigged up with a vest and sent two or three at a
time to detonate themselves outside a Shi'a target such as a
mosque or a marketplace. If they were lucky, perhaps they
could get close to a coalition patrol. Those that could drive
would be instructed to take a lorry packed with explosives to a
target and kill dozens of innocent bystanders. They had a
volunteer group here at Salim's farmhouse that would don the
vests should the Crusaders attack, to die to protect their
commander.

The educated ones, especially the engineers, would be
taught various techniques of bomb making, improvised explosive devices and armour-penetrating shaped charges. IT engineers, often trained or educated in Western Europe, would
help with communications, internet, mobile telephony and
other new technologies that were rapidly taking over the world.
The rest would become soldiers, expected to carry a gun and
shoot at whomsoever they were told. The best of the soldiers
came to Salim for sniper training.

The training was conducted on makeshift ranges in
amongst the palm groves or the verdant fields. Salim drew
upon his experiences in Bosnia to teach the principles of
marksmanship, concealment, tactical movement and, above all
patience. Sniping was, for the most part, a state of mind. He
insisted on strict discipline and many of his pupils were
destined not to be entrusted with a sniper rifle, instead having
to return to the ranks of the *jundi*. He also enforced strict obser-

vations of Islamic traditions and culture but did not instil a hatred for the Shi'a. His view was that for *Ummah* and the Caliphate to exist and grow, Muslims of all sects must unite first to defeat the infidel.

He also knew about the power of communications. He had seen the fear of snipers in Bosnia and he knew his first video had had a chilling effect on coalition troops. His spies in amongst the general population were reporting that the Americans were less arrogant and more circumspect when operating outside their fortified areas. They had adopted his moniker of Juba and associated it with the dance of death of their own enslaved peoples, the blacks. This suited his purposes and he had recruited two IT engineers to help him with video editing and distribution. DVDs were printed and handed out in the Sunni parts of Baghdad to be given free to the population. Someone had handed a copy to an Australian and it had been aired on western television and taken up by the Arabic English-speaking channel, Al Jazeera, as well as the Arabic language station, Al Zawraa. There was already a website being developed to show the Juba videos and he was now about to film his second.

He was wearing a sand-coloured shirt and black trousers, with black gloves and his face hidden by a balaclava. They had set up the camera tripod in a room of the main house whose walls had been completely whitewashed. In it was a table with a white tablecloth and a black plastic chair. When the camera was rolling, he walked into the room and laid his Tabuk rifle on the table, alongside his pistol, walkie-talkie and four bullets. He then walked to a chart on the wall and crossed off another sniping victim, the thirty seventh.

With his back to the camera, he took off the balaclava and opened an exercise book and began to write in a delicate cursive Arab script.

In the name of Allah, most gracious, most merciful. Praise be Allah, prayers and peace be upon his messenger. Oh, Muslim Nation, how can the eye turn away from the one who saw your land which was conquered yesterday by our Muslim grandfathers' blood and today it is being dese-crated by the Jews and Crusaders. How can we eat or drink while our brothers who are your sons jailed in infidel jails Abu Ghraib, Guantanamo and Afghanistan? What would we tell Allah tomorrow, when he asks what we have done when the enemy entered our Land, destroyed our Mosques and harmed our honour and abused the Quran? How will we defend ourselves in front of the newborn babies in cradles when they stand against us on judgement day? What is our answer when Allah asks us about what we have done with his orders and not applying the Islamic Law? What a wonder he who reads the Quaran and doesn't recognise Allah's verse (Unless ye go forth he will punish you with a grievous penalty and put others in your place but him ye would not harm in the least for Allah has power over all things) Al Tawba 9:39

Using a recording facility on a computer, he had read out the message with a slight echo on the soundtrack before the video cut to his first victim, an American top gunner in a Humvee. It was, he knew, a perfect headshot and on the video, the video editor inserted a red crosshair and replayed the clip again in slow motion, the impact of the bullet clearly visible on the American's helmet. Up came "Juba; Baghdad Sniper." There followed a succession of grainy images, each using the red crosshairs and the same "Juba; Baghdad Sniper." Juba was in black block letters on a yellow background and appeared to the sound of a weapon being cocked.

Salim then did a piece to camera, his faced blocked out. On reviewing the tape, he was slightly shocked about how portly and middle-aged he had become. Nevertheless, he put aside his own pride. The video was a message for two audi-ences. Firstly, the infidel crusaders and secondly, the potential recruits from the greater Muslim lands. It was a call to arms, asking for volunteers with a steady hand and an eagle eye. He had clips of the training, rows of men dressed in black receiving instruction amongst the lush green fields of the farm. All were interspersed with clips of Americans being killed by sniping, each clip ending with the new Juba logo and 'Baghdad Sniper'. He spoke again to camera:

'We have really innovated several new methods of hiding. Then the idea of filming the operations is very important because the scene that shows the falling soldier when hit has more impact on the enemy than any other weapon. Especially after we saw the great concern of the enemy and even by the western media which has interviewed one of the top ranked retired Marine snipers, Major John Plaster, the author of the Ultimate Sniper, one of the main books we use to train our snipers.'

Salim went on to outline the importance of faith for the sniper and the use of the Tabuk rifle, as well as other weapons that had been captured from the enemy. He described as "lies" reports in the German media that he had been killed, propaganda disseminated to reduce the fear of the Americans.

'It is completely wrong, a lot of news agencies publish facts, which have no relation to the truth, which makes us laugh when we hear it and, in fact, this is the way of the of the defeated. They start to spread rumours and lies. Juba, the Sniper of Baghdad, has not been killed and what was published in the German channel was just a lie and just an attempt to decrease the fear of the American soldiers especially after the fame of the Sniper of Baghdad's name, or as they call him "Juba". They realised that they must find a solution for this problem. Now the American walk in the streets full of fear and horror, looking left and right, and at the rooftops of the buildings without knowing when they will be sniped, even giving the nickname "Juba" implies how big the fear covers their hearts because if you search the meaning of the word "Juba" you will find it has the meaning of horror, being scared and a ghost or also it is an African death dance. Even if the Sniper of Baghdad is killed, then is it over? He is like every Mujahid, struggling to win one of the two good things; either victory or martyrdom. If the martyrdom comes, then welcome. We are already martyrdom seekers. The enemy must know there are hundreds of Jubas.'

After further video clips, it went on to proclaim that six

hundred and thirty-four US soldiers had been killed, two hundred and six wounded, including twenty-three officers and eleven US snipers.

'Oh, Muslim youth, that is the paradise. I see it every day in the streets of my country when I go out to snipe one of the enemies with my beloved rifle. Juba: The Sniper of Baghdad.'

The DVD would be shipped to Baghdad for printing and then distributed covertly among the Sunni faithful following prayers at the mosques of the capital.

28

Tuesday 21 February 2006
Joint Special Operations Command
Balad Airbase
North of Baghdad

Barbara had hitched a lift on a Task Force Brown Black Hawk for the short hop up to JSOC and was now milling around with several hundred other US allied intelligence operators in the Death Star Headquarters building. They had stood at the back during the morning briefing and now, as the senior commanders went into what they called the "huddle", the lesser mortals, like Barbara, took the opportunity to talk with their counterparts in other areas of the large network.

It wasn't long before Brian Mendoza had spotted her and shuffled his way over.

'Howdee, Pardner,' he opened. Barbara, somewhat surprised, thought he must have taken advice on this because it was a new departure from the usual stammered 'Good Morning, Ms. Bishop' Maybe he had been told to be more assertive or confident. She smiled.

'Good morning, Brian. What is happening today in the land of the cryptologists?'

'Well, Ma'am, I er, I th…thought you might be interested in the computer we hacked.'

As every soldier knows, even the best laid plans rarely survive contact with the enemy and Brian had reverted to the mean. Barbara flashed her eyes salaciously, and rather cruelly, she thought in hindsight. She really shouldn't be leading him on or giving him any ideas.

'What's the Bobby, then, Brian?'

'Um, B…Bobby who?'

'I'm introducing you to some British rhyming slang, Brian. Bobby Moore is score.'

He looked at her blankly. 'Ma'am?'

'Sorry, Brian. What I meant to say is what is happening in your life today?'

'Oh yes, of course. Um, I was going to say we've got some intel on tracking Zarqawi from the computer we hacked.'

'Anything interesting that I'm allowed to hear about?'

'I think you have clearance to hear everything and anything, otherwise you wouldn't be in this building.'

'I suppose I do. So, back to question one, what have you found out?'

'The computer is being used as a dead letter drop.'

'Yes, Brian, I know that. That's why we targeted it.' She was being a little cruel again, she thought.

'Right. So, anyway, it's led us to a number of AQI mid-ranking commanders and Delta and your Special Air Service have been bringing them in. A quick waterboarding at Fernandez and we get all sorts of intel.'

'Oh…kay. Not sure I'm meant to hear about the waterboarding but go on.'

'We've managed to hit some rat runs that have been coming into Rawa and we almost hit Al Zarqawi himself on the open road.'

'Almost?'

'He scooted before we could get him. Well, actually, it was worse than that. He ran a vehicle check point and a backup roadblock.'

'Please don't tell me your guys missed?'

'Not exactly. They didn't engage. The Ranger LT on the ground didn't give the order as he didn't feel he had PID.'

'Sorry, Brian, let me get this straight. You're telling me that you let Al-Zarqawi go because you couldn't positively identify him? Jeez, Brian, when has that ever stopped any American from pulling the trigger?'

'Washington are cracking down. We need to PID before firing. It gets worse…'

'How can it be any worse? He's literally the most important target we have. There are five hundred people in this room, right now, dedicated to finding Zarqawi.'

'Well, we had a Predator on him, you know, tracking him. We were following him and then the camera failed.'

'The camera failed on the drone?' Barbara was incredulous. Had the Americans been given the choice between Al-Zarqawi and Osama bin Laden, OBL as everyone was calling him, right now they would have chosen Al-Zarqawi.

Brian looked crestfallen. He felt it personally and somehow, she suspected, he also felt it might impact detrimentally on his chances with her. Which were, of course, zero. So it hadn't.

'I bet he's an ex-LT now,' she said, to take the pressure off his guilt.

'I don't really know Ma'am. Ma'am?'

'Yes?'

'Do you know about the Thursday disco in the Al Rashid hotel?'

'I do Brian.'

'D…d…do you think, I mean can we…'

'Are you hitting on me, Brian?'

'Er, no Ma'am, I mean Barbara, I mean I was just wondering, sort of…'

'If I would accompany you there one Thursday?'

'Yes, Ma'am. This Thursday, perhaps. If you are not doing anything. Which I am sure you are so it doesn't…'

'Brian, I will go on two conditions.'

'Ma'am?'

'One; you stop calling me Ma'am. And two; you understand that I am not looking for a long-term romantic commitment.'

'That's great, er Barbara. Shall I pick you up or…?'

'I tell you what Brian, why don't we meet in the Baghdad Country Club for a few sharpeners at seven?'

'Fabulousa, Ma…Barbara.'

'Brian?'

'Yes?'

'What about G.O. No 1?'

General Order Number One was that all US military personnel were forbidden to drink alcohol whilst in Iraq.

'It's fine. I don't drink.'

Barbara thought to herself, 'bloody hell, how long and painful is this evening going to be?'

29

Sunday 9 April 2006
Mission Support Site Fernandez
Baghdad Green Zone
1530 Local

The game of cat and mouse between JSOC and the insurgents was continually evolving. The insurgents knew that they were at their most vulnerable at night, when the US and British Special Forces liked to go hunting. Anyone or anything brought in was immediately analysed at Balad and a new hit list was put together for the next night. The commanders kept an unremitting pressure on the blades and the operators, who were sometimes required to make five house raids a night. So the insurgents started operating during the day, when the cats were asleep. It didn't take long for Task Force Orange to notice and so some of the troops were taken off nights and put on standby for the daylight hours. Pagers had been issued and a number system instigated. Four ones in a row meant immediate orders and then deploy to the vehicles or the air assets. As a result, those that had been shifted to daytime operations were on immediate notice to move. Which could mean sitting around waiting, the British Army's most finely honed skill.

'Boss?' said Cookie, laconically. He was lying on a Saddam era leather sofa with his feet out and his eyes closed.

'Yes, Cookie. How can I help?'

'You got a doris on the go back in Hereford?' Cookie opened his eyes and sat up.

'Not really, Cookie.' There were plenty of groupies in the pubs and bars of the garrison town but the Boss rarely was to be found in the usual watering holes frequented by the Boys.

'Ginge was telling me about the boozer you took him and John to in the Smoke. When you called him gay.'

'Hold on. I didn't call anyone gay. I just observed that the Hereford look could, in some instances, be confusing to a metropolitan civilian.'

'Whatever. He was saying you met up with a right proper posh bint. Easy on the eye, too, by all accounts.'

'Yeah, she's nice. Not sure I'm her type. Probably on the lookout for an investment banker with a chalet in Verbier.'

'Posh Rupert like you, Boss. Would've thought there was a bit of a queue.'

'Don't do it, Boss.' Stan looked up from sorting through his medical bag.

'It?' asked the Boss.

'Marry. I mean, don't get me wrong, the kids are great but the fucking missus can be a right pain in the arse. Sometimes think I would be better off on me tod.'

'Remember that time when there was a heightened car bomb threat and Banjo said before you drive in to camp in the morning, get your missus to drive the car around the block first to make sure? Made me laugh, that.'

'Rocket got hitched a few months ago, didn't you, mate?'

They all looked at Ron 'Rocket' Stevenson. He was asleep in a brown leather Chesterfield armchair.

'Oi, Ron, you dopey cunt,' shouted Stan.

'I wasn't asleep,' was his reply. 'Just resting the old eyelids.'

'We were saying you got married a few months ago, before deployment.'

'Yeah. It was brilliant, see. Nice little church in Abergavenny and a big session in the local pub. Then a week in Rhyl.'

'Well thanks for asking us, you miserable twat.'

'Not really my decision. The missus doesn't really like the army. Wanted just our old school friends and family.'

'So she's already got you by the short and curlies. Your life is now officially over,' remarked Stan.

'I dunno. Feel more settled now. See, I never had much of a family, me.'

'We're your fucking family, you Taff wanker.'

'Well, now you put it like that, yes, I suppose you are in a way. But I'm not going to have kids with any of you lot, am I, see?'

'Have you asked Ginge?' said Cookie.

The door opened and the big Scotsman walked in.

'Who wants me?'

'We were just talking about you, Ginge, me old china.'

'What youse saying?'

'No, no, my ginger Celtic friend, talking about you, not to you.'

'Look what I happen to have here.'

He opened the palm of his hand on which there lay an embroidered shoulder patch. It was a Union Jack and "Fuck Al Qaeda".

'Nice, Ginge,' said Cookie 'Weren't you tempted to get the jock flag and "Fuck Rangers"?'

'Aye, that might be the next one but not sure how well it would go down with the Ranger battalion here.'

'OK, what about "Fuck Partick Thistle"?'

'Barnie's not going to let you sew that on, Ginge,' said the Boss.

'Why the fuck not?'

'He doesn't approve of that sort of thing. What happens when we get a visit from the Prime Minister or one of those idiots in government?'

'Velcro, see Boss. Just take it off. The Yanks have got them.'

'I know they have but we are not the Yanks, Ginge,' the Boss reminded him. 'There are already mutterings about standards of dress, inappropriate mixed uniform and all that shit. Unofficial and probably obscene shoulder flashes are not going to pass muster.'

Ginge looked disappointed and put the flash in his pocket and wandered off to put the kettle on.

'Yes please Ginge. Thought nobody was ever going to ask. Julie please.'

'Whoopi for me.' These two being a Julie Andrews or a white nun and a Whoopi Goldberg or a black nun respectively.

'Fuck me, youse cunts sitting around on your arses waiting for the workers to turn up. Boss?'

'Go on then Ginge. White without.'

'Only the Brits can be found drinking hot tea in forty-degree heat,' remarked Stan.

'That's why we had an Empire.'

Staff Sergeant Barnes came in with Wolfie and Man Bat.

'Shit house rumour is that Ops are cooking up an AVI for us and Schapner's bunch this afternoon.' Aerial Vehicle Interdictions were a highlight as they were always considered high octane and gung-ho.

'Boss?'

'Yes Stan.'

'What's a Valkyrie?'

'Um, I think it's from Norse mythology, if I remember correctly. Some sort of female spirit that guides the dead warriors to Valhalla. Please don't tell me you are thinking of *Apocalypse Now*'.

'Well, I was actually, and John saying we were doing an AVI got me thinking.'

'Never advisable, Stan.'

'What music would you play out of the loudspeakers, say, on a heliborne assault?'

'You're not going to be able to hear it above the rotor noise, Stan.'

'I know, but say they were making a film of us, what music would you choose?'

'Dunno, really. Need something that instils fear and dread into the enemy. Maybe *Carmina Burana*, Carl Orff.'

'Carl Orff? Bet his nickname was "Fuck" at school.'

'I think I'm choosing *Bad* by Michael Jackson,' offered Ginge.

'Fuck's sake, Ginge. You can't have that nonce singing as we land on a hot LZ,' said Wolfie.

'Why not?' asked Ginge.

'The fucking Towel Heads would piss themselves laughing for a start.'

'I'm just messing with you, you dull twat. It would have to be the skirl o' the pipes. They have roused the Highlanders to battle for many a year.'

'So, these Valkyries, Boss. Are they hotties or gorgons?' persisted Stan.

'Don't really know, Stan,' said the Boss, 'you've sort of reached the limit of my knowledge on Norse mythology.'

'Stanley?'

'Yes, Wolfie'

'Which of the girls in *Friends* would you take to Barbados?'

'I'm not going to Barbados.'

'I know. But say you were and you could take one of the cast of *Friends*, who would it be?'

'Ginge would take Chandler,' said Man Bat.

'I think Rachel. She's a pain in the arse but looks spectacular in a tee shirt.'

'What about you, Boss?'

'Not thought about it. Phoebe, I suppose.'

'She's a nutter. She'll push you over the edge. I think you should have Monica. She would tidy you up a bit so you didn't look like a bag o' shite on parade.'

'Barnie?'

'What?'

'What about you? Which would you take?'

'I've never seen *Friends*, so no fucking idea. Can I have Claudia Schiffer?'

'Angelina Jolie for me,' said Man Bat. 'Have you seen her in Tomb Raider? Enough to turn Ginge straight.'

'Listen in youse cunts, I'm not gay. I have a wife and two wee bairns.'

'Me thinks he doth protest too much.'

'Me thinks you are about to get filled in,' concluded the Boss.

'Enough of this jollity, we've a war to win. Everybody got full mags and new batteries? We are on immediate notice to move once the hostile is spotted on the road, so I don't want any fucking around with "let me fill my water bottle."'

'Good to go John. Did the comms check ten minutes ago, frequencies all put in.'

'Sit around now. Hurry up and wait.'

30

Sunday 9 April 2006
Somewhere North of Habbaniyah
Ramadi-Fallujah Corridor
Anbar Province

Salim had been informed a new batch of Mujahadeen were
due to come across the Syrian border that night. Having
assembled in Lebanon from all over the Arab world, they had
already transited across Syria and would cross over the border
at Qa'im, an old smuggling town that stoutly resisted both
American and Iraqi army attempts to occupy and tame it. By
April 2005, the town was once again in the hands of insurgents
and a sign on the outskirts proclaimed, 'Welcome to the Islamic
Republic of Qa'im'.

The next leg of the journey would take them to Rawa, an
hour's drive away and then on to Habbaniyah, a further three
hours' drive. The road to Habbaniyah was the most hazardous
of the operation, especially after passing the insurgent held

town of Haditha. Following the snaking upper reaches of the Euphrates, it was patrolled regularly by the Infidels' helicopters, which had been known to land in the desert to stop and search vehicles.

The Mujahadeen were transported twelve at a time in the back of a nondescript truck used usually to ferry livestock. Three batches had already succeeded in reaching the western parts of Baghdad where they were quickly integrated into the resistance network. The final convoy would come this afternoon, accompanied by an SUV. The escorts, three militia, all armed, and a driver would act as close protection in case they had to run a roadblock. Zarqawi himself had told Salim how recently he had run such a roadblock and had shot his way out of an attempt to take him, killing many dozens of infidels with his trusted M4 carbine. Salim doubted the veracity of the account but someone who had been present corroborated the story, although he said that no bullets had been fired by either side.

This afternoon, the truck would turn north just before the town of Habbaniyah and cross the Euphrates. It would continue north, through the densely populated northern bank of the river and then into the agricultural belt to the Farm. Two Mujahadeen would be dropped off, with both of whom Salim had served in Bosnia. It was a decade ago now, but he was excited at meeting them again. Their experience would be a great help in training the new recruits, especially in the art of fieldcraft, tactical movement and concealment. He had ordered a good evening meal to be prepared for after evening prayers. They would sit and discuss old times long into the evening, drinking sweet tea and eating sugar coated almonds and pastries.

They were also bringing with them some weapons, including a Barrett sniper rifle that had been purchased on the black market in Pakistan. Its previous owner had been a

Marine sniper operating in Afghanistan who had left it behind after his position had been discovered by the Taliban and he had to be evacuated by air. Known as 'The Light Fifty' its half inch calibre meant that it could fire out to over two kilometres and could, with the right ammunition, penetrate the light armour of the American Humvees.

Salim had asked Abdullah to run the road from Rawa to the bridge thirty minutes in front of the vehicles carrying the men and weapons. While they couldn't rule out a helicopter stopping them, they could negate the threat of an American or Iraqi Security Force roadblock. He had texted Abudullah that he wanted to meet him and, in person, he had told him the timings of the transport, for he did not trust that the Americans were not intercepting his text messages. It was with some consternation that he received a text back confirming the meeting and asking what it was for. He would have to explain to him in no uncertain terms that such disregard for safety imperilled everyone but, for now, he left the text unanswered.

Salim was beginning to have doubts about the strategy of the Salafist insurgency that Zarqawi was propagating. While he was fighting the infidel crusaders, it seemed to him that Zarqawi was succeeding in fomenting the Sunni-Shi'ite civil war. A series of bombs carried in by Jihadists dressed as Iraqi military at the Shia al-Askari Mosque in February had killed nobody but had ignited the civil war. One of the holiest sites in Iraq, it had been badly damaged and its famous golden dome had collapsed. The next day, over one hundred bodies had turned up in canals and the waste ground in Baghdad and over a thousand in the month that followed. The Shia militias were quick to respond with attacks on one hundred and sixty-eight mosques. Ten Sunni imams were murdered and another fifteen were kidnapped. Within a week, large scale ethnic cleansing had begun in the mixed neighbourhoods of Baghdad and other major cities. Shia families left for safer areas, calling upon the charity of other Shias in those areas while Sunni refugees went the other way. Zarqawi had succeeded finally in setting Muslim against Muslim and, to Salim at least, it did not bode well for the struggle against the invaders.

He had begun making plans for leaving Iraq.

31

Sunday 9 April 2006
Mission Support Site Fernandez
Baghdad Green Zone
1530 Local

The pagers had gone off at 1530 and the Boss and Barnes had run over to the Squadron office for quick orders. There, they found someone from intelligence who told them that a two-vehicle convoy was bringing in fighters from Rawa. They were to be intercepted on the road to Fallujah that followed the Euphrates south. Task Force Brown, the US Special Ops flight unit, also known as the Night Stalkers, would be operating six helicopters. Four would be variants of the Little Bird, two AH6s which carried sophisticated weapons systems and two MH6s, which had somewhat precarious outside platforms on which could perch two snipers each side. The MH6s were also equipped with electronic warfare devices that could help find targets for their twins, the AH6s. The teams were often referred to as 'Smokey and the Bandits'. Alongside the four Little Birds would be two Black Hawk MH60Ks. A much larger airframe, these could transport the assault troop as well as host a number of high-powered machine guns and rocket systems.

The Int Officer explained that they had 'eyes on' the target convoy which had already left Rawa, using a high-flying drone. They weren't sure of the final destination but suspected the human cargo would be dropped off in West Baghdad. The mission was to intercept the convoy and arrest all military aged males. The briefing took less than fifteen minutes and by the time the Boss and Barnes arrived at the helipad that serviced MSS Fernandez, the rest of the Troop, as well as the Delta operatives under Brent Schapner, were already there.

'Right, gather round and listen to the Boss,' said Barnes.

'As we all guessed, this is an AVI on a two-vehicle convoy moving southeast out of Rawa toward Fallujah.' The Boss paused, looking at the notes he had quickly scribbled. 'Ground will be out in the desert. Mission is to detain all military aged males. Execution. We will depart here as soon as the choppers arrive on one of the Black Hawks. Yes, Ron?'

'Boss, are me and Wolfie in one of the Little Bird sniper teams?'

'No, you'll both join us in the Black Hawk and deploy on the ground. Delta have the sniper angled covered.'

'Roger that.'

'I still want you and Wolfie as fire support to cover us if we need to go in. Right, where was I? Actions on: if the vehicles stop on our command, then we are to cover the leading SUV, which I'm told is a Hilux. Delta will take the lorry carrying the insurgents. If the vehicles don't stop, then the Little Birds will obliterate them from above. If the vehicles stop but then engage us as we are deplaning, then we go into an immediate assault. Remember, we take the Hilux and the Yanks take the lorry.'

'We think there are maybe ten or twelve in the back of the lorry and they might well be tooled up. Again, watch out for suicide bombers. Anybody running towards us and fails to stop on command, even if they appear unarmed, is to be shot,' said Barnes.

'Thank you, John. Any questions?'

'Take it that once we've shredded the Hilux, we can engage the lorry?'

'Fill your boots, Cookie but I suspect if we are engaged, Delta will have already completed that task.'

There was an audible clatter of rotor blades as the choppers approached the helipad and the Troop lined up, kneeling in their positions awaiting the call forward from the loadmaster. The Americans were again taking the dogs and there were also half a dozen Iraqi Special Forces. Ibrahim, whom the Boss had managed to secure again for the operation jogged over to line up with the Troop. He gave a broad grin and a thumbs up to the Boss and Barnes before turning his head away from the swirling grit kicked up by the rotors. They all had their faces protected by masks and googles but it was still an unpleasant experience facing the helicopters as they came into land.

The pilots feathered the blades and the dust subsided a little. At the change of pitch, the Boss stood up and, at a crouch, walked towards the open side door when he saw the loadmaster signal.

Less than a minute later, with everybody seated, the loadmaster gave the thumbs up and the Black Hawk shuddered as it began to lift off.

The Green Zone diminished in size and the Boss looked out of the open door at the villa he now called home. He could see the four Little Birds flying above and in front of his Black Hawk as they banked steeply to turn west. He was grate-

ful, as ever, for the cooling breeze coming through the open
side door wicking away the sweat from the helipad. As the
pilots skirted around Baghdad, flying over BIAP – Baghdad
International Airport - and out towards the west, the countryside quickly turned into the dun-coloured uniformity of the
desert. Out of the starboard door, over the door gunner's
shoulder, he could see the green strip that followed the
Euphrates upstream. He knew that the palm groves and farms
down below were often where the safehouses of the AQI insurgency were located and he wondered now whether they were
looking up. The choppers kept a discreet distance from them
as there were credible intelligence reports of handheld surface
to air missiles now being in the insurgents' inventory. All six
helicopters were equipped with the latest state-of-the-art electronic warfare and jamming equipment but that did not
preclude a lucky shot. If the two MH6 Little Birds picked up
any hint of radar or infrared tracking, they would instantly
jam the airwaves and start firing flares to confuse the heat
seeking missiles.

The Black Hawk banked and down below he could see a
lorry and a four-by-four heading towards them down the road,
a dust plume dispersing out behind. The pilot dropped his
speed and the four Little Birds manoeuvred into position above
and behind the two vehicles. From one of the helicopters a
stream of red tracer bullets arced into the sand in front of the
lead vehicle, kicking up a line of dusty plumes as they impacted
into the desert floor. The vehicles slowed but didn't stop and
the helicopter spun round and fired again, the bullets dissecting
the road about fifty metres in front of what the Boss could now
see was a Hilux. The four smaller helicopters were swarming
above the two vehicles, their shadows flitting across the desert
floor. The vehicles slowed and then stopped in the middle of
the road and the Boss was relieved that they had done the
sensible thing. The sniper team choppers moved either side to

block off any approaching traffic, the Delta Force operators sitting on the side benches tracking their targets.

The Loadmaster signalled that they were coming in and the Troop began to unharness, ready to leave the aircraft and disperse as soon the wheels touched the ground. Ginge was already out of the door before the wheels bounced on the sand, running at a crouch, his weapon in his shoulder. Across his back was a shotgun in case they needed to blow any locked doors or boots open. The Boss jumped out third and ran to the left of Ginge who was now kneeling, his rifle pointing at the Hilux. He flicked off the safety of his M4 and trained the sight on the driver's side windscreen. The car door remained shut. Wolfie and Cookie approached the front doors from either side whilst Bat and Ron covered the rear doors, each trooper ensuring his arc of fire didn't compromise the others who might be on the other side of the vehicle with 'friendly fire'. Blue on blue, as it was called, was a common occurrence in combat and something that they had drummed into them to avoid at all costs. Ibrahim casually ambled up to the car and shouted in Arabic that the occupants were to open the doors and get out. The two front doors opened and two Iraqis got out with their hands up. Both Wolfie and Cookie now shouted and gestured with their rifles for them to get on the ground and they both knelt down. There were two passengers in the back who also emerged with their hands held high. After a quick check, Bat and Ron flattened the Iraqis with a swift boot to the back and as they were sprawling in the dusty tarmac, knelt on them and plasticuffed their hands. Always mindful of suicide vests, they did a quick search for anything that might resemble a bomb.

The Boss, satisfied that the Hilux and its occupants were secured, looked over at the Americans. With much shouting by both them and their Iraqi accomplices, they were emptying the lorry of its human cargo. As they jumped down one by one, they were ordered to lie on the ground in a line, hands behind their heads. The dogs they had brought were on a short leash, their handlers ready to them slip should any of the detainees try to make a run for it.

As he watched, the last detainee jumped from the back of the lorry and, rather than lying down, ran towards the Hilux. The Americans began shouting and the dog handler tried to unleash his Malinois. The catch failed to release the animal, who was now rearing up on his hind legs and barking, desperate to pursue his quarry, which made it impossible for the handler. Two shots, a 'double tap', rang out from behind the Boss and the running man stumbled forwards into the sand. Two American operators jogged over to the body, approaching cautiously. All the while shouting at him to stay still, they knelt down beside what was probably a corpse. A visual check was made to ensure there was no suicide mechanism in the dead man's hand and then one of the Americans checked for a pulse in his neck.

'Smoked him good. Ain't no pulse.'

Boss had a sense of foreboding. Ron or Wolfie, whoever fired the shot, had specific orders to fire at any detainees that ran towards them. It was an open and shut case. Yet he couldn't shake the feeling that this would come back to haunt them. He walked over to the body to watch the Americans search it.

'Any indication of explosives or a suicide vest?'

'No Sir. He's just got a phone and a bit of loose change in his pocket.'

'You'll bag the phone with the others?'

'Fo shiz, Sir. It'll be collated and sent to Balad this evening.'

'Any chance we can, you know, identify this phone from the rest. I'm just interested in why he ran towards us.'

'Probably just panicked and ran towards his friends to get away from the dogs. Dogs would've got him if you hadn't fired.

Some of the Hajis are very fucking scared of dogs. Who the fuck knows or cares?'

The whole operation was over in ten minutes and the detainees were led away to await transportation back to Balad for processing and further interrogation. All phones were carefully bagged as was anything in any pockets, however seemingly trivial. They would be taken back to a secure holding area by the local American infantry battalion with the help of the Iraqi Police. The Iraqi Police would take the body back for identification and, if possible, inform the next of kin that they had lost a loved one. It would be just another meaningless statistic.

It was unlikely that the men in the back of the lorry would know much about where they were going. The four from the Hilux, however, would be taken back by the Americans on a Black Hawk. Their hands and clothing would be swiped and tested for any signs of explosives or for evidence of having recently used a firearm. A number of weapons had been found in the Hilux, including a Barrett sniper rifle, and they, too, would be taken back and forensically examined. The four insurgents could now look forward to a night in the basement of the Delta villa at Fernandez.

As they waited for the choppers, the Boss discovered that it was indeed Ron who had fired the shots. He would have to put it in his operational report but nobody felt good about the death of an unarmed man, however likely it was that he was a jihadist recruit. He would ask Barnes to have an avuncular and reassuring word with Ron when they got back.

32

Sunday 9 April 2006
Mission Support Site Fernandez
Baghdad Green Zone

Back in the villa, Barnes gathered everybody in.

'Right, listen in. Everybody knows what happened today. During a stop and search of a potentially hostile vehicle, an unidentified military aged male ran towards us. Trooper Stevenson, fearing a suicide attack, engaged and neutralised the threat as per the orders he was given by the Boss. Everybody got that?'

There was a chorus of muttered 'yes John'.

'It is important you use that language. In the last few months, there have been a marked increase in suicide bombers killing coalition soldiers and therefore any *threat* can, and should, be *neutralised*, irrespective of current standing orders requiring positive identification prior to engaging. Having said that, it is best if this is not mentioned outside this room, even to other members of the Squadron. The Boss has told me that there are some ambulance-chasing lawyers getting the scent of easy money and fabricating human rights cases out of thin air. And don't fucking rely on the **MOD** helping you. Not with the shit shower of clowns currently in charge. They'd sell you down the swanee if they thought there was a vote in it or the Guardian would like them a bit more. So keep it schtum. Any questions? No? Good. Ron, come with me.'

The Boss, who had been sitting on the arm of a sofa to one side got up to go with them. They went into the villa's garden where they could hear the American's next door having a few illicit beers in celebration of a successful mission.

'Alright, Rocket?' He asked.

'Guess so, Boss. I mean, he was running towards us and the orders…'

'Yeah, I know. The orders were clear. Don't worry about that, they will be included in the report. The weapons found in the vehicle will help exonerate you.'

'Do you think something will happen?'

'I don't think so,' said Barnes, 'Dozens of insurgents are being shot every day. Yanks don't even report civilian deaths.'

'If he was a civilian,' added the Boss.

'Quite. Intel was clear that the lorry was carrying foreign combatants.'

'But he didn't have a weapon, see? Makes it sort of different. Well, it does for me.'

'I know, Ron,' said the Boss, softly, 'but you can't let it get inside your head. You are a good soldier following orders. If any shit comes along, it'll be me that gets it.'

'Thanks Boss. Appreciated. Just don't want to tell my missus this is what I did today.'

'I know Ron, I know. Which is why you won't. We are here to do a job and you are doing it brilliantly. Just keep stagging on.'

'Go and get some scoff, it's unlikely we will deploy again tonight as Air Troop are now on standby.'

'OK, Barnie. Cheers'

'And Ron?' added the Boss 'Alcohol isn't the answer. Never is.'

'Yeah, I know Boss. But thanks. Thanks for looking out for me.'

'It's why I'm the Rupert. Rank has its privileges.'

Ron turned and walked back inside the villa.

'What are you thinking Boss?' said Barnes once he was out of sight.

'That is a really tough call. Ron has been in a few engagements but they've always been about returning fire or engaging a visibly hostile and armed enemy. If that lorry turns out to be carrying workers for a building project or some such shit, then questions might be asked about it.'

'We had this in Ireland when I was a youngster,' replied Barnes. 'Shoot to kill they called it then, as if there was any other reason to fire your weapon. We knew the PIRA and INLA hoods like the back of our hand, but to some fucking civvy lawyer, they were all innocent wee lads going to visit their grans in the Divis flats. At least here we have the weapons to justify the response.'

'Yeah, I know. Police get the same treatment. Less than a second to make a decision, which, if you get it wrong, could lead to your or someone else's death yet in the press and the courts, a bunch of civvy fucks that have never even heard a car backfire want to pin a murder charge on you.'

'Twas ever thus, Boss. Boss?'

'Are you going to ask me about the obvious?'

'Just need to know you are happy that the cash can't be traced back to us.'

'It's what I've been assured. Don't touch it and nobody will realise it's there. We should just let is lie dormant for a while, happy in the knowledge that we can start afresh in New Zealand or Thailand should the need arise.'

'I've always fancied Canada,' said Barnes.

'You would. It's famous for being the biggest Sergeants' Mess in the world.'

'Is that a dig?'

'No, not at all,' said the Boss with a wry smile and a transparently false air of sincerity in his voice.

33

Wednesday 3 May 2006
Defence Intelligence Staff
Old War Office Building
London SW1

'Hello? Hello, Barbara? Fuck's sake. Barbara? Can't hear anything, David.' Eric was attempting to work the STU III encrypted telephone link to Baghdad. The Secure Telephone Unit, version 3 was developed by the National Security Agency and built by Motorola to prevent eavesdropping.

'Try again, it probably didn't patch through correctly,' said David.

'Hold on. What's the fucking number?'

'It's on the bit of paper I gave you. The one that is right there by your elbow.'

'Oh yes, so it is,' said Eric. He pushed his reading glasses back up his nose and methodically dialled the number by stabbing at the buttons with a finger. After a few seconds there was a metallic click.

'Hello Barbara? Babs? Oh good. It's me, Eric. Can you implement secure transmission?'

'I know it's you, Eric. Don't call me Babs. I'm pressing the button now.'

There was a fifteen second delay whilst the encryption algorithms initiated.

'How is sunny Blighty? Still raining?'

'Yeah, weather's shite. Must be hot with you, not that you would know, loafing around an air-conditioned office eating donuts and growing your arse.'

'Charming, Eric. I'm going to hang up now.'

'Listen, before you do that, we've been working on the Juba identification. We think he's a veteran Muj from Bosnia.'

'Seventh Muslim Brigade?'

'Yeah. Think it could be a possibility.'

'Why do you think that?'

'The video you sent. He's holding a Tabuk rifle which is an exact copy of a Zastava that they used to use. Do you remember Bugojno?' Eric knew to tread softly.

'I remember a lot of sniping for sure. Most of it from the 7th Brigade, including Adam's murderer. You think he's one of those? Oh my God. The Sniper of Bugojno. You think he's now calling himself the Sniper of Baghdad?'

'It's a possibility we are working on. We think he's called Agayli meaning from the Agayl tribe. Ring any bells?'

'No, not really. But do you remember the shit pits? We found lists of names in Arabic. Have you checked those?'

'Er…actually, no, not yet. Good idea, I'll get someone on it pronto, hold on a sec.'

Eric turned to David. 'Get Emma to see if she can find anything in the Bosnia archive. We are looking for raw int that would have been scanned around nineteen ninety-three or four.

It'll either be on a disc or one of the nineties databases. Ask her to search Agayli or any variant of that name. Failing that, anything on Sudan or Sudanese mujahadeen and then Jordanian. This is a priority.'

'Roger Dodger.' David left Eric to initiate the hunt through the archives.

Eric put the receiver back to his ear. 'The Agayl are Jordanian, so he might be linked to Zarqawi.'

'My American colleagues are obsessed with finding Zarqawi.'

'Not surprised. From what I'm reading, he's tipping the whole of the North into civil war with the Shia and the South. That will then escalate with Iran becoming emboldened to step in on ethno-religious lines.'

'You're not wrong, Eric.'

'I'm seldom wrong, Barbara. You should know that by now.'

'Modest too, as always. Have you seen the latest video?'

'Which one?'

'Have you been briefed on Op LARCHWOOD IV? Was a couple of weeks ago. When the Regiment assaulted that farmhouse? Got the M4 carbine that the Shaky Boats left behind in 03? They also found a video disc.'

'You've been hanging around the SAS too much. You don't want to let the SBS hear you call them "Shaky Boats". Yeah, I know the one. Zarqawi trying to fire the SAW and fucking up his weapon handling drills when it jams and someone burning their hand on the barrel because they didn't know it would be hot after firing off a belt of five-five-six.'

'That's the one. Also there was a call to prayer going on in the background, which he totally ignores. And ... and, even better, he's wearing New Balance trainers. Can you believe that? Anyway, AQI have released an edited version to the world.'

'Presumably through an Arabic speaking news show? Now everybody knows what he looks like.'

'*Exactly. Anyway, lo and behold, knock me down with a feather, the exact same M4 carbine is in the video.*'

'So, you are telling me that the Boys nearly hit Zarqawi?'

'*Missed him by a matter of minutes. There was a massive fire fight, suicide bombs going off all over the place. Total mayhem. But they are on to him.*'

'Interesting.'

'*Well, our American friends are releasing the original, unedited version tomorrow at a press conference. Some people are not too happy about it.*'

'Why?'

'*They think it compromises op security. Giving too much away and trying to be pally with the press. Also, quite a lot of the operators think they are giving too much prominence to Zarqawi. They are bigging him up when really he's just a small time thug out of his depth.*'

'What do you think?'

'*Well, I'll know more tomorrow because I'm going to be at the press conference. But I've heard it said that tying everything in to AQI means that there is a direct link between The World Trade Centre and the invasion of Iraq. You and I know that is tenuous to say the least, whatever the fairy tale dossier says. Oh, and another thing, there's a feeling here that the foreign muj are pissing off the local Shura. Iraqis are very un PC. They hate all foreigners, not just us. They are beginning to think that we can turn the local tribes against the imported Mujahedeen.*'

'What else have you been up to then? Any hot blokes been the subject of your attentions? Must be dozens of lonely young studs looking for a hot cougar. There's at least a hundred FBI agents alone, never mind the CIA.'

'*The Fox Bravos are OK but they're all a bit, well, immature. There's a crypto guy out here who I think might have a soft spot for me. He's almost unworkably spectral. You would love him.*'

'You getting leg over and chips then, Barbara?' Eric raised one eyebrow.

'*He's not my type.*'

'Must be some nice young British officers you can mummy out there. What about the Regiment guys?'

'The Squadron Commander is married, sadly. The Troop Commanders here are mostly pretty quiet. They are on the go twenty-four seven. When they are not out, they are sleeping. It's manic. When are you coming out? I could do with a handsome, nice, funny, like-minded colleague for company but, failing that, you'll have to do, Eric.'

'Not sure DIS would allow me out and Vauxhall are far too territorial to offer an invitation. Fucking useless civvy bastards.'

'I'm glad you haven't changed. If you want, I can see if I can blag an invite from the Americans.'

'Well, let's see if we can pin down this Agayl. Taking him out of the picture would seriously improve morale on the ground. Hold on, Babs, here's Emma. I'll call you right back.'

Emma stood before him beaming. 'We got a match from one of the ECMM discs you burnt in the nineties. There's a Salim al Agayli listed in a ration manifest that you and Barbara probably dug out of a latrine trench.'

'That's tremendous, Emma. Well done. Excellent.'

'It gets better. Guess what?'

'Let me see,' mused Eric, 'he's listed as a sniper with the 7th Brigade?'

'Spot on.'

'I think we now know who Juba is. The next question is how do we find him in Iraq. I'm going to call Babs right back and give her the good news. Right now. If I can get this fucking secure phone to work. David?'

34

Thursday 4 May 2006
Joint Special Operations Command
Balad Airbase
North of Baghdad

The Death Star was normally quiet during the morning whilst everybody caught up on sleep. Today, however, it was more busy than usual, as they were beaming Major General Rick Lynch's press conference from the Green Zone live on Kill TV.

Up on the screen, the General was speaking to a sparse audience. Barbara noted that three of the chairs towards the front were empty. Behind him were the US and Iraqi flags and a video screen showing the frozen image of a man dressed in black. The General's voice filled the room.

"Here's Zarqawi, the ultimate warrior, trying to shoot his machine gun. It's supposed to be automatic fire, he's shooting single shots, one at a time. Something's wrong with his machine gun. He looks down, can't figure it out. Calls his friend to come unblock the stoppage and get the weapon

firing again. So, what you saw on the internet was what he wanted the world to see. "Look at me, I'm a capable leader of a capable organisation and we are indeed declaring war against democracy inside of Iraq and we are going to establish an Islamic Caliphate". What he didn't show you were the clips that I showed you. Wearing New Balance sneakers with his uniform, surrounded by supposedly competent subordinates who grabbed the hot barrel of a just-fired machine gun. We have a warrior-leader, Zarqawi, who doesn't understand how to operate his weapon system and has to rely on his subordinates to clear a weapon stoppage. It makes you wonder. So, study the enemy; capabilities, vulnerabilities and intentions. Zarqawi and Al Qaeda, these are their intentions."

The General turned from the video screen and pointed to a flipchart.

"Establish an Islamic Caliphate. Remove the coalition forces and the Shi'a population from the region and destabilise the apostate government."

He turned back to the screen.

"You've seen this clip, it was broadcast on the internet last week, where he talks personally about his objectives in Iraq. And he says, specifically, that any kind of government in Iraq is a poisoned dagger in the heart of an Islamic nation. And he says, he and Zarq… he and Al Qaeda in Iraq will kill anybody who tries to join the police or who tries to join the army. That's his stated objective and those are clearly his intentions – discredit the Iraqi government, destabilise the apostate government, inflame sectarian violence, focus on the Shi'as. We are conducting operations against Zarqawi every day. And as we conduct these operations, we kill and capture terrorists and at the location of the operations, we find things. We find documents, we find information and on this particular operation, we found the complete video that Zarqawi didn't show on the internet. He showed his edited portion. The things he wanted the world to see but I found a couple of other pieces of that clip to be particularly interesting and I would like to show to you now. Next er, next clip please. Er, that's still the first one, next clip please. There, you saw this on the internet, him firing this machine gun apparently at no targets out in the middle of the desert. Very proud of the fact that he can operate this

*machine gun and proclaims that and all those closer soldiers there are very
proud of what Zarqawi does. This piece you don't see as he walks away,
he's wearing his, er black uniform and his New Balance tennis shoes as he
moves to this white pick-up truck. And his close associates around him,
his trusted advisors, do things like grab the hot barrel of the machine gun
and burn themselves. What we find in these operations, as a result of
interrogations and as a result of what we find, it leads us to subsequent
locations."*

Barbara could see the SBS M4 carbine with its distinctive
optical sight and underslung grenade launcher to the right of a
seated Zarqawi and wondered, when all this was over, whether
she should do a master's or a PHD on how weapons chosen by
terrorists can aid humint intelligence gathering. It was an idea.
She could use a period of quiet stability back home. She had a
sudden pang of longing to see her children again.

She sensed, rather than noticed, Brian was at her side and
looking up at the large screen. She sighed inwardly, a sudden
lassitude and ennui overcoming her as she remembered that
she had her hot date with him tonight.

'Hi Brian. What did you make of that, then?'

'Er w…w…what? What did I make of what, Ma'am?'

'Are we still on for tonight,' she said, hoping against hope
that perhaps the release of the video and the new information
would mean that he would have to work and thereby freeing
her from her foolish and impulsive acceptance of an evening
with Mendoza.

'Yes. Y…y…you said meet at the Baghdad Country Club.'

'It's not a salubrious watering hole, Brian, you know that?'

'Sure. So long as they have Dr Peppers.'

'I'm sure they will have that or something similar. Can't
move in the American zones without coming across fast food
and soda.'

'We like our home comforts, Ms Bishop.'

'By the way, we think we know who Juba is,' she said,

hoping to entice any American-only information he might be storing in his super-brain.

'I doubt it Ma'am. He doesn't exist. Maybe you've found out the name of a sniper but there's literally, like, hundreds of those.'

'OK, suit yourself.'

* * *

The most impressive thing about the Baghdad Country Club was its name. In reality, despite the logo, there were no rolling green fairways, azure pools, yoga studios or squash courts. It was a somewhat run-down white cinderblock building in a quiet residential street in the Green Zone. In the "garden" there were white plastic chairs around white plastic tables, where could be found the whole gamut of international personnel currently in Iraq. Construction workers, security guards, mercenaries from the major US and European security companies, as well as diplomats and staff from the many embassies and offices of the international coalition, and, of course, the military from all those countries that were not required adhere to General Order No.1. And some that were but chose not to.

It was the brainchild of a Brit, naturally, who wanted to supply food and alcohol to his international customers and promised the best wines, whiskies and cigars to be found in Iraq. To say he over-promised and under-delivered would only be half fair because James Thornett, the thirty something Brit ex-Para who had come to Iraq during the invasion and who subsequently founded the club, personally took considerable risks to keep his inventories well supplied. Liquor could also be bought from his shop, the Winery, which had so much stock pre-Ramadan that the roof nearly collapsed under the weight. But what he was really offering was an escapist bubble. It might

be, as some said, a sleazy pick-up joint for rednecks and mercenaries, but it was a very popular one, nonetheless. And, as if to
prove the insanity of the whole conflict, the next-door building
belonged to SCIRI – The Supreme Council for the Islamic
Revolution in Iraq, an organisation not known for its tolerance
of western decadence, who took a dim view of alcohol
consumption. And all they asked for was good neighbourly
behaviour and to keep the drinking discrete during Ramadan.

Barbara had been dropped off by a British HumInt
colleague who was based in the Green Zone and had access to
one of the many GMC Suburbans that proliferated the roads.
Having shown the doorman one of the half a dozen or so ID
'badges' she had to carry around, she waited in the garden of
the Club listening to the sirens wailing somewhere in the chaos
just outside the seventeen-foot perimeter wall. Inside, a group
of men were setting up their instruments for the night.

'What can I get you Ma'am?' She looked up and saw a
remarkably pretty young waitress whose nametag said 'Heidi.'

'I would love a beer, Heidi, thank you.'

'What type? We have Bud, Efes and the local brew.'

'An Efes, please. Who are the band?'

'They are a bunch of security contractors from Blackwater.
Normally, they play Nickelback covers. Pretty good really. If
you like Nickelback.'

'I'm expecting a guest. Will there be a problem if he's US
military?'

'Not with us, Ma'am but the Military Police sometimes
check ID badges.'

Barbara sat back to await her drink whilst the strangled
sounds of twanging electric guitars and the occasional drum
roll competed with the sirens and the constant backdrop of
helicopters. The night was balmy but the smell of the open
sewers wafted through on the gentle breeze.

Heidi returned with her beer and right behind her was

Brian, dressed in what appeared to be nylon slacks and a Hawaiian shirt.

'If you are quick, Heidi here will get you a drink.'

'Can I get a Dr Pepper?'

Barbara inwardly winced at the Americanism but consoled herself that Heidi probably put up with much worse than that from the predominantly young male customers she served every night. Despite the Green Zone being an oasis of civilisation, the male to female ratio was at least ten to one, with most of the males being in the age and job demographic where testosterone is at its peak. The young women that were stationed here were in high demand and some had made sure to pack their sparkly boob tubes and high heels for the disco parties held in the Al Rashid hotel. They could be found dancing the Thursday nights away atop a Ba'ath party star on the underlit dancefloor. Barbara was grateful that at her age, let's call it late thirty-something, she was less in demand. But clearly not not in demand, although she had a good ten years on Brian.

He was staring expectantly at her.

'When did you move up from Echo?' she asked, knowing he had been running the ad-hoc intelligence cell at the HQ of Multi-National Division Central South, when Clocktower had led them to the two American hostages.

'I…I completed my tour but after six months stateside, I volunteered to come back out again.'

'You got anyone at home?'

'O…O…Only my mother. My father passed a few years ago.'

'Oh, I'm sorry to hear that,' said Barbara, hoping the insincerity in her voice was not detectable and then remembering that Brian had problems detecting anything emotional in others. Then she had a pang of regret about being mean. Her own bereavement had nearly destroyed her.

'Don't be. He left when I was ten. I hadn't seen him since. Think he did a spell in prison and then lived in St Louis or somewhere.'

'So it was your mum that brought you up.'

'Yeah. She pushed me to study hard at school and I found math easy. I got accepted by Stanford and there met a professor who guided me toward coding and cryptology.'

Heidi brought the drinks, setting them on the table and Barbara watched Brian. He wasn't particularly smitten by what she thought was the prettiest girl she had yet seen in Iraq. Maybe Brian was looking for a temporary Mum substitute. Not that she was going to volunteer for that role either. But she was here to serve Queen and Country and Brian, for all his human failings, was certainly someone who had an encyclopaedic knowledge of the US electronic warfare and counter terrorism set up.

'Do you mind if we talk a bit of shop?'

'No Ma'am, I mean Barbara.'

'You think Juba doesn't exist, yet we think he's a senior AQI operative running foreign fighters into Anbar province from Syria and training sniping teams. We also think he is the brains behind the propaganda effort we are now seeing being ramped up by Al Qaeda. He would have never allowed that Zarqawi video out, so I'm also thinking that the two are not necessarily seeing eye-to eye.'

'I'm not saying they don't exist; I'm saying "he" doesn't exist.' explained Brian. 'We think Juba is just a propaganda tool for an Arab audience. Helps with recruitment. Sure snipers are being trained, foreign insurgents shipped in and videos made but it's being done everywhere, by lots of people.'

Barbara sipped her Turkish beer which was impressively cool even though the evening was still hot by most European standards, probably in the high thirties. Much like her, she thought. Brian's logic was compelling. AQI was a network, a cellular organism without much structure. The Americans had been putting considerable effort and no little expense in demonising Zarqawi and it looked like it was beginning to work. Having a second high profile operator, unnamed but nevertheless notorious, would not help their efforts either here in Iraq or in the US.

'Brian, this stays between us, right? London tells me they are hearing about the Iraqi sheiks in Anbar turning against Zarqawi and the influx of foreign jihadists.'

'Yes. We've noticed that too. And it's something that Balad want to encourage. They are calling it the 'Great Awakening'. Some foreign fighters have been attacked by Iraqi insurgents.'

'So that's why you want a clear image of someone to blame. Ideally a foreigner, he is responsible for holding back Iraq, denying it the opportunity to progress, prolonging the US occupation and all the while perpetrating numerous vicious terrorist attacks on the indigenous civilian population. And that person is Zarqawi.'

'Yup, pretty much sums up the thinking in the Death Star.' Barbara once again noticed that deep in his knowledge comfort zone, Brian didn't stammer, blink nearly as much or muddle around trying to find her name.

'We think we know who Juba is.'

'You think you know who a Juba is,' he corrected her.

'Ok, if you like. But a significant Juba nonetheless.'

'But do you know where he is?' Brian's sharp logic could sometimes be irksome at the point of use but it was a fair point.

'No. Not yet. But I intend to find out. He's called Salim al Agayli.'

'Salim is the more important name. Al Agayli just means that's where he's from. Like al Zarqawi, because he's from Zarqa, the Blue City, in Jordan. He's really called Ahmad Fadeel. Where is Agayl?'

'It's not a place, it's a tribe. Originally from where Jordan is now.'

'So you think he's also Jordanian with possible early links to Zarqawi?'

'We don't know. But possibly, although he also might be Sudanese. We think he was active in the Mujahadeen in Bosnia in ninety-three.'

'A travelling gun for hire?'

'Initially, he probably was. Was maybe attracted into Yugoslavia because Afghanistan had closed. Would have come across Bin Laden in Bosnia and may have been further radicalised about global jihad and the founding of the European Caliphate.'

'It's a credible theory, Barbara, but it doesn't really help our mission here in Iraq, unless I'm missing something. Should Zarqawi get taken out, and, sure to God he will, then we don't have this Juba on our list as the potential next leader of AQI.'

'We share that feeling. We are thinking Abu Hamza or Abu Abdul Rahman.'

'I...I...I will tell you something else, too.' The stammering was back. Barbara wondered if he was about to pronounce undying love or just say she looked nice this evening. 'Zarqawi has enemies on the inside of Al Qaeda.'

As a bombshell, it hardly registered.

'Brian, that is not breaking news. Everybody knows there is friction between him and Bin Laden.'

'But w...what you don't know yet, is one of them is talking to us...'

This was more interesting.

'What do you mean, one of them?' asked Barbara.

Brian was blinking. He was clearly having trouble with the morality of sharing highly classified information even though the whole 'two' to 'five' eyes intelligence sharing culture was well established. But, just as the British had their 'NOFORN' classification, meaning no foreign allies get to share it, the Americans would have the same.

'We don't know who, exactly.'

Another damply unimpressive squib.

'It's through an intermediary but what we are getting is cross checking and cross referencing accurately.'

'What's the means of getting this intel?'

'Can't tell you that, Ma'am. But Zarqawi will be dead in less than a month, sure to God.'

At that moment, three men approached their table. They looked different to the usual bunch of contractors and merce- naries that frequented the Country Club.

'Hey. Brian, right?'

The man must have been thirty, younger than his two companions and English. He was tall and clean shaven with pearlescent blue eyes and an air of insouciant authority about him. He held out his hand.

Brian stood up and shook it.

'N…N…nice to see you, er, Tom.'

'And you Brian. Do you remember John and Stan?'

'Y…y…yes, John. Don't think I've met Stan.'

Barbara remained seated, looking up at the four men, trying to remember where she had seen those eyes before. Like those of an arctic wolf, she thought to herself.

'Excuse me,' said Blue Eyes. 'I'm Tom. This is John and Stan.' He gestured to the two other men. We met Brian a while back on an op down south.'

So they were probably military and if they were in the Green Zone, probably Special Forces. Either SAS or SBS but probably the former.

'Was it a successful mission?' she asked, not expecting anything other than a vague response. They wouldn't discuss anything operational without knowing exactly who she was and, even then, would remain guardedly tight-lipped.

'Yes, I think so,' said Tom. She looked at his blue eyes again which seemed to have an iridescent twinkle suggesting a mischievous sense of humour.

'Right, Boss, can't hang around here, these nice people were trying to have a quiet evening.'

'No, really, it's quite alright,' she blurted out. 'I mean, do stay. If you want to, that is.'

'Got to be going, Ma'am.' He had a big moustache and was a good six or seven years older than Tom. More her age, in fact. The other man, who hadn't said anything, had early on-set male pattern baldness and what remained of his hair was closely cropped to his head.

Tom said 'He's in charge. Best do as he says.'

'But he called you Boss,' she said. For some reason she wanted him not to disappear quite yet.

'That is just a courtesy title. Anyway, nice to meet you, er…'

'Barbara. Barbara Bishop. I work with the Brits up at BIAP. Didn't we talk on the phone?'

'Part of the Int team by any chance?'

'Yes. I helped Brian with a task down at Echo in April, two years back.'

'Well, in that case, we may well have spoken. Did the Echo operation involve our Iranian friends?'

'Yes,' she replied rather too quickly. 'Were you on the kinetic end of a hostage release?'

'Can't really discuss that, Ma'am,' said the older one.

'Come on Boss, for fuck's sake, I'm gagging here,' said the bald one.

'Got to go, Barbara, but nice meeting you. And good to see you again, Brian.' And with that, the three men turned and left them to each other.

'S…S…Special Forces,' said Brian once they were out of earshot.

'I gathered that. Do you know them well?' She was really hoping that the answer would be 'yes'.

'No. They keep themselves to themselves but they are sometimes up at Balad. They work closely with,' he looked around conspiratorially, 'Delta.'

'Tom was nice,' she said wistfully hoping that the evening with Brian would conclude soon.

35

Monday 22 May 2006
Somewhere North of Habbaniyah
Ramadi-Fallujah Corridor
Anbar Province

Salim received the news of the convoy interdiction stoically. *Inshallah,* it is the Will of God. He had been looking forward to seeing his old friend from Bosnia but he was now a prisoner of the crusaders. More troubling was the manner of their capture. He was getting a feeling that there might be a spy, either working at the farm or with some sort of knowledge about movements. He would give it some thought.

He had spent numerous hours listening to *takbeers* and asking God for guidance. And now it came in the form of a letter. Some months ago, he had sent a messenger to Osama Bin Laden. He had travelled out of Iraq over the border with Iran and then into Pakistan. Very few people knew where The Great Leader was, but Salim knew where and to whom to send his emissary, even if he didn't know his exact location either. In his possession was a letter, written in Salim's beautiful cursive script and scanned onto a portable USB drive. The drive was then hidden in a date which was then mixed with a bag of other dates. The USB drive was using an encryption technique which had been explained to him by one of the German-born insurgents that had been working for Siemens before travelling to Iraq to prosecute jihad against the Infidel. He had tried, but failed to understand why the USB drive could only work with a certain computer. Something codenamed 'Tails' which worked with the Linux operating system. The end result was that the USB drive could only be read by its intended recipient and, having been read, left no trace behind once removed. In transit, it was just an unintelligible flash drive.

The letter he had written was to report his concerns about Zarqawi and the damage he was doing to Al Qaeda in Iraq. The Iraqis were turning against the Jihadists, recoiling at the vicious methods Zarqawi was using to kill Shi'a. The bombing of the Al Askari Mosque had convinced Salim and others that the strategy of killing other Muslims at prayer was to be *haram*, forbidden. It had led to tit-for-tat killings and now Muslims were killing other Muslims at a rate of ninety-four per day. There had been fifteen thousand murders since the turn of the year. He had advised Osama that it was probably best if Zarqawi was 'removed' from command and suggested giving him to the Americans. Although eighty-five percent of the Muslim world was Sunni, Osama's mother was an Alawite, an off-shoot of the Shi'a. Salim had also suggested that Abu Ayyub al-Masri, living close by to his farmhouse by the lake, should be announced as the new leader of Al Qaeda in Iraq. That way, there would be no feuding over the succession. He was especially wary of Abu Abdullah Rashid al-Baghdadi, an equally vicious psychopath who would continue the strategy of engendering violent civil war between the religious and ethnic factions in Iraq.

Salim received the reply, also in the form of a flash drive just after the release of the Infidels video of Zarqawi. Because of the video, they had mocked him, pointing to his western tennis shoes, his ignorance of weapons and for ignoring the Muezzin. It shamed all jihadists.

Salim inserted the drive into his laptop and surveyed the files. There were some voice recordings and he clicked on one.

"Our Islamic nation was surprised to find its knight, the lion of jihad, the man of determination and will, Abu Musab al-Zarqawi, killed in a shameful American raid. We pray to Allah to bless him and accept him among the martyrs as he had hoped for. Our brothers, the mujahedeen in the al-Qaeda organization, have chosen the dear brother Abu Hamza al-Muhajer as their leader to succeed the Amir Abu Musab al-Zarqawi. I advise him to focus his fighting on the Americans and everyone who supports them and allies himself with them in their war on the people of Islam and Iraq."

It was the announcement of the death of Zarqawi. Osama had spoken and had ordered Salim to engineer the death of his commander in Iraq. Salim noted that Osama had ordered his replacement be Abu Hamza. In Iraq, his old friend and neighbour was better known as Abu Ayyub. Salim was gratified the Great Leader had taken his advice and handed to him the great honour of replacing the prison thug Zarqawi with a true god-fearing jihadi warrior.

Salim had been giving the problem of a possible spy amongst them a great deal of thought, supplicating God for answers. The interception of the convoy had led him to believe that there was a traitor in their midst and that the American ambush on the trucks was not a lucky coincidence. He himself had opened a channel to the Americans via a convoluted network of dead letter drops. But he had been testing his lines of communications and whilst he was pleasantly surprised at how effective this was in disseminating verifiable but essentially useless information into the Infidels intelligence network, he was also convinced someone else with knowledge of his operations was also feeding information that he had not authorised.

'Get me Abdullah,' he commanded. He would use his principal driver to lead the Americans to Zarqawi. If they took the bait, he would both confirm the identity of his rat and be rid of his nemesis.

36

Monday 22 May 2006
Baghdad International Airport
West of Baghdad
And the
Green Zone
Central Baghdad.

War is a fickle mistress and has no favourites. Barbara's team had been monitoring Abdullah's mobile for months now. He had been given the code name 'Fishhook' and he was paid his treacherous wage in US dollars and US medicine. But he was not the only source of intelligence that was feeding the ravenous information beast at Balad. As the allies intensified their nightly house raids, prisoners were brought in for interrogations by the dozen. Most were rinsed of information and handed over to the Iraqi authorities who invariably released them. Often, they were brought in more than once, a repetitive action that annoyed and disappointed those risking their lives nightly. Occasionally, prisoners were deemed too important to release and were confined to the interrogation centres at Balad and Slayer. There, they were cajoled and flattered in turn as the gators worked in subtle ways to extract the next vital clue or piece of the jigsaw.

But today, she was going to have a day off. Or a morning off at least. The Prime Minister was going to visit. It had been kept secret for obvious security reasons but she happened to know that Eric had blagged a seat on the plane.

One of the first indications that something momentous was happening was when all communications went black, that is to say, off-line. Noticing that none of the phones worked and that the internet was down, Barbara was summoned to the briefing room and was told to be at the BIAP terminal in an hour's time. She hitched a lift in a Suburban and joined a throng milling around in the old terminal building waiting for the RAF transport to make the short flight from Kuwait. She watched as the Prime Minister and his entourage, which mainly seemed to consist of photographers, made their way down the steps to the waiting Iraqi honour guard. When the handshaking and back-slapping was done and he was ensconced in his official car, air con cranked up to max, she watched out for Eric. Numerous people appeared first but eventually, from what must have been the very back of the plane 'by the shitters' as he so eloquently informed her later, he emerged into the fierce Iraqi sun. His gut had expanded even more since she had last seen him and his old regimental New & Lingwood officer pattern shirt was straining at the buttons. He had a tatty grey and white Kufiyah around his neck, a remnant from his service in the First Gulf War, and a pair of cheap sunglasses on the end of his nose. His reading glasses were perched on his head and, she wagered, he had forgotten they were there. These second-class visitors and their accompanying hand luggage were made to wait as an old coach slowly wound its way to the side of the plane.

Eventually, he arrived at the terminal and shuffled in.

'Morning Eric.'

'Afternoon for me. Morning was about fourteen hours ago at Brize Norton. Fucking Crab Air. As much use as mudflaps on a tortoise.'

'So you've had a good flight, I take it.'

'Put it this way, Babs, I'm glad it's over.' Barbara resisted the urge to correct him as she knew he was tired and therefore crabby.

'How was the PM?'

'Fuck knows. He was sitting up at the front being his usual wanky self, lording it over his staff and minions. Do you know why he's here?'

'Visiting the troops?' offered Barbara.

'No. He couldn't give shit about them or anybody else. He's here because he wants to be the first "World Leader" to visit the new Iraqi Government that was installed a couple of days ago. Hopefully a car bomb will get him.'

'Eric, seriously, tone it down. You absolutely cannot say that here. Unless you want to be arrested.'

'You would then have to interrogate me. Could be amusing.'

'Do you have a programme for the next two days?'

'I am meant to be at an official briefing on the situation but, considering I know more than most of the muppets supposed to be briefing me, I can probably skip that. I persuaded the powers-that-be that the most important reason for coming was to have a face-to-face update from the HumInt team.'

'Well, we can get you into your CHU and then head off for lunch.'

'What the fuck is a chew?'

'Containerised Housing Unit. Not bad. Air con and your own bathroom for the officers.'

'I've got an itinerary here, one mo…oh fuck.'

'What?' said Barbara.

'I've left my fucking reading glasses on the plane.'

'They're on top of your head.'

'Oh yes, so they are.'

* * *

'Where's the Boss?' asked the Squadron Quartermaster, Jim Player, known to all as 'Banjo' because of his love of fried egg sandwiches.

'Getting his head down, Banjo,' replied Wolfie.

'Do us a favour, lad, and go and knock him up. And, if you can find him, get John here too. Got some news.'

'What's that then?' asked Bat.

'All in good time. Need you all here first otherwise I'll spend all morning briefing each of you scrotes separately, which is not a good use of senior NCO time. Meanwhile, someone get a brew on, I'm gagging.'

With the Boss, John and the rest of the Troop assembled, Banjo broke the news.

'We've got a seriously VIP visit this morning,' he announced to a collective groan.

'Fucking Walters. Who this time?' asked John.

'Can't tell you that John, as it is still classified until eleven hundred hours local. Apparently, his name begins with a 'T'.'

'And ends with Ony Blair?' asked the Boss.

'I didn't tell you that, Boss.'

'What's that clown want?'

'He wants to shake you by the hand and tell you what a wonderful job you all are doing. So wonderful that none of his family or any of his cabinet's families will need to come out here and do it as well.'

'What's the programme?'

'Squadron minus those on task will assemble in the Republican Palace at eleven thirty hours to meet the Dear Leader. CO, the Ambassador and various other headsheds will be there including Lambo, so be on your best behaviour.' General Lamb, a soldiers' soldier was known for his no-nonsense approach, having come via a Highland Regiment and the SAS to be General McChrystal's right-hand man. He did not suffer fools gladly and he had little tolerance for ceremony and bullshit. The boys loved him.

Barnes added, 'I want everybody to be in issue kit. I don't want to see anybody wearing Yank or civvy garb. Turn out is to be smart and soldier-like. Especially you, Boss. Please don't turn up in trainers like you did last time we had a dignitary.'

'To be fair, that was at Stirling Lines.'

'Don't forget, Barney, the Boss doesn't have his orderly out here.'

* * *

When the Troop did eventually meet the Prime Minister, the Boss was, in equal measure, appalled and very proud. Except for him and SSgt Barnes, they were all wearing 'Fuck Al-Qaeda' Union Jack shoulder flashes. The PM, who must have seen them, did not comment.

37

Monday 22 May 2006
Camp Slayer
Baghdad International Airport
1830 Local

Barbara decided to take Eric for a quick tour of the delights of Camp Slayer. They sat on the wall by the lakes and she pointed out the Perfumed Palace, where she had an office, the Victory Over America Palace and the Flintstones house. Then they wandered over to an American Green Bean café.

'Śubha prabhāta hajura kastō hunuhuncha,' said Eric to the Barista.

'Ma ṭhika chu sara. Tapā'īṁ āja kē cāhanuhuncha?' He replied.

'Two flat whites, please.'

'Certainly, Sir,' said the Barista.

'Shall we stay inside? Bit hot out there. Don't forget I come from the drab rain of London. Summer's yet to start.'

Barbara looked at him. 'What did you just say?'

'I said "Good morning, how are you?" and he replied "I'm well, what can I get you?"'

'What language were you talking?'

'Oh come on Babs, anyone can see he was a Gurkha.'

'Oh, yes, of course. Anyone. Silly me. And where did you learn Gurkhali?'

'In the kingdom of the blind, the one-eyed man is king. It's pretty much all I know, if I'm honest.'

They sat at a table in the corner under the air conditioning unit.

'I've essentially become a honey trap,' Barbara confided. 'This American int guy is feeding me stuff that is probably US eyes only.'

'I doubt you are a honey trap, Babs. More like a mummy trap. What's his reason, other than you're still quite hot? Or so it says here.' He pretended to read from a card in his hand. 'Or maybe he thinks you are desperate.'

Barbara sighed. She would accept hot but wondered if he meant that ironically or literally. It was difficult to tell with Eric. The desperate bit she could do without but, as always with Eric, there was perhaps a grain of truth.

'I don't know. Maybe they want us to know, in which case why not just tell us all, officially. Or he is expecting something in return, or, as you say, he fancies me. It has happened before, you know, Eric.'

'Did you tell him we know who Juba is?'

'He's not interested because the American line is Juba doesn't exist. Even if he does exist, he's just some pain in the arse sniper that releases videos every now and again.'

'Pain in the arse snipers are still killing a lot of soldiers. But he's not. He's a senior AQI operator flying under the radar that we now know served with Bin Laden in Bosnia and is probably part of the hierarchy of command. From what we know, he's instrumental in bringing foreign jihadists into Iraq and fundamental to their training. Personally, I think he's much more important. I think he's OBL's ears and eyes. OBL doesn't trust Zarqawi and I'm just picking up, from other sources that shall remain nameless, that OBL is reaching out to the Americans for some sort of peace talks.'

'The Americans are demonising Zarqawi. The thinking here is, strictly between us, STRAP 1, UK eyes only, blahde-blah is the Yanks are over-promoting Zarqawi, maybe for the purpose of coming to some sort of accommodation with Bin Laden. They are concentrating their public relations on him being the root of all the sectarian strife here.'

'Do you get the numbers?' he asked.

'Sure we do. There're suicide bombings on a daily basis. Since the Al Askari mosque bombing, around a hundred bodies a day are being found. Mixed neighbourhoods are being cleansed. The Sunni go west, the Shi'a south and east.'

'The Prime Minister came out here last December and said everything was going swimmingly and that the coalition, well, certainly the UK, would start to reduce troop numbers in six months. Which is, er, about now. What actually has happened is the murder and bombing are off the scale, the Yanks are thinking about increasing troop numbers in what they are calling a surge, and My Little Tony is left looking like the twat he is.'

'I always knew you were a Lib Dem, Eric.'

'They are fucking worse. No seriously, Babs…' she tried to interrupt but he continued, 'back home, the Government is in a spin. Everybody knows the invasion was based on a lie, even if we all thought Curveball was genuine about WMDs. Now that it's been found to be a can of shite and the whole premise was sexed up, as they are saying, even his own party wants answers.'

'And he thinks this new government in Iraq will dig him out of trouble?'

'It's the last throw of the dice. The US-UK line is now that foreigners are teaming up with extremists to throttle at birth the new democracy that we have lovingly bestowed upon the grateful nation. Iraqis couldn't give a fuck about democracy. Most of them are now missing Saddam Hussein. At least with him they could generally go about their business.'

'Don't forget he told Parliament before the invasion "Saddam Hussein will be responsible for many, many more deaths even in one year than we will be in any conflict."'

'That's aged about as well as a saucer of milk left on a radiator,' agreed Eric. 'This new Nouri-al-Malaki government hasn't a hope of succeeding.'

'Seventeen people were killed yesterday just in Baghdad,' agreed Barbara, 'but that is out of our hands right now. Remember I briefed you about Fishhook?'

'The taxi driver we are playing?'

'Exactly. Real name, Abdullah Fahzad. He was used to run the road in front of an insurgent smuggling vehicle. Interdicted by us. A number of newly arrived foreign imports and a car with four AQI players. We've hacked his phone but he's getting instructions by another means, probably an email dead letter box.'

'You think he's working for Juba?'

'Yes, I do, Eric. And I think he is going to lead us directly to him. And I've got a big bone to pick with Juba, the Sniper of Bugojno.'

38

Wednesday 7 June 2006
Joint Special Operations Command
Balad Airbase
North of Baghdad

Barbara was at the Death Star for the morning intelligence briefing and for a catch up with Brian. She was also hoping to catch sight of Tom whom she hadn't seen since the evening at the Country Club. She didn't dare confide in Eric but she had really become rather fixated on him. It was silly, she knew. But still, she was convinced their paths had crossed somewhere. Perhaps university. She would ask if she ever got to see him again.

After the commentaries from the heads of various intelligence agencies, General McChrystal and General Lamb went into their 'huddle' and she loitered around looking up at the big screens of Kill TV.

The Intelligence, Surveillance and Reconnaissance assets,

so called ISR, included a fleet of unmanned aerial vehicles, or drones, and both fixed and rotary wing piloted craft. They liked to call themselves the Confederate Airforce of North Virginia. In the Death Star they were always 'the Unblinking Eye'. Through them there was a constant stream of video playing out on the screens and Barbara was watching the tracking of a vehicle in Yusufiya, a node of the Triangle of Death. The car had started in the slums of Abu Ghraib, gone to Mahmudiyah to pick up two military aged males and was now parked outside a house. She watched as two men exited the vehicle and went to the house. The door opened and two new men handed over what was clearly a hooded and bound man. He was dragged to the waiting car and then dumped in the boot. The car drove away, heading west up Highway One towards Fallujah. The drone tracked the vehicle, keeping it central in its sights. All those watching knew what was going to unfold. A downside of the 'Unblinking Eye' was that it often shared with those watching the most gruesome of atrocities.

Once in the desert, the car pulled into the side of the road. The two men once again got out but this time they had an AK47. The boot was opened, the bound man dragged to the ground and then shot dead with a short burst of automatic fire. The second man then went up to the corpse, pulled out a pistol and fired a single shot into the still body. They left him by the road and drove back to Abu Ghraib. Job done.

The familiarity of the scene, the lack of sound and the grainy picture meant that the many observers of this murder were unmoved by what they had witnessed. Most had watched similar executions daily for however long they had been deployed at Balad. But Barbara wasn't here to ghoul over random killings. She was here, hopefully, to observe the second instalment which she knew was scheduled a bit later. Abdullah the Taxi, Fishhook, was going to drive an important cleric to a rendezvous with another car in the east of Baghdad. His passenger would be Abd al-Rahman, the spiritual adviser to Abu Musab al Zarqawi.

She wished she had Eric in here with her but his security clearance didn't allow him to enter Joint Operations Command and she knew he was killing the hours talking to other members of the UK HumInt team. The operation to find Zarqawi was so important to the allied effort that a comms black out had been imposed on Balad, so Eric didn't even know what he was missing.

Sometime after lunch, which she had skipped, there was a frisson of excitement among the assembled operators. An ISR drone was tracking a silver sedan, driving from west to east. A rotary wing airplane was monitoring his telephone, which he had switched on but wasn't using. Barbara knew that the driver of the silver taxi was Abdullah and she knew the man in the back was Sheik al-Rahman.

The car was moving slowly through the heavy traffic of a normal Baghdad day outside of the Green Zone. After a while, Kill TV indicated that Rahman had switched off his phone.

'Too late for that, Buddy. We are on to you and we are going to take you down,' said an American observer standing next to her, slurping nosily from a Styrofoam cup of lurid blue crushed ice.

The room descended into hushed concentration on the big screen. Barbara saw that General McChrystal had joined them, hands on hips, watching. The drone camera followed the silver car through the suburbs. In an area of particularly heavy traffic, it stopped beside the road and she saw Abdullah get out and wait by the back passenger-side door. After a few minutes, he opened it and a figure in clerics' robes got out and immediately got into a blue vehicle that had pulled up alongside Abdullah's car. The changeover was quick and smooth and wholly ineffectual. The drone camera began following the new target.

Barbara knew that Abdullah was now required to return to a location outside Habbaniyah. She mused to herself that she was the only person, of the many dozens in the room, who was more interested in where Abdullah was going than where the Imam was going. Her request to have Abdullah's car followed after the switch had fallen on deaf ears. The Americans were not going to risk a drone camera glitch and let off their prized target a second time.

She watched as the drone followed the new car's slow progress out of Baghdad northwards. It was, at one point, only three or so kilometres from the Green Zone and then, as it continued its journey, it skirted Sadr City, the Shi'a stronghold in Baghdad. Abd Al-Rahman was possibly the most hated man to the inhabitants of that particular slum. Had they known the car was passing through their neighbourhood, he would have been dragged out and torn limb from limb. As it was, it continued north undisturbed, picking up speed as the traffic thinned. Barbara wondered how close it would get to where she was watching at Balad Airbase but after a short while it veered slightly east and headed for the town of Baqubah. Once in the town, the car stopped and there was another well-rehearsed vehicle change. Again, the cameras stayed with the new vehicle as it left the town the way it had come in and then turned a sharp right northward towards the village of Hibhib. The silent concentration in the room was intense as the vehicle headed towards an isolated farmhouse nestled in amongst date palms.

It pulled up at the entrance to the farmhouse's drive. The driver got out and opened the door and Sheik Rahman appeared. He was clearly stiff from his journey and walked slowly towards the farmhouse. There was a murmur in the room as the camera picked up a second man, coming out of the house. He was dressed all in black and, as the camera zoomed in on him, the whole of the Death Star knew that they had got their man. Al-Zarqawi was instantly recognisable due to the video that had been captured by the SAS the month previously.

Al Zarqawi greeted his guest and they both strolled back to the farmhouse, seemingly without a care in the world. Barbara watched General McChrystal whisper some orders before he turned back to the screen. He would be gearing up an assault force, probably Delta but perhaps with UK special forces attached. The group surrounding the General were in animated conversation with a senior officer on the telephone. He was almost certainly in contact with MSS Fernandez in the Green Zone and the Delta operatives who would be already airborne.

Barbara watched the scene unravel before her, turning from the big screen to the huddle of senior American officers. She saw General McChrystal mouth 'fuck it' hand the phone back and turn his attention to the screen. She didn't have to wait long for the result of the conversation. There had been two F16 fighter bombers stacked high above the desert and one of them swooped in and dropped a five-hundred-pound bomb on the farmhouse at 1812 hours precisely.

The whole of the Death Star erupted in cheering and high fiving. There were whoops of joy, a sound Barbara only associated with Americans. The General allowed himself a wry smile and kept his attention on the screen. Exactly two minutes later, a second bomb hit the remains of the house. Eighteen minutes later, Delta arrived on Little Bird helicopters. They found that the Iraqi Police were already on the scene and that a body was being loaded on to a gurney. It later transpired that Zarqawi was still alive at that moment but internal over-pressure blast injuries meant he died a few minutes after realising that it was the Americans that had got him.

The body was loaded onto a US helicopter and brought back to Balad for formal identification. General McChrystal himself went to see the corpse and then, having made certain that they had their man, the body was taken clandestinely into the desert and buried in an unmarked grave.

It emerged only later that a catalogue of small mishaps had nearly let Zarqawi off for a second time. A helicopter engine had failed to start at Fernandez, grounding a Special Forces team; the first bomb run was aborted because the order had been wrongly drafted. And second F16 had been refuelling in mid-air when it was supposed to drop the first bomb.

But Zarqawi's luck had run out and now JSOC was getting ready to take down his murderous network. They would start with tracing the drivers of the three cars, including Abdullah. Fortunately for him, Abdullah was a known HumInt asset belonging to the British Secret Intelligence Services.

Even as Barbara was leaving the Death Star, Joint Special Operations Command was issuing orders for the next round of house raids.

39

Wednesday 7 June 2006
Somewhere North of Habbaniyah
Ramadi-Fallujah Corridor
Anbar Province

Salim al Agayli had requested that Abdullah drive to the farmhouse straight after his mission that delivered the Imam to the second leg of his journey. He did so oblivious of what was about to unfold to his passenger and arrived at the remote dwelling some forty minutes before the first F16 dropped its payload on the head of the Supreme Leader of Al Qaeda in Iraq.

Salim perfunctorily greeted the driver and asked him to wait in the little servants' quarters off the main courtyard, which had only two slit windows at the rear the room and was lit by a strip light. There he was given sweet mint tea by a newly arrived young jihadist from Saudi Arabia. Abdullah had made sure that his mobile phone was switched off prior to arriving as he knew he would be asked to hand it over on entering the compound. The insurgents had strong and, indeed, correct suspicions that the Americans were using tracking software to pinpoint locations and no personal mobiles were permitted amongst the volunteers. It was not enough. Not only was the American technology advancing at a dizzying speed but the amount of analytic manpower was also expanding fast. There was, even now as he sat in the room, a fleet of six single seat turboprop planes listening to mobile chatter, intercepting data messaging and pinpointing where both mobile devices were located. Nodal analysis of the Iraqi network was sent to various agencies both in-country and States-side. There was a Real Time Regional Gateway interactive SigInt clearing house that fed data to the Delta-run Computer Networks Operations Squadron based at its headquarters in Arlington, Virginia that, in turn, provided real time intelligence straight into the Death Star. Neither Salim nor Abdullah had any idea that they were in the sights of a F3EAD operation. Find; Fix; Finish; Exploit; Analyse; Disseminate. In the case of Abdullah's phone, it was immaterial as it was being controlled remotely by HumInt operators at the Perfume Palace in Camp Slayer and, even switched off, it was betraying him.

Abdullah immediately noticed a difference in the attitude of those based at the farmhouse. Whereas before, whilst not exactly relaxed, there had been a certain level of diffidence among the jihadists. But today, there was an air of expectant tension and the men were going about the business of what looked like fortifying the house. Everyone was carrying rifles unless they were carrying rocket launchers. The few women that he had noticed in his previous trips were now nowhere to be seen and the guards on the gate and by the main road had been doubled. There was also a posse of armed men on the flat roof of the building. They had set up a heavy DShK machine gun on a tripod and half a dozen boxes of ammunition. It was sited to fire directly down the line of the drive should the heavy iron gates by forced open. Equally, it could be used to fire at any approaching helicopters.

The afternoon was stiflingly hot and he sat with his back against the wall of the small room listening to the activity outside. There were a multitude of differing accents and at least three different languages being spoken. He got up and tried the door but it was locked and that was his first indication that all was not well.

The second and final indication came forty minutes later when the door was opened and two men were thrown in by armed militia. They were wearing the olive-green uniforms of the Iraqi army and they had been badly beaten, their faces mottled with bruising and eyes closed with the swelling. They went sprawling across the tiled floor and both lay still, one with his hands covering his bleeding head. Abdullah recoiled, edging further from the two bodies and cowering from the door. He waited, saying nothing, as the groans and whimpers of the men filled the air. One was repeating his *takbeers* in anticipation of his death. There was a tang of blood and urine.

'*Assalamu alaikum* peace be upon you,' he said softly.

The one saying his *takbeers* continued his chanting but the other looked up from the floor and gazed in fear through the bleeding slits where his eyes had been.

'Who is there?' he mumbled, his bloodied hand reaching out in front of him as he struggled to get to his knees.

'My name is Abdullah.'

'Abdullah, may God grant you mercy and a swift end. *Inna lillahi wa inna ilayhi raji'un*, surely we belong to Allah and to Him shall we return.' He knelt back on his haunches, his broken hands in his lap.

Abdullah knew better than to inquire why or who had done this. With a sickening realisation, he knew that his cover had been blown and that Al Qaeda would now surely murder him. His first thought was for his wife and children and whether the Americans, or indeed the British, would continue to pay money to his family after his death. He tried to make peace with God but his prayers were pushed aside by his fear. His brain was spinning and he replayed the day over and over in his head wondering where he had gone wrong, or whether he had been betrayed now his usefulness to the infidels had come to an end. The thought of his family brought tears to his eyes and he began to weep, adding to the gentle ululations in the room.

As the day wore on, the heat of the midday began to yield to the softer warmth of the late afternoon. He heard the *Asr* prayers being conducted outside and again he tried to pray himself but it did not come easily. He had not observed the daily prayer rituals for most of his life, only really attending the Friday midday prayers at the mosque and observing the more important of the holy days.

The sun was setting, sending a sharp beam of light into the room when the door opened again. There were four men, all with their kufiyahs covering their faces and rifles at the ready. Two each grabbed the tortured prisoners and barked at Abdullah he was to follow them. He rose to his feet and followed them out of the door into the courtyard. There were more armed men outside and the two prisoners were jostled as they were led away. Their hands were tied behind their backs and a rifle butt to the back forced them to kneel in the sand. Abdullah saw Salim come from the house, followed by a second man he did not recognise holding a camcorder. Salim had a black flag on which, in Arabic cursive script, was written, in white, the *Shahada*, the Islamic profession of faith. *"There is no god but God, and Muhammad is the Messenger of God"*. Two soldiers held the flag behind the kneeling prisoners.

Salim motioned for Abdullah to approach. He felt his legs
go weak but he held his composure, for he was still not certain
what fate awaited him.

'Abdullah, my brother, the Quran instructs when you meet
the infidel in battle, strike their necks until you have inflicted
slaughter upon them. These two infidels betrayed their country
and their God. They have sided with the Great Satan, Bush
and the Small Satan, Blair and his crusaders. They have aided
the infidels to rape and kill our children and to subjugate our
women. They have defiled the image of God with their unholi-
ness and their treachery.

'The Shi'a are continuing to kill those who call for Islam
and the mujahideen of the community, stabbing them in the
back under cover of the silence and complicity of the whole
world, and, regretfully, even of the symbolic figures beholden
to the Sunnis. Moreover, they are a bone in the throats of the
mujahideen and a dagger in the backs of their leading personalities. People without exception know that most of the
mujahideen who have fallen in war have done so at the hands
of these people. The wounds are still spreading, and they are
working the daggers of hatred and cunning assiduously, Night
or day, they do not let up.

'At this decisive historic turning point, this reality, brought
the people of truth - we consider them as such - to rise above
their own desires, step on the pleasures of the Earth, and
undoubtedly answer the call. They were brought together by
the clearness of the path, the lucidity of the vision, and the
unity of the goals; for their base is *Attawhid* unification, their
path is Sunni Salafi, their way is the Jihad, and their aspira-
tions are the consolidation of the Religion on the Earth, the
contentment of God in the Heavens, and in the end, a "Paradise of Happiness". For that, the heroes of the Mujahid
Salafist Jamaa and their brothers in *Attawhid Wal Jihad*,
convened and embraced their hearts and souls, cordially united

their ranks, and acknowledged Abu Mussab Al Zarqawi as their leader, under the group of *Attawhid Wal Jihad*. This merger is "a strength for the people of Islam, and blazing flames for the enemies of God, where they shall burn until the retrieval of the stolen rights, and the establishment of God's religion on the Earth. It is a ticket and an inducement for the groups and sects to rush for the fulfilment of this legitimate duty and factual necessity. We give our word the Islamic Nation that we shall not betray or retreat, and we shall keep our promise until we reach either one of two aspired outcomes: victory or martyrdom".

'O God, render the monotheists on this earth successful. O God, support the mujahidin. O God, let them form armies and brigades, make them sincere, and protect them. O God, watch over them with your eyes that do not sleep. O God, provide them with all that is good. O God, help all those who seek well and dispose of all those who seek evil. O God, protect them and their honour. O God, they are humble people and need your protection. O God, they are poor and need to be enriched by your blessings. O God, support Muhammad's nation and render it victorious for you are our lord. O God, let us score victory over the unjust people. O God, let us score victory over the infidels. O God, take our blood until you are satisfied, and we thank Almighty God.

'*Nuqatil fi al-Iraq wa-'uyununa 'ala Bayt al-Maqdis* We fight in Iraq, but our eyes are upon Jerusalem.'

Having finished his sermon, Salim handed a large knife to Abdullah and the horror of what he was being asked, or rather, required to do, sunk in. The two prisoners were on their knees, heads bowed. The man with the camcorder was filming all the while as Abdullah took the knife. He looked at its serrated edge and wooden handle and knew instantly that he would not be able to execute the two soldiers. And he knew it would cost him his life. He let go of the knife. It dropped at his feet as two soldiers seized him by the arms. He was forced to his knees and someone grabbed his hair and pulled his head up. He looked into face of Salim, haloed by the setting sun. The eyes were unforgiving and impassive. He neither heard nor felt the bullet that blew off the back of his head.

40

Thursday 8 June 2006
Camp Slayer
Baghdad International Airport

From the outside, Saddam's Pleasure Dome, the Perfume
Palace, looked magnificent and imposing. Despite the American engineers having built a steel and concrete mortar-proof
roof over the dome, it still dominated the surrounding lake and
buildings. Inside, it had been a paragon of bad taste. Shoddily
built, the marble walls were really just veneers, the vast crystal
chandeliers had been mainly plastic and the artwork was
amateur and tastelessly hagiographic. Once the Americans had
moved in, they had boarded everything up with quarter-inch
plywood. False ceilings and floors were constructed to conceal
the thousands of kilometres of underfloor wiring and cabling
that was required to power one of the biggest and most
powerful intelligence centres in the world. They had

constructed smaller rooms and offices in the big open areas, also made of plywood, as well as some larger meeting areas.

Barbara had asked for an assembly of the various intelligence operatives with whom she had been working for the last year to discuss the theories around 'Juba' and come to some sort of conclusion and plan. She and Eric sat at a table in front of an auditorium. Behind them was a white screen.

Barbara introduced Eric to the team with which she worked at the Perfume Palace. They were a mixture of nationalities but mainly British and American with a smattering of Canadians and Australians. When she deployed, she was initially surprised at the number of US civilian contractors that were working for the American J2 intelligence network. Most, but by no means all, were ex-US military and most, but also not all, were professional to a fault.

'I would like to present Eric Scott-Douglas, over from UK, who runs the UK intelligence analysis for the Defence Intelligence Staff of the Ministry of Defence. I first met Eric when working for the European Community Monitoring Mission in Bosnia in, when was it, Eric? Ninety-three?'

'I believe it was, Barbara.' She was slightly surprised to hear him call her Barbara. Clearly, he could behave when necessary.

'As you are all aware,' she continued, 'Coalition Forces killed Abu Musab al Zarqawi near Baqubah, yesterday. Because of a lot of hard work from everybody here, we managed to find and trace a number of low-profile couriers that were involved with the AQI network operating principally around the Triangle of Death and out west in Anbar Province. It was from this constant vigilance and int gathered from Tier One SF raids that we managed to assemble a watch list and it was from this watch list that JSOC managed to pinpoint the Zarqawi network's clandestine travel plans. But, as you all know, this is just the start. From yesterday, we traced the four drivers and are now examining the eighteen houses that were visited before and after the Zarqawi pick up. One of those involved in the first leg of the operation has been on our watch list for some time now. Code named Fishhook, he's a taxi driver by trade although we think he was part of the Ba'athist set up prior to the fall of the Saddam Regime and only took to taxiing to make a living.

'Fishhook is a UK asset and, ladies and gentlemen, that information will stay in this room. It is classified UK Five Eyes only. I will now hand over to Eric.'

'Thank you,' said Eric and pressed the button on the remote control for the projector. The screen went blank. 'Bollocks,' he murmured to himself and then, 'Um, Barbara, it seems to have broken…'

'Eric, press the two side buttons to go forward or back. I think you've turned it off.' She got up, turned the projector back on and then pointed Eric to the two buttons he needed.'

'Er…ok, thank you Barbara. Sorry about that everyone.' At least he had the good grace to look sheepish, thought Barbara.

Eric clicked the first slide which was a mug shot of Abdullah Fahzad, aka Fishhook.

'Fishhook, ladies and gentlemen. Probably mid to late forties, Sunni, almost certainly a minor functionary in the previous regime. Married with five children, one who has epilepsy. We've been tracking him through Trojan software in his phone. Trusted enough to drive Rahman on the first leg of his journey yesterday. We think he reports to this man.' The second slide showed a grainy black and white image. 'Salim al Agayli. Agayli is a *kunya* or nickname. We also think he goes by the name of "Juba".

A murmur went around the room at the mention of the name, associated by all present as The Baghdad Sniper.

'We think he cut his teeth in the Bosnian War and met Osama Bin Laden there. We know as a fact that he served in the Seventh Muslim Brigade with two of the Nine-Eleven bombers. We suspect he was a clandestine sleeper in either Bosnia or even Austria prior to the invasion, transiting to Iraq via Syria in two thousand and two or three. Whereas high profile AQI personalities such as Zarqawi and Abu Ayyub al-Masri liked to be seen to be leading the jihad, al-Agayli was requested by OBL to remain under the radar. We think his day job is reception and sorting of foreign insurgents through the ratlines from Syria, training of sniping teams, production of propaganda and the onward supply of suicide bombers into the Triangle of Death. But his real purpose was to report to OBL without fear or favour. Al-Agayli, we think, may be running a non-attributable communication link to the Coalition forces.'

To the intelligence operatives of Task Force Orange, it was not news that Al Qaeda and Osama Bin Laden had been tentatively offering an olive branch. It was well known that in 2004, on the eve of the Presidential elections, Al Qaeda tried to bribe the Europeans with ceasefire in Europe if they denounced US foreign policy in the Middle East and stopped supporting military involvement. The offer was, of course, dismissed by the European Union. This rejection led to Al Qaeda, through its spokesman Al Zawahiri, to continue its Jihad against America indefinitely.

Eric pushed his glasses back up his nose and read from a sheet.

'In January, Bin Laden had reiterated his position,' he continued.

"Al Qaeda does not object to a long-term truce with the United States… on the basis of fair conditions."

'However, he further stated that there was no guarantee of a total ceasefire as other Al Qaeda leaders might not abandon strategic priorities, including *"long term confrontation with the United States and its allies."* Again he had offered the insinuated schtick that Al Qaeda had infiltrated the US and was preparing another major terrorist strike. It all fell on deaf ears.'

Eric continued with his intelligence assessment.

'It is becoming apparent that Al Qaeda's strategy of provoking civil war between the Sunni and the Shi'a is failing and that the indigenous power base in Anbar Province, between here and Syria, effectively, is turning against Al Qaeda, its foreign fighters and the vicious brutality that they are inflicting on Iraqi citizens. It would not surprise me, and, looking around this room, you too, that OBL fed Al Zarqawi to the Americans to reset the strategy and regain the trust of the Anbar Shura.'

A hand went up in front of him.

'Yes?' he said, pointing.

'Sir, I have a question. Do you see this as OBL losing control of Al Qaeda because he is confined to his stronghold in the Waziri Badlands or is it that he is still in command but himself sees that the whole war against the West is failing here in Iraq?'

'Good question and the short answer is somewhere between I don't know and probably both. What we do know is that the tactics of suicide bombings and death by martyrdom are unlikely to change.'

'Why do you say that, Sir?' said another of the audience.

Eric continued, 'The change will be seen in Islamic co-operation. The Zarqawi strategy of fostering civil war will be dropped and the message will go out that it is every Muslim's duty to fight the West in Jihad. For example, OBL has just announced:

"The Iraqi who is waging Jihad against the infidel Americans or Allawi's renegade government is our brother and companion, even if he was of Persian, Kurdish, or Tukomen origin. The Iraqi who joins this renegade government to fight against the Mujahidin, who resists occupa-

tion, is considered a renegade and one of the infidels, even if he were an Arab from Rabi'ah or Mudar tribes.'"

OBL has picked up on the discontent in his natural Iraqi allies, the Sunni, about fighting on two fronts against the Allies and against the Shi'a. They are just not that bothered about the Shi'a, really.'

Barbara interrupted, 'Eric, if I may? It's worth adding that, in Bosnia, there was total co-operation between Sunni and Shi'a, between Saudi and Iranian sponsored groups and there was no distinction in the Seventh Muslim Brigade. OBL will be using that model for the Islamic war against the West and the foundation of the Islamic Caliphate. The ultimate goal is to found a Global Caliphate, run under Sharia law.'

'Exactly,' said Eric, 'That and destroy Israel. Al Qaeda themselves have described three foundations for the Jihad in Iraq. One, the "Quran-based authority to govern" AQI wants to found an Islamic state governed solely by Sharia Law. Man-made laws and secular governments are a heresy. Two, "Liberation of the Homelands" – there can be no elections until there is freedom in the Muslim lands and they have been liberated from every aggressor. And, finally, three, "The Liberation of the Human Being" a vision of a contractual social relationship between Muslims and their rulers that would permit people to choose and criticise their leaders but also demand that Muslims resist and overthrow rulers who violate Islamic laws and princi-ples. They reject hereditary government and identify a need "*to specify the power of the sharia-based judiciary and ensure that no one can dispose of the people's rights, except in accordance with this judiciary.*" They don't see democracy as compatible with Islam, but rather as a rival to it.

'Ultimately, they want to defeat the enemies of Ummah and destroy the Zionist-Christian crusade. Then they will take the war to the West.'

Eric clicked the remote and a slide came up of an aerial

photograph of a farmhouse complex nestled in amongst date palms.

'Yesterday evening, we tracked Fishhook to this building near Habbaniyah, Anbar Province. Unfortunately, with the large amount of new data coming in post the hit on Al Zarqawi, we can't access as many drone or ISR assets as we would like. We did get this flyover image and in it you can clearly see that this building complex houses numerous personnel. There are, in it, at least seven vehicles, including several of AQI's favourite, the Toyota Hilux. We would like to examine the surrounding areas but lack of airtime means that we can't. However, I would suspect we would find some evidence of training areas and ranges where Al Agayli's task to train snipers is apparent. We are going to request a Tier One Special Forces raid on the complex, see what we can find. If we can pin down Al Agayli, we might find intelligence that leads directly back to OBL and possibly information of his whereabouts in Afghanistan, or wherever the fuck he is. This raid is likely to be given to Task Force Black, the British.'

A hand went up in the audience and a voice spoke out.

'When are the SF due to go into the targets? I'm in the meteorological section and there is a pretty heavy dust storm gathering, which could hit Anbar Province as early as tonight. That will ground all air assets including helos.'

'Thank you for that,' said Eric, 'Planning for site exploitation is up to JSOC at Balad who will, I'm certain, have the latest met int. Just to conclude, AQI is in a state of flux in Iraq, its leadership has just been decapitated and we think we can start to work on the second-tier leaders. We will start with Salim Al Agayli, if not tonight then in the next twenty-four to forty-eight hours.'

41

Friday 9 June 2006
Mission Support Site Fernandez
Baghdad Green Zone

After midday, the sky turned a foreboding hue of dark orange. What the meteorologists call a dust event, everybody else called a sandstorm and the best place to be was inside. When the low-pressure systems rumble in from the west, the wind picks up dust and sand from the arid deserts of Saudi Arabia, Syria and Western Iraq and dumps it as it travels east, often all over Baghdad. Approximately ten days each summer were lost to this type of weather in the capital.

The Boss watched the sky redden and was grateful that nothing would happen for the next twenty-four hours. The Squadron were coming to the end of their tour and, as the days counted down, there was a growing trepidation about getting back in one piece. A day off was a welcome break from the incessant stress of night operations. Following the visit of the Prime Minister and the death of Zarqawi, there was a brief interlude as the President of the United States also decided to visit the new Iraqi Government. A quick photo-opportunity handshake with those that risked their lives to make it happen was an essential stop on his lightning tour of the Green Zone.

The next phase of operations would be to take down the exposed Zarqawi network that Task Force Orange had so assiduously mapped out over the last year. This would involve a series of house raids and it was already the Squadron gossip that the British had a particular target they wanted to go after. Quite who or why he didn't know and, frankly, didn't really care. It would be another target to add to the long list of objectives already taken. All would be made clear in the orders when they came.

In the meantime, he thought he would go and find Staff Sergeant Barnes. The age gap between them was less than ten years but he had grown to rely on his second in command, not just for his experience in all things military but also for his Manichean outlook on life. Besides, he wasn't really a second in command. In the British Army, the senior non-commissioned officer was considered the 'backbone.' A few tried to take more power than they could handle and some seemed to relish their officers' mistakes. But the really good NCOs, men like Barnes, understood the actual reason why officers existed in the first place. Rather than loading everything onto a class war, they realised that a young officer was both intellectually better equipped and educationally better trained. This also wasn't a class statement, as anybody with the right educational qualifications could apply. A good NCO would take those two qualities and nurture them to produce a future senior officer of exceptional quality. It was for that reason that senior NCOs were tasked with training cadet officers at the Royal Military Academy Sandhurst. The obverse face of the coin was that the young officers, and the Boss was not so young these days, would rely on their NCOs for their guidance. And the really good young officers would shoulder the blame if things went awry as they sometimes, or, actually, often did. But it would be naïve to think there weren't numerous exceptions to this generalisation on both sides. The Boss thought of his Troop as a team but he thought of Barnes as a sage to whom he should listen. Besides, the rest of the Troop did not mess with their Troop Staff Sergeant. Or, if they tried to, it only ever happened once. Best stay on the right side of him.

'Turned out nice again, Boss.' He was sloshing a tea bag around a mug by its string.

'That a special tea bag? What's wrong with the compo tea bags?'

'It would be an understatement to say the Yanks don't really get tea but I found these in the PX. Earl Grey, whoever he was. Probably related to you, Boss.'

'Don't have any Greys in my family, John. I think he was Prime Minister and, if I remember my Victorian history from uni, he took down the East India Company monopoly amongst other things. The nice aroma, though, is from Italian Bergamot oil.'

'Has anyone ever told you, Boss, that you have a stupid amount of useless information in your head?'

'Yes. You. Quite often.'

'Anyway, Jacksons of Piccadilly.'

'Who are they?' asked the Boss.

'They make the tea. I've come to like it since we've been here.'

'Well, you'll find loads of it in Tesco's in Hereford, I should think.'

'Jim tells me we are brewing up for a big hit on an AQI training camp. Will be at least half a squadron. Maybe Delta as well. The weather is holding everything back, of course, but once it clears, we will be off.'

'I'm surprised we weren't stood to for the Zarqawi hit,' said the Boss.

'Yanks wanted it for themselves. It was a big statement from them, despite the large part B Squadron played in the build-up. Anyway, they just bombed the fuck out of the house with a JDAM. Delta were ready to go, rotors turning, but were stood down until their F16s had twatted him. They just went and swept up the pieces.'

'Apparently, he was still alive.'

'Yup. That's what I heard. Didn't last long, though. Over pressure from a JDAM is going to turn your internal organs into mush.'

'This sandstorm will last at least another twelve hours. We'll probably deploy just before first light, do you think?'

'Yeah,' agreed Barnes. 'The Crabs will need some time to dust off the choppers so I can't see us going before tomorrow.'

'Whereabouts is this training camp then?'

'I think somewhere out west. The problem is that until it clears, we don't have any drones in the air. Need at least aerial photos of the objective.'

'Would prefer a predator up there as we go in,' said the Boss.

'You know the Yanks are stingy with air assets. We may be in this together but some are more together than, er...'

'Are you reaching for the "All are equal, but some more equal than others"?' offered the Boss. 'Animal Farm describing when the pigs took over.'

'Yeah, that's the one,' said Barnes with an abashed smile. 'Anyway, they seem to hog the predators.'

'Very good. I can see what you did there,' said the Boss with a smile. Barnes looked slightly puzzled but the Boss continued 'You never know, we might be sharing the op with Delta, in which case I'm sure we'll get all the toys. By the way, how's Rocket? He holding up after the AVI?'

'Think so, Boss. Hard to tell. He's always been quiet. Think he's OK.'

'He's not come to you or anything?'

'Nope. I might ask Ginge if he's noticed anything.'

'Everybody is exhausted. Time to pass the baton and go home for a rest.'

'Still got nearly a month Boss.'

'Don't I know it.'

'You OK Boss?'

'Me? Yeah, fine. Couldn't be better.'

'How's the kipping? Are you getting your beauty sleep?'

'I get about four hours and then I wake. Usually in the middle of a stress dream. But it's nothing I can't handle.'

'You need more than four hours, Boss.'

'If I'm lucky, I can go back to sleep. But that's quite rare, if I'm honest.'

'You seen the doc?'

'Only socially.'

'You should go and see him.'

'He'll only put me on some sort of medication or give me sleeping pills. I don't want to get hooked on any of that stuff.'

'Well, another month and we can have some down time. You can pop up to London and see your posh totties.'

'The trouble with most of them is they are attracted more to high earning men based in London. Not some wandering soldier who's never there and can't afford a place of his own.'

'Come on Boss, less of the negativity. You would make a great catch for someone. Quite who, I don't know. She would have to be madder than a box of frogs.'

'Well, exactly.'

'What about that bird in the bar, whenever it was. You know, the one with that Brian geek.'

'What bird?'

'Come on Boss, you're not fooling anyone.'

'Oh her, yeah. I think I've met her before, somewhere.'

'She was quite tasty. And quite posh. And she's security cleared. She'll be up at Slayer. I thought she took a bit of a shine to you.'

'When am I going to find the time to get to Slayer?'

'Wouldn't be too hard to get her name.'

'She's called Barbara Bishop. She said.'

'There you go. Halfway there.'

'Anyway, don't worry about me, how's your missus?'

'We've been married fifteen years, Boss. She's used to life in the quarters. There's quite a gang of wives and they tend to look after themselves. The SSM's wife takes charge and makes sure they are all looking after the new pads. It's the youngsters that need the help.'

'They looking after Ron's wife?'

'I'm sure they will be but good point, will ask in the bluey I send home tonight.'

'You still sending letters every day?'

'Not quite every day, but certainly once a week.'

'You do know you can call home on the computers?'

'Yeah, I do that but the wife doesn't have a computer at home and, to do that, she needs to go into camp and it's all a bit of a faff. Good old Mark One airmail has served me fine for twenty years.'

'Stick to what you know, eh?' said the Boss. 'Right, I'm off to get some scoff and then try for an early night. Maybe a big day tomorrow if the weather clears.'

42

Friday 9 June 2006
Somewhere North of Habbaniyah
Ramadi-Fallujah Corridor
Anbar Province

The dust storm had enveloped the compound in its gritty, dark, billowing arms and all the Mujahadeen were sitting it out. Some were puffing on hookah pipes, drinking tea and gossiping the day away whilst others read their Qurans or cleaned their rifles. Salim kept a strict house and idolatrous pastimes such as cards or listening to music were *haram* or forbidden. Nevertheless, the cooks were busy preparing the evening meal and two of the goats had been butchered according to *halal*. They had met their end by the Islamic custom of slaughtering animals or poultry, *dhabiha*, being killed by a cut to the jugular vein, carotid artery and windpipe while still alive. The cooks all the while reciting their *shahadas* and blessing the meat. But despite the storm, the compound was still on high alert for any signs of attack. Sentries were still outside, now covered in red sand from top to toe but watching intently from their fire positions. Some of the young volunteers were ready to don suicide vests and run towards any attackers, their thumbs on the detonators. For them, it would be a glorious martyr's death and everlasting paradise.

Salim had spent the day getting ready for a trip over the border to Syria. He had hoped to leave that very afternoon but the storm had prevented any travel. He had informed his sub-commanders that he was going away for as much as a week to visit the safehouses that operated on the routes taken by the in-coming Mujahadeen. The death of Abdullah had been neces-sary as it was agreed with Osama that once he had been used to transport Al Zarqawi on the first leg of his meeting with death, he should be disposed of. There was a suspicion that he might be working for the Infidels and no chances could be taken. Nevertheless, Salim felt his absence as he was a good and reliable driver. He would now have to make do with a young man from Baghdad who, it transpired, had no aptitude for sniping, or, for that matter, shooting at all. Still, Salim liked the boy and was loath to send him forward as a suicide bomber. There were plenty of others for that. He decided to try to train him as a driver for he had, somehow, already obtained the necessary licence.

He packed his meagre amount of worldly goods into a canvas bag. Under his loose-fitting white thobe, he concealed a money belt in which he had twenty thousand US dollars, ten thousand euros, both in large denomination notes and his Bosnian passport. It still had a year left before it expired. For the trip out of Iraq, he would use his Iraqi identity papers for any roadblocks manned by the police or the army he might encounter.

He had felt for a while that this day would come. The strategy of slaughtering the Shi'a to provoke a civil war had

always run contrary to his beliefs for the world domination by
Islam. For how could they triumph if they were killing each
other? The signs of failure had become more apparent by the
day and now it was clear that the al-Sawah, or the 'Sons of
Iraq' had turned their weapons on to the Mujahadeen. The
tribal elders that he had used extensively on the rat runs for
foreign fighters, the Albu Mahal tribe, were being forced out of
this lucrative people-smuggling business by the al-Salmani
tribe. The Salmanis were much favoured by al-Zarqawi and he
had encouraged them. They were the dominant AQI force in
the smuggling town of Qa'im. Now the obvious response had
happened. The Albu Mahal tribe had gone to the commander
of an American Marine Corps battalion to offer him their
services. The Americans agreed to give them weapons and
training and they were attacking the Mujahadeen. There had
been accounts of foreign Mujahadeen being killed or
kidnapped and murdered by the local Sunni. There was
evidence that they were not only co-operating with the national
police and the Iraqi army but taking the local population with
them - pinning their flag to the Infidel Crusader mast.

Salim had kept his own counsel but he knew now it was
time to reinterpret the war against the Great Satan. The military successes against the Serbs and Croats in Yugoslavia and
against the Soviets in Afghanistan seemed a distant memory.
Halcyon days when it seemed possible that the word of the
Prophet, peace be upon him, would rule the world. But now,
the Americans and their allies had sent their crusaders to
Muslim lands, had defiled them with their satanic practices and
crushed them under their heels with superior military might.
But the West at home was weak and dissolute. The decadence
was like a corrosive substance eating away at their souls. The
new phase of the war would take place in Europe and America
itself, against the weak peoples who prided themselves on their
democracy and human rights. Freedom was nothing if it was

not used to adhere to the Word of God. There were no human rights other than those prescribed in the Quran. And it would be that freedom and tolerance, so highly valued, that would bring them down. For a silent army was assembling. It would infiltrate the West using their own weakness against them. When the time came, the Infidels would realise what exactly they had let in to their lands. By then, it would be too late.

Two months ago, in April, the Ruler of Libya, Mu'ammar Al Gaddafi had spoken in Timbuktu to a large crowd. It was widely reported on the Arabic news channels and shown around the Arabic world.

"We have fifty million Muslims in Europe. There are signs that Allah will grant Islam victory in Europe, without swords, without guns, without military conquests. The fifty million Muslims in Europe will turn it into a Muslim continent within a few decades. Allah mobilises the Muslim nation of Turkey and adds it to the European Union. That's another fifty million Muslims. There will be a hundred million Muslims in Europe. Albania, which is a Muslim country has already entered the EU. Bosnia, which is a Muslim country has already entered the EU. Europe is in a predicament and so is America. They should agree to become Islamic in the course of time. Or else declare war on their Muslims."

Salim placed his Quran at the top of his bag. Its birthplace, Juba, had given him his *kunya* and he knew he was feared. The videos would continue to be made but he could do that from anywhere now that the Mujahadeen had taught themselves about American technology and turned it against its maker.

He had long since lost count of the number of men he had slaughtered with his Tabuk. Probably over a hundred in Yugoslavia. Maybe over a thousand in Iraq. It was a faithful weapon and he had no need of the supposedly superior rifles that many of his fellow snipers chose. He sensed there was an unholy pride in the possession of the latest, the best, the most expensive, that was contrary to his teachings. Al Zarqawi had prided himself on his British M4, a weapon he himself had not captured and knew not how to use. The American video had brought shame and ridicule on the Mujahadeen and that was unforgivable. But Osama had already decided on his fate. The video merely confirmed that it had been the right decision. But now his successor showed no signs of altering the course of fomenting civil war and so it was time for Salim to leave. He would pursue his own Jihad away from the chaos of Iraq and into the heart of the Great Satan.

He waited for the storm to abate listening to *takbeers* on his Walkman. He had positioned a dirt bike in the palm groves at the back of the house and intended to leave by the rough track that led out into the fields so that people would not see him going. He would then travel towards Rawa and the Qa'im. Once in Qa'im, he would rest in a safe house belonging to a trusted AQI lieutenant before being smuggled over the border to Syria. Once there, he would be in the hands of the people smugglers that were supplying the insurgency with young Muslim men. From Syria, he would go to Turkey, having changed appearance from Middle Eastern to European. From Turkey he would take a ferry to Italy and then on into Croatia. To the world, he would appear as a Bosnian returning home.

He had no plans other than to find a safe place to hide whilst he considered his options. He remembered the first time, over ten years ago, when he arrived in Austria. Then he had found many fellow Muslims who were prepared to take him in, to introduce him to the Mosque and the Muslim neighbourhood. He had enough money for several years. He would not go cold and hungry for God would provide.

43

Saturday 10 June 2006
Joint Special Operations Command
Balad Airbase
North of Baghdad

Joint Base Balad had been called the Al-Bakr Airbase prior to the invasion. Since being occupied by the Allied forces in 2003, it had been renamed Logistics Support Area Anaconda, or the Big Snake. In the heart of it was the Death Star and it formed one apex of the Americans' own Triangle of Death that was intent on taking down the Muslim insurgency. Together with Camp Victory, which housed within its demesne Camp Slayer at Baghdad International Airport and the Green Zone, in the heart of Baghdad City, it formed the central network of the Allied Command in Iraq.

Barbara, alongside Eric, had put together a rushed paper requesting that Tier One Special Forces, particularly Task Force Knight, the Special Air Service, be used to hit the farm complex out towards Fallujah in Anbar Province to the west of Baghdad. In order for this to happen, the paper had to convince the Americans that it was worth committing the resources and persuade the British that it was worth risking lives to achieve. Through her numerous conversations with Brian, Barbara knew that the name 'Juba' was insufficient to galvanise interest. However, what was of interest were the rat runs of new recruits coming in from Syria and the provision of training facilities to meld them into soldiers. It was on these two aspects that the request for force was focused. Nevertheless, both Barbara and Eric were convinced that Salim Al-Agayli was both Juba and a direct link to Osama bin Laden. That he was unknown to the Allies up to this point made the sell hard but not impossible.

They had mooted the theory to the assembled intelligence community forty-eight hours ago at Slayer and it had been very much accepted as plausible. Now they were being asked to present to JSOC and to give the details of exactly where they thought the enemy complex was and exactly who they could expect to find there.

'The question is, Babs,' said Eric from the back of the Suburban as they drove to the helicopter, 'Is whether we allow a good forty-eight hours of aerial reconnaissance after the storm or go in once the weather clears.'

'That is an operational decision out of our remit, Eric. But why would they not over-fly the target?'

'Because, if they suspect Fishhook was compromised, they will be packing up as we speak and fucking off out of it. There's a chance the Regiment assault an empty house, or worse, one filled with Iraqi civilians minding their own business.'

'That's just the luck of the draw, Eric. The Regiment assaults houses most nights. Some nights they do two or three. More often than not, they achieve nothing other than annoying the occupants in particular and the community at large. Other times, they might enter into a shitstorm of resistance and take casualties.'

'So worth rolling the dice on this one?'

'Deffo, Eric. I need closure. For me, it's personal.'

'I get that, Babs. We will get him, don't you worry.'

The Suburban pulled up at the helicopter landing zone and an RAF Puma already had its rotors turning, billowing clouds of red sand left from the storm. There was a hotchpotch of personnel going to Balad, mainly British military but also some civilians that Barbara didn't recognise and two Polish officers, whom she presumed were up from Forward Operating Base Echo in Central Iraq.

The flight to Balad was uneventful and they were soon in a briefing room in the Death Star that was already occupied by British and American Tier One Special Forces. They wore a hotchpotch of uniforms with no one person dressed the same. There was a lectern in front of a large projector screen, displaying the JSOC logo of four crossed swords in front of a globe and Barbara spotted Brian hunched over a laptop. The soldiers were deep in discussion as they entered. One of them detached himself and walked over with his hand held out.

'Hello Barbara, you must be with the Int detachment from BIAP?' He was taller than she remembered and looked lean and strong in his uniform. 'I'm Tom. I think we met a while ago. At the Country Club? I hear you want to brief us about a target out towards Habbaniyah?'

She pretended she didn't remember. 'Yes, hi, Barbara Bishop. Currently attached to HumInt section at Camp Slayer.' Oh god, it sounded contrived. He'd just called her Barbara. He knew who she was. 'Can I introduce you to Eric Scott-Douglas, who is over from DIS in London, where he runs the Iraq desk.' Barbara flicked her hair, forgetting it was, as usual, in a tight bun and stood a little straighter. Perhaps pushed her chest out a bit, too, if she was being honest with herself.

Eric stepped forward and looked the young officer in the eye and Barbara saw that his brain was whirring.

'Tom? You didn't happen to be involved with the hostage release of a couple of American captives about, when was it, must have been two years ago now, um…?'

'April 04,' offered Barbara. She found herself really hoping that the answer to Eric's question was 'yes'. She had almost teased it out of him at the Country Club but Moustache Man had interrupted.

'Yes, actually, I was,' said the Boss to Eric. 'Did you know that or was it a lucky guess?'

'Call it intuition. Barbara and I were running an asset we called Clocktower. It was him who led us to the eventual farmhouse.' The Boss looked at Barbara, who looked away. He turned back to Eric.

'The guy with the beret stuck in his epaulettes? We were under strict instructions not to slot him.'

'Clocktower, with your help, Tom, managed to take down a very embedded Iranian Quds operation.'

'We never get to hear the full story. I remember one of the American hostages was killed which put a dampner on it as far as we were concerned. It's probably not a coincidence but Brian Mendoza, over there, was also part of that operation. Actually, as was Brent Schapner. Oi, Brent, over here mate.'

'I know Brian well,' said Barbara, desperately. She gave Brian a wave. 'We quite often work together. He's a whizz with computers.'

'Much like me then Babs,' said Eric.

'Er, I don't think so, Eric.' She silently mouthed 'and don't call me Babs'.

The officer, Barbara presumed he was a Troop Commander from Task Force Knight, signalled over to another older man, who wandered over with an American. The other Brit was the one she had also met with a big moustache and a very slight strabismus that gave him something of an air of menace.

'This is John,' the officer said to Eric, 'He's in charge until things go wrong and then he lets me take over. And this is Brent from Delta.'

'That's not very fair, Boss. I'm always in charge. What have you got for us today?'

'Hopefully a really big cog in the AQI machine.'

'We took out the really big cog a few days ago,' said Brent.

'Yes, well, we'll come to that. All in good time,' said Eric.

'Shall we get going?' said Barbara. 'Eric has put together something that we have been working on for at least six months.' She motioned over to Brian who had finished peering at the laptop.

'Brian?'

'Y…y…yes Ms Bishop?' His round pebble glasses magnified his eyes, which were now blinking out some sort of morse code.

'Can you load this into the laptop?' She offered him a thumb drive.

'I…I…I can't load an uncleared flash drive into a JSOC computer, Ma'am. Against standing orders.'

'Brian? Just load it. It's come from Slayer. We have the same protocols as you.'

'B…b…but, it's…'

'Brian?' said Eric taking the drive, 'load the fucking thing or I can't give my presentation and then General McChrystal will have to come over here rip your head off and pull out your lungs.'

Brian looked at the Englishman, his magnified eyes still blinking rapidly. Corpulent with two sweat patches under his arms and a little bow of tummy showing through his stretched shirt, he was holding his gaze with one arched eyebrow and the drive held between forefinger and thumb.

'It'll take me at least half an hour to clean this machine once you are done,' he mumbled.

'Good man, Barbara told me we could rely on you.'

Brian took the drive over to the laptop and Eric went in front of the lectern.

The Boss gathered the Troop in the row of chairs at the front. Behind were some American helicopter pilots and other assorted American troops, including dog handlers, signallers and intelligence personnel from Task Force Orange.

Eric's briefing covered the reason why British Intelligence thought Salim al-Agayli was an important high-ranking AQI operator. He gave a quick recap of his activities in Bosnia ten years previously.

'We think he's the sniper called Juba but we don't know why he's chosen that name. In one of his videos, he claims it is from the indentured African American community of the eighteen hundreds, where Juba was associated with a drum beat that foretold death but he may have picked that up from following on-line comments after he posted his first video nearly a year ago. Have you all seen that video?'

In the front row, the Boss said, 'I, for one, haven't'

Eric fiddled with the laptop, swearing under his breath and then, exasperated, summoned Brian over to help him. After a slight pause the first Baghdad Sniper video began playing with the masked Juba explaining how he was going to shoot American soldiers.

"I have nine bullets in this gun and a present for George Bush."

'It was the Tabuk rifle that first alerted us to his possibility of having come via Bosnia. We don't actually know where he's from, the name al-Agayli suggest Jordan, Juba suggest Sudan, but, to be frank, we don't actually know.'

'Tabuks are quite common in this country, Eric,' observed the Boss.

Barbara found herself staring at him and he turned to her and gave her a smile. She looked away and only just stopped herself flicking her hair. She must stop doing that, she thought. She was a trained SIS operative and she was acting like a schoolgirl.

'I know but I don't think they are for sniping purposes. When I was in Bosnia, the Muslim Brigade used them almost exclusively. Or rather, their Yugoslav predecessor, the Zastava.'

'OK, so he's a sniper. I get why you want to take out a sniper but almost any Jihadi with a rifle wants to be and, actually, is a sniper.'

'Good point, Tom. We think he's running the sniping school that is featured in his videos. We know AQI love making these propaganda vids but there has been an increase in lethal sniping in the areas around Baghdad. We think he's training them…'

'But there's more' said Barbara from the side.

'Yes, there is,' continued Eric, 'We think al-Agayli is also running the ratlines in from Syria, through Anbar and into Baghdad. The suicide bombers are coming from all over the Muslim world but a large number are coming in through Syria. But this is the clincher…we think he's effectively the second-in-command of Al Qaeda in Iraq. Or rather, we suspect that he is in direct contact with Osama bin Laden and he's reporting everything back to him directly without going through the formal communication channels. In fact, we have a theory it was him that fed Zarqawi to us on the direct orders of bin Laden.'

'Why would he do that?' asked Barnes 'Why not just slot him quietly?'

'Again, it's all to do with optics. Zarqawi had turned into a liability and his psychopathy was severely damaging the AQI cause in Western Iraq. It's noticeable that the indigenous Sunnis are turning against the foreign Jihadis. This would be a disaster for AQI. They are now running the risk of having a civil war within a civil war.'

'So, if I'm reading this correctly, you would prefer us to capture him? We hit the sniper school and try to detain everyone we find in the hope of him being one of them?'

'Ideally, yes,' confirmed Eric, 'As you are aware, there are so-called reconcilables and irreconcilables. We think he might be the former.'

'You think the two i/c of AQI is a reconcilable?'

'There's that possibility, although I might have been hasty to call him second-in-command. What I think he is, is a sleeper for bin Laden within his own network. He's OBL's spy, if you like. Eyes and ears on the ground.'

'Have you tried to contact him?'

'Well no. We only knew where he was yesterday. We think personally he is having second thoughts about the strategy but those around him are still hardcore irreconcilables.'

'So why don't you stake out the area with drone surveillance and when he moves, intercept him?'

'Another good point. Because we think they know they have been compromised and the recent sandstorm has grounded all ISR assets. By the time we get clearance, bid for the drones, try to persuade the Americans, no offence guys, that this is actually a priority, he may have moved to another location.'

'You do realise that if this is an ultra-high net worth target, then we can expect resistance on the objective? They will have thought about defending this area and will be prepared. Especially if Juba has ten years' worth of military experience.'

'I appreciate what you are saying and I hope very much that the operation can be conducted without it turning into a bloodbath,' said Eric.

'Me too, I guess,' agreed the Boss. 'So it's a classic F-three EAD.'

'Um…which is?'

'Find; Fix; Finish; Exploit; Analyse; Disseminate. We do the Fs and you lot do the EAD.'

'I guess it is then,' said Eric and then turning to Brent 'Excuse me, do you know where I can bum a fag?'

There was an awkward pin-dropping silence with the two Americans looking at Eric aghast until Barnes snorted and the Boss quickly called to the team. 'Anyone got a cigarette? You'll have to smoke it outside, Eric.'

Barbara let out a giggle and rolled her eyes at the Boss. He smiled back. She went red. Then Eric went up to the Boss and whispered something in his ear.

44

Saturday 10 June 2006
Task Force Knight Forward Operating Base
Balad Airbase
North of Baghdad

The Troop had left the briefing with Barbara and Eric to prepare for the assault on the farmhouse which would go in at last light. The Boss had poured over the detailed maps of the area and the available aerial photography. Being the senior Troop Commander in the Squadron, his commanding officer had left the final preparations and orders to him. There would be two Troops committed to the assault plus a cordon from the resident Parachute battalion. 'Infil' and 'exfil' – getting to and from the objective, would be by helicopter on account of the high chance that the compound was surrounded by improvised explosive devices. The Boss and Barnes were under no illusion that the main target, Juba as they now called him, was an intelligent and experienced soldier and would have prepared his defences well.

'The good news is that we'll be flown in by Crab Air.' The RAF Special Forces pilots were renowned for flying so low that it was impossible to engage them either with a missile or gunfire. The Americans, for a reason that had something to do with too high a casualty rate in training, flew in the 'Death Zone' between five hundred and a thousand feet, giving ground fire a much better chance of hitting its target.

'And the bad?' asked Barnes.

'The bad is that they are going to hear us coming. This is going to be a hot LZ so we need suppressing fire from the air.'

'Suggest we ask for an Apache, Boss.'

'Already have and hopefully we'll get one from the Night Stalkers.'

'Then I suggest we also have a couple of snipers on the skids of a Little Bird.'

'Agree, John. We've got the Paras coming in on a Chinook and we can land them here and they can secure the perimeter.' He pointed with a pencil to the area on the aerial photo he had laid out on the table next to the detailed map of the area. 'Most likely area of counterattack is from these buildings here because we don't know if they are occupied by enemy forces or just innocent farmers.'

'Two things that always scare me shitless, Boss. Suicide bombers and IEDs. We have to assume that the approach from our LZ, say, here, will be free from IEDs but we also have to assume there are suicide bombers ready to go as soon as they hear the choppers.'

'We'll have Ron and Wolfie on the Little Bird as snipers. We just have to hope they spot them before they get too close to us.'

'Do you want Ron on the sniping task?'

'He needs to get back on the horse, John.'

'In which case, you'll need to make it clear that potential suicide bombers are to be engaged without hesitation. Needs to be a quick double tap headshot. No fannying around with is he or isn't he.'

'Ron will be left in no doubt but you might back it up John. Just shoot any cunt that approaches us. Forget PID or any of that shite.'

'What about MOE?' Methods of Entry were crucial to a building assault.

'We could go route one, land here and assault through the front. We could also fast rope onto the flat roof and take both the top floor and the ground floor simultaneously.'

'Or, Boss, we could go through the wall with a charge, or perhaps blow a hole with an M203.'

'We need to be careful. If there's civvies, women and children the other side, then there's going to be a shit show of an enquiry. Prefer a frame charge, if we're to go through an outside wall. Less chance of collateral.'

'OK, Ginge can get a couple from Banjo after the 'O' group.'

'Looking at the ground, I think I would prefer the frontal assault landing the choppers here and here. Hopefully, we can suppress any ground fire on the approach with the miniguns in the Apaches.'

'Boss, we are meant to be capturing people. An Apache would destroy everything and kill everyone. Needs to be used jusdish…jid…'

'Judiciously,' said the Boss.

'Yeah, that.'

The door to the briefing room opened and Banjo, the Squadron Quartermaster, popped his head round. 'Want the good news or the bad news?'

'Fuck. What now?' said Barnes.

'Op's been postponed.'

'Fuck's sake. Why?'

'A Lynx and a Puma are grounded. Something to do with the dust storm. Probably the Crabs fancied an evening in the disco at the Al-Rashid.'

'Cancelled or merely postponed?' enquired the Boss.

'Postponed, Boss. Ground crew are trying to get it sorted asap. Been told to tell you stand down until at least tomorrow.'

'Have you told the boys?'

'Not yet Boss. They are having a brew. All kit and ammunition has been issued, so we stay here until we get the word that either we are going or it's cancelled.'

'Thanks, Jim. Let's go and give them the good news.'

'Apparently Boss,' said Banjo.

'Yes, Banjo?'

'Shithouse rumour is that you've caught the eye of the HumInt bird.'

'Yeah, I noticed that,' said Barnes with a wry smile. 'Boss has got previous, too. Remember the Polish int officer at Echo?'

'Oh come on, lads…'

Barnes continued 'There must be something about the slightly older lady. Mummy issues, perhaps Boss?'

'Fuck's sake.'

'Long loving gazes and lingering glances I'm told,' said Banjo.

'Who told you that?'

'Couldn't possibly say, Boss. Other than, perhaps, it's someone whose name begins with an 'M'.'

'Fucking Man Bat'

'Need to know Boss. If you need to ask, you don't need to know.'

The Boss looked at the two senior NCOs who were grinning broadly.

'She's not really my type,' said the Boss.

'What are you looking for? A blood donor?' replied Banjo.

'She is quite cute, Boss, got to admit,' said Barnes.

'Long dark hair, nice figure, tidy arse. You should have a nip at that Boss,' added Banjo.

'Divorced, I'm told.'

'How come, all of a sudden, you two are experts in my love life? Or lack of it.'

'Men of the world Boss. Seen it all before. Brung up in the school of hard knocks. No fancy schooling for me and John. We are men of the people and we know how this shit works.'

'And you are always moaning about not having a girlfriend,' added Barnes.

'I'm not always moaning, John. You are always bringing it up. Usually at embarrassing moments.'

'Fucking spare me Boss, what about in that pub in London.'

'Let's not go there, John. We all know what happened after that.'

'I don't,' said Banjo.

'Need to know mate, but I tasered a mugger. Was after the keys to the Rangie.'

'I'll pretend I didn't hear that,' said Banjo.

'Right, I'm off to tell the lads to stand down til further notice.'

'They are in the cookhouse. As is the Int officer and her Boss. Which is just a coincidence, I'm sure.'

45

Saturday 10 June 2006
Joint Special Operations Command
Balad Airbase
North of Baghdad

'Where can I bum a fag? Seriously, Eric?' Barbara had waited until everyone had left and then had taken Eric to the Green Bean Café. He was smoking his second cigarette and nursing a cup of coffee.

'Never fails to shock 'n' awe,' he said with an exhalation of blue smoke. 'Yanks are so easy, sometimes, it's almost not worth bothering.'

'Can you blow that poison away from me, please? And can I remind you, you are here to observe and assist, not cause a diplomatic incident.' Barbara was vigorously fanning her hand.

'Relax, Babs…'

'Don't call me…'

'I've been working closely with the Americans for a decade

now. One suspects they have a jejune sense of humour but they really don't. Or, at least, most that I meet don't. That Delta Captain knew it was a piss-take. You could tell. Not sure about the goofy bloke with the Naafi ashtray glasses.'

'Brian.'

'Thought he was going to break into a Beach Boys' song. Bar Bar Bar Barbarbar Ann.'

'Don't be mean Eric.' She paused, thinking. 'Eric, what did you whisper to the Troop Commander?'

'Tom? Wouldn't you like to know?'

'Come on, don't be a dick.'

'If you must know, I told him if they couldn't take Al Agayli alive, "then please make sure you kill him." For old time's sake. Time to move on Barbara.'

Barbara's mobile pinged and she looked down at it.

'Some people think it is quite ill-mannered to examine your mobile telephone whilst in the middle of a...'

'The operation's off,' she announced.

'What? You're fucking joking,' said Eric.

'I'm not.' She showed him the text.

'Any reason?'

'None given so far. Could be a whole number of things. Most likely troops or assets are being prioritised elsewhere. Don't forget the Americans are only quite impressed by our theory. They still like to be the big gorillas in the room.'

'Not much room for a gorilla, what with the fucking elephant in there too,' said Eric.

'They can't see the elephant. To them, Salim is a middle manager running a few ratlines and training a few snipers. No big deal. They've killed Zarqawi and now they want to take down the whole edifice. Salim's a sideshow.'

'I think they are grossly under-estimating him.'

'So do I, Eric. But we are destined to be second fiddle in this war.'

Her phone pinged again.

'Postponed until tomorrow. Aircraft maintenance issues, apparently. Probably hoovering the sand out of the choppers.'

'Barbara?'

'Yes?' she replied cautiously. He rarely called her Barbara unless in polite company or he wanted something.

'That Troop Commander, Tom. Have you met him before?'

'Not formally, seen him around a bit. But for some reason, I feel we might have met briefly in another life.'

'You mean like "Brief Encounter"?'

'Dunno. I've seen those eyes before somewhere.'

'You quite like him, don't you?'

Barbara felt herself blush and hated herself for it.

'Look, you are going all red.' Eric was beaming with mirth now. 'You fancy him, don't you?'

'Oh shut up, Eric, I'm old enough to be…'

'The older woman. Yanks call your type 'cougars'.'

'What do you mean "my type"? I'm hardly a cougar. I've only just met him.'

'So you are not denying it.'

'Denying what? What are you insinuating?'

Eric looked her in the eye with a knowing glint in his. 'Barbara Bishop. Who would have thought…'

'Can we just rewind this please? Technically, this is harassment. I can speak to my senior officer about you.'

'OK, OK,' said Eric, gesturing with the palms of his hands in submission. 'I was only asking. Course, none of my business.'

'You're right. It isn't.'

'Ha. I'm right. You've gone coy now. Look, for what it's worth, he looks quite nice. Fit, obviously. Seems quite bright. No visible tats, isn't ginger. What have you got to lose?'

'I've got two small kids and an ex-husband'

'So? There's a big market for milfs these days. I'm told.'

'Eric, honestly, you should spend less time on the internet. Anyway, I'm too old. What's he going to see in me?'

'Babs, you are just feeling sorry for yourself now. Get a grip. I'm sure you could scrub up quite nicely if you tried. Maybe you could do something with your hair and get a new wardrobe. Perhaps lose…'

'Fuck right off, Eric, you are not someone who should lecture people about losing weight.'

'I was going to say, lose the attitude…'

'Pah.'

Eric started humming tunelessly, '"And here's to you, Mrs. Robinson, Jesus loves you more than you will know." Why do they call it a flat white?' he asked, summoning over the waiter and lighting another cigarette.

46

Saturday 10 June 2006
Somewhere North of Habbaniyah
Ramadi-Fallujah Corridor
Anbar Province

Once the worst of the sandstorm had abated, a battered car drove up to the gates of the compound. The driver was recognised by the guards as a ratline smuggler. In the back were sitting two young men, no more than boys really.

'Tell Salim we have delivered two *istishhādi*.'

The Guard opened the car door and gestured for the two youngsters to follow him.

'What are your names?'

The younger looking one replied 'Mahmoud.'

'Where are you from Mahmoud?'

'Morocco.'

'Mahmoud the Moroccan. And you?'

'Mohammed. I am from Tunis'

'Come Mohammed and Mahmoud. I will show you to your quarters. Follow me.'

Salim was informed of the arrival of the two martyrs. They had volunteered in their local mosques, Mahmoud in Rabat and Mohammed in Mahdia. They had illegally entered Spain and then travelled up through the country to southern France where they lived for a few weeks in a safe house in Marseilles. Forged French passports then enabled them to fly to Turkey and from thence into Syria.

In Syria, they attended a training camp that would finish the indoctrination first started in France. They were constantly taught that martyrdom was a religiously legitimate, honourable way to conduct Jihad. To attack the Americans and their allies, including other Muslims, was permissible. Selected tracts of the Quran were used as well as the numerous *Hadiths*. Infidels were imprisoning and violating the women and girls of Muslims. The Shia, who were Kuffir were also legitimate targets. They used decrees by religious scholars and cited the precedent of the famous commander and companion of the Prophet Muhammad, Khalid bin Walid, whose outnumbered army fought bravely against the enemies of Islam. They would tell stories of past suicide bombers who appeared in their dreams telling them what paradise was like. Sometimes, they were even shown videos of suicide bombings but never of the aftermath. They were not permitted to interact with the common Jihadi for they were *fidai* and superior to those that wished to live.

The Quran has over one hundred and twenty verses on military jihad with a great deal written on those who die fighting. It promises much to those who are killed in God's cause and that they will be rewarded in heaven as *shaheed* or martyrs. But, as Salim knew all too well from his deep studies of the religious texts, there was a theological problem with suicide. There are no religious texts that condone suicide, whether military or otherwise. In fact, it was explicitly *haram*. "*He who kills himself with something in the worldly life, will be tortured with it on judgement day."* Although introduced by the Iranian Shi'a, the tactic had been widely adopted by the Sunni, especially the Salafist groups like Al Qaeda. Imams and religious scholars had explained away the Quran by stating that the suicide bomber was 'already dead' having been *'doomed to death'* by non-Muslim tyranny and were choosing the *'most beautiful of deaths.'* They were like the valiant knights of old, throwing themselves onto the enemies' line, sure in the knowledge of a glorious death for the greater good and the glory of God.

To recruit the volunteers, Al Qaeda had created the glorious 'cult of the martyr.' The spiritual benefits of martyrdom, rewards in heaven and the remission of sins amongst them, were strongly stressed to the impressionable young men in the Mosques of the Arab world. Yet, although these rewards are stressed, any scholar worth his salt knew these rewards were also given to anyone who died whilst fighting Jihad. More prosaically, volunteers were also persuaded by the rich monetary rewards given to their families once they had died and many a poor son had been persuaded by the earthly rewards alone. And, of course, there was the promise of *'houris'* the female companions of devout Muslim men in heaven. They were described in the Quran as *"companions of modest gaze well matched"* with *"large and beautiful eyes"* and *"untouched beforehand by man or jinn".* And in the *hadith*, it was written *"There are six things with Allah for the martyr. He is forgiven with the first flow of blood he suffers, he is shown his place in Paradise, he is protected from punishment in the grave, secured from the greatest terror, the crown of dignity is placed upon his head—and its gems are better than the world and what is in it— he is married to seventy-two wives among the wide-eyed houris."*

O Bou Bakr, o Baghdadi
Terror of the enemy
Heaven's houris are calling me

Sign me up as an istishhādī

But for Salim, the theological problem remained. And with it was the political problem that most of the suicide bombers recruited and sent to Baghdad ended up killing not infidels but other Muslims.

Many had passed through his compound and were transported up the ratlines to Baghdad and he had no doubt these two would follow in the others' footsteps. However, for now, he would keep them here for he was sure that, were Abdullah working for the infidels, an attack would come soon. For the two boys to prepare, they were handed over to the Salim's camp's suicide squad commander, the *rahbar*.

They were issued new clothes and told to bathe and shave all their body hair. Once prepared, they would see nobody but the *rahber* and would remain at his command. Each was given a vest lined with explosives, with which they were familiar from their time in Syria. The *rahber* would be the person that sent them out to their deaths if and when the infidels came. For that reason, total obedience to the *rahber* was inculcated into every suicide bomber's psyche. Mahmoud's *rahber* taught him a simple verse to recite continuously:

And we have put a barrier before them, and a barrier behind them, and we have covered them up, so that they cannot see

This would protect them as they approached their intended target. God would make them invisible to the infidels.

Mahmoud was finally given his suicide vest. He was

instructed to wear it under his shirt so that it would not be obvious. The orange detonation cord was connected to the explosives and then taped down his left arm to the striker in his left hand. The striker was a ring that would be pulled by Mahmoud's right hand. It would detonate immediately, he was told, so he needed to be as close as possible to his target. Mahmoud mumbled that he was honoured to be chosen by God. His *rahber* assured him that his family would be told of his glorious death.

47

'Hi, I'm Mike.' The pilot extended his hand and the Boss read Bewley on his name tag.

'Morning Michael,' he replied, shaking the hand.

'Actually, it's Mycroft. Don't ask. Father was a Sherlock Holmes fan.'

'I think Mycroft Holmes was always meant to be the genius in the family,' replied the Boss. 'Cleverer than his younger brother Sherlock.'

'Lucky he didn't call you Sherlock then,' said Barnes 'You'd get sick of hearing "no shit Sherlock".

'I hear that a lot anyway,' replied the pilot.

'No shit,' said Barnes.

'Anyway, come and look at the aerial photos we have of the objective. Outlined in red is the compound boundaries and it comprises three separate buildings here.' The Boss pointed his pencil. 'This is the main door and we think this, on the flat roof, is some sort of sandbagged area probably with an automatic weapon like a Dushka.'

'There's an Apache that is going to fly top cover, I believe,' said the pilot. 'He can take that out as we come in. Don't fancy taking incoming twelve-point-seven rounds on approach.'

'I think we have four Little Birds as well, flown by our American cousins. We will have a sniping team in one and the second will have the OC in. The other two will be AH6 fire support.'

'Will the OC be in an MH6?' asked the pilot

'Yeah.' said the Boss 'The AH6s should have seventy-millimetre rockets and a minigun. Enough to take out the top roof position.'

'Should cover it.'

'We think we should have the LZ here,' said Barnes. 'That gives us the option to assault straight into the front or go around the side and go through the walls.'

'Providing the AH6s can suppress the ground fire to get the choppers in safely. Second Puma can land here and take on the two other buildings. I'll liaise with the pilot to make sure there's no fuck ups on the ground as we come in.' He paused and then added, 'looks like a goer to me.'

Once he had left, Barnes turned to the Boss and said, 'He's a proper wingnut but he's also a top pilot, I'm told.'

48

Tuesday 13 June 2006
Joint Special Operations Command
Balad Airbase
North of Baghdad

The operation, codenamed ENDSLEIGH, was finally cleared by those in the Death Star to commence the following early morning, with H Hour set to be zero-five-thirty hours on the objective.

The troop assembled at the helicopter LZ at four in the morning. The night sky was clear with a gibbous moon but it was still very warm even at that time and the heavy equipment meant everybody was sweating under their body armour.

The Boss did a comms check on the radio as the troop waited at the side of the hard standing. There was desultory chatting with other members of the squadron who were tasked to assault the second and third buildings. As the target had been identified as hostile, there were no dogs on the task. Ibrahim would accompany them in the Puma.

Mike and his copilot wandered over and told them engines would be started at zero-four-fifty. The flight time to the objective would be twenty-nine minutes. Loading would take place at zero-four-fifty, in twenty minutes time. He also had some bad news. The Apache wouldn't be coming due to a technical issue. It wouldn't stop the mission.

The Boss looked at his watch and then put on his combat gloves. They were fire-retardant, something they had learned to wear from the Americans. If a helicopter went down, it was important to be able to free trapped personnel from a burning fuselage, so all troops were issued with fire-proof clothing.

'You got the frame charges, Ginge?' he asked.

'Aye Boss, not managed to lose them in the five minutes since you last asked.'

'And the Barclaycard?' This was the specialist automatic shotgun for removing door hinges.

'Aye, not managed to lose that neither.'

The Boss then went over to Wolfie and Ron, who would be sitting on the bench seats outside one of the Little Birds with the sniper rifles.

'Remember, anything that looks like a suicide bomber approaching us will be deemed to be hostile and should be engaged.'

'Roger that, Boss,' said Wolfie.

'Ok Ron?' said the Boss.

'Sure Boss. No probs.'

'Good man.' And he tapped him on the back before looking at his watch and then going to find Barnes.

'OK, John, let's line them up for emplaning.'

Ibrahim casually joined the line, his hands in his pockets. The Boss was always slightly impressed that he joined these missions without any weapon whatsoever, not even a pistol.

The pilots were in their seats now and the ground crew were making the final external checks, removing one by one the red flags hanging off the helicopters. Finally, the thumbs up were given and the rotors began their slow turning as the engines caught. There was more dust than usual and everybody turned away from the blasting grit. The loadmasters signalled for the troops to move forward and everybody climbed aboard and sat in their usual seats. The airframe shuddered as the Puma prepared to lift off, the door gunner behind his weapon.

The Boss plugged into the intercom to listen to the pilot chatter.

<*OK, Mike, clear for take-off*>

<*Roger that. Fuel on, quick set of scans done*>

<*Sweet*>

<*Wind negligible we'll just come in straight*>

<*Control Tower to Ironside six-one, clear for take-off*>

<*Roger that, Control Tower*>

<*Lifting off. Twenty-five minutes to target*>

<*How did your date with Heidi go, Mike?*>

<*That would be telling*>

<*Yeah, but did you scruff her?*>

<*A gentleman never divulges that sort of info*>

The airframe left the ground and the Boss could see the second Puma, carrying the other troop, beside them. They would fly side by side to the target with the Little Birds in front and above. He watched as the Balad LZ grew smaller. They would go as low as possible to evade ground fire and, more importantly, the man-portable air defence weapons that had been used recently against some American flights. It was thought that Russian made SA16s were being smuggled into Anbar Province from Syria. Fired from the shoulder by a single operator they were sophisticated enough to ignore the flares ejected from the aircraft.

The Boss saw the Little Bird MH6 with Ron's legs dangling in the air above the skids, his sniper rifle cradled in his arms. On the opposite side would be Wolfie. The other Little Bird was carrying the Squadron Officer Commanding who would, if required, direct the assault from on high. The two AH6 gunships, known as the "Killer Eggs" were carrying rapid fire M134 chain gun and a 70mm Hydra rocket pod on each side. Whilst not quite the killing power of an Apache, they would be used to engage any enemy from about eight hundred metres or more. For such a small helicopter, it could pack a very hard punch.

<Five minutes from target, going to come in straight>

<OK, Mike. Cool>

<Target in sight. Being engaged>

<Ironside six-one this is Viper five-five, you're clear to engage>

The Boss saw the flash of a tracer go past the door and immediately knew that they were expected. The aircraft dropped even lower and he could see the tops of the palms rush by so close it felt he could lean out and touch them. Through the door, he saw the Little Bird pivot and fire rockets. They left the pod in rapid succession but he couldn't see the impact.

<Ironside six-one, that was right on the money. Good shooting>

Above the clatter of the rotors, the Boss could now hear the Little Bird firing its chain gun as it strafed the target in front. He toyed with the idea of undoing his seat harness to get out of the fuselage quicker on landing but didn't want to risk being flung into the rotors should it crash and tip on to its side.

<Height good. Two hundred, one fifty, fifty, four, three, two, down>

The Puma hit the ground hard and bounced slightly but Ginge was already out and running from the plane. Behind him was Man Bat and then Cookie. The Boss jumped onto the sandy ground, trying to get his bearings in the dark. Already, behind him, the engine noise changed and he sensed rather than saw the big Puma lift off into the night sky, swivelling on its axis and flying out of the firefight. There was a loud ripping noise and the Little Bird fired a long burst into the house seventy-five metres to his front.

From the side of the house a flatbed Bongo truck drove at them. The Boss shouted a warning, dropped on one knee, his rifle already in the shoulder. He fired a short burst through the windscreen, the glass shattering and falling inwards. He fired again but the Little Bird had spotted the threat and opened up with its chain gun. The impact of the rounds shredded the cab and through his night vision goggles, he saw each strike glow a bright green. The rapid ripping sound of the gun following almost immediately. The Bongo slowed and then stopped; its driver slumped over the steering wheel. One of its tyres had caught fire.

The Troop was now running towards the side of the house, avoiding the closed large iron gate that led onto the inner courtyard. They paused at the corner of the wall and Ginge and Man Bat went forward. Ginge slapped the frame charge against the wall and they both retired behind the corner to await the detonation. There was a thump and the Boss felt the pressure of the explosion but was already following his men around the corner and into the gap blown into the wall. They were in some sort of storeroom and Ginge was already at the door. He tried the handle once and then placed the shotgun against the top hinge and blew it out. He kicked the door in and then they were into the main living room of the residence.

There was movement at the far end as a shadow ran up the stairs. A burst of automatic fire cut him down and he fell. A second burst hit his back. A dark pool of blood was already oozing down the steps.

The Boss made a quick assessment of the layout of the room and saw two doors leading off to other parts of the house. 'John, take Cookie and…' He was cut short by the scream of 'grenade' and saw it bounce down the concrete stairs. He flung himself flat as the blast and pressure ripped through the room.

'Fuck…I'm hit.'

The Boss looked up at Cookie bent double, clutching his left arm. Stan was already running towards him as Barnes leapt to the bottom of the stairs, tentatively looking up. He was joined by Man Bat who had slotted a grenade into his M203. He fired up the stairs and both men rushed up, taking the steps three at a time.

'I'm ok, Stan. Just some fragments in my hand,' said Cookie. Stan left him and followed the other two up the stairs.

The Boss heard firing from upstairs but wanted first to clear the ground floor. He signalled to Ginge to blow off one of the doors leading from the main living area, and then peered into a kitchen. Inside, sitting in a huddle in a corner were three or four women and several children. The Boss looked around for Ibrahim but couldn't see him.

'Where's the Terps?' he shouted at Ginge but was met with a shrug. He shouted at the women to stay where they were but had little faith that they understood English.

'Ginge? Ginge?' Ginge seemed unable to hear him so he prodded him on the shoulder. Ginge turned and shouted 'Wha? I've gan a bit deef, Boss.' He had a cut across one cheek, probably from the fragmentation grenade and blood was dripping off his chin. The Boss pointed to the second door and Ginge pulled the shotgun around from his back and blew out the top hinge and then the bottom. It fell in.

They were in a corridor and the Boss could see nothing through his night vision goggles except some whisps of smoke. All he could hear were shots from somewhere else in the building. He crept forwards soundlessly, aware of Ginge on his shoulder. There was a door at the end of the corridor and he tried the handle. He pulled it open and he and Ginge stood flat against the wall in case someone was waiting the other side. The Boss cautiously peered through the open door. They were looking into the outside courtyard. At the far end was standing a man, no more than a boy really. He stared at the two soldiers without moving, his hands down and away from his sides. The Boss, through the luminescent green of his goggles, immediately saw the pull handle of a suicide vest.

49

Tuesday 13 June 2006
Somewhere North of Habbaniyah
Ramadi-Fallujah Corridor
Anbar Province
AKA Objective Alpha Operation ENDSLEIGH

Salim was listening for the distant sound of helicopters. In the night skies over them it was a common sound but right now there was silence. Salim was experienced enough to know that if they were to be a target, the infidels would have put a no-fly zone over the compound. He also knew that it was unlikely that a vehicle borne assault would be considered as the fear of booby traps would deter them. He had put the compound on full alert, and the women and children were confined to the kitchen of the main farmhouse. There were two mujahadeen on the roof manning a heavy machine gun and they would shoot down the helicopters before they could land the soldiers. If that did not work, a truck bomb, driven by Mohammed the

Tunisian, would accelerate toward the landed machines and detonate. Mahmoud the Moroccan would wait for the infidels in the courtyard and when they stormed through the big iron gate, he would detonate his vest. At that stage, the defenders would withdraw from the compound out towards Ramadi and leave the women and children behind. The Americans would hand them over to the Iraqi police who would invariably release them within twenty-four hours.

His own plan was to leave before the Americans got there. He had no fear of dying but he knew his death would be an act of ungodly futility. Osama, his mentor, would not approve of him sacrificing himself in the defence of a farmhouse, however glorious might be the death. Their original idea of taking the battle to the Great Satan had not worked out as it should have. The crashing of the jets into the twin towers had merely roused the crusaders and now the caliphate's stronghold of Afghanistan was over-run. The jihad against them in Iraq was also not progressing as planned, with more and more Muslim deaths. The Iraqi Sunni were growing tired of civil war and the *Shura* were turning against the foreign fighters here to liberate them.

He heard shouting from the roof and then the throb of helicopters. He was right in his assessment about Abdullah and now the Americans were coming for him. He grabbed his Tabuk and went to the back of the farmhouse. The sound of engines was growing louder and he knew they had sent at least three or four. The big machine gun on the roof started firing, the muzzle flashes lighting up the night sky. He watched as the tracer arced through the darkness but, from the ground, he still couldn't see the helicopters. He suspected the gun crew were firing blind. The second staccato firing was interrupted by a series of detonations, the flashes blinding and the impacts deafening. The top of the farmhouse had been destroyed and the gun silenced. Then, all around, the earth erupted as numerous bullets hit the walls and sand. The helicopters were very loud now but he still couldn't see them from the back of the house. As the rotors changed pitch, he knew they were landing and he made his way down a path away from the house and toward the palm groves. There was another burst of fire but Salim was expecting the loud explosion of the suicide truck. Running as fast as he could to the shelter of the trees, he heard a helicopter fly low over him and then pivot on its axis to face the way it had come. He waited for the impact of the bullets but they never came. He looked up, his face blasted by the down wash and saw the bottom of the Killer Bee, two pairs of legs dangling. He paused to unsling his Tabuk. Sliding a round into the chamber, he aimed at the helicopter but it once again swivelled and moved off at speed. He fired and the burst must have hit something but he now needed to get away before he was spotted. He ran into the palm groves and then between the trees to where the motorbike was parked. He kicked it to life, slung the Tabuk and put his bag on the tank and drove off down the path into the night leaving behind him the sounds and flashes of an intense firefight.

* * *

'Let me talk to him, Mr. Boss.' It was Ibrahim whispering next to him.

The Boss realised the young boy in the vest couldn't see them in the dark and was waiting for the iron gate to open. He had turned down his radio so that no voices or static could be heard.

'OK but let him know we will shoot him as soon as blink if he moves towards that handle.'

Ibrahim spoke gently in Arabic and the Boss, through his sights, saw the boy startle. He could see he was terrified but he had not yet made a move with his right hand to the trigger on his left wrist. The boy shouted back in Arabic. Again Ibrahim, no more than murmuring, spoke. The Boss could hear raised English voices coming from the house behind him and indicated to Ginge to go back down the corridor and not let anyone through the door. Through his sights, the Boss observed the boy slowly turn and walk towards them.

'Tell him to stop right there,' whispered the Boss. Ibrahim spoke again, calmly but firmly and the boy stopped. He shouted something back. Still his arms were at his side.

'Tell him to take off his jacket and then the suicide vest.'

The instructions were relayed but the boy just stood staring, still unable to see into the dark shadows that concealed them.

'He is called Mahmoud, Mr. Boss.'

'Well, tell fucking Mahmoud he needs to remove his suicide vest.'

'I'm telling him that if he surrenders, he will be taken care of.'

The boy shouted again into the darkness. Ibrahim again calmly answered.

'He says don't shoot.' The boy slowly and deliberately shrugged off his jacket and underneath the boss could see six sticks of explosive, wired in tandem and the det cord taped to his left arm.

'Tell him to undo the gaffer tape, Ibrahim. One false move towards that handle and I shoot.'

The boy stopped and looked again. He made a slow and deliberate move and began to pull at the tape at his bicep. The Boss watched as he tugged again, this time at the tape around his wrist, the cross hairs of his night sight on the head of the young man. The handle, suspended by the det cord hung at his side and with slow deliberate movements the boy began to move his shoulders.

The Boss had shut out all sound, although there was still shouting and some sporadic fire coming from one of the other houses. He felt sweat drip down his back, his finger on the trigger, safety off. His heart was pounding in his ears.

He sensed the sound and blast of the Little Bird as it flared up over the wall, held in the air and then, through his sights, he saw the bullet hit the boy's head. He dropped to his knees and then fell face down in the sandy courtyard.

'Fuck,' was all he could muster. The chopper was overhead now, blowing the sand in a whirlwind of grit and debris before moving off out of sight.

'Fuck,' he said again as the sound of ululating and keening broke through to his consciousness. The women of the house, confined to the kitchen, must have seen the boy get killed through a window and were now screaming in terror and rage. The Boss ran forward and was startled to see the boy's eyes moving as he approached. He lifted the limp body and removed the suicide vest, first one arm and then the other. He put it next to the wall away from harm's reach. Ibrahim came over.

The boy made to speak and Ibrahim bent down towards his mouth. He murmured back in Arabic but the boy continued to talk.

'He is telling me that he didn't want to die.'

The Boss had no words.

'He is a good Muslim. From Morocco. He is saying that the Muslims here are bad Muslims. They forego their prayers, drink alcohol and watch the dirty porno videos. He did not want to die for them but he had no choice.'

'Ginge, Ginge, get Stan,' shouted the Boss.

Ginge came over to them and said, 'Stan's hit pretty bad Boss.'

'What? Where's he hit? Where is he?' All this time on the tour, all the nightly house raids, month after month and now someone gets badly wounded just before they were due to go home.

'He went up the stairs with John. Think a round hit him. They are evacuating him now.'

'We need someone here to get this casualty out,' said the Boss, standing up.

'I think, Mr. Boss, we are too late for that.' The Boss looked at the young boy and saw that he was staring up into the sky, not moving.

'Ginge, see if you can find a pulse. I'm going to find John.'

'Aye, Boss. But he's a goner.'

'Then come with me.'

The Boss crossed the courtyard and went back down the corridor. In the main living area, the lights were on, so he removed his night vision goggles. The place was a mess of smashed furniture, broken glass and spent cartridge cases under-foot. The troop were moving through the room looking for anything that could add to the intelligence picture. Sensitive site exploitation, as it was known, would feed the endless demand for intelligence generated by the Death Star. In all probability, it would inform the following night's – no, make that tonight's, house raids.

The Boss knew he would hit the wall soon, he always did, coming down from a kinetic operation. But he felt truly exhausted by the night's events. He looked at his watch and realised they had been on the ground for twenty minutes.

'Where's John?' He asked Man Bat.

'Outside by the choppers Boss. Stan's not in a good way.' Man Bat was looking gaunt and pale even though he was now a seasoned veteran of dozens of raids. But this one was different. One of their own had been seriously wounded.

The Boss went out of the hole in the wall, through which he had entered the house and saw a medivac Blackhawk being loaded with a stretcher. A medical orderly was holding a drip as two others loaded the stretcher. There were three Iraqis sitting on the ground being guarded by two paratroopers.

He spotted Barnes.

'How bad is he, John?'

'Hard to tell, Boss. Don't think it's life threatening but it may be what the press euphemistically call 'life-changing.' Entry wound is lower back, just below the body armour. Stan says he can't feel his legs and can't wiggle his toes. But we need to get him back for a full assessment.'

'What about Cookie?'

'Cookie's alright, Boss. Took some grenade shrapnel to the hand. He's on the chopper with Stan.'

'At least Stan's got someone with him'

'Yeah, Boss.'

'Wolfie and Ron about?'

'Yeah, though they were lucky. A round came through the Plexiglas and hit the pilot in the foot. Luckily, the co-pilot took over. They are down now and helping with the site exploitation. Ron hit a suicide bomber in the courtyard with the sniper's rifle.'

'I know, I was there.'

'Why didn't you shoot him Boss?'

The Boss felt the tiredness and despair in that simple question. 'It's complicated. I'll tell you later.'

50

Tuesday 13 June 2006
Camp Victory
Baghdad International Airport

Barbara had been at Balad watching the feeds on the Kill TV video wall during the assault. She had seen a few live assaults prior to Operation ENDSLEIGH, as well as numerous CCTV feeds from drones and helicopters eliminating designated hostile targets. But this operation had been different. She knew why, too. She was desperate for nothing to happen to the young Troop Commander she only knew as Tom. It was ridiculous. She kept telling herself she was at least eight years older than him. She had two small children and an ex-husband. He had almost certainly forgotten about her, didn't know her name, didn't even remember meeting her. He would have a girlfriend in England, may be thinking about marrying her, possibly already engaged. It was unlikely she would ever see him again. But, even so, during the half hour in front of the screens, she felt a gnawing fear something would happen. When it didn't happen, at least not to him, the fear was replaced by an unedifying nervousness that she might never see him again. In her years as an SIS operator she had taught herself to think logically and dispassionately but, even so, she couldn't get him out of her mind. What would make matters worse was that Eric had sussed her. He had a knack for knowing things about you that nobody else knew. What did he call it? Metagnomy; she had had to look it up. Divine inspiration or the acquisition of information by paranormal means. It was one of his arcane words that he liked to trot out.

But Barbara was also self-consciously aware that the target of the raid was the Baghdad Sniper and she was convinced he was the Bugojno Sniper who had killed Adam and effectively destroyed her world. She had carried with her, these last ten years, a morbid fascination about these hidden killers and since first seeing the video showing the shooting of that young American medic, she had a feeling that the Bugojno Sniper's malign presence was here in Iraq. It might have been metagnomy, but it was also nemesis, or rather, she would be his nemesis. The Greek Goddess of revenge, who would bring retributive justice to the killer of her love, the father of her child. Tom and his Troop would exact a terrible vengeance.

Eric was due to fly home tomorrow, so, for now, her secret would be safe, she thought. She had dealt with his jokey quizzing, knowing he was fishing. But now he was more concerned about Juba not being killed or captured. The enormous effort in pinpointing him to the farmhouse had been for nothing and he was angry at himself for not getting it right. As he had said, he would have bet his mortgage, if he had one, on Juba being there. He felt the failure personally. Barbara was more sanguine. She knew that the military aged males that were captured in the raid were, even now, being worked on by the American gators. If Juba had been there and slipped away in the night, like Zarqawi had during the LARCHWOOD IV raid that found the now infamous video, they would soon know. She was glad the Americans had the job as she was not permitted to use 'robust interrogation techniques'. But with Juba, she might have ignored her strong moral compass and got medieval on him. She wanted to know if he was the Sniper of Bugojno. The author of her decade of sorrow and sadness. And if he was, she wanted him to know he was going to suffer for the rest of his life as well, preferably locked away in somewhere like Guantanamo.

There was a knock on the plywood door of her office. Here he was now, though he didn't usually knock.

'Morning Barbara.' Not a good sign. "Barbara" signified seriousness.

'You packed up then, Eric?'

'No, but then it's only going to take me three minutes to stuff my kit into my holdall.'

'You look a bit pissed off, Eric'

'The MAMs they took haven't spilled the beans yet, I'm told. I've read a few of the transcripts and they are just new arrivals, not even trained. Someone said there was a senior AQI but nobody knew his name. Agayli and Juba did not provoke a reaction.'

'So, we will never know,' said Barbara. 'Was he the sniper in the videos. Was he a direct link to OBL or were we just fooling ourselves? Did he kill Adam?'

'Correct, Babs, we don't know. We now must wait for him to resurface and then we go after him again.'

'Any news on our casualty?'

'That's the point, Babs. Have we just ruined a life pursuing a chimera?' Barbara thought to herself that is what Brian had called it. 'We were so sure and yet it was all for nothing.'

'Come on Eric, this is unlike you. Everyone knows the

score. Certainly the boys from Hereford. They don't ask for sympathy.'

'You're right. They will be out again tonight, working on someone else's theory about where the bad guys are. Jaysoc doesn't abide rest and reflection.'

'If the insurgent networks are going to be taken down, then it has to be done at pace,' she said. 'The squadrons will be rotating soon, as will I.'

'Yes. I suppose you are right. You usually are. What's next for you then?'

'Back to Vauxhall. Need to make some big decisions but first I'm going to take some leave. Then I'll see how I feel.'

'Did you get his phone number?'

'Whose? Oh, right. No. No, Eric, I haven't.'

'Want me to get it for you?'

She thought for a while and then said, 'if you can get his email and if you can keep it confidential between us – what did they call it? 'Need to know,' then yes. OK. Eric, that would be great.'

'I'll see what I can do. I mean, if I can't find the email I might as well give up and go fishing.'

51

All wars are fought twice, the first time on the battlefield, the second time in the memory

Viet Thanh Nguyen

According to a Veteran's Administration study
Half of the Vietnam combat veterans suffered
From what psychiatrists call
Post traumatic stress disorder
Many vets complain of alienation, rage, or guilt
Some succumb to suicidal thoughts
Eight to ten years after coming home
Almost eight-hundred-thousand men
Are still fighting the Vietnam War
None of them received
A hero's welcome

Paul Hardcastle Nineteen

52

Stirling Lines
Credenhill
West of Hereford
UK
About a Year Later

'Boss, CO wants to see you.'

'What've I done now?'

'Dunno, he's in RHQ.'

The Boss was in the squadron interest room having a cup of coffee and reading the papers. Putting on his beret, he sauntered over to 'Puzzle Palace' where the Commanding Officer, the Second-in-Command and the Adjutant all had their offices.

'Go straight in, Boss,' said the Chief Clerk.

He stopped at the door, briefly calmed himself and then knocked.

'In' came a brusque instruction and he pushed open the door, saluted and stood in front of the Colonel's desk.

'You wanted to see me, Colonel?'

'Yes, Tom. Have a seat.'

He pulled up a chair and sat opposite his commanding officer who seemed busy reading an official looking letter. He looked around the office. There were numerous photos on the wall of Troop or Squadron groups. They had mainly been taken in deserts, jungles or in arctic wastelands. Two were formal pictures of the Officers' Mess taken below the famous Clocktower. There were also framed prints of other regiments, usually with a message of thanks. He saw Delta Force and the Seals and one in German from GSG 9, their counter-terrorism police unit.

'There's a bit of nause, Tom.'

His heart sank. 'What about, Sir?'

'MOD were contacted by a team of ambulance chasing lawyers. They filed a complaint, alleging that the Regiment were murdering civilians in Iraq.'

'Are they saying the Squadron did it on the last tour? That's crap, as far as my Troop is concerned.'

'Apparently, these lawyers have been retained by the families of some dead insurgents. They are alleging that they were shot after surrendering and when they were posing no further threat.'

'They will need more details than that, Sir.'

'In the letter sent to the MOD, one was shot after surrendering during an AVI. Apparently, he was unarmed at the time and they have several witnesses. The other was shot surrendering to you, Tom, it says. On a house raid. Witnessed by several females who were there at the time. Do you know anything about any of this?'

'If it's what I'm thinking, they were both shot as suspected suicide bombers after being given an opportunity to surrender.

It's impossible to know, Sir, if someone is running towards you whether…'

'Tom, I'm aware of what operational requirements are for suspected suicide bombers. But the second one had his hands in the air and had taken off his suicide vest when he was murdered, they say.'

'With all due respect, Sir, that's bullshit. I took off his suicide vest after he was shot.'

'The witnesses say he had already removed the vest. Tom, work with me here. These are allegations that have been made via a registered UK law firm. They will have to be investigated and the SIB are asking me for a date when they can come up and interview you and the Troop.' The Special Investigations Branch of the Royal Military Police were notorious for their thoroughness and, some, indeed many, thought, rather too zealous in their pursuit of a result.

'I believe both incidents were on your watch?'

'There were occasions when we hit would-be suicide bombers, yes Sir. I can't say if those described are the ones, exactly.'

'Can you recall who pulled the trigger in each of the two instances?' asked the Colonel.

'No Sir.'

'Was it Trooper Stevenson?'

'Can't exactly remember, Sir.'

'I expected that answer. Nevertheless, the SIB will take statements. They will want to interview you and Staff Sergeant Barnes as well as any members of the Troop who were present at those two incidences.'

'Do I, or rather we, need a lawyer, Sir?'

'Not for now, Tom but if this goes any further the MOD will get you someone. Listen, I know it's distressing, especially after a long and, as I've already told you, very successful tour.'

'If it's the raid I'm thinking it is, then Ibrahim the interpreter was a witness. The suicide bomber hadn't taken off the vest.'

'Ibrahim was killed a couple of weeks ago I'm afraid Tom.'

'How was he killed?' Tom repressed his sudden feeling of weary sadness.

'IED, travelling in a Humvee. Sorry to let you know in this way, Tom. I gather he was a valued member of your team.'

'He was a good man. Brave as fuck and always cheerful,' Tom tried to focus, 'So, they are saying we shot two people in cold blood after they surrendered and the only reliable Iraqi witness is dead?'

'That's the gist of it, Tom. Yes.'

'They will be vexatious complaints, Sir. Scumbags after money. Trying to screw the Government for compensation.'

'Tom, and I say this as a friend as well as your Commanding Officer. The MOD is very aware of certain firms in the legal profession running no-win-no-fee compensation claims against the Army. You are not the first to be accused of wrongdoing over there. But there is a due process and you have to follow that due process. You have to forget that these people stand to make a lot of money if they win.'

'Yes Sir.' But the Boss was feeling the anger well up inside. The injustice of it all. The false pretence of the reasons for war, the failure of the Government to supply them with even some of the most basic kit. The loading of responsibility on to those like Ron, at the very tip of the spear taking instant life and death decisions. Of people like him, having to issue orders, formulated from above but given to him to disseminate so that the buck stopped with him. The relentless nature of operations, the lack of sleep, the constant anxiety and fear of death or serious injury. And now, some wanker in a shiny M&S suit and a micky mouse law degree from a shitty polytechnic was trying to make a fast buck.

'There is some good news,' said the Colonel. 'Stan came out of Selly Oak hospital at the weekend. He's gone home to his parents in Melton Mowbry.'

'Right Sir. Might go and visit, if that's OK.'

'Course. Chief Clerk will get you the address and phone number.'

'Might take Staff Barnes, too Sir.'

'You might want to know that Staff Sergeant Barnes is to be made up to Sergeant Major. He does know but it's not been officially gazetted yet.'

'About time, Sir. No disrespect.'

'I think that's all, Tom. Unless you have anything for me.'

'No Sir.'

'Good. Remember what I told you about due process. Being in the Regiment is about clarity of thought. Revenge is a dish best eaten cold and all that. We will do our best to look after you. Most importantly, we will endeavour to keep your name out of the media.'

'Yes Sir. Thank you, Sir.'

* * *

Ron Stevenson had packed his Bergen and taken his car down towards Merthyr Tydfil. It was a gorgeous early summer evening, with clear blue skies, as he parked next to the Storey Arms mountain rescue centre. He cast his memory back to the first time he found himself in this car park. Day two of his SAS Selection. The training staff had been curt and professional but, as he had found out after eventually passing, with a good sense of humour as well. He had been given a grid reference and told to make his way to it. The grid was at the top of Pen Y Fan, the highest point in the Brecon National Park. At the summit was another member of the Training Wing who, he later learned, was Ginge Campbell. He was drinking tea and had half a roll-up cigarette hanging out of the side of his mouth.

'Name?'

'Stevenson.'

'Wiz ye?'

Ron looked at him. 'Pardon?'

'Is ye deef? I said, where is ye?'

'Oh…' Ron pointed to his map.

'That'll be a five poond intae the fund, you crap hat Taff wanker.'

Ron remembered that pointing with a finger onto a map was a Regimental no-no, so he picked a blade of grass and pointed 'Likely here see, trig point on top of the Fan.'

'Reet, this is ye next grid checkpoint.'

Ron bent to look at the map.

'Show me on ye map,' said Ginge. Ron pointed with his grass. 'Cheer up. Is nae meant to be easy otherwise every cunt would do it. Wa' ye waiting for? Fuck off now.'

And hoisting his sixty-pound Bergen and his old rifle without a sling, Ron made his way down the far side of the Fan and down the Roman Road towards the Talybont Reservoir.

But this evening, he made his way in the opposite direction towards the Fan Fawr trig point. It was a steep climb, over tussock grass and numerous small streams. Some sheep watched him as he approached the concrete block with its stencilled red dragon and he sat down and surveyed the view. God's own country, he thought. Sheer majestic beauty of the hills. Hills that he knew so well. He picked himself up and setting his compass, made his way further west towards his final destination.

He saw it up ahead just as the sun was low over the ridge. It would be dark soon. The enormous primitive monolith of Maen Llia, stood against the skyline. It was fully twelve feet high and nine feet wide and shaped like a diamond. Nobody really knows who put it there, or why, but the sheer effort of doing so was awe inspiring, especially given that a quarter of the stone is buried under the ground. At over five hundred and seventy metres above sea-level, it is the highest standing stone in the Principality. Legend has it that, at sunset, the stone goes to drink from the nearby stream and Ron wanted to see if its shadow did indeed extend that far.

As the light faded, he took the hooped bivvy bag from his bergen and flipped it open. His sleeping bag was already inside. He thought about his wife and child. How, since returning from Iraq, he had failed them. His quickness to anger, his violent thoughts, his hurtful actions and words to those he loved the most and who loved him the most. How the slightest noise could set him off, how the thump of helicopter rotor blades could reduce him to tears and despair. He had asked to go back with the next squadron rotation but had been refused. He was under investigation, he was told, for murder. The Boss and John had told him not to worry. The Boss even knew the Government lawyer, Sir Somebody-or-other, with whom he had been at school or something. 'Don't worry, Rocket, we've got this. The man is the sharpest legal mind in the business. No worries.' But the haunted nights and catatonic days just piled up on him and he felt he was going mad.

Then his wife had accused him of abandoning them, of being married to the Regiment. Of 'not talking' and 'bottling everything up.' Eventually, she had taken the child, that most precious person in the world, and moved back to her mother's 'until we sort something out.'

Well, he was going to sort something out. As the sun went down, he wandered down to the little brook where the shadow was having its drink and filled his mess tin. He then opened a little hexamine stove and boiled up some water to make a brew. Strong army tea is what the military operated on. Once he had his brew, he sat and looked at the view. He then opened a small Ziploc bag where he had been storing the sleeping pills the medics had been giving him over the last few months and swallowed all fifty-one tablets with the last of his tea. He lay down in his sleeping bag, his face up to the darkening skies and closed his eyes.

53

Edgbaston
South Birmingham
UK
27 July 2007
1015 Local

Using his Bosnian passport and his large amount of cash, Salim had found it straightforward to get to Austria once he had negotiated the Iraq-Syrian border with the people smugglers. A bus took him to Damascus and from there he flew to Vienna. He had considered going via Sarajevo to renew the passport but then decided against. It had been issued in Vienna and he would approach the embassy directly in Tivoligasse once he had established lodgings. He chose the district of Vienna with the largest Muslim population, which was Bezirk Rudolfsheim-Fünfhaus. The Muslims in all parts of Europe were growing exponentially in number and Austria was no

different. The Muslim population had tripled in the past fifteen
years.

For Salim, it was the confirmation of his theory that the
Great Satan would not be defeated by war in Muslim lands.
The weakness and decadence of the West was Islam's greatest
weapon and the inability to coalesce as one people, *Ummah*,
their greatest weakness. But by moving to the infidels' lands,
Muslims were forced by circumstance to live side by side. To
refrain from taking arms against each other and to face the
true enemy. It was a growing trend that had started with the
war in Yugoslavia when hundreds of thousands of people
began to move west to the more prosperous countries. Even
though the West had helped them both in Bosnia and then
Kosovo, the migrations continued and grew. Wars in Algeria
and the Horn of Africa and, indeed, all over Africa coupled
with almost no border controls to speak of, allowed tens of
millions to move. Mu'ammar Al Qadhafi had been correct
when he had said that to defeat the West and establish Islam as
the dominant religion, all that was needed was time. Time for
the movement of peoples. With the help of God, their families
would out-produce the decadent whores of Europe with their
painted faces and immodest clothes. Already colonies of
devout Muslims were settling in areas, establishing Mosques
and schools. Money was pouring in from the Middle East and
while the Americans and their allies were spending vast sums
on prosecuting their wars, Islam was spending money on establishing itself right at their heart.

Salim had decided that once he had renewed his Bosnian
passport he would move to the United Kingdom. His Algerian
heritage would normally have suggested France as a place to
settle but he had left Algeria long ago and had no particular
liking of the French, whom he had encountered in his homeland after returning from Bosnia. But in the United Kingdom,
the Muslim population had grown from almost zero to five

percent of the population within the last fifteen years and with a considerably higher birthrate outstripping that of the decadent native population, that number would continue to grow. The government of the country was unquestioningly generous with its money and getting a house and lavish benefits were said to be easy. The mosques in the large cities were helpful in settling newcomers, finding jobs and earning money either legitimately or not. The British judges were especially lenient and the stupid authorities could not tell one foreigner from another. He knew that he could choose to be Kosovan, Bosnian, Turkish or any number of Arab countries, even Iranian and he would be taken at his word. He would find a wife and start a family, raising them as devout Muslims rather than devout Sunnis.

He had picked Birmingham as the city in which to settle. There was the Jame Masjid Mosque, which, until recently, had been called the Saddam Hussein Mosque on account of the two and a half million dollars the former president had donated to have it built. Birmingham had a large Muslim population and a number of other thriving Mosques. He had settled there, but in the south of the city, near the Jalalabad Mosque and the cricket ground. He had come from humble beginnings in Algeria and had no great need for anything other than a simple life. But he would keep his contacts with Al Qaeda and when the time came, would once again be a soldier of Holy Jihad.

* * *

'Right, Stan, let's get you up the steps. Wolfie, grab the chair.'

'Not there, Wolfie. Got to hold it by those bits there. Yeah there. They are the handles. Boss, make sure you got me at the back. I don't want to tip up.'

'Relax, Stan,' said the Boss, bracing his back and bending

his knees. 'You're bobbing about like a turd on the Thames. Got it John, on me, two six lift.'

'What's wrong with "one two three"?' asked Barnes, once they have hefted Stan up the three steps.

'Nothing really,' said the Boss. 'I think two and six were the gun crew in Nelson's navy that pulled the cannon back after it had fired. Or something. Matelot speak.'

'You're sounding like a shaky boat, Boss.'

'We are all on the same team now, John.'

'Where's the ground, then?' asked Wolfie.

'We just follow the crowds. Close to here.'

'Selly Oak is just down the road. Me mum used to come down the Bristol Road when she came to visit.' Selly Oak with the hospital which had looked after Stan. Emergency trauma had been seen to in Baghdad and then he was flown home to the military wing of the hospital. After several months he had been discharged and sent to Headley Court, the Defence Medical Rehabilitation Centre near Epsom. He had spent nearly a year learning to try to walk once more. He couldn't manage more than a few steps with crutches and that was only because of his upper body strength. The bullet that had hit him in the Farmhouse had done too much damage to his lower spinal column to make walking realistically feasible.

'Put a couple of Gimpies on the front here, Stan, paint it pink and off you go,' said Wolfie.

'I wish,' said Stan, 'There's some people round here that could do with a few rounds of seven-six-two. Actually, funny thing happened, you know.'

'What was that, then?' asked the Boss.

'Me Mum has just got into email and…,'

'She's already ahead of John, then,'

'Yeah, but anyway, she got an email from some lawyer geezer.'

'What did he want,' asked Barnes.

'Said he represented my dad,'

'OK,' said the Boss 'And?'

'He said my Dad had left me a big sum of money. I mean, really big.'

'How big?'

'Quarter of a million quid big,' said Stan.

'You should delete that immediately,' said Wolfie

'Yeah, I know,' said Stan 'but anyway, me Mum, bless her, replied and it seems that me Dad, who I didn't ever know, is some big shot businessman in Mauritius.'

Barnes and the Boss looked awkwardly at one another. 'Stroke of luck, then Stan.'

'It's in my Mum's account. Couldn't fucking believe it. Really going to help. Start off by getting an electric wheelchair rather than this army issue one.'

'Good one, Stan,' said Wolfie 'I was always led to believe those emails from Nigerian princes were a scam.'

'My advice, Stan, is to keep that quiet. Need to know only.'

'Yeah, only told you guys.'

'You got the tickets, Boss?' asked John, keen to change the subject.

'Oh, fuck. No, fuck…'

'You utter muppet, Boss. Honestly, you had one job…'

'Just joshing with you, John. Here we go, three grandstand tickets, right at the front. Best seats in the house thanks to you, Stan.'

'Well, at least there's a small token of appreciation for those of us that can't walk.'

'Who are you supporting, then Stan? England or India?' asked Wolfie, keen to change the subject.

'Me mum would be disappointed, so don't tell her, but actually I'm an England fan. Obviously, Leicester Football Club first and foremost, but England in the cricket too.'

'Right, Boss, get the beers in. Don't forget Ron's.'

'Others might, but we will never forget Ron,' replied the Boss.

* * *

Salim had an occasional part time job at the cricket ground as part of the security team. At the entrance he had to check the bags of the spectators. He had almost no vetting before being given the task and, were a bomb to be smuggled into the ground, then it would be the easiest thing in the world. He despised the *Kuffirs* he was meant to be protecting. Their picnic bags contained pork and alcohol but he was careful to hide his true feelings and went through the motions of searching. His shift finished at lunchtime and then he would pick up the intox-icated *Kuffirs* in his taxi, again, always with a smile hiding his contempt.

His attention was caught by a group of fit looking men pushing a wheelchair and he wondered if they were from the military hospital nearby. Tanned and lean, two with drooping moustaches made a contrast with the majority of the over-weight male spectators.

He stopped what he was doing and looked at the men. He wondered if the one in the chair had been wounded in Iraq or Afghanistan. He turned away, thinking to himself *'Ma Sha Allah'*. It is God's Will. He gave it no more thought and carried on his search. At the end of his shift he would go to the benefits office. The money would pay for the fuel for his taxi. It wouldn't be too long, he was told, before he would be eligible for a British Passport.

SIFTING FACT FROM FICTION.

As with Closer to Paradise, this is a novel and therefore it is entirely fictional. Well, not entirely. The characters in it are imaginary and everything they do and say is imaginary too. Again, I would emphasise, as before, this is not autobiographical. I wasn't present during the conflict and the characters in it are not real people in disguise. However, I have made every attempt to weave this story into the fabric of historical events and so there are descriptions of real people, both allied and insurgent. While there was an Al Qaeda sniper who called himself Juba, he was never identified and both his fate and whereabouts remain unknown. Numerous people have claimed that they killed him. The number of different departments and all the people they employed cannot be conveyed in a work of fiction such as this and therefore, literally, dozens of organisations and thousands of specialists and ordinary servicemen and women don't get a mention. They, too, should be remembered for the part they played. Their omission here is not to belittle their huge achievements but to simplify the narrative for the reader.

I have used *italics* to indicate either that the word is a transcribed Arabic word or to provide real translations of actual documents, such as the letters or speeches of Al Qaeda. Most of the translations come from US or other Western Government archives.

I have also listened to some of my readers of my first book 'Closer to Paradise' and have tried to reduce the TLAs[1] whilst trying not to compromise authenticity as I did so. Anybody familiar with military life knows that they are both rife and prone to multiply and mutate at an astonishing rate.

The massacres at Ahmici and Trusina took place on the same day in 1993 and marked the start of the 'gloves off' phase of the tripartite civil war in Bosnia. There are harrowing transcripts from survivors testifying at the International Criminal Tribunal for the Former Yugoslavia (ICTY) during the trial of some of the alleged perpetrators. The war would become a brutal and uncompromising conflict that followed no logic or reason. Historians still find it hard to explain how and why, for example, Croatia would allow foreign Muslim fighters to travel across their country to fight against their own people in Bosnia. Or why the American CIA would not only allow but actively encourage arms shipments from the Middle East, including Iran. It is a matter of fact that Osama bin Laden was given a Bosnian passport in Austria and that the Mujahadeen were allowed to open fake humanitarian organisations in Austria and other European countries, such as the Third World Relief Agency and Muvafak, for the sole purpose of sending fighters to Bosnia. Even after the World Trade Centre bombing in 1993, American 'black flights' flew arms into Tuzla with the permission coming from the very top of the Clinton administration, to arm both Al Qaeda and Hezbollah. It is also well documented that Osama bin Laden visited Bosnia in 1993 and 1994 and the 9/11 bombers, Khalid al Midhar and Nawaf al

---

1. Three Letter Acronym

Hazmi were fighting in the El Mudzahid brigade. There is also overwhelming evidence that the Iranian sponsored Hezbollah and the Sunni Al Qaeda were prepared to co-operate in order to set up the first Muslim caliphate in Europe. Muslim governments globally gave both arms and money, including Saudi Arabia, Turkey, UAE, Sudan, Pakistan, Malaysia and even Brunei. The West, NATO, the EU and the US all knew this and turned a blind eye. Whilst the excesses of Serbian military and paramilitaries are well documented, with Srebrenica being the most infamous, numerous other atrocities were taking place regularly in Bosnia. The El Mudzahid executed 52 Serbian soldiers of the Vojska Republika Srpska, some by beheading. Only one man, Rasim Delić, was ever convicted of war crimes at the ICTY. The American Private Military Contractor MPRI was training, equipping and funding both Croatian and then, after the Dayton Accord, the Army of Bosnia Herzegovina, including arms shipments worth over $100,000,000 and training invoiced for $190,000,000 paid for by the US Government's Department for Defense. Early flights of men, money and equipment were also conducted by Eco-Trends, an American-Russian joint venture Private Military Contractor. Russian planes transported 120 tons of former East European weapons into the airfield at Maribor in Slovenia, disguised as 'humanitarian aid'. Osama bin Laden even set up a "humanitarian" aid agency in London in 1994 called the 'Advisory and Reformation Committee'. It is also a matter of fact that the Bosnians knew that 'aid' came with Salafi strings attached especially *Sahwa* – world domination by Islam, *Jihad* – holy war and *Dawa* – the teaching of Islamic law, traditions and culture.

The Battle for Bugojno was an intense ten-day struggle for the town that saw the superior numbers of the Muslim Bosniaks triumph. The aftermath of the battle saw numerous atrocities, with HVO prisoners being beaten and murdered in various holding areas including the Slavonija Furniture shop, the Bugojno convent, the Gimnazija where the character Luka surrendered, the Vojin Paleksić school, the BH Banka building and, most infamously, the FC Iskra stadium. Josip Kalaica, a native of Bugojno and a pre-war aspiring association football player, was interred on July 23rd, 1993, spending 239 days in the camp. He was exchanged from the Bugojno Stadion Concentration Camp on March 19th, 1994.

However, what Bugojno Bosniaks would call a "stain on their existence", and the one thing about which they agree with the Croats, is the decision of the so-called "Bugojno War Presidency", to mark people such as: Miroslav Dilber, Ante Markulj, Dragan Miličević, Zoran Galić, Zdravko Jurišić, Niko Zlatunić, Nikica Miloša, Perica Crnjak, Branko Crnjak, Mihovila Strujić, Željko Miloš, Frano Jezidžić and Stipica Zelić as "special HVO extremists" and transferring them to Zenica. On their way to the city, in a motel at Ravni Rostov, they were handed over to the 7th Muslim Brigade, after which they weren't heard of again. It is thought that they had been executed, despite the fact that their remains still, to this day, haven't been located.

There were two British regiments at Gorjni Vakuf during the autumn of 1993. The Cheshires, commanded by Bob Stewart and their armoured reconnaissance squadron which came from the Light Dragoons. They handed over to the Coldstream Guards. However, the imaginary officers of the unnamed regiment in The Unblinking Eye should not be confused with anyone from those illustrious regiments.

The 'Fish Heads' did indeed operate on Tunnel Road but were never bought to justice. Gornji Vakuf, the location of one of the British Battalions bases, was on the front line between Muslim and Croat forces. In January 1993, Corporal Wayne Edwards, of the Royal Welch Fusiliers, attached to the Cheshire Regiment was driving a Warrior armoured vehicle escorting an ambulance when a sniper shot and killed him. The fictional death of the character Adam Lonsdale should not be conflated with that tragic incident.

The massacre of Bosnian Croat civilians at Uzdol and then slaughter of Bosnian Muslims at Stupni Do in the autumn of 1993 were both investigated by the War Crimes tribunal. The German ECMM monitor who first entered Stupni Do was called Rolf Weckesser and his testimony to the International Criminal Tribunal for the Former Yugoslavia can be found in the transcript of proceedings at page 9,041. In that transcript, Colonel Weckesser told the court that the scene had also been visited by three UKLO, the official name for the Special Air Service. To those soldiers, I would apologise in borrowing your presence there to enhance the story for this book. Further information from the war crime trials can be found in the United Nations document 'The International Tribunal for the Prosecutions of Persons Responsible for Serious Violations of International Humanitarian Law Committed in the Territory of the Former Yugoslavia Since 1991'

The Dayton Accord bought a semblance of peace to Yugoslavia and its terms required the foreign Mujahadeen to leave Bosnia. Many of the veterans slipped away to fight in other Islamic wars, including the vicious insurgency in Algeria. The hijacking of Air France flight 8969 that occurred on Christmas Eve 1994, was a real event. The hijackers killed three passengers and intended to fly the plane into either the Eiffel Tower or the Tour Montparnasse. Inexplicably, they decided to refuel in Marseilles whereupon the French GIGN, the elite counter terrorism group of the National Gendarmerie stormed the plane and released the hostages. All four hijackers were killed. That this was the inspiration for 9/11 is purely speculative on my part but it must have been noticed by Al Qaeda.

As well as Algeria, there were on-going guerrilla wars in Lebanon, Palestine and especially Afghanistan, where the Taliban had filled the vacuum in the wake of the Soviet withdrawal. Osama bin Laden was welcomed in and set up various military training camps. It is well documented that Al Qaeda had men in Mazar-i-Sharef in August 1998 when the Taliban slaughtered thousands of Hazars, Uzbeks and Tajiks. That this crime was on a par with Srebrenica but remains almost unknown in the West is a sad and indicting reflection on both our governments and our media. The only accounts come from eyewitnesses collated by Human Rights Watch.

Osama provided money for Abu-Musab al Zarqawi to set up his own independent Jihad camp in Herat on the Iranian border. The relationship between the two Mujahadeen was neither straightforward nor friendly. However, post 9/11 and the fall of the Taliban, many Mujahadeen left Afghanistan to fight the Multi-National Force Iraq, entering the country through the so-called rat runs via Syria or Iran. The Allied Forces were concentrating on the mythical weapons of mass destruction and rounding up 'former regime elements' rather than trying to prevent the country descending into an anarchic civil war.

The al-Zarqawi letter quoted in the book comes from the US Department of State official translation and provides prima facie evidence that Zarqawi's main ambition was to prosecute a war against anybody who did not adhere to the strict Salafi interpretation of the Koran. He thought he could usher in the Caliphate by using the Sunni-Shia civil war to destroy everything that stood in the way. This was, ultimately, his undoing. That he was an unhinged violent psychopath can be seen from the way he killed people by whatever way his warped imagination could think up. In the end, his attacks on the Shia majority civilian population alienated even his Sunni sponsors and the

Great Awakening, the *Sakhwa,* began in Anbar Province, west of Baghdad, around the end of 2006.

The intelligence operation, under Task Force Orange, during the timeline of this book was commanded by (the real) General Mike Flynn. It started off short staffed, with little equipment and an enclosed secretive culture. General Stanley McChrystal, (real person) knew that to destroy the insurgent network he had to build his own network and together they set up Joint Operations Command aka 'The Death Star' at Balad Airbase. 'Kill TV' was one aspect of this but more importantly for the effort against the insurgency, was Gen McChrystal's drive to destroy AQI. He achieved a huge amount, often against entrenched political and military scepticism and hostility. Possibly his two biggest culture changes were the relentless nature of the operations and the sharing of information. Anyone who was part of the team could access information and, thereby, he moulded a large multipart team of operators who were all aligned in their objectives. The archetypal 'warrior monk', he demanded an enormous amount from both himself and the staff in JSOC. An example of this is that in August 2004, JSOC (which included both UK and US Special Forces) conducted 18 missions. In August 2006, it conducted more than 300. Gen McChrystal, together with General Graeme Lamb, his UK deputy, had realised that to break the cellular nature of the AQI, they should not necessarily go for a 'decapitate' strategy but rather 'eviscerate the middle managers' quicker than AQI could regenerate them. This was confirmed as after the death of AQI leader al Zarqawi in June 2006, the number of bombs and murders climbed ever higher. To go after the local commanders, the so-called 'middle managers', JSOC needed to process intelligence in a matter of hours rather than the weeks or even months that it used to take. This speedy processing, as well as the AQI reliance on the rapidly expanding Iraqi mobile phone network, led to a snow-balling effect of intelligence gathering and target acquisitions. By the middle of the conflict, The Death Star at Balad was the most sophisticated, focussed and ferocious war machine ever seen on the planet.

The first video of the novel, that of the shooting of Stephen Tschiderer was released in July 2005 in DVD format and soon made its way onto the internet and into the studios of the English and Arabic language television news networks. For a time, Tschiderer was feted by the western media.

Juba, the Baghdad Sniper, released four videos in all, starting in November 2005, when a DVD was handed to an Australian journalist. They were published on the internet and, at the height of his notoriety, he had over 30,000 followers on his dedicated website, www.jubaonline.org which has subse-quently been taken down. They received increased publicity when they were aired by al-Zawraa TV. In one video, he showed off his copy of "The Ultimate Sniper: An Advanced Training Manual For Military And Police Snipers", written by U.S. Major John Plaster. Following the video's appearance on television, it was picked up by other stations and aired widely and often, in the Arab world. From my research the card found at one of the firing points saying *"What has been taken by blood, cannot be regained except by blood. Baghdad Sniper"* was found by an American Quick Reaction Force.

In the first video, Juba is holding a Tabuk rifle, which was an Iraqi copy of the Yugoslavian Zastava rifle. As a snipers' weapon, it was not sophisticated and there were plenty of better rifles to be had at the time, including a number of captured coalition weapons and imported Soviet sniper rifles that could use armour piercing bullets. The word 'Juba' was said to be based on the Juba dance which was originally brought by enslaved peoples from the Congo (where it is called Giouba) to Charleston, South Carolina. It became an African

American plantation dance that was performed by slaves during their gatherings when no rhythm instruments were allowed due to fear of secret codes hidden in the drumming. It was thought that the constant dodging and jockeying that infantry do when facing a sniper threat, resembled the Juba. Standing still for any period of time invites a shot. This is all speculative, as Juba was never caught.

The second Juba video was a more sophisticated affair, with Juba and Baghdad Sniper highlighted in block colouring and a red crosshair superimposed to show the target. The quality of the film is still poor by today's standards mainly because it was taken on a Sony Handicam at the extreme of its telephoto ability. In the video, a somewhat portly man ticks off his thirty seventh victim and then writes a meticulously calligraphed letter in an exercise book, as transcribed in the novel. Two more videos of increasing sophistication were released. The third was released in nine languages.

The Americans were never much perturbed by Juba and his videos, or so they claimed. Sniping, whilst a psychological weapon, only accounted for 1.3% of coalition deaths and they believed that "Juba" was not a single person but a propaganda tool for spreading fear and uncertainty. This technique has been used before, notably in the Russo Finish War of 1939 with Simo Häyhä the "White Sniper" and Vasily Zaitsev the Soviet sniper at Stalingrad in 1942. In June 2004, four US Marine snipers from Echo Company, Second Battalion Fourth Marines were to be relieved in place on a rooftop in Ramadi. When their replacements got there, they were found dead, all shot in the head and their weapons taken, including two sniper rifles and a PAS-13 thermal imaging sight. One had had his throat cut.

There was an Iraqi taskforce, called Task Force Raptor, which was formed to find him. They were formed into counter-sniper teams armed with M24 sniper rifles. Various claims as to the identify of Juba have been put forward, including Celebi Osman, betrayed and killed in 2007 and Abu Othman. Othman was an Iraqi army deserter who lived as a shepherd on the Iraqi-Syrian-Jordan border. He was originally from Fallujah and was noted as a calligrapher. Various Americans claimed to be the ones that eventually killed Juba but again, there is no direct evidence. It is said that the publicity surrounding Chris Kyle, labelled the most prolific sniper in history, was an attempt to counter the publicity surrounding Juba. His story was made into the film 'American Sniper' by Clint Eastwood in 2014. In 2008, a short film titled 'Juba the Sniper; the Untold Story' was released in Kuwait but was not overly successful at the box office despite some critical acclaim at Cannes Film Festival. It can be seen on Amazon Prime. Amazon also commissioned the film 'The Wall' in 2017 about a US sniper team encountering Juba in the desert.

The other taskforce, described in this book, is that of the 'Mohawks'. They were Iraqi volunteers recruited by JSOC and were vetted and provided with credible back stories. They were used by Delta to spy and inform on the general population to help build an intelligence picture of the local insurgent networks. The use of internet cafes and their bugging by the Mohawks was an important and very dangerous part of the surveillance effort. The description of how Trojans were introduced and then analysed is both accurate and from open sources.

The video of Al Zarqawi, which can be found on the internet, was captured by B Squadron, 22 Special Air Service during Operation LARCHWOOD IV on April 8th 2006. The assault was particularly violent with a number of insurgents killed and five wounded among the assaulting forces. They narrowly missed Zarqawi himself. However, they did recover the M4 carbine that identified the terrorist as well as computers and other electronic data. The computer held a video, which was used in the famous press conference by Major General Rick Lynch and described in the narrative. Again, italics in the book indicate an actual transcription of some of what said at the press conference. The description of the hunt and final death of Zarqawi is taken from contemporary accounts at the time.

The description of torture that Barbara has laminated is from the "Convention against Torture and Other Cruel, Inhuman or Degrading Treatment or Punishment" published on 10th December 1984 by the United Nations General Assembly. It is Resolution 39/46. The British were very aware that the Americans were less concerned with bending UN resolutions on Human Rights and this led to a short period when British and US Special Forces were not co-operating. It was not until a framework had been adopted that allowed the UK to opt out of certain tactics (for example, 'special renditions') that the two countries fully co-operated again. That the Americans sought their own legal interpretation of 'torture' and 'combatant' is also well documented and there seems to be convincing evidence that waterboarding and tasering were, if not common, then certainly prevalent in prisoner interrogations. The descriptions of the interrogation sites at Camp Nama and the High Five Paintballing Club are from contemporary sources. As a result, prisoners taken by the British would be handed to the Americans on-site.

The "Unblinking Eye" of the title refers to the name given by coalition intelligence staff to the constellation of airborne ISR assets (Intelligence, Surveillance, Reconnaissance) that watched and eavesdropped around the clock. Both manned and unmanned fixed and rotary winged aerial vehicles were used. By 2006, when the book is set, the number of aircraft had grown from one Predator drone in 2004 to Mike Flynn regularly having no less than three sets of airborne eyes on each live target. Equally, the aircraft were equipped with the state-of-the-art surveillance and electronic warfare technology. This in turn, led to an increase in nightly operations.

The Baghdad Country Club was indeed a bar in the Green Zone set up by James Thornett. And it did have a very pretty waitress called Heidi, who no doubt everyone hit on. And, indeed, it was located right next to the Supreme Council for Islamic Revolution in Iraq. Really, you couldn't make it up and I didn't.

The Union Jack shoulder flashes with 'Fuck Al Qaeda' were also real, an idea copied from the Americans. There is a photograph of members of B Squadron 22 SAS with Tony Blair. Some of the blades are wearing the flash in his presence.

'Italics' have been used to denote transcriptions from real documents. I cannot attest to their authenticity in this world of 'fake news' but many of the quotations come from trusted archives such as, for example, the National Archives in Washington DC. This should not be confused with *<italics>* which I use to denote radio transmissions.

The descriptions of the preparation for suicide bombing and the theoretical discussions have come from my research into the subject using reputable academic sources. For example, al-Qaradawi, arguably the most influential living Sunni theologian, states: "to call these operations suicide attacks would be a mistake and misleading. These are examples of heroic sacrifice." However, as always, there are many that disagree with him.

Nobody knows the true fate of Juba and, of course, Salim al Agayli is a fictitious name. The story of his hunt by the British SIS is also wholly imaginary. Legend has it that he was betrayed and killed. Others think he joined ISIS or even fought against ISIS. There is no evidence whatsoever that he is living in Edgbaston. Finally, the cricket test against India in 2007 was actually played at Trent Bridge.

In December 2024 Phil Shiner, an "award winning human

rights lawyer" from 'Public Interest Lawyers' was convicted of fraudulently accusing British soldiers of human rights abuses in Iraq. He had invented charges of prisoner and civilian abuse and had paid 'witnesses' to testify. It was all a tissue of lies to make him money. Although barred from practising law, he was only given a suspended sentence.

The wars in Iraq and Afghanistan took a terrible mental and physical toll on those that were asked to fight them. This is no less true of Special Forces than anyone else. Coming to light now is Military Related Mild Traumatic Brain Injury (MTBI) which is thought to be caused by multiple exposures to explosion over-pressure resulting in microstructural brain aberrations. This can lead to chronic post-concussion symptoms including cognition problems, memory loss, sleep disturbance, vision and hearing impairment. Since those wars, there have been huge demand placed on the charities that look after wounded veterans, including The Royal British Legion, Help for Heroes, Blesma – The British Limbless Ex-Servicemen's Association, and Combat Stress, to name a few. If you enjoyed this book, or at least found it interesting and informative, I would encourage you to give a small donation to any one of these charities.

Finally, I would like to remember Chris Waddington, a colleague and contemporary Troop Leader in my SAS Squadron, who died during the writing of this book. Chris was both the youngest platoon commander and point officer for 2 PARA at Goose Green in the Falklands War. He revealed in a BBC documentary, made in 2020, the harrowing events of that attack – telling the interviewer that he had never told anybody about what happened during the intense hand-to-hand fighting and how badly it affected him. Although Chris went on to serve both in Bosnia and Iraq, he tragically died when the light aircraft he was piloting nosedived into the ground, shortly after the documentary was broadcast. Air crash investigators found no mechanical faults. I do not want to speculate on the crash but rather to remember an incredibly brave man asked to do unimaginable things as a nineteen-year-old young officer who had the courage to admit on television he had hidden it all away and not told anybody of his suffering.

GLOSSARY

AQI: Al Qaeda in Iraq
Bosniak: Bosnian Muslim as opposed to Bosnian Croatian or Serbian
Box: Technical name for MI6
BUA: Battle Update Assessment
BRIXMIS: British Exchange Mission to Soviet Forces Germany
Chetniks: Serbian Nationalists in WW2
Dushka or DShK: Soviet-made heavy machine gun
Druganov: Soviet-made sniper rifle
ECMM: European Community Monitoring Mission (Yugoslavia)
F3EAD: Find; Fix; Finish; Exploit; Analyse; Disseminate.
Five Eyes: Intelligence restricted to UK, US, Australia, Canada,
New Zealand
GCHQ: Government Communications Headquarters
GPMG/Gimpie: General Purpose Machine Gun (UK)
INIS: Iraqi National Intelligence Service. Funded by the CIA
ISR: Intelligence, Surveillance and Reconnaissance

JSOC: Joint Special Operations Command. Combined Tier 1 Special Forces

Jundi: Soldiers (Arabic)

Kufiyah: Arab Headdress often red and white checks

Little Bird: AH6 or MH6 Little Bird four-man helicopter

LZ: Helicopter Landing Zone

MAM: Military Aged Males ie possible terrorists.

Mil Mi-8 Hip: Soviet era Transport Helicopter

MSS: Mission Support Site

MSS Fernandez: Co-located compounds with SAS and Delta

'O' Group: Orders Group

OBL: Osama bin Laden

ORBAT: Order of Battle – List of units and formations

Pads: Marrieds or Married Quarters (UK)

PID: Positive Identification (of potential targets)

PMC: Private Military Contractor

PX: Post Exchange. Large, subsidised shopping centre (US)

RHQ: Regimental Headquarters.

Scoobie: Scoobie Doo or clue. (UK rhyming slang)

SOPs: Standard Operating Procedures (UK)

SSM: Squadron Sergeant Major (UK)

STRAP 1 (UK): Highest category of security. UK Eyes Only

Terps: Interpreter

TOW: Tubed-launched, Optically tracked, Wire guided anti tank
missile (US)

UNPROFOR: United Nations Protection Force

Ustasha: Croatian fascist group fighting for the Germans WW2

Zastava M72: Yugoslavian Automatic Rifle

Zil 131 and 157: Soviet era military 6 wheeled lorries

Zulfika: Bosnian Muslim Special Forces Unit

ARABIC WORDS

Qibla direction towards the Kaaba in the Mosque in Mecca
Istishhādi Literally 'martyr' but can refer to suicide bombers
Haram 'Forbidden' under Sharia Law
Kuffir Unbeliever or apostate
Kunya Nickname
Rahbar Literally 'guide' often used for suicide bomb trainers
Sahwa 'Awakening' to the Muslim way of life
Shahada Islamic martyrdom during Jihad
Shura Islamic Council of Elders
Takbeers Repeated religious chanting
Takfiri The denouncing of Muslims as Kuffirs
Ummah A Commonwealth of Muslim Believers
Takbeers Repetitions of prayers such as Allahu Akbar

ABOUT THE AUTHOR

'Scott Leigh' was an officer in the British Army for 10 years. He was commissioned into a Challenger Regiment before passing Selection for Special Forces. He spent a number of years as a Troop Commander with the Special Air Service and a tour commander with BRIXMIS.

Since leaving the Army he has established a successful business career and is a director of a number of companies that operate in this country and in frontier markets in tropical Africa.

He is married with two children and divides his time between Oxfordshire and London.

ALSO BY SCOTT LEIGH

Closer to Paradise

'Gritty authentic and unputdownable!' **Bear Grylls**

'This is fiction but it reads like fact - and captures what it feels like, smells like and is like on real world operations - a very good read' **Lt General Sir Graeme Lamb**, former Deputy Commanding General, Multinational Force, Iraq

An explosive, compelling, searingly authentic thriller about the Iraq War.

A stunning first novel by a former SAS officer.

Good Friday 2004, and a US logistics convoy sets out to carry a precious cargo on the long journey from Baghdad to Kuwait. Several hundred kilometres to the south, a covert SAS patrol is on the lookout for weapons of mass destruction. Meanwhile the Mahdi Army prepares to launch its ultra-violent insurgency against the Occupying Allies that very day.

Convoy, patrol and insurgents all collide with terrifying consequences. With the veneer of civilisation stripped away, young men and women are forced to fight a brutal battle for survival, reliant only on themselves and their closest comrades. The only rule is there are no rules, and civilisation is whittled down to survival of the fittest.

And in the ruthless reality of twenty-first century warfare, it's not just about who fights and who survives. It's about trust and betrayal… and some very tempting treasure…

Published by Chiselbury and available in hardback, paperback and ebook

Printed in Dunstable, United Kingdom